Valkyrie: Attrition
Book III


Lucas Marcum

*This book is dedicated to all of those who have borne arms in defense of their nation, both living and dead.*

## Prologue

The war against the enigmatic enemy race known as the Elai had raged for nearly four years, but finally the tide seemed to be turning. Forced to withdraw from system after system at great cost by the United Earth Alliance forces, the mysterious aliens were now forced back to their final defensive perimeter: a ring of heavily defended systems surrounding their home world. Anxious to avoid further casualties and force an end to the devastating conflict, the leadership of the Earth Alliance has chosen to make a risky assault on a key enemy system. If successful, the war could be forced to an end. If unsuccessful, the conflict could drag on for years. Knowing this, the political leadership has voted to allow the military operation to proceed... but in war, both sides get a vote.

# Chapter 1

## "A Thousand Lives Lost"

*Offices of the United Earth Alliance First Fleet,*
*Huxley City, Mars.*
*February 14, 2248*

General Salifi Abbasi looked at the man across from her. His pristine white dress uniform and rank insignia marked him as a fleet admiral in the Earth Alliance Navy. He noticed her gaze and nodded, almost imperceptibly. Standing, the petite officer moved to the front of the room. There was a mix of political staff members and lower ranking officers from all of the branches of the Alliance military in the room, but none of them truly mattered.

At the front of the room, three people sat at a table that faced a display screen, with a podium off to one side. The governmental officials were as varied as the worlds they came from. In the middle sat a slender woman with a kind face and dark eyes, wearing a traditional kanga. Its deep blue color, trimmed with silver, stood out in contrast for its simplicity in the room full of suits and dress uniforms. To her left, a blonde man with piercing blue eyes in a plain gray wool suit. To her right sat an older woman with a clean shaven head and pale, almost translucent skin.

General Abbasi moved to the front of the room and stood behind the podium. The soft buzz of conversation died down and after a moment she began to speak, her normally soft voice clearly audible through the small room.

"Prime Minister, Minister Gerhardt, Minister Otoro. Welcome." Abbasi looked quietly around the small room. "Today, we will informally brief you on the proposed course of action regarding the war with the Elai. We will also seek your guidance as the commander in chief of the armed forces on our proposed courses of action moving forward, before we present this plan to the Alliance Parliament later this month."

She paused, looking out at the small room, then continued in a grave tone. "To this date, the war has been going on for four years. We have lost three hundred seventy thousand, two hundred and six soldiers, sailors and Marines, with many hundreds of thousands more grievously wounded. The Navy has suffered particularly heavily. We have lost three fleet carriers, two assault carriers, twenty two cruisers, a hospital ship and dozens of destroyers. We have fought eight major naval engagements, five major ground campaigns and countless skirmishes, raids and probes. All of this has led us here."

Tapping a key, she illuminated a star map on the wall behind her. Four systems shone in red in the center of the map. In a measured voice, the general continued. "The fighting on the jungle world of K3254, known as 'Paradise', while extraordinarily savage, was notable for one thing: The acquisition of a series of data cubes of a hitherto unknown starfaring race. As the war has continued, we have located many such ruins in dozens of systems." She paused, regarding the map for a moment, then continued, "While this race remains largely unknown, the data extracted from the cubes was able to assist us with a crucial piece of information: The location of the Elai home system. This information was subsequently confirmed by long range stealth ship patrols."

There was a murmur in the room. The three leaders sitting at the table sat quietly, listening intently. Tapping a key, the view zoomed in on the four systems highlighted in red.

Stepping back and gesturing at the screen, the officer continued, "These four systems form the core of the Elai industrial worlds." As she spoke, each system blinked. "This Draconis 324, is the location of their primary shipyards and heavy industry. It also has substantial agricultural output. This one, Draconis 327, is a sparsely populated industrial and resource system with a rich asteroid belt and multiple gas giants for starship fuel production." Another system blinked on the screen and she continued, "Kappa Cygni II appears to be their oldest and most prosperous settled planet outside of their home system, similar to Tau Ceti for us. This binary system here is Alpha Draconis- their home world. The old name for the system is Thuban- which, appropriately enough, is Arabic for 'Head of the Serpent'. These systems are code named Topaz, Onyx, Ruby and Diamond, respectively."

After a measured pause, she continued. "At this point in the war, we must now choose a course of action. Attacking and neutralizing any one of the three populated systems as a military target will deal a crippling blow to the Elai war effort. It must be noted, however, that all of the populated systems are heavily fortified and will be defended ferociously. The casualties will be high, with some estimates running into the hundreds of thousands. Taking this into consideration, it is the opinion of the Allied High Command that we need not assault any of them directly, if we act decisively. Admiral Onoda?"

The admiral stood and moved to the dais, nodding gravely to General Abbasi. He spoke in a precise, clipped tone. "The Office of Combined Intelligence, in conjunction with the UEA civilian intelligence departments, have determined that if we deny the Elai access to the raw materials that they need for starship fuel production, the remaining fuel reserves will last their Navy less than three months of combat operations." Pausing for a moment, the Admiral continued, somberly. "They undoubtedly have anticipated this move and have prepared defensive counters. To maintain the initiative, we propose a triple pronged naval assault, with the Second, Third and Fourth Fleets and their associated combined arms task forces attacking each of these systems simultaneously."

He tapped a key and three arrows appeared, pointing at the three Elai industrial worlds. He continued, gesturing at the star map. "The three separate fleet actions will tie up resources to prevent the Elai from concentrating their naval forces to oppose our ground landings on our true objective, which will be on the three primary moons orbiting the second gas giant in Draconis 327." The map zoomed in to show the gas giant and its multiple moons, with the largest highlighted.

In his customary, precise tone, the admiral continued. "Our primary objective will be M3254. It is the largest moon of the gas giant, which the planners have code named 'Onyx', on which a Marine space-ground task force will make a forced landing, in an operation known as 'Safecracker'. The Marines will then overcome the defenses, establish a fighter-bomber base and utilize the base to disrupt the collection of raw materials for fuel and starship component production in the system."

Tapping a control, he continued, "We anticipate that this will draw an immediate defensive naval response from the Elai, resulting in the stripping of all naval forces not actively engaged in the diversionary assaults to reinforce the system." He gazed directly at the Prime Minister and spoke in a firm tone. "At that point, Prime Minister, the Earth Alliance Fifth Fleet will engage and destroy the reinforcing Elai vessels."

The Prime Minister nodded thoughtfully. After a moment, she spoke in a soft, accented voice. "And what then, Admiral? When their fleets are destroyed, what happens then?"

The Admiral tapped a control and the screen changed, displaying red arrows moving from one system to the next and spoke gravely.

"We anticipate that there are two probable responses to this course of action. The first and most likely is that with the collapse of their defensive line, the Elai withdrew their remaining naval and ground forces back to their home system to prepare for the final defense of their home. The second and less likely possibility is that they do not withdraw. In that case, we will shift the fleet from Onyx to each of the other systems in sequence, linking up with our attacking fleets and destroying them in turn." The red arrows marched from system to system, then pointed at the Elai home system.

The admiral stood for a moment, then spoke. "We anticipate substantial losses in both lives and warships, as the Elai response to the attack at Onyx will likely be prompt and ferocious. Simply because our ships are better technologically does not mitigate the fact that they are brilliant strategists and their logistics systems and general staffs are as good or better than ours." The naval officer frowned slightly and remarked somberly, "I must observe that had this war occurred in another fifteen or twenty years, that the outcome may have been very different."

There was quiet for a moment, then the blonde man at the end of the table spoke, "Admiral, you said there would be casualties. What is your estimate?"

The Admiral met the man's gaze and responded quietly. "Minister Gerhardt, The Naval and Army General Staff estimates for Operation Safecracker, including Naval, Marine and Army losses could range up to fifty to seventy five thousand servicemen during the operation and possibly up to fifteen capital ships."

The man nodded soberly and responded, "I see." He paused for a moment, then asked, "And the campaign to take the Elai Home System?"

The Admiral looked down momentarily, then back up and answered in a clear, firm voice, "If we must take the Elai home system by force, our projected estimates are that we will suffer between one to one point five million Earth Alliance casualties for the initial invasion. The campaign that follows will cost hundreds of thousands more. There will also be extensive casualties amongst the Elai, with civilian and military infrastructure being heavily damaged. We cannot estimate their civilian casualties, but our estimates are that their home world contains between seven and ten billion Elai civilians." He hesitated for a moment, then added, "I must add that the number of military casualties could be reduced significantly by orbital bombardment, but that enemy civilian casualties would go up by orders of magnitude. It is not the recommended course of action."

The Prime Minister nodded and spoke in her calm, lilting voice. "Thank you, Admiral, General. While I find the idea of that abhorrent, we will do what we must. We must strike hard and fast, lest we allow them to regain the initiative. Every moment this war continues is a thousand lives lost on both sides." Abbasi and Onoda nodded silently.

The graceful woman regarded them for a moment, then spoke. "I do have one additional requirement." Her piercing brown eyes bored into the two senior officers.

"As the direct representative of the Earth Alliance government to the military, I am hereby directing you to order a fleet to be put together...a relief fleet. Military led, but staffed with anyone and everyone that can be of assistance. It should consist of every expert we have on the Elai. Doctors, scientists, engineers, combat veterans, agriculture and industrial specialists. Everything we need to prevent their world from tearing itself apart or rebuilding it if needed. Our own people have seen too much of that in these last few centuries." The Prime Minister stopped for a moment, then spoke again. "I want it ready to go the moment the fighting stops. We must plan for the peace as thoroughly as we have planned for the war." She leaned forward slightly and spoke in a deliberate tone. "After this is over, we will still share the galaxy with them. We will not let them lay where they fall."

General Abbasi and Admiral Onoda nodded silently, then Abbasi replied soberly. "It will be done, Prime Minister."

# Chapter 2

## "Assemble the Fleet"

*August 1st, 2248*
*Aboard the UEAN* Infiltrator
*The Mars Trojan Fleet Yards, Sol*
*Six Months Later*

"I guess that's it." Captain Mitch Harris pushed the datapad across the desk in his cramped office aboard the stealth ship *Infiltrator.*

His executive officer, a slim, dark eyed commander named Greta Von Kant, picked up the datapad and scanned it rapidly. Her eyebrows raised after a moment and she looked up.

"No fleet carrier support?" She asked with a raised eyebrow.

"Nope. It looks like the carriers are going to be staying outsystem." Mitch frowned and gestured at the small star map hanging over the desk. "Only a jump away, but still…" He left the statement unfinished.

"Shit." Von Kant frowned, then looked up at the display. The latest additions to the task force blinked silently in light green. After a moment, she added thoughtfully, "Ok. So, seven heavy cruisers, two light cruisers, two assault carriers and one lone stealth ship." She raised an eyebrow, ironically, "The mighty Task Force 3.1." She set the data pad down and added, "If this is the main effort, this is a damn light force."

Harris nodded. "I agree, but if we pull too heavily from the Second and Third Fleets, the sharkies will know there's another maneuver force out there someplace. Fleetcom wants to do this quick, quiet and to own the place before the Elai know we're there." With a faint grin, he added, "'Silent and Deadly', right?" Von Kant shook her head and laughed at his sardonic use of the UEAN Navy's Stealth Warfare school.

"I guess." She drummed her fingers on the desk for a moment, then added, "So what happens after we take the system? It's going to be the Wild West out there if there's any serious kind of counterattack and that close to their home system, you can bet your boots it's a matter of 'when', not 'if'."

Harris's grin faded as he replied, "You aren't kidding." The two fell into troubled silence as they stared at the holodisplay.

\*\*\*\*

*Aboard the UEAN* Stalwart
*Flagship of Task Force 3.1*

Admiral Laura Kensington watched the holodisplay in the center of the dim compartment blink slightly and update. From her left, the accented voice of her operations officer, Captain Dimitry Sokolov, spoke. "There's the last one. Commander de la Cruz. Fleet status report, if you please."

Across the display table, the tiny woman spoke quickly. "Yes, ma'am. *Stalwart, Independent, Forthright, Audacious* and *Steadfast* report manned and ready. *La Venganza* and *Bravado* are breaking Martian orbit, along with the assault carriers *Phantom Fury* and *Thunderbolt*. Their estimated time to the rendezvous point is six hours." The woman paused and tapped a control, then continued. "Waiting at the rendezvous point, Quebec, are the *Mont Blanc* and the *Denali*. Also, somewhere up there is the *Infiltrator*."

Captain Soklov leaned forward and rumbled, "Has the *Infiltrator* engaged her stealth systems?"

"No, sir. She's just damn hard to see even with the systems off and if she didn't have her transponder on, we probably wouldn't see her at all."

In a humorous tone, Admiral Kensington broke in, "Wouldn't be much of a stealth ship if she was easy to see."

Turning to the fourth officer in the compartment, she asked, "Captain Destin, as soon as we make the jump to Bernards Star, I'd like a fleetwide conference with the command teams." The pale, shaven headed Martian native nodded somberly, acknowledging her request.

The UEA Admiralty had insisted on strict secrecy, even though the chances of a spy in the war against the sharp toothed, saurian race known as the Elai was slim. Due to the secrecy, the only people aware of the fleet's destination were the Flag officers, the Marine planning contingent on the assault carriers and the captain and crew of the *Infiltrator,* who'd extensively surveyed the target system several months before.

"Captain Soklov, signal the fleet: Form on the flagship and proceed to Point Quebec."

Soklov nodded and replied, "Aye, Admiral." He tapped several keys on his console. A moment later, he reported. "Task Force 3.1 is under way." Kensington nodded acknowledgement. The thrum of the massive engines of the *Stalwart* could be felt through the deck as the warship picked up speed and headed towards the rendezvous point.

\*\*\*\*

*Aboard the UEAN* Phantom Fury
*Shipboard Operations Center, Fifth Battalion, First Marine Division*

"Any time now." The tall, somber-faced man wearing the silver eagles of a colonel and a nametape that read 'Nelson' said, distractedly. He checked his watch. A few seconds later, the deck of the massive assault transport began to thrum as the antimatter engines increased power, pushing the starship and its thousands of crews forward into the darkness. "There we go." He looked over at the younger man next to him. "Major

Harris. Schedule the drop briefing for the task force. "

"Yes, sir," the younger man with sandy blonde hair replied, making a note on his datapad. "I'll brief it tomorrow, if that's ok with you. It'll give the company commanders time to go through their ops plans and get back to us if there are problems."

The colonel turned, with a frown. "You think there are going to be problems, Tony?

"Sir, there are *always* problems with military operations and ever more so when dealing with the sharkies. You know that, sir." Tony set the datapad down and ran his hands through his hair. He looked tired, with big circles under his eyes.

Colonel Nelson regarded him for a few seconds in silence, then asked bluntly. "You think this plan is a bad one?"

Shaking his head, Tony replied. "Not exactly bad, per se." He motioned at the datapad. "There's just a lot of moving parts. It makes it more likely there's going to be problems." He looked at Colonel Nelson and added somberly, "And where we're going, we don't have a lot of room for error, sir."

"I see." Colonel Nelson fell quiet for a few moments, then abruptly asked, "Tony, when was the last time you slept? I know we've all been busy getting the task force ready to go, but as my exec, I know you've got a lot of irons in the fire." His face turned stern. "And I don't mean catnaps in the tactical operations center. I mean uninterrupted sleep– as in 'sleep in a bed'?"

Rubbing his face, Tony sighed and replied, "What day is it? Tuesday?"

Nelson nodded silently.

"Then I got about six hours on Wednesday, right after we broke Martian orbit."

With a frown, the colonel replied. "Major, that was almost a week ago." He picked up Tony's datapad, glanced at it then set it down. "You are hereby off duty for the next fourteen hours." Seeing Tony open his mouth to protest, Nelson held up a hand. "No, Major. None of this is critical. We have a week left in transit and most of this stuff can be handled by the staff." With a hard look, he added, "Without you."

"Yes, sir." Tony replied, simply.

"You may consider that an order, if it helps." The older officer grinned. Tony laughed and shook his head. The colonel slid the datapad back across the table and turned to look out the window in the cabin. The hard-yellow spot of Sol in the distance outshone all other stars in view, despite being over ninety million miles away. After a moment, he spoke again. "For what it's worth, I think you're right. There are a lot of moving parts here and the margin for error is small." He turned back to Tony with a serious expression on his face. "After you get a good night's sleep, get the staff together. We're going to make some contingency plans of our own."

"Yes, sir." Tony replied. After a moment, he asked, "What do you think we're walking into here, Colonel?"

The colonel turned back to the starfield in the window, his face worried. After a long silence as he stared into the stars, he replied, "I don't know." He turned back to Tony. "And that worries me."

Tony nodded silently in agreement, his exhaustion suddenly replaced with a deep sense of foreboding.

\*\*\*\*

*Aboard the Assault Carrier UEAN* Thunderbolt
*Aft Cargo Bay Twelve*

"Sign here, sir." The slender, red headed petty officer held out a data pad. Major Micheal Manderson accepted the data pad and pressed his thumb to the screen. It blinked once, then chirped. He handed the pad back wordlessly. "Excited, sir? This is the big one." The chief asked, her tone belying her own excitement.

"Not really." Mike replied, flatly. He turned and looked at the assault shuttle. The deck crew were sealing the doors on the large spacecraft, now packed with medical supplies and sighed.

"They say this could end the war." The sailor stated. Her tone was much less certain than before. Mike noted her name tape read 'O'Reilly'. "They say that if we do this, the sharkies will either collapse or surrender." Her eyes searched his face, her expression worried.

"Yeah." He replied, then his phone buzzed. As he reached for it, he said flatly, "Well, *they* say a lot of things." He tapped the phone and answered brusquely. "Manderson."

From the phone came the calm voice of Colonel Loyo, the field hospital executive officer. "Major Manderson, this is Colonel Loyo. Calling to get an update on the supply situation."

"Afternoon, sir." Mike replied. "All the supplies you wanted to go down in the first wave are packed into two assault shuttles." His voice took on a wry tone. "The Marines weren't happy about sacrificing the extra ammo and life support packs, but when I told them we were jamming in extra medical; they gave us as much space as I needed with minimal bitching."

"Good." Loyo replied. "So, you managed to get all three of the drop team's equipment and shelters into the shuttles?"

"No. I got all of the 355th's and 410th's onboard, but we may have to make a second trip for the 336th's hard shelters." He paused, then added, "If push comes to shove, we can put most of the 336's supplies into a Valkyrie, along with about half of their surgical crew." Manderson hesitated, then asked, "Sir, why are we pushing these medical elements this far forward? Why not a typical early entry element of the hospital? Doctrinally, it only takes thirty-six hours to drop the full hospital." He paused, then answered his own question, "Unless you don't think we're gonna have thirty-six hours to land…"

Flatly, Loyo replied. "You got it. There's a reason you're on that side of the operation, Major. I and most of the hospital staff think we won't have time to drop the full hospital so we're doing what we can to get as much down as fast as we can and having you as a liaison is helping tremendously."

"That explains me shuffling all this shit into Marine shuttles, instead of yours." Mike observed. "So, they go in with the first wave."

"Exactly." Loyo hesitated, then added, "Mike. I got a bad feeling about this one. You're going to be the senior medical officer down there in terms of both combat and operational experience. You guide and advise those commanders. If they're wise, they'll listen to you. If they're not..." The colonel's voice turned grim. "Well. We both know firsthand what happens when the people in charge don't listen to their expert guidance."

With a grimace, Mike replied. "Ain't that the damn truth."

"I'll be briefing them in a few days. They'll know to look for you dirtside to get things coordinated. Take care of them, Mike. They're green and this is a no-shit operation."

"I will, sir."

"I know you will. It's why we picked you for this." The colonel paused, as if he was going to say something else, then said abruptly, "I'll be in touch. Loyo, out." The phone disconnected and Mike put it thoughtfully back on his belt. Having overheard the conversation, the young petty officer asked in a worried tone, "This isn't going to go like we think, is it, sir?"

"Nope." Mike replied. Without another word, he turned and left the cargo bay at a fast pace, leaving the sailor staring at him as he walked away.

# Chapter 3

## "Cold Forge"

*Aboard the Assault Transport UEAN* Phantom Fury, *39 Draconis*
*Task Force 3.1.1*

"Room...Teeench-CHUN!" The throaty bark of the master gunnery sergeant standing by the door snapped through the murmur of conversation in the compact briefing compartment, bringing the officers and senior enlisted to their feet in one motion.

"As you were." A low, gravelly voice came through the silence in the room. Moving through the hatch at a fast walk came Major General Piasecki, followed by his Command Sergeant Major, a tiny woman with an icy expression on her face. Without pause, the general moved up to the podium at the front of the room and nodded at the officer standing to the side of the room and began to speak.

"Ok, Marines. I don't have the time nor the inclination to sugar coat it. We're in for a hell of a fight in this system. I'm going to make sure everyone knows their roles and the overall plan. You'll get the detailed operations order afterwards." He gestured to a major standing near the wall, who dimmed the room lights. As the lights dimmed, the podium control screen illuminated his face from below, sending into stark relief the stainless-steel prosthetic of the right side of his face and the unblinking camera lens that served as his eye. The control lights glinted off of the polished metal and lens, making it look like a metal skull, with the flesh stripped away. He pointed a finger at the screen and started to speak.

"Operation Safecracker." The image on the screen blinked on, showing a starfield with four highlighted systems. "These four systems here are the core sharkie worlds. I won't overcomplicate this. This one is their home, this one here feeds them, this bad boy here is a shipyard and industrial world and this lonely ass pile of rocks in the middle of nowhere is a resource rich system where they mine rare ores and get materials for starship fuel." One of the systems blinked, then zoomed in on a beautiful blue and white planet.

The general continued in his gravelly voice. "This is Topaz. The Fifth Marine Division is going for the shipyards and the 82nd Spaceborne and 2nd Infantry Division and three colonial divisions will assault the planet's surface. The bulk of the Second Fleet is supporting them. It will appear to be the main attack."

The screen flashed again, showing another blue and green world, with massive icecaps and emerald green seas. Pointing at the screen, the officer continued. "Same story here at Objective Ruby, except they have the 3rd and 5th Colonial Armies, supported by the Fourth Fleet." With a dark grin, he added. "If those colonial troops give the Elai half the trouble they gave us back during the insurrections, those sharkheads are in for one hell of a fight." There was a grim chuckle in the dim compartment. The tenacity, ferocity and inventiveness of the colonial troops was well known throughout the UEA military from previous clashes with the colony worlds.

The Marine officer stabbed the control again and continued in his gravelly tone.

"However, all that song and dance is just a diversion to give us cover for what we're really doing." The image changed to a ringed gas giant with multiple small moons orbiting it. "This is the real objective of Safecracker, code named 'Onyx'. The system is Draconis 327 and the objective is these three moons orbiting the largest of the gas giants. These two smaller ones are defensive installations and will be bombed out of existence by the Navy. This big one here is our primary goal. It's got a major anti-ship missile installation, several squadrons of fighters and at least a division sized element of Elai infantry."

He tapped the control again, with the view changing to show the icy black and blue of the frozen moon.

In a confident voice, the general continued. "The operation name to capture Onyx is 'COLD FORGE'. We will seize it, kill every last sharkie we can find, neutralize the anti-ship missiles and set up fighter bases to interdict the fuel harvesters and mining operations in the system. We cut off their fuel and their capital ships run out of gas in about three months." The old Marine grinned, his metal prosthetic giving him a decidedly nightmarish look, "Can't fight a space war without gas in your spaceships." Turning to regard the map momentarily, he then turned back to the assembled Marines. "Marines, these moons are ours, those sharkheads just don't know it yet." He turned back to the assembled Marines. "Now, since they couldn't trust those mouth breathers over in the Fifth Division with this job, it has fallen to us here in the First to take care of business, as usual. 'Rah?"

The Marines in the room responded with the ancient, guttural cry of their service. "Uuu-RAH"

Nodding, General Piasecki pointed at the screen. "Damn right. Now, here's the nuts and bolts of the plan, Marines. We're going to drop in fast and hot and overwhelm these fuckers before they get their bearings and get those big anti-ship missiles launched. We'll be in our drop pods before the Navy jumps into the system and come right from the jump into orbit around the gas giant. It's gonna be a single pass, low orbital drops with high velocity insertion." He grinned and added, "In the finest traditions of the Marines, we're coming in fast and loud." He grinned again and gestured to the steely eye's woman next to him. "Sergeant Major Adana."

The tiny Marine with the hard eyes stepped up to the podium and started speaking in a precise, accented voice. "We will be dropping two operational forces, code named Hammer and Anvil. The plan is for the smaller of the two forces, Task Force Anvil, led by Colonel Nelson's Fifth Battalion will secure a landing zone then immediately dig in. The objective of this force is to secure a base of operations and establish a fixed position to draw the Elai defenders towards. The second and larger force, Task Force Hammer, with the Second, Third and Fourth battalions will be the mobile force. They will drive the Elai forces onto the fixed defenses of First Battalion and destroy them. First Battalion will remain aboard the *Phantom Fury* as an orbital reserve." She paused, then with a glint in her eyes added. "As you can see, we're going to fix them between a rock and a hard place…the old hammer and anvil, hence the operation name."

The lights came up and she looked around the small room. "Most of you know each other. Most of you are combat veterans and have tangled with the Elai before. Make no mistake. This is going to be a nasty fight in a nasty place. Onyx is an icy, nearly airless planetoid. Cold enough to flash freeze flesh, but with volcanoes that go off like tactical nukes. Light gravity, rough terrain. Close enough to the Elai home system to be easily reinforced and important enough to be well defended. They will be dug in deep and they will fight hard. This is a bad place in every sense of the word." Her hard eyes swept the room, meeting the return gazes of the officers and senior enlisted present. She continued quietly. "They will fight savagely for this moon because if we take it, the timer on the end of the war starts. The Navy will get us there but cannot guarantee that we won't be cut off. In fact, we probably will be, at least temporarily. Your job as commanders and first sergeants is to keep your men organized, motivated and in the fight."

From the back of the room came a low drawl. "Hell, Sarn't Major. We cut 'em off, it just means the little critters can't get away. Me'n the weapons company from First Battalion got a little bit'a discussion ta' have with these fellers about Paradise. They acted right uncivilized over there."

Sergeant Major Adama smiled a tight, hard smile. "You'll get your chance, Gunny. You'll all get the chance. "She looked down at the podium and tapped a control, then continued in a calm, professional tone, "The drop sequence will be…."

## Chapter 4

**"The Best Laid Plans"**

*35th Combat Support Hospital (Spaceborne)*
*Aboard the UEAN* Thunderbolt, *39 Draconis*
*August 20th, 2248*

"All right, people. Pipe down." The stocky man with a neatly groomed salt and pepper mustache at the front of the compartment waved a hand in the air. He wore a name tape that read 'Assad' and the eagle insignia of a full colonel on his collar. The chatter in the room died down. The man flipped a switch and the screen behind him illuminated, showing a slide with a single word on it; 'Onyx'. The stocky man spoke again in a booming voice, "Listen up. There's been some changes to the plan and they significantly impact our operations for the first thirty-six to forty-eight hours on the surface." There was groaning by the assembled personnel in the room. Most of them were officers, with a senior noncommissioned officer here and there. The man grinned humorlessly. "For most of you, it's a good thing. You'll be coming in on the shuttles, nice and civilized. For the forward dropped surgical teams, it is going to be just like the bad old days."

Two captains and a major sitting off to the side next to several senior NCO's scowled and started whispering amongst themselves. The man continued, "I'm going to let the Hospital Operations Officer, Colonel Loyo, brief it from here. Colonel?"

The lean man took the front of the room and said in a clear, easy voice. "Thanks, Colonel Assad. Next slide, please." The slide clicked forward and showed a closeup of what appeared to be a crater with a rugged floor and high steep walls. Colonel Loyo gestured at the image and started to speak in a measured, even voice. "Our initial plan to get the field hospital down as the early entry element has changed, due to the nature of the LZ. We knew from pre-drop reconnaissance of the moon that the Marines would need to clear it and bring in engineers to clear space and cut tunnels before we can bring the entire combat support hospital down." Gazing at the assembled leaders in the room he added, "However, the initial plan to bring down the forward dropped resuscitation teams to support operations has been scrubbed due to the fact that a big chunk of the crater floor is apparently not stable enough for the deployable shelters. Navy says that until the Marines secure it, they can't get down there with enough engineers to get us a place to set up." With a dry smile, he added, "The Navy assures us that we can begin moving the remainder of the hospital down within forty-eight hours."

There was a disgusted murmuring from the soldiers in the room and a number of muttered curses directed at the Navy.

Loyo held up a hand and declared, "We don't like it either. Our contingency plan is to send three beefed up forward surgical teams in with the first waves of shuttles. They'll be loaded with extra personnel and equipment to support the jarheads until we get the bulk of our assets onto the surface. Until the remainder of the early entry element equipment comes in, they will be operating out of the tunnels dug by the Marines and the Seabees."

The man looked at the three scowling commanders at the side of the room and said, "336th, 355th and 410th Forward Dropped Resuscitation Teams. You're in the pipe. Major Miller will make contact with Major Manderson once you're dirtside. He's our Army medical liaison assigned to the 5th Battalion, 1st Marines. He'll make sure you have all the assets that the 1st MARDIV can get you and will help coordinate with the Marine command teams." Major Miller scowled and nodded acknowledgement. Colonel Loyo looked at Colonel Assad. "Sir?"

Colonel Assad stepped back up and looked at the three

officers and their detachment sergeants. "Ladies and gentlemen, I'm not going to kid you. It could be a hairy few days down there until the rest of us get down there. You need ANYTHING, the hospital will give it to you. Coordinate requests through Colonel Loyo here." His sharp eyes swept the rest of the leadership from the hospital in the packed room. "Anything they need, they get. Clear, Lunar Medics?"

There was a chorus of quiet 'Yes, sir's' from the group. After a moment, the colonel said firmly, "Get to planning, people." He pointed at the surgical detachment commanders and ordered flatly, "You three, come with me." The three officers stood and followed the colonel as the room started to clear, the buzz of talking once again filling the compartment.

\*\*\*\*

As the two captains and the major followed Colonel Loyola into a small conference room, there was a tense silence. The colonel gestured at the table.

"Sit down." He ordered brusquely.

The three soldiers sat and exchanged glances, then one of the captains, a woman named Etti, spoke up.

"Sir. I don't like that we're going to be liaison with Major Manderson. Everyone knows about what he did on Desolation…"

With a hard look at the younger officer, Loyo replied, "'Everyone knows, do they? What, exactly, do they know?" He locked eyes with the young captain.

Again, looking at the other two officers for support, Etti replied cautiously, "Well, we heard that on Desolation…" She paused and looked sheepish. "I mean. There's rumors that he got most of his unit killed and…" Her voice trailed off.

"We heard he used wounded Marines in stasis pods as a fortification, sir." The other captain, a man with the slender build of a Martian native with the name tape that read 'Abunto' broke in. "Is that true? Because if it is…" He shook his head angrily. "That's fucked up and I don't understand why he's even still in uniform."

Loyo tilted his head at the man and asked quietly. "Were you there?"

With a scowl, Abunto replied, "No, sir. I was in drop training in Tau Ceti."

He shifted his hard look to Etti. "Were you there?"

The woman replied defiantly, "I was. There's no excuse for it."

Suddenly, Major Miller broke in. "Etti, you were on the *Temperance* when the Elai counter attacked. I know that because I was up there with you. Did you ever make it to the surface?"

With a dark look at Miller, Etti replied. "Not until a few months later."

"Yeah, well I did." With a frown at the younger officer, Miller added, "We got sent down to replace the 378th Forward Drop Surgical Detachment after they got wiped out and I saw what they did to Forward Operating Base Humpback." He shook his head. "Not two months later. The week after and it was still a disaster." He looked back at Colonel Loyo. "What actually happened, sir? Were you there?"

Shaking his head, Loyo replied, "No, but mostly by luck. I was about three miles away at division headquarters. We listened over the radio as their perimeter was breached and the Elai overran most of the installation, including the aid station." The colonel grimaced. "When they pushed aside the mech battalion on the perimeter and broke through the walls, the installation commander ordered everyone that was able to move to fall back to the eastern half of the camp to try to re-establish the line." Loyo pulled his data pad out of his uniform and tabbed through it. Pulling up a picture, he slid the pad across the table. As Miller silently picked it up and looked, Loyo continued. "The Elai overran the command post before the staff could get out. Colonel Elias and his staff were cut down where they stood. The remaining soldiers pulled back as they were told, but the 914th Surgical Team either didn't get the message or didn't have enough staff to defend their patients as well as themselves. They had to choose to either run and abandon their patients and maybe get cut down as they did or make a stand in the aid station."

Miller silently passed the pad to Etti, who took it with a faint look of horror on her face. Loyo continued. "Manderson saw them coming and knew that there was no one left to cover them as they withdrew." Etti silently slid the pad to Abunto, who took it. "The Spaceborne had been in the thick of it for a week and the stasis pods with wounded were stacked outside the aid station, awaiting transport to the hospital ship. Manderson was unwilling to abandon his patients and unwilling to let his soldiers die without a fight, so he ordered everyone out of the aid station. He told patients and staff to get out and ordered them to take cover behind the stacks of stasis pods."

Staring at the picture, Abunto muttered, almost to himself, "You know...they do have a durasteel frame and reinforced nanoweave exterior casing..." Shaking his head, he handed the pad back to Loyo.

"They do." Loyo replied. "And while the stasis pods didn't hold up well to the Elai energy bolts, they held up better than the nu-aluminum walls of the aid station." He put the pad back in his uniform pocket. "The 914th managed to hold the Elai off for almost an hour by themselves." He looked hard at the three commanders across from him. "Alone...No infantry. No fire support. No weapons bigger than their rifles. Just the nurses, doctors and medics fighting alongside their patients, led by a man who made the best decision a commander could make in a bad situation." His tone grew gentle. "There's a lesson there, soldiers."

"Yeah." Miller replied sourly. "The Elai don't respect medical facilities."

"They haven't attacked one deliberately since Desolation when they wiped out the Valkyries." The colonel replied, with a slightly reproachful note in his voice. "The General Staff Intel division thinks that it was an accident on their part." Miller shook his head silently at that. Loyo continued, "No. The lesson here is that sometimes even the best prepared and best trained among us will have to deal with something we aren't trained for, because you *can't* train for it and when that happens..." The colonel paused, then continued somberly. "Well, let's hope you're adaptable as Major Manderson was."

There was a long, silent pause at the table. After a moment, Etti asked, "How bad do you think it's going to be down there, sir?"

"Bad." Loyo's tone was grim. "Technologically behind us or not- the Elai are extremely capable soldiers and we're on their turf now. They're fighting for their home and backed into a corner." He paused for a split second. "Be glad you have Manderson down there as your liaison. His reputation is complex, but the man can think on his feet and knows a thing or two about being in a tight spot. When he advises something, listen. You don't have to do what he says; you're the commanders of your units; but given his experience, I strongly recommend you listen to his guidance." His gaze moved to each of theirs in turn. "You three will be the only medical units down there for a few days. Work together, be smart and we'll be down as fast as we can."

"Yes, sir." The three officers replied as one.

Loyo nodded. "Very good. The reworked drop plans are in your mail. Go get your teams ready." He stood, as did the three junior officers. "Dismissed."

The three officers saluted and left the room, their minds turning towards the daunting task ahead.

# Chapter 5

## "Opposed Landing"

*Aboard the Assault Transport UEAN* Phantom Fury
*Low orbit over M3245, Draconis 327.*
*Two Weeks Later*

Major Anthony 'Tony' Harris laid his head back in his armor and blew out a breath, trying to slow his heart rate. He picked up his rifle, checked the function, then loaded a magazine. Checking that it was on safe, he then secured it in the stand built in next to the hatch, then locked his powered armor into place. The rigid armored shell froze, immobilizing him inside the drop pod. The speakers in his helmet crackled and then the gravelly voice of the division commanding officer, Brigadier General Piasecki, broke through.

*"Thirty seconds. Feet first into hell! Go get 'em, Marines!"*
Tony grabbed the bars on either side of the hatch in front of him and braced himself in the seat to prepare for the drop pod's re-entry.

Taking another deep breath and blowing it out, he watched the timer in his helmet clicking down towards zero. At fifteen seconds, he made a quick decision and keyed the comm playback in his suit. A small picture appeared in the lower right of his view, of a pretty brunette woman smiling into the camera with a stunning blue ocean behind her. He focused his vision onto her image. The timer continued its inexorable countdown, hit zero, then chirped twice. He took a deep breath and tried to force his muscles to relax inside of the locked armor. The only thing he could move was his head inside his helmet. There was a series of bumps, then sensation of increasing speed, then another bump, then he was falling. Outside the pod was nothing but silence as he dropped towards the icy landscape below. Commanding the image to play, he fixed his eyes on the woman.

She was speaking to the camera. "Hey Tony! Just wanted to drop you a quick note and say hello, so...Hello!" The woman smiled cheerfully and continued talking as the sensation of falling increased. "I came down to the beach this morning and was just thinking about how much you'd like it here. I mean, how could you not? Look at this!" The view panned to a sun-drenched beach, with the ocean a stunning shade of blue, stretching out until it met the cloudless sky.

Tony smiled slightly at this and checked his displays. There were another series of numbers in his helmet, altitude, speed. The display showed the relative position of the wave of descending pods, screaming towards the planet's surface.

Elizabeth's image continued speaking. "I was also thinking that we ought to think about taking some time off. You know, nonmilitary time and just going exploring. South America, or some of the outer colonies maybe. I hear the scuba diving on Edrani 32 is spectacular. You know...when you're back from wherever you are."

In Tony's other ear on the command net, he could hear speaking; multiple voices and call signs all jumbled together.

A calm voice broke through the confusion, speaking quickly and clearly, *"Witcher Three, Gunfighter Nine Six, Ident, mark six."*

A rapid, tight response, *"Gunfighter, Witcher Lead. I see them. Witcher Six, break left! Left!"*

Another voice broke through the confusion, in a flat, dispassionate tone, *"Spindle, Dropbox. On the hill there at your nine is some sort of gun emplacement. We gave it a pass but took heavy ground fire. Keep an eye on that."*

*"Witcher Lead, Three. Six is hit! He's going in!"*

*"Dropbox, Spindle. Uh...roger, we'll keep an eye...."* The chaotic radio traffic faded into static.

Elizabeth's voice continued. "You know, I was worried about being apart. You know. Even though we haven't ever really had any time in real life. We ought to try that sometime...You know. Real life. The food's better, or so I've been told!" She laughed merrily at her own joke.

The pod was shaking, a dull roar was now audible through the walls of the pod as the atmosphere thickened. The numbers in the altimeter decreased rapidly. The pod began buffeting and shaking hard. There were several loud banging noises from outside, shaking the pod with each impact as the decoys blew themselves free of the pod. On the display on the screen in Tony's helmet several of the symbols indicating the falling pods winked out, either breaking apart or falling to enemy fire.

Elizabeth's voice continued, softly, "I was thinking about how important you are to me." She paused sheepishly, then continued. "I don't know. Maybe I'm just being dumb, but I feel closer the further apart we are." The altimeter in Tony's helmet blinked red and he clenched his teeth together and forced his head back in the helmet. Her voice had taken on a soft, but resolute tone. "I know that we have deliberately not said it because of this stupid war and all. Well, I don't care."

There was a tremendous explosion under him as the retro rockets on the pod fired, feeling as if he had stopped dead in space. There came another few seconds of silence as the pod fell again. Tony locked his eyes on Elizabeth's face on the screen.

Looking down, then back at the camera, Elizabeth spoke again. "I don't really know how to say this, so...Here goes. Tony, I lo..."

There was a massive crash as the pod hit the ground, bounced twice and rolled disorientingly. His head slammed backwards and forward inside his helmet. The pod rolled to a stop, then shuddered as it righted itself. There was a series of teeth-rattling popping from directly in front of him as the explosive bolts blew the door off. The restraints released at the same time and, snatching his rifle from its secure point next to the hatch, Tony hurled himself out of the pod into the smoke and sounds of gunfire.

As he hit the ground outside, he hit a chunk of rock with his armored boot and promptly tripped, falling onto his face. Picking himself up with a muttered curse word, he activated the thermal imaging system and friendly position overlay indicators in his helmet, trying to see around him.

Seeing a group of symbols in his display that marked a group of Marines nearby, Tony moved in a low, fast crouch towards the rally point. Several seconds of sprinting later, he was able to see where the cluster of Marines were positioned and moved towards them.

The group had rallied in a pit in the ground. It had a tattered canvas cover over it and what appeared to be formed walls. It was large enough for the six or seven armored Marines already in the position to not be crowded. Another half dozen were outside, busily opening cases of different types of drones. Loiter drones that acted as long-lasting aerial mines shot skyward, followed by swarms of beetle sized decoy drones that mimicked an individual Marine's heat and signal signatures. Another Marine was launching stealthy recon drones. As the private opened the case, dozens of them shot skyward and vanished almost as soon as they were out of the case. In the distance, Tony could see dozens of other Marines engaged in other tasks, all working calmly and quickly at a multitude of different tasks.

Tony slid into the pit and looked around for his commander, Colonel Nelson. Not seeing him, he made his way to the senior noncommissioned officer present, Sergeant Major Carlos Jimenez. The short, stocky figure of the senior NCO was easily recognizable, even clad in the bulky power armor. As Tony stepped across the hole, he stepped on something. Looking down, he saw a dead Elai soldier in an armored pressure suit, laying on its back. Its faceplate was shattered and it's terrifying reptilian features were already covered in a layer of frost from the lethally cold atmosphere of the moon. Carefully stepping over the body, he moved to Sergeant Major Jimenez, who was snapping instructions into his comlink.

"Alpha, Bravo and Charlie get to that rim, now. Leave cleanup of the stragglers to Delta and Echo." He paused, listening. "Well until he shows up, the company is yours, Lieutenant. Listen to Gunny Singh and don't do anything stupid…. Yeah….Ok. Anvil 7, out."

Jimenez turned to Tony and reported sourly, "Well, sir. As usual, shit isn't going according to plan. We're scattered all over this god damn crater." He motioned to a nearby lance corporal, who was finishing setting up a tactical display.

Looking around the group and seeing mostly senior noncommissioned marines and staff officers, Tony replied, "Yeah. Usually doesn't. Where's Colonel Nelson?"

Jimenez shrugged. "No idea, but this is a big LZ. It might take him a while to get here. You're the big man until he gets here, sir." He gestured at a nearby console. "Here, the tactical display is up."

Tony stepped closer and looked intently at the display. The holographic map illuminated, displaying the landing zone inside the caldera of a long extinct volcano. Markers indicating the moving units of Marines were steadily fanning out towards all sides of the crater and beginning the climb towards the rim, where they had been instructed to dig in. Throughout the floor of the crater, there were red markers, indicating enemy contact.

Tony pointed at the red markers. "Lot more of them than we thought, Sergeant Major. Why?" He looked at the alien body lying on the ground nearby.

Shaking his head, the stocky Marine responded. "No fucking idea, sir. Me and Jenkins landed together and the pod doors popped out and we landed right into this pit here. Poor little fucker never knew what hit him."

Jenkins, the private manning the tactical display, laughed grimly and held up a power armored fist and spoke. "Turns out their faceplates don't hold up that well to a power armored fist, sir. We pushed that little tidbit upstairs so if we find ourselves in close, the guys will know what to do."

The sergeant major spoke again, "Anyways, these little holes are all over the fucking place. Some have Elai in 'em, some don't. They're fighting positions, but sort of half-assed ones and not well laid out. There's also these things all over the place." He pointed at the map, which zoomed in on a flat metal disc, about ten meters across dug into the floor of the crater.

Tony cocked his head and stared hard at the display. "Those the missile silos?" He asked.

Shrugging again, the Sergeant Major replied. "Probably, but who the shit knows. As soon as we get dug in on the ridgeline, we'll pry one open and see. They don't seem dangerous right now, so let's just leave 'em alone."

While the sergeant major spoke, Tony was watching the symbols on the map blink with contact reports. The teams heading for the walls of the caldera were bypassing any Elai they could by running past and shooting as many as they could and leaving the rest. The map symbols for Delta and Echo companies formed into a long skirmish line, preparing to sweep around the crater floor like a clock, sweeping up Elai stragglers.

Satisfied, Tony nodded. "Ok. Except for the fact that we didn't know these guys were here and the scattered drop pattern, the plan is holding." He turned to a captain working a radio nearby. "Captain Shin, call the Navy. Tell 'em to drop the heavy pods with the fire support mechs as soon as Delta and Echo have cleared half of the LZ." Turning to another officer nearby, he ordered, "Captain Lew, as soon as those Gorgons are on the ground, I want targeting data for them. Your observer teams should be on the rims of the crater now and their drones ought to have a pretty clear view. If there's any hint of sharkheads within fifty clicks, I want them turned into a smoking crater." The two officers nodded and turned to their radios. Turning to an enlisted Marine nearby, Tony ordered, "Get us a head count of casualties from the drop and find those missing pods," the Marine acknowledged and turned to his task.

Jimenez pointed out the side of the captured Elai fortification. "The auto turrets are up, sir. We shouldn't take much indirect fire." In the distance, a small team of Marines had opened a bulky drop pod. Out of the pod, on an expanding frame rose a smooth, glass ball. In the tactical display, the symbol for anti-missile defense system blinked on, followed by others around the crater, twelve in all. As reports came in, the display became rapidly more complex, with equipment and units coming online or moving around.

A nearby enlisted Marine reported, "Sir, Sergeant Major. Echo company just found two more pods that burned in. One of 'em was Colonel Nelson. Looks like his decoys popped early and they got him."

Nodding, Jimenez looked at Tony and spoke in a matter of fact tone. "Well, that answers that. Looks like it's your show for the time being, sir."

Tony nodded grimly and replied, "Yeah. Hell of a way to go." Forcing his former friend and commander out of his mind for the moment, he turned back to the Marine, "Let the sweep and clear force know to keep their eyes out the rest of the missing pods, but that the primary objective is to secure this crater."

The Marine nodded, "Yes, sir. The sweep force reports that they have cleared half of the crater. The Navy shuttles are two minutes out with the Seabees and the medical teams are right behind them. The Gorgons are launching from the *Fury* now and Spindle reports that Witcher is on station for top cover."

Tony nodded and replied. "Good. The second they hit the surface, tell them to start boring into the crater wall. We need those bunkers up."

"Yes, sir." The Marine turned back to his radio and started manipulating the controls.

Tony put his hands on his hips and stared at the display, thinking. After a moment he spoke. "Sergeant Major. If you were the sharkie commander, what would you do if we dropped in?"

Jimenez chuckled drily. "Me? I'd already be pummeling the dogshit out of this LZ with arty and follow it up with a rapid counterattack on the ground. Personally, I'd use armor but if not I'd use whatever I had. They have to know once we get dug in, we're going to be a real pain in the ass to get out. Whatever they're gonna do, it's gonna be soon."

The Marine manning the tactical display spoke up. "Sir, Spindle is reporting that we have multiple Elai fast movers inbound. Witcher Flight is withdrawing until Gunfighter has secured the airspace."

Tony nodded, thinking about this. Witcher Flight was their primary close air support; flying the squat, sturdy and heavily armed Banshee ground support fighter. Gunfighter was a Navy squadron of Apparition fighters; fast, stealthy and supposedly better than anything the Elai had in their inventory. If the command and control crew in the spaceboard command aircraft known as 'Spindle' said there were inbound threats…He turned to Captain Shen and ordered, "Tell the Navy that…"

The Marine on the tactical station interrupted, "Sir, drones are showing a large collection of vehicles at two seven four, at thirty clicks." He paused, listening, then spoke again. "And the scout platoons confirm enemy armor identified. Estimate twenty plus medium enemy vehicles, no type ID at this time."

Tony looked at Sergeant Major Jimenez, who grinned and said, "Here comes the arty." The senior noncommissioned officer closed the heavily armored blast shield on his helmet.

The Marine on the tactical station shouted, "Incoming! Bearing two five three, two seven four, forty vampires!"

A moment later, an automated voice came over the general area broadcast frequency, booming in its distinctive mechanical voice, "INCOMING, INCOMING, INCOMING".

An insistent alarm began to hoot and Tony could see Marines all over the crater floor diving for the nearest cover, some into the scattered and now mostly abandoned Elai fighting positions, some throwing themselves prone and trying to get as low as possible. Tony sat down in the bunker and kept his eyes fixed on the glass globes of the Zeus missile defense system that he could see sticking some fifteen meters above the crater floor. There was a brief red streak that shot out of it, then another and another, the laser beams catching just enough dust to be visible to the naked eye. A split second later, there came a series of faint popping and muted flashes from above. In the tactical display, the rapidly moving red dots of the incoming missiles were winking out as the laser defense system knocked them out of the sky.

Tony looked at the Sergeant Major, who was leaning back and watching the missiles detonating above. Catching Tony looking at him, the smaller man grinned. "Hell of a light show, sir. Oops. Heads down." Almost faster than Tony could react, the noncommissioned officer rolled flat into the pit and onto his face, dragging Tony with him. As he did there was a tremendous roar as something streaked by extremely close overhead, then a flash. The shock wave bounced the Marines around in their pit. For a moment after, there was silence, then the automated voice spoke again.

"ALL CLEAR. ALL CLEAR. ALL CLEAR." At the tactical Station, the Marine spoke dazedly, "Sir, all rockets intercepted by the Zeus. Negative hits inside the perimeter."

Sitting up, Tony gave a hard look at the Marine and pointed in the direction of the explosion. "If no rockets hit, what the hell was that?"

Sergeant Major Jimenez spoke, "Sir, that wasn't a rocket. That was a fighter."

Standing and peering in the direction of the explosion, Tony asked, "Whose fighter?"

Captain Shin spoke up. "Uh...We just heard from Gunfighter Flight. Apparently, that was one of the Elai suborbital fighters, sir. They just greased one of the Navy heavy shuttles coming in. Gunfighter Lead says he had a shot and took it but the Elai was too low to avoid crashing inside the crater. He also reports that all the Elai air in the area is neutralized for the time being. They're vectoring Witcher Flight onto the armor." He paused a moment, then reported, "We have a fix on the shuttle crash site. Combat search and rescue is not available yet, since the Valkyries don't come down until the second wave."

"They'll have to wait," Jiminez replied bluntly. "We'll get to them when we secure the DZ."

"Agreed. We'll get to them when we can." Tony replied and clambered to his feet just in time to see a heavy lift shuttle come roaring in low over the wall of the crater, closely followed by two others. They swooped down into the middle of the mile wide crater, their massive cargo doors already opening. The moment the shuttles touched down, vehicles and Marines started pouring out. From the lead shuttle, four massive tracked vehicles appeared, two from each side. On one end of the vehicle was a dozer blade, controlled from a heavily armored crew cabin. The aft of the vehicle was a large, round surface with cutting bits protruding from them. Tony nodded in satisfaction. They had a technical name; The D-32A4 Tactical Combat Construction Vehicle, but the Marines called them 'Killdozers'. The giant armored tractors didn't even pause as they came off the ramps of the shuttle, just ground their way towards the crater rim, each heading in a cardinal direction to begin the construction of the bunker system.

Behind the construction vehicles, the massive four-legged combat missile platforms came into view. The sturdy legs supported a large, rounded, beetle-like body that had earned them their nickname: 'Humpbacks'. These were the M37-B 'Gorgon' Fire Support/Missile platforms; and could fire and maneuver to avoid counter battery fire.

Tony smiled savagely and turned to the Sergeant Major. "Sergeant Major, think we can whip up a little surprise for our friends outside the crater?

Jimenez grinned and replied. "Way ahead of you, sir." He

pointed at the Humpbacks. The rear of the large walkers had elevated, showing dozens of missiles in the tubes. As Tony watched, the missiles began to flash, sending flashes of fire skyward. Tony nodded in satisfaction, watching dozens of the precision guided munitions racing into the sky to rain down fire onto the Elai vehicles.

The Marine on the tactical station spoke again. "Sir, Alpha, Bravo and Charlie companies report the rim positions are secured and that they have begun to dig in. Prefab bunkers are on the way up the crater wall now. Delta and Echo report the crater floor is clear."

Tony nodded and looked at the tactical display. The construction vehicles were at the crater wall and had started chewing into their tunnels. The symbols for fighting positions and crew served lascannons had popped up on the rim of the crater and the markers for the construction troops were now fanning out all over the crater. Setting onto the hundreds of tasks that would transform the extinct volcano crater into a foothold on the moon.

"Sir; Ironjaw 6 actual is on the horn. He wants a sitrep." The Marine on the comm panel tapped a control and there was a brief burst of static then the small image of General Piasecki appeared in Tony's helmet display. The old Marine General's scarred face in the tiny image was like something from a nightmare.

The apparition spoke in a gravelly voice. *"Status report, Major Harris."*

Tony responded, "Sir, the LZ is secure. There was some scattered ground resistance, but it seems pretty disorganized. I think we caught them with their pants down. One attempt so far at indirect fire; neutralized by the Zeus systems, one air sortie countered by the Navy, but not before they got one of our heavy lift shuttles. We have counterbattery fire going out now. The Navy caught an armor column headed our way and chewed it up with Banshees. They're chasing down stragglers now. Bunkers going in, tunnels in progress. Patrols will start within the hour."

General Piasecki nodded and asked, *"Casualties? Where's Colonel Nelson?"*

Tony shook his head, grimly. "Don't have totals yet, but he was one of them. Pod was hit on the way in. We also have a Navy shuttle down outside of the perimeter. We're putting a team together to secure the crash site now. We'll get numbers for you as soon as we have them."

The frightening visage of the general officer regarded Tony for a moment, then spoke. *"Ok, Tony. What's your no bullshit assessment? These little bastards are fast, so we gotta be faster. So, I have two questions. Are you operational and can we start the offensive?"*

Tony thought about this for a moment, then replied. "Yes, sir. Forward Operating Base Anvil is online. Start landing the troops."

Piasecki grinned, making his face even more terrifying. *"Good man. Now, Major, what do you say to us going and paying these little fuckers back for what they did to us on Paradise?"*

Tony's grin matched his commander. "That, sir, sounds like a hell of an idea.

## Chapter 6

### "Into the Void"

*Aboard the Assault Transport UEAN* Phantom Fury
*Low orbit over M3245, Draconis 327.*
*August 26, 2248*

"Commander Nelson?" Lieutenant Commander Nelson, the bridge operations watchstander, turned as his name was called. Moving over to the petty officer on the sensor station, he replied in a low tone, so as not to disturb Captain DiGenova sitting nearby in her command chair.

"What do you have, sailor?" he asked, looking over her shoulder at the sensor readouts.

The sailor gestured to the display in puzzlement and said, "We have a ton of high frequency interference, sir. It just started all of the sudden."

With a slight frown, Nelson responded, "You run a console diagnostic?"

"Yes, sir. It didn't really clear it up. I did get broader spectrum interference here, here and here." The sailor indicated a section of her display. She added, "I thought it might be solar interference, but we're kind of far out from the primary for a flare to screw things up that bad." Nelson nodded and tugged at his lip thoughtfully, then glanced at the captain. Deciding against bothering her, he picked up his comm panel, tapped a few keys and then spoke,

"Sudden Strike, this is Silent Death." The call sign for the *Phantom Fury's* sister ship, *Thunderbolt,* was a reference to an ancient military philosopher, although Nelson didn't know it.

After a moment, the ship communications officer responded, *"Silent Death, Sudden Strike. Go ahead."*

Keying his mic again, Nelson said, "Hey, can you do us a

solid? We're picking up a ton of fifty to seventy thousand gigahertz interference at two two five. Might be solar activity. Since you're closer, can you run an active sweep and see if you have anything on that bearing?"

*"Will do, Silent Death. Standby."* The ship to ship radio fell silent for a moment, then blared, *"Silent Death, Sudden Strike, we have multiple unidentified contacts, bearing two two five. No ident, Assume hostile, assume hostile."* There was a hiss as the *Thunderbolt's* communications officer broke the connection abruptly.

Nelson stared at the display. He didn't want to bother the captain for a jumpy sensor watchman on the...

The petty officer on the sensor station in front of him suddenly shouted, "Multiple contacts, two two five, mark three and seven! No ident, negative IFF!"

Nelson spun and snapped, "Captain DiGenova, we have multiple contacts bearing two two five, estimate four hundred thousand kilometers. Assess probable enemy heavies, unknown number."

Captain Valentina DiGenova nodded calmly and replied in a firm tone. "Very good. Mr. Miller, take the ship to general quarters. XO, prepare to break orbit. Mr. Perry, sound the maneuver alarms. Tell the launch parties they have twenty minutes to get what they can off the ship, then we thrust." She paused as the crew sprang into action and alarms began to chirp all over the ship. Seeing the flurry of activity, she turned to her executive officer and spoke in her lilting voice, "Signal the flagship. We have sighted the enemy fleet."

\*\*\*\*

*Flag Bridge, UEAN Heavy Cruiser 'Stalwart'*
*High Orbit over M3245*

Rear Admiral Laura Kensington's display chirped, providing an update on the progress of the troop landings. She looked up from the deployment status update for the remainder of the First Marine Division. About half of them were on the moon, in two major fire bases. Her staff was telling her that another forty eight hours and they'd have most of the Marines and all of their armor and artillery on the moon with them. She smothered a yawn and lifted her coffee cup, only to find it was empty. Looking at her liaison officer, a Marine colonel, she said, "Mitch, I'm going to get another cup. Want one?"

The stocky Marine shrugged, "If you're buying, ma'am." Grinning, she moved towards the hatch of the flag bridge.

As she grabbed the handle, a watch stander said, "Ma'am, Captain DiGenova from the *Phantom Fury* is on the line. It's flash traffic." Cocking an eyebrow, Admiral Kensington moved to the panel and hit the accept key.

DiGenova's dark complexion filled the screen. Her face was serious and professional. She said in a calm, firm tone, *"Admiral. Sensors report that we have between seven and ten Elai heavy cruisers with multiple escorts inbound. Estimated time to contact three zero minutes."*

Kensington swore under her breath then replied, "Captain DiGenova, launch what you can and prepare to break orbit. I'm going to get the fleet underway. Kensington out."

Turning and walking back to her display, she said rapidly, "Commander de la Cruz, alert the fleet. Tell all transports and assault carriers to prepare to break orbit. If they can launch their dropships in fifteen minutes, to get them going. If they can't, just go." De la Cruz nodded and bent to her communications console. Staring at the display for a moment, the admiral then ordered, "Captain Soklov, signal cruiser divisions One, Two and Three and destroyer divisions Seven, Nine, Fifteen and Sixteen to advance to contact along two two five. Execute Operational Plan Kilo." She frowned, thinking. Plan Kilo ordered the fleet to engage the enemy fleet until the assault carriers were clear of the gravity well. It worked well when the enemy force was evenly matched. This time, they weren't.

She stared for a moment longer, then turned to her Marine liaison, "Colonel Thompson. Get me General Piasecki, now." The stocky marine wordlessly held out his handset, having anticipated the order. She took the handset and said, "Alex?"

The gravely tone on the other end responded immediately, *"How many, Admiral?"*

Turning to look at the display, she replied, "Ten or so heavies, with a couple dozen destroyers. I'm going to try to buy some time with the cruisers, but I have to pull the assault transports. They'll be heading outsystem. I told their captains to launch everything they have in the bays and get ready to go."

There was a moment of silence from the other end, then the gravelly voice again, *"Well. We planned for this. Hoped it wouldn't come to it, but shit happens. Launch every ready bird you got, as well as many fighters as you can spare. We're gonna need em."*

Kensington nodded her head and said quietly into the mic, "Good luck down there, Piasecki."

The old Marine's voice was gentle, *"You too, ma'am. Give 'em hell. I'll see you on the other side."* The connection broke as the thrum of the *Stalwart* engines picked up speed as the warship turned to intercept the incoming enemy vessels.

\*\*\*\*

*Aft Ready Room, UEAN* Phantom Fury
*Low Orbit over M3245*

The chiming of alarms woke Major Ross 'Rocco' Genova from a sound sleep in the recliner in the pilots ready room. Looking around, he didn't see anyone and there was no emergency warning directed at the medevac birds, so he leaned back and tried to close his eyes again. Moments later, his phone went off. Swearing, he dug it out of a pocket and answered irritably, "What?"

His co-pilot, Captain Jeremy 'Icepick' Moretti's image appeared, "Dude. The *Fury's* breaking orbit."

With a scowl, Rocco responded, "So what?"

"So, that means the Elai fleet is coming," Moretti responded.

Rocco sighed, "Didn't you get enough of those little bastards on Paradise? I say if the Navy's bugging out, we go with 'em."

Moretti glared at him from the phone screen, "And leave the Marines with their nuts hanging out down there? Don't be a dick. We're not doing that. Get the fuck on the phone and ask for emergency clearance. We'll get the Valk warmed up. The med crew is already loading."

After a few seconds of glaring at the phone, Rocco sighed, "I fucking hate it when you appeal to my conscience. I'll be right down." Sighing, he tapped the phone to disconnect and thought for a minute, then punched a contact.

After a moment, a woman's face appeared. She looked stressed and snapped, "Rocco, this had better be good. We're really busy up here."

With a grin, the pilot replied, "When do I ever contact you without a reason, Angie?" The woman's face darkened and she moved to disconnect.

Quickly, Rocco said, "Wait! Listen. We know the *Fury's* breaking orbit. We got one Valkyrie on deck in the launch lineup and another that can lift with thirty minutes of lead time. Talk to the space boss. Let us get down there and help those Marines."

The woman glared at him for a moment then sighed, turned and spoke to someone in the background, her words inaudible. After a minute, she turned back and said quickly, "He says fine. He's gonna send some stuff down with you, so they're loading your Valk now and you'll get expedited clearance. Get your ass moving. You have twenty two minutes to get out of the bay before we thrust."

Rocco breathed a sigh of relief. He didn't have the best

relationship with the commander of the air/space group, due to an inebriated misunderstanding some months before. Angie continued, "He also says good luck and to not get your dumb ass shot down."

Nodding, Rocco responded, "You be safe up here, Ang. Tell Pierre thanks and I still think he's still an asshole and also to try not to die." The woman nodded and broke the connection wordlessly. Rocco looked at the clock, then stepped towards the head right off of the pilots ready room. Moments later, relieved, he started moving rapidly for the hatch and called Jeremy as he did.

His co-pilot's face appeared on the screen. Behind him Rocco could see the dark, familiar confines of the cockpit of their specialized search and rescue craft that was known throughout the Earth Alliance forces as a 'Valkyrie'.

Moretti snapped, "Rocco, hurry your ass up. We just got expedited clearance. I can time it between the fighter launches." He stopped to tap a control, then continued, "We also have a bunch of sailors throwing a big pile of shit into the back and a bunch of passengers. No idea what it is, but they said it came right from the CAG."

The deck bucked and a different alarm began to chime. Rocco stumbled, then caught himself. His co-pilot yelled from his phone, "Get your ass down there! I'm starting preflight! Katerina…." The connection broke as Jeremy and the flight engineer Sergeant Katarina Dagoyavitch began preparing the craft for launch. Increasing his jog to a sprint, Rocco flew down the passageway and nearly fell taking a ladder three steps at a time. Cursing, he made the last turn to the wide passageway that led to the *Phantom Fury's* primary flight deck. As he turned he could see two sailors in vacuum suits and helmets with visors up, getting ready to seal the door.

Rocco raised his voice and waved as he ran, "Yo! Hold up!"

One of the sailors turned and said something to the other, then paused. Rocco came up to the hatch, paused and gasped, "Thanks. I'm heading for Three Alpha."

Looking him over, the sailor said, "You'd better fucking hurry, sir. We're taking fire. The captain's breaking orbit in twelve minutes. You know where it is?"

"Yeah." The deck lurched again under their feet.

With a jerk of his head, the sailor indicated the hatch, "Go. You got seven minutes before we depressurize the hangar. Do NOT be on the deck when we do."

"Yeah." Rocco gasped in reply and slipped through the hatch, noting the yellow flashing lights that preceded the atmosphere evacuation of the entire hangar deck. Entering a full sprint, he put his head down and raced across the cavernous hangar, heading for the docking station where their Valkyrie was moored.

Ahead of him, he could see that the rear crew compartment door of the big craft was open. Two of the hulking power armored suits of the medical crew were in their seats and half a dozen armored combat pressure suits were piled into the back as well. The deck bucked again and he fell to his knees. Scrambling to his feet, he could see the armored figure pointing at him, then gesturing to him to hurry. Covering the last few meters in a record time, Rocco reached out for the armored figures' hand. The augmented strength of the armor hauled him into the air and into the back, dumping him in an undignified heap across the laps of the suited figures.

Looking up, he could see the figure that had just pulled him in speaking, "We got him. Sealing crew cabin, ready for lift." The cabin wall screens flicked to life, displaying the flight deck around them. The figure opened his helmet visor; revealing the flight nurse, Captain James Matthews. The young man grinned and said, "God damn, sir. You know how to make an entrance."

Rocco unentangled himself from the pile of figures and struggled toward the cockpit, saying as he went, "Make sure they're strapped in, it's gonna be rough." He squirmed through the hatch and closed it behind him. The pressure hatch light came on over the door.

Regarding the sudden entrance of the pilot, one of the suited figures spoke in a muffled voice, "Who the fuck was that?"

The lead flight medic, Master Sergeant Brian Agawa, replied, "That was the pilot in command of Valkyrie One, Major Genova."

One of the figures, their faces obscured by the helmets muttered, "That's the *pilot*? Then who's flying this fucking thing?"

Agawa smiled slightly and replied, "Hey, Doc. Icepick and Rocco are mostly qualified and almost not completely retarded. I flew with them on Paradise. We're probably going to be fine." He paused, then added, "You might want to buckle up, though." He reached over and sealed the big side door of the aircraft, as the engine noise started to increase with the power ramping up.

One of the suited surgical team said to Matthews, "*Probably* gonna be ok?"

The nurse grinned, "We're fine, sir. Major Genova and Captain Moretti are way more competent than they seem." He paused for a second then added, "But like he said; you should definitely buckle in. This is gonna be a rough ride."

There were a series of bumps from underneath them, then the sounds of alarms faded away as the atmosphere was evacuated from the hangar.

Casually, the stocky medic said, "Rocco's doing a no count lift. Here we..." There was a sudden push from behind the large craft, then the hangar vanished around them. For a few seconds, the massive assault carrier looked like a wall in space, then rapidly shrunk.

Suddenly, Sergeant Agawa pointed at the side viewscreen, "Captain Matthews. There. See those?" The side of the massive assault carrier had three large scorch marks on the side of its hull, about a hundred meters from the hangar bay doors. As they watched, three more bright flashes hit the ship, then dissipated in rapid bursts. There was a burst of light from further out as something exploded and they could see the ruby light sparkling from the dome shaped missile defense turrets on the hull of the ship as the turrets came to life. Amid the silent light show, another hangar bay door flew open and the chunky gray bulk of an assault shuttle could be seen powering out of the bay, its engines already flaring as the bulky craft attempted to clear the beleaguered carrier.

Watching the flashing and silent flowers of explosions in the void, the young officer asked in an awed voice, "Missiles?"

The sergeant nodded and replied, "Missiles. Those are small ones, but small for the fleet is more than big enough for us. The defense turrets target the bigger ones and let the hull armor eat the small ones."

Watching the ship as it grew smaller, Matthews asked, "Do we need to worry?"

With a shrug, the senior NCO answered, "I doubt the Elai give a shit about us right now. They want the carriers. We're small fries compared to the ship." More streaks of light headed towards the carrier then disappeared as their craft rolled away from their mother ship. The two Valkyrie crewman and the frightened surgical team watched in silence.

Rocco's voice came over the intercom, *"Ok, we're re-entering in about sixty seconds. This icy shitball doesn't have much of an atmosphere, but it's got enough to be bumpy. Plus, we're going in assuming there's bad guys down there, so hold onto your butts and keep your suits sealed."*

Up in the cockpit, Captain Moretti keyed the radio, "Anvil Station, Valkyrie One."

The Marine forward ground controller's voice was distorted and tinny through the static of the return connection. *"Valkyrie One, Anvil Station."*

"We're inbound bearing two seven one, estimated time enroute seven minutes, tactical approach. We'll be coming in low and fast. We have a high priority load, so clear an LZ."

The response came rapidly, *"Valkyrie One, we don't have any prepared LZ's set up yet. Land at the pinged coordinates. It's the best we're gonna get for now. See you on the deck and watch out for gomers. Squawk two two seven seven and good luck. Anvil Station out."*

"Two two seven seven, Valkyrie One." Moretti disconnected the radio and started rapidly snapping switches, preparing for entry into the atmosphere. As he did, he muttered, "Fucking white-knight boy-scout bullshit is gonna get me killed."

Putting his helmet on, Rocco replied, "This was your idea. Don't forget that." He reached out and took the controls. "My bird." He rapidly tested the flight controls, then asked, "Who are the jabronis in the back?"

Moretti shrugged, his eyes locked on the controls. "No idea. I think it's a surgical team. They were due to drop later today, but the admiral wanted them down early, since the *Fury* had to break orbit." An alert chimed on the console and he added, "One hundred thousand. Time to start re-entry." Rocco nodded and started tapping in the re-entry sequence. Rocco looked at Moretti, frowned and keyed his mic to speak to the whole crew, "Here we go. Hold onto your nuts."

The Valkyrie began to shudder as it dropped rapidly towards the moon's surface.

\*\*\*\*

*Flag Bridge, UEAN Heavy Cruiser 'Stalwart'*

The heaving deck and a massive shower of sparks caused Admiral Kensington to turn her face from the console and hold on tightly as the impacts shook the warship. The acrid smoke from the shorting console was making her eyes water and she could hear her flag staff coughing and swearing at the smoke as the powerful ventilation systems cleared it. The lights and display dimmed momentarily, then came back up as the power surge abated. She looked to her left at the lieutenant commander standing at the station that monitored and communicated with the *Stalwart's* bridge.

The officer was staring intently at his display, then looked up and said, "Captain Kayser reports mission capable. No more missiles inbound."

The *Stalwart* remained in the fight for now, despite the hits. Kensington nodded and turned her attention to the display. Nothing she could do about it. Captain Kayser would fight the ship; she would fight the fleet. In the middle of the dim flag bridge, the holographic display showed the bright red spots with identification tags on the reported locations of the Elai ships. The human ships were in blue, with the icy blue-black color of the moon towards the bottom of the display. Frowning, she tried to put herself in the position of the Elai fleet commander and asked herself what she would do, were she them.

Her fleet operations officer, Captain Arun Destin, a slender man with the pale, smooth skin that came from growing up in Earth's asteroid belt, reported in a firm voice, "Admiral, they're splitting up. Designate enemy forces as Force Alpha and Bravo. Deviate course three seven five, three seven seven. Looks like...five heavies per group, with escorts." In the display, the Elai vessels began to diverge. At the bottom, the two large blue dots that indicated the *Phantom Fury* and the *Thunderbolt* were visible. She could see from the tiny numbers in the display that their captains were thrusting, desperately trying to break orbit, but deep in the moon's gravity. Well, it was going to take some time– time they didn't have.

Pausing to consider the tactical situation, Laura scowled at the display, then stated flatly, "They're going for the carriers." Biting her lower lip in concentration, she thought, then turned to her staff, "Ok. We probably can't hit them both at once and they know it. Options?"

Captain Destin replied promptly, "Doctrine says to hit in force. Pick one and hit it, then get the other. We'll outnumber them locally."

Another member of her staff, a tiny, dark eyed commander named Penelope de la Cruz, retorted, "At the possible cost of one or both of the carriers? I'm not sure that Casey and her two light cruisers can hold off five Elai heavies while we isolate and destroy the other."

A stocky man with a crooked nose and a Russian accent spoke up from the other side of the display, "We can run up the middle of the two groups, if we burn hard now. We'd probably damage them badly enough to give Casey a shot."

Staring at the display, Destin responded slowly, "We're gonna get hurt, Dimitry."

Shrugging, the Russian officer responded, "We have a better chance than the *Fury* and *Thunderbolt*. They still have half the First Marine division aboard and not nearly the firepower, armor, or defensive armament that we do. Commander de le Cruz, we outgun the Elai cruisers, yes?"

With a shrug, de la Cruz replied, "Historically, yes. These ones are already proving more capable than the others we have on file."

Dimitry grimaced. Turning to Kensington, the stocky man said in a formal voice, "Admiral, as I see the tactical situation, we have little choice. We must meet them head on."

Admiral Kensington thought for a moment, then nodded and said firmly, "I agree. Captain Soklov, order the *Fury* and the *Thunderbolt* to drop every smart mine they have aboard and to get every transport they can scramble to the surface, then to break orbit and drop sunward. If we can't hold orbit, I'll be damned if I let the sharkies have it either." She turned to the slender officer next to her, "Destin, notify Captain Casey that she is to protect those carriers at all costs." She stared hard at the man for a moment, then said again, "At all costs, Arun. Get those carriers outsystem."

The pale man nodded and responded quietly, "Understood, Ma'am."

Turning to de la Cruz, Laura Kensington took a deep breath and said, "Commander, order the fleet to come to two three five and to advance to flank speed. Prepare for action to port and starboard. Report ships manned and ready." She paused for a moment, listening as her experienced and highly trained staff gave the orders that turned the seven heavy cruisers and their destroyer escorts of the task force towards the onrushing Elai fleet. Watching the display, she said, thoughtfully, "The way they're diverging, we're only going to get one shot at both of them."

Captain Sokolov replied, "Agree. If we burn hard now, then turn and decelerate prior to contact, it will prolong our time in the engagement window. If they are seeking to neutralize us as a force, they'll slow. If they're aiming to hit the carriers, they'll accelerate and try to blow past."

Kensington nodded slowly, then said, "I think if they blow past us, we come around and try to hit them as they enter the gravity well. I don't think they'll leave us out here in their rear. They'll fight."

Captain Destin looked up at this and asked, "How do you know, ma'am?"

Regarding the man with a tight smile, the admiral responded, "Because that's what I'd do. I'd blow past us, hit us as hard as possible, then come around and finish the job. The carriers are easy pickings if they take us out."

The other officer nodded somberly in agreement and turned back to his console.

Commander de la Cruz spoke thoughtfully, staring at the display, "Well. If we hit them hard and then keep going, then they can't commit to a landing operation, can they? We'll just hit them when they try. They have to know we'll be on their asses until our heavies in Task Force 3.s gets here."

Drumming her fingers on the edge of the display, Kensington responded, "Yeah. While we wait for our heavies, that begs the big question: Where are their heavies? Are we being lured into a trap?" The small command staff fell silent, staring at the holographic display as the two fleets inched closer and closer together.

\*\*\*\*

*Aboard the UEAN* Infiltrator

Commander Von Kant frowned at the display and said, "Well, it looks like Admiral Kensington's picked the brute force option."

Captain Mitch Harris sighed, "Well, subtlety never was Laura's strong suit. Let's hope she's as tough as we think she is." He paused for a moment, then ordered in a firm tone, "XO, take the stealth systems online. Rig for dark running. Put us on an intercept course between those gomers out there and the carriers." He paused, staring at the display and said thoughtfully, "Vicky Casey is good, but those two light cruisers of hers aren't going to last long if those big bastards break through."

Von Kant nodded and replied, "She's gonna need help, on that we agree; but if we break stealth we aren't going to last long either, Skipper."

Rubbing his chin, Harris nodded absently then suddenly grinned, "I think I've got an idea. Come right to zero five two and get me the Chief Engineer and the Weapons Officer. We're going to have to get creative."

\*\*\*\*

*Flag Bridge, UEAN Heavy Cruiser* 'Stalwart'

The shaking of the deck finally ceased. The emergency lights popped on, throwing pools of light in the inky black of the flag bridge, previously only lit by sparks from blown out equipment. Feeling for the edge of the command table, Kensington pulled herself to her feet. The compartment was eerily quiet, with the only sound the distant hooting of alarms from outside. The emergency lights cut beams of light through the smoke from the consoles and Laura could smell the scorched plastic and burnt metal from the damaged equipment.

In a voice that was calmer than she felt, Laura called out, "Fleet status, Commander de la Cruz." In the darkness, she could hear a low, steady mumble in Russian from Captain Sokolov. Even though she didn't understand it, she knew cursing when she heard it. She could see him making his way to his feet, cradling his left arm with his right, the unnatural angle in it obvious even in the gloom.

Commander de la Cruz began to call out in a clear, steady voice, "Admiral, fleet status. *Stalwart* reports damage to port side and scattered power losses. *Independent* reports damage to maneuvering systems but can keep up with the fleet. *La Venganza* reports multiple hull breaches but is operational. *Bravado* reports no damage and is volleying all remaining ready anti-ship missiles at the enemy."

Admiral Kensington nodded. *Bravado* was at the end of the line of cruisers and was ensuring that the enemy cruisers had plenty to discourage them from pursuing. The petite commander continued to call out status reports, "Cruisers *Forthright, Audacious* and *Steadfast* are not answering hails and are no longer responding on the fleetnet. Destroyers *Sling, Arrow* and *Dagger* are not answering hails and no longer responding on fleetnet. *Bowie* is heavily damaged and her captain has ordered the crew to abandon ship." The woman paused, her face pale.

Next to Laura, Captain Sokolov muttered, "Damn."

Laura clenched her eyes tightly shut for a moment, trying not to think about the thousands of Alliance sailors dead and dying in the hulls of those ships because of her decisions. Opening her eyes, she snapped at Captain Destin, "Report on the enemy fleet, Captain Destin."

The pale skinned man nodded and said in a clear, calm voice, "Admiral, Alpha One has suffered a catastrophic loss with confirmed core detonation. Alpha Two is powered down and adrift. It appears to be launching lifepods. Alpha Three, Four and Five are damaged but remain operational. Group Bravo has had two catastrophic losses, with Bravo One suffering a core detonation and Bravo Two breaking up. Bravo Three has suffered extensive structural damage but is keeping up with the group. Bravo Four and Five appear undamaged and remain on an intercept course for the carriers. Multiple Elai destroyers knocked out...four, I think." The man paused, then said again, "Admiral, Group Alpha is coming around. They're going to try to make another pass at us."

Laura leaned on the edge of the display, thinking rapidly. She had four cruisers left, all but one heavily damaged. The Elai had three in Alpha group and two in Bravo with minimal damage.

Next to her, Dimitry rumbled, "Not good odds, Admiral. We might want to think about falling back until the heavies get here."

Standing and looking at the display again, with the flickering numbers updating next to her four remaining cruisers, she thought rapidly, then came to a decision.

"Captain Destin, signal the fleet. Set course three zero five, ahead flank. We've got a speed advantage, so we're going to run until they turn, then hit them in the ass if they try to go for Captain Casey and her group. As long as we're out here, they can't commit to supporting the assault."

"Aye-aye, Ma'am." The man bent to his communications station.

In a low tone, Captain Soklov muttered, "Well, at least we gave Captain Casey better odds."

Admiral Kensington nodded and replied grimly, "Yeah. I hope it's enough."

\*\*\*\*

*Aboard the UEAN* Infiltrator

Commander Von Kant turned from her display and announced, "Group Bravo is entering engagement ranges for the stationary weapons."

Mitch nodded and said firmly, "Make ready to fire the stationary weapons in synch with our volley and prepare to break contact. Activate drone decoys on my mark." He turned to a lieutenant sitting at a weapons station, "Lieutenant, open tubes 1-10. Arm and target all missiles, maximum warhead yield. Set to synch fire with stationaries."

The lieutenant nodded and replied, "Aye, sir. Tubes 1-10, Arm and target, max yield, synch fire."

He turned to the sailor manning the weapons station, "Chief, open tubes 1-10. Set yield to 15 kilotons. Arm all weapons, with the following pattern: Bogey One, four missiles. Bogey Two, three missiles, Bogey Three, three missiles."

The sailor whispered rapidly into his headset, then reported, "Tubes 1-10 open, set for 15 kilotons, targeted as ordered. On your mark, sir."

The lieutenant looked at the captain and said, "Boat reports at Condition Red firing stations, sir."

Mitch turned slightly to Von Kant and said, "Commander, you may trigger the decoy when ready."

Von Kant nodded and tapped a control on her station. Several hundred thousand kilometers away, behind the charging Elai cruisers, the drone activated, sending a sensor ping at the rear of the enemy spacecraft. A few seconds later, the stationary weapons, three stationary AR6M 'Ragnarök' anti-ship missiles with nuclear penetrators, activated from where the *Infiltrator* had deployed them into space. The electromagnetic pulse of the jury rigged EM emitter behind them simulated the launch tubes of a stealth ship. The Elai ships decelerated rapidly and began to turn, their defensive weapons systems flickering; reaching out for the slow moving missiles. The drone increased power, appearing on the sensors like a stealth ship trying to break contact.

As the broadsides of the three Elai cruisers came into view, Mitch nodded at the lieutenant on the weapons station, "Fire tubes 1-10. XO, prepare to break contact."

The weapons officer ordered, "Chief, fire all tubes!" The petty officer stabbed a button on the console and watched his indicators. The crew could feel the familiar shudder of the massive anti-ship missiles being hurled out of their tubes, sped up by an electromagnetic accelerator. As the missiles were fired, a series of indicators on the chief's station turned from green to red.

As the last light blinked red, the chief reported, "Missiles away."

Not waiting for the lieutenant's report, Commander Von Kant began snapping orders, "Set course zero nine zero, mark three, ahead flank. Deploy decoys."

"Zero none zero, mark three, ahead flank, aye!" The helmsman replied. The deck of the small ship started to thrum as the engines picked up speed, attempting to clear the area from where they had launched their volley.

From the weapons station the chief petty officer reported calmly, "Decoys away." The THUMP of the decoy drones launching and racing in different directions could be heard throughout the ship.

As the *Infiltrator* settled into its new course, the captain turned to the weapons officer, "Weapons, report."

The young officer calmly watched his scope as he spoke, "Missiles running hot, stealth systems online. Doesn't look like they see them yet... There they go. They just saw 'em."

On the screen, the enemy cruisers could be seen attempting to swing back onto their previous course, to narrow their cross section to the onrushing missiles, but were too late. The first cruiser was hit broadside by all four missiles aimed at it. For a moment, nothing happened, then there was a brilliant flash, temporarily blotting out the optical sensors. Seconds later, there was another, then six more flashes in rapid succession.

Mitch waited a moment, then ordered in a calm tone, "Report."

Blinking to clear the afterimages from her eyes, Commander Von Kant replied, "I think...Yep. We got two of them. Bravo One and Bravo Two are destroyed. Bravo Three is heavily damaged. Looks like her drive is offline and she's venting atmosphere." She paused for a moment, then added, "She's breaking up."

On the sensor station, another officer spoke up, "Captain, we have incoming enemy vessels. Seven light units, bearing two six four mark twelve. It looks like their surviving destroyers." The man paused then added, "They're hauling ass too, sir. Zero point four-right at us. They want us bad." The officer looked up at the captain. "Looks like you pissed them off, sir."

Nodding, the captain ordered, "Yeah. Slow to one third and rig the boat for stealth running. Get the tubes reloaded."

Von Kant grinned darkly and said, "Now comes the really fun part."

\*\*\*\*

*Flag Bridge, UEAN Heavy Cruiser 'Stalwart'*

Captain Destin said in a professional but tense voice. "Admiral, we have explosions in Group Bravo! Two...Three...multiple detonations!"

Laura snapped her eyes to the holo display. The simulated detonations were fading. As they did, she could see the display change the status on the enemy cruisers on Group Bravo. She grinned darkly as Destin reported, "Looks like multiple kills... Correction. Two catastrophic kills, one disabled, probably breaking up."

With a dark chuckle, Dmitry commented, "Looks like Mitch Harris and his gang of pirates in the *Infiltrator* decided to join in the fun."

In a relieved tone, Kensington responded, "Good timing, too. Casey and her ships ought to be able to handle the destroyers."

The holo table chirped, updating. After a moment, Destin

reported, "Ma'am, the surviving destroyers from Bravo are after the *Infiltrator*. Seems like they're setting up a screen."

Commander de la Cruz observed from her station, "We haven't seen them do this before. Do they have anti stealth tactics?"

On the screen, there was a flash over the indicators of one of the Elai destroyers, which then changed to the symbol indicating destroyed. Kensington grinned and said, "Captain Harris has seeded the area with stealth mines." She frowned at the display and added, "And no, we haven't seen them use anti stealth tactics before, but the Elai are nothing if not adaptable." Another symbol flashed and winked out on the screen. She continued thoughtfully, "If he leaves any of them alive, it won't be so easy next time."

"Admiral, the remaining destroyers from Bravo are breaking contact. They're coming to heading one two one. Looks like they're linking up with Alpha." Destin paused, then continued, "Alpha is changing course, too. One niner three. Looks like they're heading outsystem." Laura nodded silently and folded her arms, thinking about the next series of moves.

Breaking the silence in the compartment, Dimitry said in his ponderous voice, "Admiral, we are in no shape for a second engagement. If they catch us in the gravity well again or jump in additional forces…well. We might want to consider jumping out of the system and linking up with Admiral Halleck's task force. Preserving our forces needs to be a consideration."

The admiral stared at the display for a heartbeat longer, then came to a decision, "Commander Destin, signal the fleet and set rally point Omicron. We're going to link up with Task Force 3.2 and regroup." She paused and turned to Dimitry, "Signal the *Infiltrator*. Tell them to do what they can to buy those Marines time if the Elai come back." Turning back to the display, she said again, "Commander de la Cruz, I need a burst tightbeam to the Marine commander on Onyx."

Several seconds later, the commander nodded and said,

"Ma'am, you're on."

Laura tugged her uniform top down and tapped the record key, "General Piasecki, this is Admiral Kensington. We did what we could, but we have to move outsystem. We took a pretty good beating but the Elai are also withdrawing. We didn't win, but neither did they. We will be linking up with Task Force 3.2 and returning in force. Dig in and hold on, Marines. We will be back for you. I promise. Kensington out."

Nodding at de la Cruz, Laura turned and issued one of the most difficult orders of her career, "Commander Destin, signal the fleet. Take us to rally point Omicron and prepare to jump."

## Chapter 7

### "Unfriendly Skies"

*335th Forward Inserted Surgical Team*
*Currently aboard Valkyrie One*
*Approaching LZ Anvil*

The Valkyrie rolled hard to the left, throwing the frightened members of the surgical team against their restraints, then dove for the ground. From the right side of the big craft, Moretti yelled into the intercom, "Rocco, bogey at seven high! He just got the shuttle!" Rocco didn't reply but whipped the aircraft into a hard right turn. There came a flash and what sounded like gravel hitting the outside of the aircraft. In the cockpit, Katharine Dagoyavitch, the flight engineer, reported in her usual cold voice, "Minor damage to the hull on the port side. No pressure loss."

Captain Moretti, the co-pilot, suddenly made a decision and reached for a control. "Fuck this." He muttered. "Kat, I'm dropping the Spuds. Put them on active engagement mode." The Valkyrie continued to swerve wildly as Rocco tried to shake the Elai fighter on their tail.

"Wilco." The engineer worked her controls rapidly, then replied, "Spuds hot! Drop 'em!"

Moretti tapped the control and felt the aircraft lurch as the wing mounted tactical deception drones fell out from underneath. On his display, he could see them powering up and accelerating, then bank sharply around, their AI guided weapons systems seeking any nearby threats.

There was a bright red burst of lascannon fire that streaked by the cockpit windscreen and Rocco again sent the Valkyrie into a sharp series of wild banks. He grunted as he did, "Icepick, get us some goddamn fighter support. I can't dodge this guy much longer. Kat, use the tail cannons to keep him off our ass." His voice was calm, but his forehead was beaded with sweat over his mask.

"Firing!" Katarina yelled from her position and opened up with the tail mounted remote lascannon. The bright green energy bursts seared through the dark sky and the Elai fighter banked away before climbing, then diving back at the fleeing aircraft. Suddenly, the tactical drones opened up with their dual lascannon, the smoky red bolts flashing towards the Elai fighter. The fighter nimbly rolled away and snapped a burst into one of the tactical drones, causing it to detonate in a ball of fire. It then looped and riddled the second with a precise burst, even as the drone fired at the aircraft. Taking a half dozen of the Elai fighters energy bolts, the drone lost power and silently fell from sight. The Elai fighter again settled onto a path that would allow it to use its cannons to fire at the search and rescue aircraft that was wildly jinking.

Moretti looked up and flinched. There was a massive wall of rock right in front of them. Rocco hauled back on the stick, standing the Valkyrie on its tail for a moment then shoved the nose back down, flashing over a ridge line. Moretti saw a brief glimpse of several power suited figures diving for cover as the aircraft cleared the ridge with meters to spare, then felt the sensation of falling as the craft dove down the other side. From behind them, there was a bright flash of light and again the hard smacks, like gravel on a roof, of objects striking the outside of the Valkyrie. A split second later, the Valkyrie leveled out and the nose thrusters fired to kill forward speed, bringing the ship to an abrupt standstill. As they did, the flaming wreckage of the Elai fighter that had been chasing them came screaming past, impacted the crater floor and exploded in a massive ball of fire.

Watching the fireball dissipate, Moretti blew out a shaky breath and muttered, "Holy shit."

Shaking his head as if stunned, Rocco replied, "Hell yeah, holy shit. I can't believe we survived that." Blinking rapidly, he asked, "Kat, what happened?"

The engineer responded, "No idea. It wasn't me. Maybe he hit the wall?"

Moretti shook his head. "No. Someone shot that fucker down. If he'd hit, he'd have tumbled in." He pointed to their left. "We can figure it out later. There's the LZ."

Seeing the flashing IR strobes illuminated on the computer augmented screens of the cockpit, Rocco pivoted the Valkyrie, flew another dozen meters and sat the aircraft down hard in a clearing between two large rocks. As they set the aircraft down, they could see power armored Marines rushing at them, waving their arms.

Reaching over and snapping his comm panel to the local ground circuit, Rocco could hear one of the ground crew yelling, "Out of the bird! OUT! We got incoming!"

"Shit!" Rocco toggled the intercom. "Everyone out! Follow the Marines! We got incoming arty!" He joined his co-pilot and flight engineer in hastily powering down the Valkyrie. Several seconds later, Katarina yelled, "We're good! Helmets!" Rocco slammed his visor down and hit the power on his combat survival suit. Feeling it pressurize he turned and checked the other two, then yelled, "Pop it, Kat!"

The engineer nodded and turned from her station to the tiny door that led to the crew compartment. She popped it open and the cockpit depressurized in a quick gust of escaping air. The three scrambled out as quickly as the tight space would allow and clambered out. A Marine in the bulky power armor was waiting and helped them down and then pointed at a nearby pit in the ground. "There! Go, go!" Rocco could hear a hooting as the local area net alarms started to go off and the robotic voice started to speak in his ear. "INCOMING. INCOMING. INCOMING."

The three flight crewmen sprinted to the trench and joined the medical team, who was already crouched in the hole.

Rocco found himself face to face with one of the surgical team members. He could see her face through their helmet plates. She was very pretty but was scowling ferociously.

Rocco almost burst out laughing. "What's going on?"

The woman looked at him crossly and snapped, "I hate to fly and that was a terrible landing. You call yourself a pilot? You suck."

With a grin, Rocco replied, "Hey, you know what they say about landings, right?"

"Yeah? What's that?" The woman cautiously raised her head and peered at the Valkyrie, then ducked again as there was a flash of light from overhead and a slow rumbling boom that rolled over the crater.

"Any landing you can walk away from is a good one." He flinched as an explosion boomed and echoed across the crater, then added, "Being alive is sort of my thing. I'm actually pretty good at it." Rocco grinned at the woman, who scowled again, then flinched as several more flashes came from above the crater. There came a tooth rattling series of explosions from behind them.

The woman twisted to look in the direction of the explosions, then responded crossly. "Yeah. I guess we'll see just how good you actually are at that, won't we?"

"Yes we will!" Rocco replied. He cautiously lifted his head over the edge of the trench. Straining to see in the low light, he muttered. "Shit." He sat back down.

"What now?" The woman asked crossly.

"The shuttle didn't make it." Rocco replied. After a moment he swore bitterly, "Fuck!"

"Oh my god." The woman's face was pale behind her helmet visor. "That shuttle had most of our supplies and half of our surgical team in it."

"I know." Rocco responded. There was a brief burst of static, then the distinctive chirping; followed by the emotionless voice of the anti-missile system spoke in his ear. "ALL CLEAR, ALL CLEAR, ALL CLEAR."

Nearby, a Marine clambered out of the trench. His power armor was covered in the fine dust that made up the floor of the crater. He waved his arms and pointed at a nearby cliff face. The local radio circuit crackled and a hoarse voice shouted, "Everyone who just unassed that bird, get into the tunnel. Go!"

The nurse looked at Rocco. "Ok, flyboy. It's showtime." She rose to a crouch, looked at the sky for a split second, then took off at a sprint, the boots of her combat suit leaving little puffs of dust as she ran.

With a last look at his damaged Valkyrie, Rocco shook his head, swore under his breath and followed the rest of the crew into the dark mouth of the tunnel.

Inside the tunnel, a hastily placed portable airlock stood open. Rocco followed, squeezing in behind the half dozen others. A few seconds later, the buffeting of wind told him they were pressurized and the inner door flew open. A Marine with lance corporal's stripes on his power armor motioned them out and hurriedly ushered them down the tunnel, which was dimly lit with a single strand of lights. Another fifty feet in, the Marine gestured towards another airlock, this one sturdier, made of roughly welded durasteel plate.

"In here, hustle!" There was a rumble through the rock and the ground trembled under their feet. A couple of armored Marines charged by, their power enhanced boots slamming the tunnel floor. They disappeared in the direction of the airlock. Following the others into the airlock, Rocco emerged into a small room with buttresses on the walls and bright red lockers full of survival gear. The airlock clanged shut and suddenly there was silence.

"Holy shit." Moretti muttered, next to him. He undogged the neck seals on his helmet and pulled it off, his dark hair wet with sweat and his face pale.

"Tell me about it." Rocco replied. He also pulled his helmet off, just in time to see a stocky man in power armor enter the room.

The man's voice cut through the chatter. "Everyone ok?" The man's eyes swept the small group, inquiringly. After a muttered chorus of replies, the man spoke again, his voice firm "Good. Listen up. I'm Major Micheal Manderson, the Army medical liaison to the First Marine division. Welcome to Firebase Anvil. As of right now, you are the only medical assets higher than a battalion aid station on the planet." There was a murmur of surprise and shock at this statement. Manderson held up his hand. "I know. Not ideal, but it is what it is. We have a job to do. Who's your CO?"

The blonde nurse spoke up. "It was Captain Etti. He was on the shuttle." Her voice was flat and drained of emotion.

"And your exec?" Manderson replied.

"Lieutenant Taro. Also on the shuttle." A short, stocky medic replied.

"Then who's senior, goddammit? We need to get you up and operational." Manderson snapped. He paused, seeing their faces, then sighed and added gently, "I'm sorry about your team. I really am. We'll have a memorial for them later- you have my word. But for now, we have casualties stacking up and we're already running low on stasis pods."

A stern faced man with hard eyes shouldered his way forward. His combat armor bore the black oak leaves of a lieutenant colonel. "I'm Colonel Douglas. I'm the surgeon and probably the senior medical officer here. What are we working with?"

"Sir." Manderson replied, "We're working with an improvised aid station, a damaged surgical unit we pulled off of a cargo drop pod that burned in and a mishmash of supplies. The Marines are engaged in constant firefights on the perimeter and the Elai are hurling salvos of unguided rockets into our perimeter on a constant basis." He shook his head and added, "If anyone survived the shuttle crash, we'll get them in here if they're mission capable. We have a patrol headed out to evaluate the crash site now."

Manderson regarded the colonel for a moment, then said, "I have a secure set of tunnels for you to work out of and you get complete priority on any incoming med supplies, since you are the only surgical asset on the surface."

Acerbically, the colonel replied. "Superb." He turned to the frightened group. "Captain Dahl."

The blonde nurse replied from the crate she was flopped on, "Sir."

"Get a by name list of who we have here and what their specialty is. Let's get organized." Dahl nodded in acknowledgement. The colonel pointed at the three flight crew, standing together uncertainly. "You three, you're with us."

Rocco looked at Moretti and Katerina, then replied, "Sure thing, doc. Tell us what you need. The bird's broke anyway."

Colonel Douglas turned back to Manderson. "Ok, Major. Here's our surgical team. Let's get to work." Manderson nodded. Douglas continued, "I'm gonna be busy once things get spicy, so you are going to handle the command aspect of this, Major. You have a better operational picture than I do anyway."

Grimacing, Manderson replied. "Kinda thought you might ask." He shook his head. "I can, but only until more of your hospital command element drops. I've got my hands full coordinating with the Marine command teams."

"You don't have to like it, major. Just do it." Douglas replied brusquely. He turned to Brian. "Master Sergeant, you're the detachment NCO. I need the rest of them to keep surgical ops running. Your flight nurse is with me, I need every trained provider I have to keep surgical operations going."

Brian nodded calmly. "Yes, sir." He nodded at Manderson. "Me and the Major will handle it."

"Make it happen, Master Sergeant." Douglas turned back to Manderson. "One other thing, too. We're gonna need power armor. These armored combat suits aren't going to cut it." There was a series of echoing booms that made the floor tremble. The surgeon gestured towards the roof, "And those little bastards are persistent, if nothing else."

Grimly, Manderson replied. "I agree. I'll see what I can do." There was another series of explosions and the ground trembled underneath their feet again. As the shaking died down, Manderson spoke again, "We need to get moving."

As another round of rockets began impacting the surface above, the team stepped through the airlock and headed down the dimly lit tunnel.

\*\*\*\*

*Crash site of Shuttle 355*
*349th Special Forces Detachment, 'Thundercats'*
*2 kilometers Southwest of LZ Anvil*

"There, sir. Two five two. Another one. Designate Tango Two." The flat, emotionless tone of Master Sergeant Chan, his detachment sergeant, whispered in Captain Shawn Tulp's ear and on his display a small red triangle appeared, highlighting the tagged enemy soldier. "Looks like a standard patrol. Probably more of them behind that ridge."

"I see him. Anything on thermal in the wreck?" He replied, cranking the magnification up on his power armor optics as he panned the view over the remains of the assault shuttle.

"No, but there's a lot of heat signatures in there from the crash. It can't have been here for more than a half hour, tops."

"So. We can't tell if there's survivors." The young captain considered this, then sighed. "All right. Let's get a microdrone over there and take a look."

He zoomed out of the view in his armor and gestured at a boulder a dozen paced from where they lay on the frozen ground. A shimmering shape like a heat wave slid out from behind the rock and surged towards him, distorting the landscape behind it as it moved. A few seconds later, it flopped to the ground beside him and dissipated, leaving the slate grey power armored figure of Sergeant Tran, the teams communications specialist. She had a hard sided case with her that she flipped open. Reaching inside, she removed a tennis ball sized drone, flipped a switch on it, then tossed it into the air. It vanished almost immediately as the stealth system activated. A few seconds later, the feed appeared on a small inset screen inside his visor. The view rushed forward as the drone flew towards the crash site. A few moments later, Sergeant Tran slowed the drone and tapped the light amplification system. Two Elai soldiers could be seen cautiously approaching the wreckage, their movements slow and deliberate.

Lingering on the two enemy soldiers for a moment, Tran then brought the drone up in height and swept the drone's view up. A moment later she spoke in a satisfied tone. "And there's their buddies. Looks like a squad sized element." The view showed the dark shapes of the enemy soldiers crouching behind a ridge of rock on the far side of the wreck.

"Master Sergeant, what was in this bird? Anything critical?" The younger soldier asked.

"No idea. We're just closest available. Airspace is contested, so no search and rescue available." Chan replied.

"Hmm," the young woman replied. "Oh, look, someone's curious." She panned the drone feed back to the Elai at the wreck. One of the black clad figures was peering in a large breach in the hull. Suddenly, there was a burst of brilliant blue bolts from out of the wreck and the Elai stumbled backwards and fell scrambling backwards, as his companion opened fire, sending a stream of smokey red energy bolts towards the rent in the hull.

"Holy shit!" Tulp exclaimed. "We got survivors down there!" Tabbing his low frequency squad radio, he snapped, "Shooters front!" There was a burst of movement as two more shimmery shapes rushed forward and crashed down. The shimmer faded to reveal two soldiers with the long, deadly shapes of the long range electromagnetic accelerator rifles the special forces team used.

"Daniels, take those two gomers down! Engage when

ready!" Tulp ordered. "Kim, get some loiter drones on those fuckers in the rocks. Keep them pinned down. When you get the drones up, support Daniels and call it in. Top, you're with me. Let's get our people out of there."

The soldiers scrambled to carry out the tasks. Daniels lay still as a stone, his armor locked in place and linked to the sniper rifle. A moment later, he spoke calmly. "Firing one." The rifle kicked and the hypersonic round left a cloud of dust on the ground as it left the barrel at fifteen times the speed of sound. The enemy soldier closest to the shuttle crumpled to the ground in a spray of black blood and a large hole appeared in the hull of the shuttle. Tulp grimaced at this, but said nothing, only motioned to the big Korean master sergeant to follow. As he did, he caught a glimpse of Kim opening a case of small loiter drones. The drones shot skyward, almost immediately vanishing into the space black sky.

Tulp looked at Chan. "Ok. Get in, get out." Chan nodded. The two rose to their feet and sprinted towards the crash site below.

As they did, they heard Daniels announce over the radio, "*Firing two.*" The piece of hull plate that the second enemy had taken cover behind suddenly had a softball sized hole in it and the remains of the alien fell to the ground, motionless. Thirty seconds of power augmented sprinting later, Chan and Tulp reached the edge of the crash site. Tulp motioned Chan to take cover and the two men crouched behind a piece of wreckage.

Sergeant Kim's voice came through their helmet speakers. "*Drones have locks. Going hot.*" Overhead, there were brief streaks of light as the rocket motors ignited on the stealth drones, sending them hurtling downwards towards their targets. There was a series of hard thumps from over the ridge, then a second series of sharp explosions.

"*Targets neutralized,*" the young NCO reported. "*No other targets in sight. We'll keep our eyes out and I'll let you know when I hear from Anvil.*"

"Roger." Tulp replied. He pointed at the breach in the hull. "I'll do it." Easing out from behind cover, he toggled his suit lights and activated his suit radio on the emergency frequencies. "ATTENTION THE SHUTTLE. FRIENDLIES OUTSIDE!"

There was no response from inside the shuttle. A few seconds later, the young special forces officer called out again. "WE'RE FROM A RESCUE TEAM FROM THE MAIN LZ."

There was a burst of static, then a defiant voice responded on the emergency band, "Bull shit. There's no way a ground force could have gotten here this fast."

"WE WERE ALREADY OUT HERE. WE'RE A TIGER TEAM DOING RECON. CAN I COME CLOSER AND SHOW YOU?"

There was another long pause, then the voice yelled back, "Fine, but turn your lights off and open your blast shield."

Turning off his exterior lights, Tulp raised his blast shield and slowly walked forward, slowly moving in front of the breach in the hull. A flashlight beam stabbed out of the dark for a moment and aimed at his face, then switched off.

A youthful face in a light combat armored suit appeared in the breach. "Thank Christ you're here. We got wounded in here, the hatch is jammed shut and we have a high priority cargo."

"I don't know if we can get your cargo, but we can get your people out. How many survivors do you have?" Tulp replied. He looked at the mangled shuttle.

"Five," the man replied, then turned and looked inside as someone spoke to him. His face hardened for a moment, then he added, "Four, now."

"Ok. Sit tight. We'll get the cabin door open in just a second." Chun approached and using his augmented armor, began to pull at the warped hatch of the main cabin.

"Sir, incoming message from LZ Anvil." Kim's voice reported. She paused for a moment, then forwarded the message, which appeared in Tulp's visor.

*"Thundercats- Acknowledge survivors at crash site. Marine QRF en route-Call sign 'Rattlesnake'. Secure site for high value cargo recovery until relief arrives. -TF ANVIL CO'"*

"Shit." Tulp replied. "Hang on, Top." Spying a bar in the wreckage he forced it in the door and the men leaned on it together. After a few seconds of force, the hatch screeched open. The four trapped soldiers scrambled out, clad in the light combat armor issued to support troops. On the shoulders of the armor was painted a red cross.

"You're medical?" The officer asked. The last soldier out, the man he had been speaking to through the breach, replied. "Yeah. We're the 336th Forward Surgical Team." He looked at his three comrades. "Or what's left of it, anyway. We lost six of our people in there and the entire flight crew." The man's suit was battered, with emergency suit patch tape covering most of one of his arms and sealant foam on his pressure helmet obscuring part of his face.

"Damn." Tulp replied. He pointed at the hill they'd just come down. "I've got two soldiers up there. Get up there with them, they got air and power packs for your armor. Go."

"Got it." The soldier motioned to the three other survivors and they began to make their way up the hill.

From behind him, Tulp heard Master Sergeant Chan mutter. "God damn."

Turning to see what he was looking at, Tulp saw the man with his head in another large crack in the hull towards the rear of the ship. "What do you have?"

Chan straightened up and replied, "I got an extremely dead major and a shitpot of smashed up medical supplies." He looked at Tulp. "They weren't kidding. This bird probably had half of the landing force's medical resupply on it."

Shaking his head, Tulp replied, "Well. Let's hope we can hold it until the reaction force gets here. We need this shit."

"That we do, sir. Let's get on that hill and scrounge for intel on them dead gomers. Might as well do our job while we wait for reinforcements. "

"You got it." Tulp clambered over a piece of wreckage and the two men began to walk up the far side of the ridge. As they did, Tulp glanced above them at the stars. Seeing the hard moving points of light of primary ship engines flaring above, he wondered who was winning and what was going to happen next.

## Chapter 8

### "Dig in and Hold On"

*Forward Operating Base Anvil,*
*Planet M3245; Draconis 327.*
*August 28, 2248*

Tony stood in the entryway of the completed portion of their newly dug bunker system and stared, the awe breaking through his exhaustion. He marveled for a moment at the ingenuity of the Navy construction crews. They had pried up the doors from the now disarmed Elai missile silos in the floor of the crater, flipped them on their sides and converted them into massive doors, making a main airlock big enough for the heavy equipment. The Seabees, as they had been called for hundreds of years, had lived up to their reputation for performing engineering miracles with minimal resources. All around the inside of the rim of the kilometer-wide crater, they had carved a massive tunnel with multiple entrances, forming a giant ring. Towards the inside of the crater, massive offshoot tunnels housed the single squadron of fighters and the lone Valkyrie that had made it down before the fleet had been forced to withdraw. The scavenged silo doors now formed airlock doors. Up towards the rim of the crater, smaller tunnels let the Marines access their bunkers and observation posts without having to go on the surface.

Waiting for a moment for the giant airlock to cycle, Tony entered the main ring. Inside, Sergeant Major Jimenez was waiting for him. He was still clad in his power armor, but with his helmet off. With him, his back towards Tony, was a figure that seemed familiar...

Sliding his helmet faceplate open, Tony said, "Sergeant Agawa?"

Brian turned and nodded calmly at Tony, "Hey, sir. Nice setup you have here. Those Seabees can really dig a tunnel." He gestured at the massive tunnel stretching off in both directions, packed with equipment, the hulking missile mechs and dozens of Marines, all busily toiling at various tasks.

Working the helmet off of his armor, Tony ran a hand over his short cropped hair, "Yeah, they're pretty good at what they do. It's good to see you. I had no idea you were on the *Fury*. When did you get aboard?"

With a shrug, the man replied, "Couple hours before the jump. The Valkyrie squadron needed a senior NCO and I was up for a deployment anyway, so I pulled a few strings. Plus, I told Liz I'd keep an eye on you." He grinned and reached out and shook Tony's hand. Tony grinned back and shook firmly in return.

Sergeant Major Jimenez nodded sympathetically, "Babysitting officers, Master Sarn't? Seems that there isn't too big of a difference between the Corps and the Army sometimes." He grasped Brian's hand and shook it firmly. "Speaking for myself, I'm glad to have you. We can always use more experienced NCO's, especially ones that know their way around these shark toothed fucks. We got a lotta boots out there on the line." Tony shook his head in silent agreement. The vast majority of the Marines that had landed with the First Marines had little or no combat experience; 'Boots' in the old Marine slang.

Brian nodded grimly, "Yeah, well, they aren't going to be boots when we're done here." He looked at Tony, "I guess we're kicking off the offensive now we're dug in here?"

Grimly, Tony nodded and replied, "Yeah. Was supposed to be tomorrow. Took longer to get dug in then we originally planned with only half our people getting on the ground. We're supposed to be pushing patrols north and keeping tabs on the Elai for Task Force Hammer as they push south. "Theoretically, we're supposed to catch the enemy main body in a pincer maneuver."

Brian's face flickered with a half-smile, a rare expression for the stoic noncommissioned officer. He said drily, "Theoretically?"

Tony shrugged, "Well. you know the Elai. They have their own plans, regardless of what we do, hence why we're cut off with less than half our forces and maybe a third of the supplies we need."

"Shit." Brian observed, laconically.

Sergeant Major Jimenez grinned, "Oh, come on, Sergeant Agawa. No supplies, no reinforcements, no Navy in orbit for either us or the sharkies and we got a whole mess of pissed off, heavily armed Marines with no adult supervision. If it helps, try to remember we aren't stuck down here with them. They're stuck down here with *us*."

Brian looked at Tony, who just grinned in reply. Seeing the grin, Brian sighed and said, "You know, if I didn't know better, I'd say you guys were enjoying this."

With a cheerful slap on the smaller man's armored shoulder, Jimenez responded cheerfully, "Agawa, you dropped with the Marines this time. We do things a little differently."

Shaking his head, Brian looked reproachfully at Tony, "And here I thought you were one of the normal ones, sir."

Laughing, Tony replied, "I'm not the most 'Marine' of Marines, but I *am* still a Marine, Master Sergeant," Tony paused, "It's good to have you here, Brian."

Brian nodded in return, "Glad to be here, sir."

While they spoke, two men approached them. One of them was in power armor, with the Valkyrie logo painted on the left shoulder and captain's bars in the middle of his chest plate. The other was an older man with a buzz cut, piercing blue eyes and a commanding face. He was in an unpowered combat armored space suit, with red crosses painted on the shoulder armor. On his chest was the black oak leaf of a lieutenant colonel. Tony nodded respectfully, "Sir."

The older man nodded in a silent acknowledgement, as the

young man said, "Major Harris, I'm Captain Matthews, off of Valkyrie One. This is Colonel Douglas. He's the lead surgeon from the 335th Forward Drop Surgical Team."

The older man offered his hand and Tony shook it, trying to remember if any medical units had landed.

Beating him to it, the surgeon said, "What's left of the FDST, anyway. We squeezed a team into the Valkyrie as the *Fury* broke orbit. Didn't get a lot of equipment down and the rest of the surgical team didn't make it down. Their shuttle went down as we landed. Captain Matthews here," He indicated the young officer, "Managed to get us some equipment and got us on board." He paused, then looked sourly at the young man, "Bumpy ride, my foot." Matthews shook his head silently as the surgeon continued, "Anyway. Major Manderson had the Seabees dug a couple of side tunnels for an operating room and a ward. It's not exactly a station hospital, but it'll do."

"I heard." Tony replied. "Will it work?"

"For now. Manderson's done a damn fine job, given the circumstances. He and I do have a request from you, however."

Tony nodded, "Sure, sir. What do you need?"

The older man replied promptly, "Power armor. Your liaison told us you had spare sets and I want my team set up in them. We need it in case we need to get out of these tunnels and I'd prefer that we go up there in something more substantial than this armored underwear they call a combat suit."

Tony and Sergeant Major Jimenez traded a look, then Tony said carefully, "Sir, power armor is...usually for the line troops. I don't know that we have enough to spare..."

The surgeon replied in a dismissive tone, "Bosh. The aid station already has fifteen Marines stuffed in stasis pods, waiting for evac and we got another six in beds in the hospital. They aren't using theirs. We only need ten sets and we can repair the least damaged using the more beat up suits. That way we get armor and you aren't tapping into your spares."

Tony turned to Sergeant Major Jimenez, "Sergeant Major?"

The stocky man frowned for a moment, thinking, then shrugged, "If they don't mind wearing suits Marines got hurt in. Seems like bad juju to me, but if you guys are ok with it, I guess it's fine with me."

Tony turned back to the hard faced surgeon and replied, "Well, sir. There's your answer. We'll get the armorers to give you a hand getting them fitted. That work for you, Colonel?"

Nodding, Colonel Douglas said, "I appreciate it, Major. We're not trying to be a bother; we just want to be able to keep up if we have to scoot outta this little fort of yours if we need to."

With a tight smile, Tony nodded, "Yes, sir. But if they force us out of here, it's going to be with something so big power armor won't help a lot."

Shrugging, the colonel replied, "Probably. I'd still rather have my team kitted out in it than not. I was in command of a forward surgical team in the Epsilon 32 campaign. We sure as hell could have used it then. That blowing sand ate through our combat armor seals like a hot knife through butter." He paused, his craggy face somber, then continued, "At least we could breathe there." He stopped and shook his head, then added sternly, "You send someone to get those suits up and running, Major."

Tony nodded, "Yes, sir. We will." The older man nodded, shook Tony's hand again and turned and walked off into the crowded tunnel, with the young Valkyrie crewman following.

Watching him go, Sergeant Major Jimenez commented thoughtfully, "Doc's jumpy."

Brian nodded slowly and responded, "Some people have a nose for trouble, Sergeant Major; and Colonel Douglas has been in the Army for a long time. Let's talk, you and me. I have some ideas about a few things."

The senior Marine NCO turned to Tony and said, "Meet us in the new operations center in fifteen minutes, sir. We're going to update you on what we have here and then we brief the boss at fifteen hundred. Ordonez will take you up." He gestured to a lance corporal waiting nearby, "Lance, get the Major up to the new ops center."

The young Marine nodded, "Yes, Sergeant Major. Sir, if you'll follow me." She gestured down the tunnel. With a nod at Brian and the Sergeant Major, Tony followed the young Marine.

As they moved down the tunnel, a voice called out, "Major Harris? Got a minute, sir?" Tony turned around. A young, cheerful looking man with a lieutenant's insignia in a powerful naval construction variant of the combat armor was approaching him. Next to him was a hard faced older man with salt and pepper hair in the same heavy duty armor, wearing the insignia of a senior chief.

Tony responded politely, "Lieutenant, Chief. What can I do for you?"

"Well, sir. Couple of things I wanted to discuss before your meeting with the General and something I wanted to show you."

"Ok. What's up?"

The lieutenant gestured down a side tunnel and replied, "This way, sir." As they started down the tunnel, with the lance corporal in tow, the young officer said, "So, we have the entire perimeter tunnel dug and compartmentalized and all the hangars and bunker access points. It's about as good as it's gonna get." He paused then added, "We did have an idea to float at you though. Actually, it was Chief Sullivan's idea." He gestured at the senior petty officer next to him and continued, "It occurred to us, sir, that we might need to get out of here in a hurry. So, with your permission, I'd like to get the men digging exit tunnels to the outside of the crater, too." He paused, then said, "We won't break through, but we'll get within a few feet then set demo charges so all we have to do is hit the clacker and bang! Instant exit."

Tony considered this, then replied, "That seems prudent. I

can't see a real downside and we might need to make an exit tunnel anyway. Go ahead and start digging them, let me know what you need." He paused for a moment and then added, "Just in case, make them nice and wide...You know. The fire extinguisher principal-better to have them and not need them, than need them and not have them."

The young engineer nodded, "Yes, sir. We can do that. We'll make 'em big enough for the mechs, just in case." He paused, then pointed ahead of them, "Here, sir. Check this out."

Ahead of them, was a gaping black hole in the wall of the tunnel. Several pieces of yellow tape were crossed across the entrance and a bored looking sailor stood guard outside. Approaching, the engineer said to the guard, "We're going to show the major. Hit the lights." He ushered Tony in front of the hole. The young sailor nodded and hit a switch on a box bolted to the tunnel wall. The pitch black in front of Tony began to sparkle, with what seemed like millions of glinting sparks of light. As the engineer swung his flashlight beam, the light was caught and refracted into thousands of tiny rainbows, reflected and re-reflected. The color was dazzling and Tony had never seen anything like it. He took a couple of steps forward, then ducked under the engineer tape, followed by the naval officer.

After a moment, Tony said, "What are they?"

Shrugging, the engineer replied, "Near as we can tell, it's a variant of diamond but I haven't ever seen ones that do this before." He stooped and picked up a fingernail sized piece and played his light over it. As he did, the color of the crystal shimmered and changed, flashing through the primary colors as the light beam moved around it. The young man continued talking, in a distance voice, mesmerized by the stone, "We think it's got some sort of crystalline structure that changes frequency as its exposed to radiation, but the stone itself doesn't change like terrestrial diamonds, just the refractions. Watch." He keyed the infrared lights on his suit and the reflections of the tiny chunk of crystal became a brilliant blue. He then tapped another key, switching the light to ultraviolet and the reflections from the diamond became deep purple. Switching the light off, the reflections went back to the sparkles of multicolor. He added, "I bet these'll be incredible when cut properly. This are just its properties raw. Pretty neat, huh?"

Tony nodded, taking the small stone from the man and turned it over in his hand, watching the lights sparkle and dance off of the uncut gem. After a moment, he looked up, "Can I have this one?"

The engineer laughed, "Sure, sir. It's not like we don't have plenty. We can get you a bigger one, if you want. We got a pile of baseball sized ones back there a ways."

Shaking his head, Tony replied, "No, this one is good. Thanks." Carefully tucking the stone into a container and then into a belt pouch, he looked around the cavern again, "Quite a find, lieutenant. If we ever come back here, these are going to make someone *very* rich." Looking at the lance corporal, he said, "Ok. Duty calls. Thanks, Lieutenant, Chief." He nodded to the young Marine waiting at the door. "Lance, get me to this new ops center everyone's talking about. We got a shark hunt to plan."

The corporal grinned and gestured to the hall, "After you, sir."

\*\*\*\*

Fifteen minutes later, Tony entered the newly constructed operations center. Located high up in the crater wall, a long, narrow window dominated one side of the room. Interested, Tony moved over to the window, marveling at the sturdiness of the construction. It appeared that the Seabees had used a massive piece of clear, half meter thick plaststeel and embedded it directly into the rock, then covered the outside of the window with strategically placed boulders and nanomesh camouflage netting. The result was a concealed window that offered a dramatic, sweeping view of the entire crater and all of the activity happening on the crater floor.

Seeing Tony looking at the window, another man in Naval construction armor came up to him and said, "It's a shuttle windscreen. We took it off of what was left of Shuttle 355, after it got shot up on the way in. Makes for a pretty decent view, don't you think?"

Tony nodded and looking at the man, said, "It sure does. I don't think we've been introduced. Major Harris, acting commander of Fifth Battalion and interim commander of Firebase Anvil. You must be Commander Thornton."

The man smiled with a lopsided grin and shook Tony's hand, "Indeed I am. Good to meet you and sorry for the delay. We've been busy building this fort of yours. Quite the challenge, given the circumstances."

Tony laughed, tiredly, "I'll say!" He snapped his fingers. "Hey, that reminds me. One of your guys, Lieutenant Mitchell, has an idea for egress tunnels. I think it's a good idea. Let me know if you guys need anything to make them happen."

The commander nodded, "Sure thing, sir. We'd discussed the idea and I was actually going to bring it up here but if you're good with it, we can start the cuts right now."

Clapping the man on the shoulder, Tony said, "Get it done. Let me know if you need anything." The man nodded and picked up his comm device and started speaking. Tony made his way to the briefing table and found his chair set out for him, with a hot cup of tea already sitting by it.

Picking up the cup appreciatively, he nodded at the Sergeant Major, who waved an arm for silence and said, "Ok, people. Let's get started. Keep it brief, we don't have time to sugarcoat it. Bottom line up front. Captain Shen."

The young captain rose and said, "Sir, I'm going to brief as to who we actually have on the ground, then Captain Saint is going to brief equipment and supply, followed by Major Reys, with our latest intel reports. We will then conference in with

Brigadier General Piasecki and get his guidance on the overall plan of action moving forward," He tapped a button on the conference table and the wall lit up with a list of units and names. The young officer began speaking, "In terms of personnel, we have 1,232 personnel in Operating Base Anvil. We had planned for 700 for the Fifth Battalion and our support elements, but when the carriers got jumped, we took what was in the shuttles and ready to go, so we have a whole mishmash of people here we didn't plan on. Next slide."

The screen changed, displaying another set of data. Captain Shen continued, "Intact units include us here in the Fifth Battalion, First Marines, the 352nd Naval Construction Company and Alpha Company of the 1/17th Mobile Missile Battery and their lance of four Gorgon-class missile mechs." He paused checking a datapad in front of him, then continued, "Partial units include the 12th Space-Ground Fighter Wing with five Banshee fighters and their field support elements, one shot up Valkyrie from the 6253rd Aeromedical Search and Rescue with its crew, twelve functional assault shuttles and their crews we inherited since the Navy's gone." He looked up from his list and added, "In terms of medical elements, we have a six person forward surgical team off of the *Phantom Fury* as a last minute gift from Captain DeGenova and half of another that survived the crash of Shuttle 355. We also have, for some reason, a fifteen person electronic warfare team off of the *Thunderbolt* and all their equipment." He paused, reading down the list. "There's also the six person Special Operations detachment 3515 off of the *Infiltrator*, call sign 'Thundercats'. They're one of the long range recon tiger teams we've been hearing about." The young officer looked up from his notes, "They're already outside the perimeter. They've been out since they hit the dirt and are due back sometime later today." He looked back down at his notes and continued, "And last but not least, we got an infantry company from 2nd Battalion, so that's another two hundred Marines we weren't counting on. That brings us to our total of 1, 232 people on the ground inside the firebase, right now." He paused again then said, "Sir, in terms of bodies, we have way more than we planned for this position. We're good on people and guns. I'll let the S4 talk about our supply issues." He looked at Tony, "Questions, sir?"

Tony shook his head, frowning, "No. Not at the moment. Continue."

Another captain stood up and said, "Sir, I'm Captain Saint, the battalion supply. I'll be blunt. We got plenty of air, ammo and power but we're gonna get damn hungry after a few weeks here if the Navy don't come back." The young man ran a hand through his sandy brown hair and blew out a frustrated breath and continued, "We dropped with a basic ninety day supply for our battalion. Since we doubled the number of troops, we cut that in half. Call it forty-five days, maybe sixty if we stretch it by cutting meals. Same with med supplies. Those folks are damn low on expendable medical supplies already, to say nothing if the shooting starts again in earnest." The man paused, "Either way, sir, it's gonna be tight. I talked to the supply guy over at Operating Base Hammer and they're in the same situation."

Tony nodded and replied, "Well, captain, we'd better wrap this up before then, shouldn't we?" Around the table, there were a few grim chuckles.

At the nearby communications station, a Marine reported, "Major Harris, General Piasecki is on the line. I'll patch him through." Tony nodded and turned back to the screen.

On the main screen, a picture of an operations center similar to their own appeared. In the center sat General Piasecki, with a grim-faced major with a rifle standing to his right. His power armor was scorched and battered and the poor light made the stainless steel prosthetic half of his face glint menacingly.

In his low gravelly voice, the scarred officer began to speak, "*Major Harris, we just got hit in force here. They jammed.....omms and sensors....tried to overrun us. They used....*" The screen flared into static and then cleared enough to hear the general say *"Some sort of experimental...."* The static swelled up again and the connection dropped.

The communications sergeant spoke up, "Jamming, sir. It looks like it's on their end. I'll try to get them back."

With an absent nod to the comm sergeant, Tony turned to Sergeant Major Jimenez, "Sergeant Major?"

The stocky enlisted man was staring at the screen, his face hard. After a moment, he spoke slowly, "I think they're about to try our lines again, sir. Wish he'd gotten a few more seconds to talk. 'Experimental' don't sound too good."

"I agree." Tony frowned and turned to Captain Shen, "Captain Shen, get extra people up in the bunkers. I want them using bare eyes to scan the terrain. The Elai can be damn quiet when they want to be and their electronic fuckery is top notch. Anything funny at all, we need to know about it."

The young officer nodded and turned to his communications sergeant. Tony looked at the rest of the people at the table and said, "Let's wrap this up. We'll continue...."

A nearby Marine on a sensor station suddenly shouted, "Vampire, vampire, missiles inbound! Bearings zero zero one, zero nine zero, one eight zero! Estimate forty plus!" The chirping alarms of the automated missile defense system began and the automated voice of the Zeus system went off again.

"INCOMING. INCOMING. INCOMING." Through the thick slit window, Tony could see the few personnel left above the surface diving for cover. The globes of the Zeus system glowed briefly, then a faint beam shot out, then in rapid sequence, dozens more. Moments later, Tony could see a silver cloud gently drifting through the air, slowly settling to the ground.

Turning to the Marine on the sensor station, Tony demanded, "Marine, what am I looking at?"

Sergeant Major Jimenez replied before the tech could speak, "Chaff, sir. It's an ancient radar countermeasure. It's usually not that effective but combined with that goddamn jamming…"

In the floor of the crater, there was an explosion and Tony could feel the floor tremble. Another explosion, then another.

Captain Saint said in a distracted voice as he stared out the window at the explosions in the crater below, "Those clever fuckers. They're blinding our Zeus with the jamming and chaff to get unguided rockets through and having us distribute their chaff for them when we zap their rockets." The floor trembled again as another rocket hit.

Tony turned to Sergeant Major Jimenez, "Sergeant Major, get the Humpbacks out and get a location on those goddamn launchers. I want this rocket fire stopped before they breach a tunnel."

Across the command post, a slender man with a shaved head and pale skin called out, "Major Harris, I have them triangulated. Drones have visuals now. Looks like four standard Elai heavy rocket vehicles per launch site. The drones have the targets painted now." The man paused, then said in a firm voice, "Targets acquired."

"Get them," the sergeant major ordered in a hard voice.

With a broad grin the Marine reached for his handset and said into it, "Hellhound Lead, this is Anvil Control. Standby for fire mission-Counterbattery."


\*\*\*\*


*Forward Operating Base Anvil,*
*Crater Access Tunnel Four, Crater Floor*


"Roger that, Anvil Control. Moving into position. Hellhound Lead, out." Captain Tara Chalee, a young woman with a shaved head and crystal blue eyes, was sitting in the commander's hatch of a massive, Gorgon-class missile mech affectionately known as a 'Humpback'. She looked down into the hull of the machine and said, "Spin 'em up, boys. Counterbattery." Slapping the thick hull next to her over the painted words '*Bad Mama*', she carefully locked her helmet onto her power armor. Tossing a jaunty salute to the engineers manning the airlock, she slid down into the hull of the mech and dogged the hatch.

She toggled her mic to speak to her lance, "Hellhounds, this is Hellhound Lead. Lance One, exit tunnels and prepare for counter battery fire on my mark. Acknowledge."

In Hellhound Two, Sergeant Harris's calm voice came over the radio, followed by Three and Four, "*Lead, Two. Acknowledge.*"

"*Lead, Three. Rog.*"

"*Lead, Four. Let's do this, baby!*"

Captain Chalee grinned and keyed her radio, "Anvil Control, Hellhound Lead. We are on the move."

Her driver, Corporal Yang, pushed the throttle forward and moved the big machine into the airlock. As the airlock cycled, Tara ran her eyes over her commander's console. The status indicators shone steadily, with screens giving her fuel, ammo, armor integrity and a dozen other metrics showing her the health of the mechs under her command. Several lumbering steps brought the large, four legged machine out of the hangar. Behind her came the other three mechs in their lance, each step of the forty ton, armored hulls making the solid rock of the tunnel floor tremble. Their adjustable camouflage systems had been tuned to the local environment, giving each mech a smoky gray color, matching the rock of the crater floor. Changing her screens to look behind the mech to check the rest of her team, Tara could see the hulking shape of Sergeant Harris's Hellhound Two, with the words '*The Sizzle*' painted on the side of the hull. Behind Hellhound Two, out of sight behind the massive mech, were Three and Four, right where they were supposed to be.

With a nod, Tara toggled the mic. "Looking good, Hellhounds. Firing pattern Charlie." The four heavily laden machines moved into a diamond pattern, several hundred feet apart.

From below, the mech engineer, Sergeant Dieter, said in his precise, clipped voice, "Reactor within norms, heat sinks operational. All secondary armament active and safe."

Keying her radio, the young officer commanded, "Hellhounds, lock position and rotate tubes to firing position."

Over the radio, a new voice broke in, *"Hellhounds, Flamestrike Control. Target coordinates as pinged; first salvo load high explosive, second salvo area denial delayed munitions, report firing status and standby for fires."*

Hearing her control panel chime, Tara responded to the Fire Control Officers orders, "Flamestrike Control, Hellhound Lead. Target coordinates received, confirm high explosive, followed by area denial. Over."

Below her, Yang reported, "Leg locking pins in place; ready to deploy." There was a series of bangs under the mech as the titanium alloy pins shot down from the legs, securing the mech to the ground. Yang reported seconds later, "Pins secure."

Seconds later, her gunner, Sergeant Ubuntu reported, "Primary missile systems online, rotating tubes." A mechanical whine filled the hull of the big machine as the large, rounded rear section of the mech lifted up and then rotated skyward. Ubuntu said again, "In firing position. Selecting high explosive, followed by delay cluster. All positions, scan firing area."

Tara scanned around her with her monitors. Seeing no ground personnel, she keyed her mic, "Commander, area clear." Her crew quickly followed suit.

"Driver, forward clear."

"Gunner, right and left, clear."

"Engineer, rear clear."

Ubuntu said again, "Commander, all positions report clear. Targeting data received, Hellhound One is condition alpha."

Tara clicked her mic and acknowledged, "Acknowledge,

condition alpha." Tapping on the radio, she said to the other four missile mechs, "Hellhound Lance, report firing status." Even through the thick armor of the hull, the crews could feel the trembling of the ferocious but inaccurate Elai return fire hitting the floor of the crater, shaking the rocky floor.

From the driver's position, Corporal Yang opened his face plate, leaned over and commented sourly to Sergeant Dieter in the engineers station next to him, "Well, now we see just how good this 'experimental' fire control upgrade package is."

Diter grunted in agreement, "No shit. Well, no test like live fire, right?"

Yang rolled his eyes and shut his faceplate again, turning his attention back to his instruments.

In Hellhound Two, Sergeant Harris responded briskly to the lance commanders status request, *"Hellhound Two is condition alpha."* Immediately after, the vehicle commanders in Hellhounds Three and Four acknowledged that they were in position and ready to fire.

Seeing the indicators for the other three vehicles wink green, Tara keyed her radio again, "Flamestrike Control, This is Hellhound Lead. In position and ready for fires."

From the radio came the voice of the Marine fire control officer, *"Hellhound, Flamestrike. Commence counter battery fire on my mark...Mark."*

"Roger, Flamestrike. Commencing fire." Tara keyed the mic to her lance and said, "Hellhounds, on my command, commence fire...fire, fire fire."

\*\*\*\*

Inside the tactical operations center, Tony looked up from the tactical display just as Sergeant Major Jimenez said, "Sir, you oughta watch this."

Moving over to the slit window, Tony peered down at the scene below. The four mechs looked small from their position high on the crater wall. As the operations staff watched, the rear of one of the mechs shot fire and then, a split second later, a streak shot skyward. Two seconds later, another and another. Soon, the four mechs were at the base of what appeared to be a pillar of fire aiming into the sky, volleying rockets at the distant target identified by their drones. Tony nodded and grinned. Without looking away from the scene below, he said, "Sucks to be the Elai artillery guys right now."

The sergeant major chuckled and replied, "Yep. Whole lotta hurt heading down right now. Hold the fuck up...What's this?" He pointed down into the crater. Squinting, Tony looked at what he was pointing at, then saw it. The explosions of the Elai rockets were getting closer to the positions of the missile mechs as they poured rockets into the sky. Tony frowned, thinking as Jimenez snapped orders to the Fire Control officer, ordering the mechs to switch positions.

Tony turned to the Marine on the sensor station, "Corporal Radgast, do they have drones up? They're zeroing in on our artillery."

The young man shook his head, "No, sir. Scopes are a mess because of the jamming and chaff, but our outposts haven't reported anything in the air."

One of the captains in the back of the ops center spoke up, "Think they left cameras or some other kind of sensors behind?"

Turning back to the scene below Tony scowled and said, "Shit. They could be anywhere, if that's the case."

Tapping on his screen, Captain Shen said, "Sir, we do have that electronic warfare team. I just pinged them to get on sweeping and clearing the crater again for anything we might have missed."

Nodding, Tony agreed, "Good call. Get them moving." After a pause, he said again in a thoughtful tone, "These little fuckers never do anything without a reason. What's their game here?"

Major Reyes answered promptly, "To knock out our artillery?"

Frowning, Tony replied, "They have to know that we have better anti-missile systems than that and this adjustment fire is just going to let us grease more of their launchers. No, this is harassing fire. They're trying to get us to look away from something else." He paused, then, trading a look with Sergeant Major Jimenez, he said suddenly, "The crater walls."

The old NCO nodded, somberly, "It's what I'd do, sir."

Almost simultaneously, the Marine manning the sensor station said, "Sir, we have sensor trips on perimeter stations seven, twelve, thirty five, thirty seven...." The young man paused, then said, calmly, "Three major areas of sensor activity. North, east and southwest sectors."

Sergeant Major Jimeniz observed sourly, "And there it is: the attack."

Nodding, Tony replied, "Ok, people. Showtime. Get the Marines up in their holes. As soon as the Gorgons neutralize that artillery, get the fighters in the air. Send a flash message to 3rd Battalion and General Piasecki if you can reach him. Message reads: 'Anticipated enemy counterattack underway. Will advise.'" The Marines burst into action.

Turning back to the holo display, he picked up and locked his helmet into place. Taking a deep breath and blowing it out, he commanded his suit to play a saved file. A woman's voice started playing in his ear, *"I was also thinking that we ought to think about taking some time off. You know, non-military time and just going exploring. South America, maybe. When you're back from wherever you are."*

With a tight smile, Tony paused the recording and started giving orders.

\*\*\*\*

*Forward Operating Base Anvil, 'Hellhound Lance'*
*Crater Floor*

Captain Chalee keyed her radio, "Flamestrike Control,

missiles expended. Fire mission complete. Entering reload cycle." The mech began to shake with the familiar rhythmic thumping of the rocket tubes going into their automatic reload process.

Through the radio the fire control officer responded, *"Roger, Hellhound. Be advised, Elai rocket fire is correcting, maneuver to avoid."*

"Flamestrike, Hellhound. Roger. Maneuvering." Tara keyed her intercom and said to the crew, "Ok, gang. Looks like these guys want to play rocket tag. They're trying to zero in. Yang, let's go. Evasion pattern Delta."

"Yes, ma'am. Pattern Delta." Yang started the sequence that withdrew the titanium pins locking the mech to the crater floor.

As he did, the engineer, Sergeant Dieter, commented, "We got a lot of dud rockets out there. I've seen at least four or five without explosions. Weird."

From her position in the commander's seat, Tara said, "Just keep an eye where they came down. We don't want to step on one by accident."

The radio crackled and then Sergeant Davis, in Hellhound Four's voice came over the radio, *"One, this is Four. Uh...Do we have friendlies on the surface in the crater? My guys are reporting seeing someone out there. Looks like five or six ground personnel at my nine, about fifty meters out."*

With a frown, Tara responded, "None I know of, but let me check upstairs. Standby." Switching the radio she said, "Anvil Control, this is Hellhound Lead. Can you guys advise if we have anyone on the surface? One of my guys is reporting that we have personnel inside of our minimum safe zones for launch."

The communications sergeant in the operations center responded promptly *"Hellhound lead, I don't think so, but let me check with ops. Standby."*

"Roger." Tara spun her camera and scrutinized the area that Sergeant David had reported seeing people. After a few seconds she keyed her radio and said, "Hellhound Four, I don't see…Wait. There's one. Behind that boulder, the bean shaped one?"

Davis responded, *"Yeah, that's the…."* The shape stepped out of the shadows and as Tara watched, raised a tube to its shoulder, which flashed and sent an orange streak shooting at Hellhound Four. There was an enormous orange-red ball of fire as the rocket hit the side of the vehicle. The radio emitted several bumps then went to static.

Shocked, Tara hesitated a split second, then keyed the radio and screamed, "HELLHOUND LANCE, CONTACT LEFT!!" As she watched several more figures popped up and aimed the tubes and again the red streaks shot towards the massive missile mechs, one of them aimed right at her. There was a dazzling flash and the Gorgon shook, as if it had been kicked by a giant. Blinking to get the afterimage of the flashes out of her eyes, Tara yelled, "Yang, get us moving! Now!" The machine started to take its lurching steps, as more streaks shot towards them. Almost as an afterthought she smashed the button to activate the anti-missile systems, not seeing that it was already activated.

Ubuntu's accented voice cut through the noise of the alarms with a deadly calm, "Anti-missile systems active. Anti-personnel weapons hot."

Keying her radio, Tara took a deep breath to steady her voice and called, "Anvil Control, Hellhound. We have an unknown number of hostiles on foot in the crater, repeat: hostiles in the crater. Request QRF immediately."

Keying her lance radio channel, she said, "All Hellhounds, maneuver independently. Weapons hot!" Looking at her instrument panel she could see that Hellhound Four had sustained damage to its front left leg and that it had multiple systems offline. Its reactor was also running extremely hot. Tara tapped her radio, "Four, Lead. Report."

Over the radio she could hear indistinct words, then Davis's voice cut through the static, *"Lead, Four. We took two, maybe three hits to the left. Crew is ok, but both of the Mark 30's on the left are out and we have a bad leg. We got a heat sink going bad too. Might have to dump if we want to move."*

Breaking in on the radio came the voice of Hellhound Three's vehicle commander, Sergeant Thuoc. Her high, melodic voice belied the seriousness of her tone, *"Hellhound Four, you have seven tangos moving in on your left. We are moving in to support, two minutes."*

There was a scream from the radio, *"They're right on top of us!"* Tara clenched her controls tightly as the radio went dead.
****

*Hellhound Four, Crater Floor*

Inside of Hellhound Four, Sergeant Aaron Davis watched the figures approach his badly damaged mech, stopping to fire rockets as they moved from cover to cover. Reaching up, he triggered all of his smoke generators. It wasn't much, but.....

Sergeant Thad, the engineer declared, "Sergeant, those weapons on the left are fucked. I don't think they're offline, I think they're gone."

Muttering a curse, Davis responded, "Shit. What do we have left?"

The weapons sergeant, a solid, plain faced woman named Jen Holtz, responded, "We got the ones on the right, but since we can't really turn, I can't use them."

The engineer added, "Radios are fucked too. External antennas are probably gone."

From below, the driver, Private Kim chimed in, "Sergeant, I have an idea. You aren't going to like it, but it might keep those things off of us."

Rapidly, Davis responded, "Spit it out, private." He noticed that he could no longer see the enemy on the thermal cameras and started to pan them around trying to reacquire the figures.

Kim said, "Emergency dump the heat via the plasma vents. When we're cool enough, I'll jumpjet us outta here. I can do it on three legs and in this gravity, we're gonna bounce like a grasshopper."

With a muttered curse, the mech commander responded, "Fine. Thad, you better do it fast. I just lost the little fuckers. They might be underneath us."

With a sidelong glance at Thad, Kim muttered, "Underneath us, huh?" Reaching to his controls, he yanked the leg height control lever and the massive mech sank, dropping its forty tons of weight into its belly. There was a sickening crunch from underneath the big mech and the screeching of tortured metal transmitted through the hull. With a smirk, Kim raised the mech back up and reported mildly, "Underside secure for plasma vent."

Rapidly snapping switches to vent the reactor plasma, Thad muttered, "Fucking little psycho. Creative, though." Tapping a final button, he declared, "Ready to vent!"

From his command position, Davis snapped, "Do it!"

Keying the override switch, Thad pulled a lever. There was a massive roar as the plasma exhaust from the reactor was vented through specially designed heat dumps underneath the Gorgon, shooting an arc of several thousand degree white hot plasma out underneath the mech. Thirty seconds later, the engineer reported, "Reactor core temps within safe parameters. Clear for jump."

Grabbing the handholds in his commander's turret, Davis ordered, "Go!"

Kim tapped the controls and said, "Hold onto your nuts, gang." The mech dropped again, then shot up, the jumpjets firing as the massive legs pushed off of the now red-hot glowing rock. In the light gravity, the forty ton machine flew skyward.

As the mech launched, the gunner said calmly, "Multiple targets acquired. Engaging." The plain faced woman at the gunners station triggered all of the remaining anti-personnel weapons as they did, sending streams of green bolts towards the ground.

\*\*\*\*

*Hellhound Lead, Crater Floor*

Tara watched with her lips pressed tightly together, as the smoke enveloped Hellhound Four. Keying her radio, she said, "Four, Lead. Report." The radio only issued static, "Four, Lead. Davis, respond." Swearing again under her breath, she snapped to her crew, "Bring us around and get us over there. We have to cover him."

Below her, Ubuntu responded in his tight, accented voice, "Target, eleven o' clock. Firing."

Tara spun her view around just in time to see the brilliant green stream of the bolts from the leg mounted Mark 30's catch a figure in the process of moving from rock to rock. The stream of energy hit the figure, who staggered but astonishingly didn't fall. The figure scrambled into cover. Tara responded, "Negative kill. He's still back there."

In a grim tone, Ubuntu responded, "Not for long." Switching to the side mounted grenade launchers, he fired, expertly dropping several of the high explosive rounds behind the bounder the figure had ducked behind. The brilliant flashes backlit the figure as it stood, then fell, partially out from behind the rock. Ubuntu walked the Mark 30 bolts into it and kept firing into the figure until it began to smoke. Finally satisfied it wasn't moving, he ceased fire.

Tara snapped her eyes back to the massive cloud of smoke that still enveloped Hellhound Four. She watched in horror as the smoke illuminated with a brilliant white searing light that made the cloud illuminate the entire area.

As the sheets of flame illuminated the clouds of smoke, her radio crackled with the impartial voice of the Marine on the communications station, *"Hellhounds, QRF is inbound on your position from the north, callsign Rattlesnake. ETA Six minutes. Break contact to the north."*

She could hear Yang asking in a low voice, "Was that their

reactor?" No one answered him.

Seconds later, the brilliant flare died down, replaced by smaller lights that illuminated the cloud brilliant white and shot upwards. Suddenly, out of the top of the cloud flew the massive bulk of Hellhound Four. Its left side was charred and smoking and one of its jumpjets wasn't firing–but it was very much still in the fight. As Tara watched, the guns and the grenade launcher mounted on the right of the mech started spitting fire, aiming down towards Hellhound Three, clearly seeing targets from their elevated position. As it moved through the air, the pilot corrected its orientation with brief bursts from the jumpjets.

Breathing a sigh of relief on seeing the big vehicle operational, Tara toggled her radio again, "Hellhound Lance, use jets and break contact to the north. Verify IFF is on." The green acknowledgement lights shone from her master control as the crews acknowledged the order to activate the friend or foe identification system. Corporal Yang manipulated the controls and the mech flew into the air. Tara's stomach dropped out from under her, as it always did. As the mechs of Hellhound Lance bounded away, she caught sight of a low slung, fast moving armored vehicle; a Marine ground assault vehicle with the quick response force. It was screaming southward, a plum of dust from the crater surface rising behind it.

\*\*\*\*

*Inside the Tactical Operations Center, Forward Operating Base Anvil*

"Sir, the QRF has engaged the tangos in the crater," the comm sergeant paused, listening to his headset, then said again, "They're saying that they are taking multiple small arms hits each to bring down."

Tony nodded, his mouth set firmly. He turned to Major

Reyes and Sergeant Major Jimenez, "We need to figure out how the hell they got in and stop it." The two men nodded, watching the flickering of red and blue bolts from the crater floor below as the Marines in the response force traded fire with the Elai in the crate.

The comm sergeant said again, "Hellhound Lance is clear, sir."

Sergeant Major Jimenez commented, with a dark note of amusement in his voice, "Well. That settles what they were after. They wanted to zorch our arty. Rocket fire to draw them out, infantry assaults on the walls to distract us and then special forces to zap 'em. Feints within feints within feints. Clever little bastards."

Tony shook his head silently, watching the firefight. As they watched the returning smoky red bolts slowed, then stopped. Several moments later, the comm sergeant reported, "Sir, Rattlesnake Six reports tangos neutralized." The sergeant listened again for a moment, then said, "They're requesting you down there as soon as you can, sir. They're saying there's something you need to see." He paused and reported again, "The perimeter reports that the forces assaulting the crater walls are withdrawing."

In a grimly satisfied tone, Jiminex commented, "Looks like we drove 'em off."

Tony nodded and turned back to the tactical display and replied, "Yeah. They'll be back though."

\*\*\*\*

Thirty minutes later, Tony, the sergeant major and Major Reyes approached the small team of soldiers standing on the floor of the crater. They were standing in a circle, standing around something lying on the rock. As Tony approached, he noticed the rock was scorched black and blasted clear of dust. In the center of the burned area lay a pile of burnt and crushed armor; only recognizable by the extremities visible in the heap.

Nearby, a still figure lay, its bulky suit of armor seared and warped by the immense heat.

Seeing him approach, one of the soldiers nodded respectfully, "Sir." He gestured down at what Tony could now see was a body. One of the other figures waved at him and he could see Brian's face through the visor of the power armor.

Looking at the scene in front of him, Tony cocked his head and regarded the dead Elai. After a moment he asked, "What the hell am I looking at?"

Brian responded, "It looks like rudimentary power armor, sir. Hayes here," he gestured at a Marine standing nearby, "is an armor tech. He says that it looks like a copy of ours, but a lot less sophisticated."

Hayes spoke up, "It looks like they took some of our armor and reverse engineered it. It's low tech but sturdy as hell, I'll give them that."

"Sir." The lieutenant in charge of the quick response force approached, her rifle still in hand. Tony nodded at the young woman in a silent greeting. She began to speak, "Looks like there were fifteen of them. They came down in unguided glide pods mixed in with the rocket fire and dodged the counter missile fire by using the chaff as cover." She looked down at the scorched armor of the dead alien at their feet and continued, "Looks like they were trying to get the Humpbacks. They were using rockets to immobilize them and then were going to get underneath and use charges to take them out." The young officer gestured at the nearby mangled pile of metal, "Those guys were underneath one trying to set a charge on the hull when the crew inside figured out what they were up to and set it down on top of them." She indicated the scorched figure at their feet, "This poor bastard was caught in the plasma blast when the crew vented their reactor heat. Cooked him in his own armor."

Tony nodded somberly and said, "Nasty way to go."

The lieutenant nodded, "Yes, sir." She looked around the crater, "There don't seem to be any more. These guys had to be on a one way mission."

The group stood in silence for a moment staring at the charred corpse, when there was a flash of brilliant white from the sky above, rapidly followed by another, brighter flash that illuminated the crater with a chalky white light. Blinking to clear the spots from his eyes, Tony looked up. Overhead, there was a wash of light slowly expanding, with dark flecks of debris visible, slowly moving as the ball of gas slowly expanded.

Brian observed in his usual, calm tone, "Well. Looks like the Navy is back." He looked at Tony and the Sergeant Major.

Staring skyward, Sergeant Major Jiminez muttered, "Well. Someone's Navy is back, anyway." He looked at the small command team. "Let's get back inside. We have work to do."

# Chapter 9

## "Do What You Can With What You Have"

*355th Forward Drop Resuscitation Team*
*Inside the Tunnel Complex*

"Ok, people." Manderson spoke firmly. The small group of people in dirty, mismatched armor turned and looked at him. "It's time to get organized. Here's the situation. Of the three forward dropped surgical teams that were supposed to drop, we have half of one. One surgeon, one anesthetist, three nurses and two medics. That's the entirety of the original 355th FDRT." He tossed the clipboard onto the crate in front of him. "What we scrounged up are three line medics from the Marines, a flight medical crew and a pharmacist's mate." His eyes swept the room, meeting the eyes of the soldiers there. "The thirteen of us are all the medical assets on this fire base right now. Us and the corpsmen with the line units are it until the Navy comes back."

"Super," the blonde nurse, Dahl, observed sourly. "When are we getting relief?"

"Maybe tomorrow. Maybe a week. Maybe longer." Manderson replied. "I'll be honest. I don't know. I talked with Major Harris and he says the fleet had to, quote, 'temporarily fall back' end quote."

"What the fuck does that mean?" A huge, barrel chested man wearing navy medical insignia demanded. "I mean…sir."

"It means that that light show we saw overhead was the Navy getting its shit pushed in." A short medic replied. "We all saw the fireworks, Sven."

"Pipe down." Brian spoke, his voice firm, his eyes locked on the two enlisted men. "Let the major finish."

"Sorry, Master Sergeant," the medic replied, looking

abashed. The big medic glowered for a moment before scowling and looking at his boots.

"As I was saying," Manderson continued, "What we have is what we've got. We have a team scrounging supplies from what's left of the shuttle, but it's not looking like a lot made it." He looked down at the clipboard on the crate and asked, "Ok. First things first. Can anyone fix an octodoc? The FRST's was damaged in the drop and the spare went down with the shuttle."

The soldiers and sailors traded looks, then the short medic raised his hand. "I took the short course, sir." He hesitated, "I can't promise anything, though. It was mostly maintenance."

"Better than nothing." Manderson replied. He nodded at Brian. "Get him on it."

Brian nodded wordlessly. The officer continued, "The rest of you, let's get to setting up a better layout for the hospital. These crates here are what we have so far. "He gestured at the mess of crates in the room. "It's almost all of what we have, so be wise with supplies."

Dahl spoke up. "I can start an inventory while the medics set up a trauma station. Do the Marines have a battalion aid station set up yet?"

"Yes, but they don't have a provider. His pod didn't make it down. It's being run by a senior medic and we stripped his assistant for our team here." Manderson replied, gesturing at the hulking corpsman. "Assume that I have stripped the Marines of everything they can spare." He smiled hollowly. "Because I have."

Dahl nodded thoughtfully but didn't say anything.

Colonel Douglas suddenly spoke up. "If we can fix the octodoc, that's good. If not, we can do it the old fashioned way." He looked at the short medic. "Does it have the surgical tip recovery tray with it?"

"I honestly don't know, sir. If it's like the ones we had on the 'docs in the FRST, then, yes. A recovery tray is part of the kit."

"What's a recovery tray?" Manderson asked, listening to the interchange.

"It's a steel tray about this big." The surgeon held up his hands, indicating a size. "It's intended to recover 'doc surgical tips in case there's an arm failure. It's got a set of old school microsurgical tools in it." He grinned, humorlessly, "Not that I'm saying that the military octodocs are unreliable pieces of shit, but they have been known to fail…from time to time."

"Ok." Maderson made a note of this on his datapad. "The shuttle was smashed to shit but maybe we can find what's left of the 'doc and see if there's another kit on it." He looked down at the datapad again. "Ok. We've got Master Sergeant Agawa putting together rosters, Captain Dahl on inventory and Specialist Mathers and Colonel Douglas on trying to salvage a 'doc." He looked up. "Ok. Next item: Workspace." He tapped a button on his datapad and a small holographic map appeared. It showed the volcanic crater that formed the firebase. Inside of the massive walls, the tunnels could be seen outlined. Manderson stuck a pen into the hologram. "This here is the south main entrance. It's big; because the Marines had the Seabees cut it big enough for combat support mechs, but it's currently here we have the aid station, right off the side of the main hangar. It's good because it's on the far side of the crater from the main enemy forces." He paused, "Or we think so anyway. Who the hell knows." He pointed at a different area on the north wall. "This is the north entrance. Smaller and still being dug by the Seabees. It's not far from the operations center, so we'll be able to communicate with the command team if there's a mass casualty or we need extra hands." He looked up. "It's closer to the action, but that might actually be better for the surgical team." He pointed back at the south wall. "I propose that we set up a lower acuity area of care here. Walking wounded, troops who only need a day or two to get back on their feet. Nothing critical. We'll put the critical patients and the surgical team here." He gestured at the smaller tunnel.

Colonel Douglas leaned forward and inspected the hologram. After a moment, he gave Manderson a hard look and asked in a low tone, "Is it wise to split us like that? We are already mighty short on people."

Gazing back steadily, Manderson replied. "No, but it's also for another reason. If we lose part of the tunnel, we don't lose all of the medical assets."

Douglas nodded thoughtfully but said nothing. Manderson continued speaking, "I've got extra non-medical hands to staff the minimal care station. You'll have to train them in simple stuff, dressing changes, IV bag changes, med pump changes, that sort of thing- but they're Marines. They're nothing if not adaptable." He looked up at Captain Dahl, who was leaning against the wall nearby. "Who do you have from the nurses that can run it?"

Dahl looked startled and turned to the two women and single man standing behind her and looked helplessly. After a moment, a stout woman with Asian features wearing lieutenant's bars stepped forward. "I can do it." Manderson leaned forward and peered at her nametape.

"Nakahara, sir. Kelly Nakahara." She smiled and added, "I've run minimal care dets before with less than this. Just run me a phone line and get me a couple crates of medpacks and I can improvise the rest."

"Thank you, Lieutenant Nakahara." Manderson scrawled her name down, then looked up at the small group. "She needs a medic."

The hulking medic with a permanent scowl raised a single hand without a word. Manderson nodded, "Name?"

"Johansen. Corpsman," the man rumbled. "Will we be directing the marine casualty collection teams to bring casualties to either location, sir?"

"Good question." The officer looked at Colonel Douglas. "Sir?"

The surgeon rubbed his chin for a moment, then asked, "How far apart are the stations?"

"Mile across the crater, maybe. Probably a couple if we have to take the tunnels around the crater."

"Do we have medical transport?" Douglas asked. "Ambulances, armored vehicles, anything?"

"I'll have to check." Manderson replied. "We might be able to take one of the non-combat capable armored vehicles and use it as a med transport."

The young flight nurse from the Valkyrie crew spoke up. "If you can get the vehicle, sir, I can man it. I'm comfortable with enroute care."

Colonel Douglas nodded and added, "If we get one, casualties to either location and transport per the captain here. If not, the Marines need to bring them to the north station where the surgical team is."

"That works for…" Manderson stopped and frowned at his datapad, then reached for his comm unit. He looked at it for a moment, then bluntly said, "Well, we're out of time. Casualty collection point Charlie has four seriously wounded and is bringing them to the south aid station now."

With a brusque nod, Douglas replied, "Well. Here we go." He gestured to the short medic and snapped, "Dahl, bring the troops and what you can carry. Resuscitation supplies and the synthblood that we have are priority, as well as ventmasks and medcuffs." The nurse nodded and turned to start giving orders to the soldiers in the room.

The colonel jerked his head at Manderson, "I'm going to go see what we've got." He turned to the medic, who had shouldered a large aid bag. "Let's go." He swept out of the room, gesturing to a Marine standing outside to serve as a guide.

With a nod to the departing colonel, Manderson spoke to the remainder of the team. "Grab what you need. I'll have some of the sailors move this shit to the aid station. I got this here." He clapped his hands. "Hustle. The Marines will take you to the south station." The room burst into activity as the soldiers and sailors grabbed what they could take and hurried out the door.

\*\*\*\*

*Thirty minutes later, in the South Aid Station.*

Manderson entered the tunnel leading to the aid station and immediately heard it: The sounds of the organized chaos of a trauma resuscitation. Stepping through the door, he found himself in a wide room carved out of the solid rock, with a low ceiling. It was brightly lit by powerful light sets bolted into the rock. To his left and right were rows of stretchers running down either side of the room with an aisle down in the middle. Two soldiers in power armor lay still on stretchers, with monitors plugged into their armor and a box plugged into the bedframe with a tube running into the armor. Both were tended by a single medic. Closer to the far door, a group of people stood crowded around a bed. Manderson couldn't see the patient, just a pair of bare feet protruding off of the end of the stretcher. He paused and listened to the voices and watched the hurrying medical personnel as they worked.

"Pressure is 80/45, weak pulses, cold extremities." Dahl's normally icy tone was brisk and businesslike, cutting through the hubbub.

"Give him two more units of synthblood." Colonel Douglas calmly ordered from where he stood at the foot of the bed with his arms folded.

"We don't have a lot of synthblood left." A medic nearby stated. "At least until I can run another batch in the synthesizer. Only have six left right now."

"That's fine." Douglas turned and asked, "How's the scanner coming?"

A specialist looked up from an instrument console. "About another minute, sir. It's rebooting. It took a pretty hard hit in the crash but I think I got it working." He looked down at his console. "There we go." To the colonel he said, "We're up, sir."

"Scan him." Douglas ordered. "Is the airway secured? Is the ventmask on and working?"

Someone from the head of the bed replied, "Yes, sir. It's in." Manderson could see the black mask covering the injured Marine's face. The tiny instrument panel on the side of the mask flashed as the man's chest rose and fell rhythmically as the machine forced air into his lungs.

The tall corpsman that Manderson had noted earlier called out in his thickly accented voice, "Scanning. Step back please." The team stepped back, giving the officer watching a view of the wounded man. He was still partially in his armor, but the chest and abdomen had been opened, exposing the pale skin underneath. On his abdomen was a large, blood soaked dressing. Johansen ran a long slender rod connected to a handle over the wounded man's body, then rapidly passed under the bed. A few seconds later, the handle beeped and the team moved back towards the man, once again obscuring him from view. He nodded to the technician on the console, who nodded back without looking up. Colonel Douglas was leaning over the man's shoulder staring at the screen intently as the images appeared.

"Fragments throughout the abdominal cavity.' He muttered. The surgeon looked up and asked, "Is there any biofoam in his urine?"

Dahl leaned over and looked at something out of Manderson's sight, then called back, "No, sir." She stood back up, "But there's a lot of blood in there."

With a curt nod, Douglas tapped the screen for a moment, then stood up and turned to the far side of the narrow room, where the stocky medic was sitting cross legged on the floor, with his head stuffed inside a large, rucksack sized piece of equipment. The pack had four mechanical arms on it, neatly folded into their storage position.

"Mather, is it up?" Douglas asked.

The medic pulled his head out and replied, "I think it got

ice inside the main circuit out there, sir. Everything inside here is fucked." He gestured at the open panel. "The arms will probably work, but the computer system is cooked, so no scanner guidance, no virtual reality augmentation, nothing."

With a grimace, Douglas replied, "Ok. We're going to do this the old fashioned way." He nodded to Dahl. "Let's get him to the OR. Prep for an exploratory laparotomy."

The nurses hesitated, then looked at the nurse across from her, Lieutenant Nakahara. Nakahara shrugged. "If you go to the OR with the colonel, I can watch those two." Dahl nodded and the chaotic scene continued.

Turning from the scene, Manderson looked at the two nearer patients, then spoke to the lone medic tending them, "How are they?"

The medic looked up from his clipboard. "They'll live." He gestured at one of them. "His suit emergency medical system saved him when it tourniqueted and sealed off his arm. He'll probably lose it, but he'll live. I've got him sedated for now." He nodded at the other one, who was sitting up slightly. The woman nodded back with a grimace. "She's got nasty frostbite. Her suit power failed after they got hit and the emergency backups shunted heat from her arms and legs."

"Damn." Manderson replied. He stepped up to the side of the stretcher and spoke to the injured woman. "How are you doing, Marine?"

"It hurts like a bitch, sir." She replied through gritted teeth. "My suit medpack is out of painkillers and he's telling me that we don't have any to spare for minor injuries."

Reaching for his belt, Manderson grabbed his spare medpack, intending to offer it, but the Marine shook her head. "Keep it. I can hang." She nodded her head at the far end of the room. "Plus, Ivan needs it more than me." She regarded the scene for a minute, then asked in a pensive tone, "Is he going to die?"

"Not if we have anything to say about it," the medic declared flatly.

The injured Marine looked at him, then nodded, seeming to relax slightly. After a moment she closed her eyes and said, "Williams is dead, isn't he." Her tone was flat.

"Yes," the medic replied, his face a carefully composed mask. "We tried, but he was dead before he got to us."

Without opening her eyes, the woman replied, "I thought he might be. The rocket hit right between him and Ivan. I think he took the brunt of it." She opened her eyes and looked at the medic. "Did he suffer?"

"No," the medic replied quietly. "I'm quite sure of that."

"Good." The Marine closed her eyes and fell silent for a few seconds. "I'm glad for that." He paused again, then added, "He was a good dude. I'm going to miss him." She pushed her lips tightly together, then turned her face away from the medic and squeezed her eyes tightly closed.

The medic squeezed her shoulder briefly, then stepped around the bed. He leaned close to Manderson and said in a low, grave voice. "We ain't gonna be able to sustain this for long, sir."

"No," the officer replied. "We aren't." He met the man's eyes, "But we have to, because what choice do we have?"

"Not much," the medic replied. The younger man held his gaze for a moment then added, "We'll do what we can."

"That's all I ask." Manderson slapped the medic's shoulder. "That you do what you can." He turned to leave.

As he did, he could hear someone call out from the far side of the room. "Major Manderson, the operations center says they have another set of casualties inbound, ETA twenty minutes. They also need our comm plan and emergency freqs."

Manderson wearily raised his hand in acknowledgement and picked up his comm handset and got to work.

# Chapter 10


## "Iron Dice"

*39 Draconis, United Earth Alliance Task Force 3.2*
*Aboard the UEAN* Stalwart

Rear Admiral Laura Kensington stood in the dimly lit flag bridge on the *Stalwart* and watched the holographic image of Fleet Admiral Halleck addressing the fleet commanders.

"As we push in-system, we expect heavy Elai resistance. In the first engagement they met Admiral Kensington and her cruisers. She hit them hard but suffered losses." Laura frowned darkly. 'Suffered losses' was a polite way to say her task force had been damn near destroyed and thousands of sailors lost. The fleet admiral continued, "As we make our way in system, the heavy cruisers and their escorts will engage any mobile forces. The *Phantom Fury* and the *Thunderbolt* will do a high combat drop to reinforce the Marines on the surface. All other vessels package and transfer anything you want dropped to Captains DeGenova and Strasser." The admiral frowned and continued, in a tight tone, "We expect that we won't have a lot of time to drop if we can't hold orbit, so make those drops count. Food, munitions and as many reinforcements as we can get down. The *Phantom Fury* and the *Thunderbolt* are going to try to get the rest of the First Marines onto the surface. The fleet will try to buy them time to accomplish that."

The admiral paused as the holographic map in each of his fleet captains' ships updated, then continued speaking, "I will lead the battle group with the *Courageous* serving as flagship, joined by *Daring, Reliable, Indomitabl*e and *Noble*. We will add *Bravado* as it is the only undamaged ship from Admiral Kensington's task force." Laura winced at this but said nothing as the task force commander continued, "The reconstituted escort force will be the *Stalwart, La Venganza* and the light cruisers *Denali* and *Mont Blanc,* commanded by Admiral Kensington. They will escort and protect the *Phantom Fury* and *Thunderbolt* as they complete the second drop." Admiral Halleck looked at a datapad in his hand and said added, "We will run quiet until we identify Elai forces or are engaged." Glancing at the images of each of the captains of the vessels, he continued, "Immediately after we jump, Captain O'Toro in the *Avenger* will go dark and attempt to link up with the *Infiltrator.* We haven't heard from her, but we assume she is still operational in-system, as we haven't picked up her beacon." With a look around at the images, he asked, "Are there any questions?"

Laura asked, "Admiral, if we encounter numerically superior forces, what is our strategy?"

With a grim half smile, Halleck responded, "If we are forced to fall back, our rally point is here at the jump point in 39 Draconis. The Fifth Fleet is sending the fleet carriers *Shiva's Wrath* and the *Athena's Bow* and as many cruisers as they can spare from Sol, but they're a week out, at the earliest. Those Marines might not have a week if the Elai can reinforce the system." Looking back around, he said, his voice more gentle than his normal stern tone, "This might be a show of force and it might be the fight of our lives. I think we all know the Elai well enough to know what's more likely. Stay alert, stay calm and we will emerge victorious. Captains, ready your ships. Admiral Kensington, a moment if you please. Dismissed."

The conference call ended, the images of the captains vanishing. After a moment, the older fleet officer said, "Laura, I didn't put you in charge of the escort force because of a lack of confidence. I put you there because you have the discipline to stay with them." He paused, then continued somberly, "We can't lose any more capital ships– particularly carriers. That little mess out over Solace put the *Gloriouso Espana* and the *Jade Emperor* in the fleet yards for a year plus and destroyed seven heavy cruisers, with half a dozen more probably unsalvageable. The new United Nations class battleships are under construction but won't be ready for at least six months." He gestured at the holo display, where the fleet was slowly moving into its new configuration, "Those two assault carriers represent a fifth of all assault carriers left in the fleet. We can't lose them." The small image's eyes locked on hers and continued speaking, "I'm counting on you. If this goes sideways, you get those carriers out of the system."

Laura nodded and replied simply, "Yes, sir."

Halleck suddenly gave her a lopsided grin, "It'll be like old times, Laura. Remember the insurrectionists in Tau Ceti?"

Despite herself, Laura laughed, "Sir, Tau Ceti was a fucking disaster. We god damn near lost our ship, our careers AND almost got killed. I don't know if that's the comparison we want to go for here, Admiral."

Laughing, the senior officer replied, "I meant more as in 'We made it through that mess together and we will make it through this' but your point is well taken."

Shaking her head, Laura responded, "I guess."

His face becoming serious again, Halleck said, "In all seriousness, Laura. Be careful. If it goes to shit, get the carriers and your force out. That's an order. This war has enough dead heroes."

Laura looked down for a long moment, then back up at the holo, "Yes, sir. It sure does."

\*\*\*\*

*Aboard the UEAN* Stalwart, *Task Force 3.2.2 'Escort Force',*
*Draconis 327, Entering high orbit over M3245*

Several hours later, Laura remained on the flag bridge, her bladder full to bursting, but unwilling to leave. The two improvised task forces had jumped into Draconis 327 expecting a fight as they transitioned into the system but had found nothing. The approach to the gas giant and their objective of the small moon with the beleaguered Marine contingent was completely uneventful. Frowning at the display again, she turned to her operations officer. The taciturn Russian was tapping awkwardly into his console with one hand, the other arm in a light cast.

Laura said, in a thoughtful tone, "Dimitry, are we missing something? It's not like the Elai not to contest a system with everything they have, as soon as they see us."

The man looked up and replied, "You are thinking it's a trap, Admiral?"

"If you were them and you saw us heading in with fresh ships, what would you do?" She went back to staring at the display.

Looking into the holo display, Captain Sokolov looked thoughtful, but didn't reply. The other two officers on her staff were silent for a moment, then Commander de la Cruz suddenly said, "If I were them, I'd let the strike force pass, then hit us. We're obviously a softer target. We have two damaged heavy cruisers, two light cruisers and two carriers."

Captain Destin, her logistics officer, disagreed, "If they come after us, we run and let the assault force hit them in the rear. We still maintain a speed advantage. We can also seed our path with mines. It'll make us a very hard target to catch."

"While leaving the Marines down there under the guns of their cruisers," De la Cruz responded, testily.

Destin shot back, "Not like we haven't done that already. What does a few more days matter?"

Laura sighed and turned back to the display for a moment, half listening to her staff going back and forth. The stress of waiting was getting under everyone's skin, as her officers didn't usually argue much, particularly not in front of her.

Making a sudden decision, the admiral announced, "Enough, you two. I'm going to hit the head, then get us coffee. Dimitry, Penelope, the usual?"

The two officers stopped their tense debate and the petite officer responded, "Yes, ma'am!" She ran a hand through her hair and eyed the slender, gaunt eyed officer across from her as she did.

Turning to Destin, Laura said again, "Tea?"

The pale skinned officer nodded and answered, "Thank you." Heading to the hatch that led to the passageway outside of the flag bridge, she made her first stop at the head. As she was washing her hands, her communicator went off. With an annoyed look, she dried her hands and saw the message that read 'STRIKE FORCE REPORTS MULTIPLE CONTACTS'. With a muttered curse, she exited the restroom at a run and entered the flag bridge just in time to see the tactical display update, showing Admiral Halleck's' forces moving into a combat formation.

As Laura moved to the command table, Dimitry reported flatly, "Admiral, fifteen minutes to the gravity well. The *Fury* and *Thunderbolt* will do a high drop, in one pass. Captain Strasser on the *Thunderbolt* says that if they do not have to maneuver, they can get the pods and shuttles launched in less than thirty minutes."

Laura's eyebrows shot up. "Half-hour for fifteen hundred Marines and their equipment?"

With a nod and a slight smile, the staff officer responded, "Yes, but he says not to ask how. I suspect Captains DeGenova and Strasser might be...how do I put this...getting creative with their launch procedures?"

Shaking her head, Laura replied, "No questions. As long as he gets the job done." The display chimed and the red markers indicating enemy vessels began populating as the sensor data from the Strike Force began to fill in the display. She continued grimly, "Looks like we don't have a lot of time anyway."

\*\*\*\*

The chirping of the alarms came faintly through the thick walls of the flag bridge as the *Courageous* went to general quarters. Fleet Admiral Halleck waited patiently for the reports to start coming in.

"Sir, we have seven contacts, designated Alpha One through Five as Type I cruisers and the other two..." The lieutenant on the sensor station stared at his display momentarily, then continued, "Uh...The other two are not in the database. Just a second, sir..." The young officer leaned forward, whispering into his headset. Admiral Halleck sat in his command chair calmly and watched the holo display. Several seconds later, the lieutenant reported, "Sir, the sensors are reporting that the two unclassified contacts are estimated in excess of a million tons." He twisted in his seat to look at the Admiral behind him, "I've pinged the rest of the strike force to confirm."

Nodding, Admiral Halleck turned to the captain standing beside him, "Captain Koa, anything in fleet intel about this?"

The fleet intelligence officer was standing at his station staring at the screen. After a moment, he responded, "No, sir. This is something new."

Considering this for a moment, Halleck responded, "Carriers, maybe? We've been waiting for an Elai fleet carrier to show up. We know their fighters are space capable."

Koa shook his head. "Initial optical analysis of the hull isn't showing any launch bays or tubes yet. I've got the fleet intel section doing an analysis on them now." On the main screen in front of them, the image of one of the massive enemy ships appeared. It was the size of an Earth Alliance fleet carrier, dwarfing the Elai cruisers around it. Koa pointed at the image, "What the hell are those things?" He indicated several dome shaped structures with short, tube-like protrusions on the fore and aft of the vessel.

With a humorless smile, the admiral responded, "I think we're about to find out."

The lieutenant spoke up again, "Sir, Captain Hall reports seven minutes to the engagement envelope." At the same time, another officer at a station next to the communications station reported, "Admiral, the escort force has started the drop. They estimate thirty minutes to completion."

Halleck replied, "Thank you. Whatever those things are, we're about to kick them in the teeth. We're going to make an initial pass and give them everything we've got. We'll break contact, then see where the escort force is with the landing and reevaluate. Signal the Strike Force to form line abreast, set course one three five, Indigo Six"

The lieutenant on the comm station responded, "Aye, sir. Line abreast, one three five, Indigo Six. Signaling the fleet."

On the holo display, the strike force began to form into a line, the seven heavy cruisers maneuvering so that each would flash past the enemy vessel in succession, launching their missiles then peeling away, minimizing their time in the missile fire from the Elai warships.

Admiral Halleck opened his mouth to speak when the deck began to vibrate, then shuddered violently, knocking sailors off their feet. Around the flag bridge, alarms began to scream and consoles exploded in showers of sparks. In a matter of seconds, the vibration had turned into an ear splitting roar, punctuated by sharp snapping and cracking he could feel shaking the deck. A violent gust of wind blew Halleck forward out of his command chair and into a nearby console. He could feel bones snapping in his shoulder and followed by sharp, stabbing pain in his chest as ribs broke. The undulating wail of the depressurization alarms filled his ears, along with the screeching of tearing metal. He opened his mouth to scream and couldn't seem to get a breath of air. Struggling to breathe, he gasped once, twice, then the darkness swallowed Fleet Admiral Thomas Halleck.

\*\*\*\*

*Aboard the UEAN* Bravado, *Task Force 3.2 'Strike Force'*
*Draconis 327, Interplanetary Space*

"Captain! The *Courageous* just got hit! She's breaking up! My god! They're hitting the *Daring*! She's breaking up too! Her core just blew!" The young officer's voice was high and had a note of panic in it.

Commander Ripley Piasecki ordered immediately, "Weapons, volley fire all ready missiles, maximum warhead yield. Helm, set course two six three, ahead full, lateral roll to port. Get us out of here, Mr. Casey!"

The helmsman responded immediately, "Two six three, port roll, ahead full, aye!" The deck of the cruiser started to thrum as the massive engines increased their power.

The officer on the sensor station shouted again, "They just hit the *Reliable*! She's off the net!"

Ripley snapped, "We can all hear you, Mr. Stone. No need to yell." Turning to her left, she ordered, "XO, fire every drone and decoy we have off the starboard side. We need as much flying junk as we can get between us and that thing."

Her executive officer, a somber-faced giant named Lars Knutson, said in a cold, matter of fact tone, "We can move behind the hulk of the *Reliable* if we have to."

A watchstander at the engineering station reported, "We have the hull temps rising fast in frames thirty eight, thirty nine...forty, forty one" The officer looked up, his face pale, "Looks like whatever that thing out there is targeting us but increasing distance and our movement is keeping us out of effective range."

The damage control officer reported in a flat voice, "No damage reported. I think the range and our roll are keeping any one section from burning through. We still ought to get further away, though."

Blowing out a shaky breath, Ripley ordered, "I agree. Signal the fleet as to what the engagement range is and keep us out of it." She lowered herself into her command chair and stared at the tactical display. On it blinked the symbol for 'Signal Loss' from the *Courageous*, the *Daring* and the *Reliable*; the first three cruisers in the attack formation. The other two warships in line behind her, the *Noble* and the *Indomitable* displayed damage indicators. Somehow, the *Bravado* had come through unscathed, again. As she watched, the other two cruisers came around and followed behind her in the *Bravado*, heading away from the massive enemy vessels.

The sensor officer, his voice calmer, reported "Captain, the Elai vessels do not seem to be pursuing. They've set a course for Onyx." Ripley nodded grimly, acknowledging the report.

A moment later, the communications officer spoke up, "Skipper, we have a flash traffic coming in from Admiral Kensington. Text only." He tapped a control and the message displayed in the bottom of the main screen in the front of the bridge. 'STRIKE FORCE DISENGAGE. PROCEED AT BEST SPEED OUTSYSTEM. LINK WITH ESCORT FORCE AT RALLY POINT OMICRON. TASK FORCE 3.2 COMMANDER'

Her executive officer observed in a low voice meant for her ears alone, "Looks like we just got our asses handed to us, ma'am." He paused and added somberly, "Again."

Ripley pressed her lips tightly together, unable to find any words that seemed appropriate and not trusting herself to speak, nodded silently.

\*\*\*\*

*Aboard the UEAN* Infiltrator

Commander von Kant stared at the viewscreen and shook her head silently, as the wreckage of the task force dissipated and the survivors turned and began to accelerate towards the system jump point. After a moment, she turned to Captain

Harris and said quietly, "Sir?" Her tone held all the questions she needed to ask.

Staring at the display, Captain Harris nodded slowly. Suddenly, he said firmly, "Right. Those big bastards are going to be a tough nut to crack. We're gonna have to get close and get the missiles inside 'em before whatever that thing was that they used on the cruisers can tear the guys on the surface apart." He turned to the helmsman and said, "Make your heading three five two, ahead one third. Stay ahead of that thing. We can't get silhouetted against the gas giant." As the helmsman acknowledged, Mitch turned to the senior chief petty officer of the *Infiltrator*. She stood glaring at the display with her hands on her hips and a scowl on her face, "Chief Chara, what the hell was that weapon?"

The senior enlisted sailor answered promptly, "If I had to guess, sir, I'd say it was a particle beam and a godawful powerful one at that. Not a new technology, but we don't use it. Takes too much power away from propulsion. We had a few ships with 'em back in the 2230's, if I remember right, but they never really caught on." She frowned at the display for a moment longer, then turned and said, "Sir, that thing's gotta have a fuckton of armor. We build our defenses to counter our weapons, so why wouldn't they? It'd also account for the mass."

Mitch nodded and stared at the imposing bulk of the Elai ships. One was now clearly vectoring towards the planet and the other and its escorts were heading towards the jump point, keeping between the planet and the fleeing Alliance warships.

Pointing at the display at the one heading for the planet, the captain stated, "Commander von Kant, start our approach. Let's get this big bastard before he gets that cannon in range of the Marines." He turned and added in a low voice, "Greta, this needs to be perfect. With all those escorts, I don't know that we're going to get a second shot at this. We need to hit him hard and immediately break contact." Turning back to the display, he leaned on the edge of the table and stared at it again, then said, "Let's get to work." His executive officer simply nodded and began to issue orders.

\*\*\*\*

*Aboard the UEAN* Infiltrator, *High Orbit over M3245, six hours later.*

"Shoot!" Mitch ordered. The *Infiltrator* shuddered as the missiles left the launch tubes. The chief petty officer on the weapons station reported, "Weapons away!"

The hours of stalking the massive alien ship had ended at this very moment. The familiar shudder of the massive anti-ship missiles shook the deck under their feet. Immediately, Commander von Kant, the executive officer, ordered, "Helm, roll 180 degrees on the axis."

The helmsman, in this case, a slender young woman with the distinctive shaved head of the residents of Mars answered, "180 degree roll on the axis, aye." The indicators began to flicker on the displays, as the *Infiltrator* rolled in space, exposing the second set of missile tubes on its starboard side. The sailor at the helm reported, "Roll complete."

Von Kant ordered, "Open tubes 11-20 and prepare to fire."

The chief on the weapons station reported, "Tubes open...ready to fire!"

Mitch ordered again, "Shoot!" The shuddering again rocked the stealthy warship. Several seconds later, the chief reported, "Weapons away."

Von Kant nodded and said, "Helm set course two three four, mark four. Engines ahead one third." Across the dimly lit control room, a lieutenant sitting next to the chief at the weapons station said, "Missile group one running, still at low power. Missile group two running, also at low power."

Mitch nodded and asked his exec, "What did weapons end up targeting?"

The young woman responded, her eyes glued to the screen, "Five at the big one, two at each of the cruisers. We left six for follow up in group two."

Von Kant checked her watch, then responded, "Ok. Hit the mines."

The chief nodded and tapped the console in front of him. On the display at the front of the compartment, there was a series of bright flashes, outlining the massive Elai battleship as it moved towards the moon. Several seconds later, the large bulk of the Elai battleship started to shift, turning away from the remotely detonating mines.

The weapons chief reported, "Fifteen seconds. Going to full power." The propulsion units on the missiles suddenly glowed brightly and the missiles accelerated. The Elai warship and its escorts were now broadside to the missiles as they attempted to turn away from the minefield in front of them. As the weapons approached the enemy warships, the warheads separated from the body of the missile, rapidly moving ahead as a small rocket motor drove it ahead of the body of the missile. The duranium slugs punched large holes in the armor plate of the enemy warships with the nuclear warheads a split second behind, tearing through the rends in the armor left by the mass of the penetrators. There was a flash as the first of the nuclear penetrators detonated, causing the crew on the bridge of the *Infiltrator* to turn their heads from the screen.

All of the weapons aimed at the Elai battleship struck within milliseconds of each other, boring five massive holes through the ship, incinerating armor, subsystems and crew as they tore broadside through the warship, detonating inside the hull. The big ship immediately began to drift, with atmosphere venting from the holes and sparks spitting from the edges. Multiple smaller explosions could be seen inside of the damaged areas as internal systems failed.

The remaining missiles each targeted an Elai cruiser, with similar results. Seconds later, as the afterimages cleared from the screens, Captain Harris asked in a calm tone, "Report."

The commander on the sensor station said, "Sir, looks like we have five solid hits on the big one. We got three of the cruisers though... There's two of them left and another damaged and adrift. The big one is...." On the screen, the massive Elai warship detonated in a blinding flash. A second later, they could see a wave of energy and debris being hurled outward, consuming the smaller warships around it.

Captain Harris snapped, "Helm, put us bow on to that energy wave. Chief, sound the collision alarms." The *Infiltrator* heeled over as the helmsman tried to get the bow of the ship towards the blast wave but wasn't fast enough. The energy wave caught the stealth ship, striking it broadside. Mitch clung to his command chair armrests as sparks showered down from an overhead panel with a loud crackling. and then the lights went out. There were a few yelps and screams of pain as the electrical wave arced through panels and instruments. The crackling stopped and there was dead silence. After a moment, the dim red emergency lights popped on, cutting through a smoky haze. Groaning nearby caught his attention and he saw the young sailor at the helm now lying on the deck, clamping her hands to her face, blood dripping between her fingers. Mitch snapped a control on the arm of his command chair and said, "Medical emergency on the bridge. Corpsman to the bridge." Climbing out of his chair, he knelt to check on her, "You ok, sailor?"

The young woman lowered her hands, showing a crooked nose with blood pouring from it. She answered in a pained voice, "Yes, sir. Console bit me and I got smacked pretty good." She looked at the blood on her hands and said unsteadily, "I think I'm ok."

Looking around and seeing his command dazedly pulling themselves back to their stations, he stood and said in a clear, loud voice, "Damage report."

From her station, Commander von Kant said, "Propulsion is offline. Internal comms is spotty. Active stealth is offline. Primary weapons offline. Hull integrity is holding. Looks like...Life support is ok." The normally stoic officer's voice was dazed. "We got a shitload of fried noncritical subsystems."

The weapons chief called from his station, "Sir, the missile load systems are offline. We can load by hand but it's gonna take a while. Probably a couple of hours. We're empty until then."

Mitch nodded and said, "Ok. Get me casualty reports. Commander, get down to engineering and get a feel for where we're at. Tell the Chief Engineer that the priority is propulsion, then stealth. Go."

"Aye, sir." The young woman stood and unsteadily made her way off of the bridge. The commander at the sensor station said, "Sir, I have limited sensors back online."

With a nod, Mitch responded, "Good. Any of the Elai left?" The officer bent to his instruments. A corpsman with an aid bag came into the compartment and was tending to the young sailor, who was now sitting up, a nasty cut at the bridge of her nose now visible. The corpsman was holding pressure to the cut and speaking quietly.

The sensor officer replied, his voice shaky, "Sir, we have three Elai destroyers inbound, moving at point five. They're coming right at us."

With a sinking sensation in his stomach, the captain responded, "How far out?"

The young officer said in a low tone, "Ten, fifteen minutes, tops."

Mitch put his hands on his hips and thought for several seconds, then tapped the comm panel, "XO, Commander Niece, status?"

The distinctive French accent of the chief engineer answered, "Sir, we can get propulsion back online in a couple hours. The EMP blew out a bunch of subsystem surge protectors. Nothing we can't fix, but it will take time."

In a grim voice, Mitch responded, "Time we don't have. We have three Elai destroyers bearing down on us. Can you get the secondary weapons online?"

There was a moment of quiet from the communicator, then

the chief engineer replied, "We will surely try, sir."

The young woman sitting on the floor was now unsteadily making her way to her feet, helped by the corpsman. Standing for a moment, she then turned and made her way back to the helm, with the corpsman protesting quietly. Seeing this, Mitch said, "Sailor, you can go with the corpsman."

The young woman shook her head and responded, "No, sir. My duty station is at the helm. I'm ok." She wiped her face again gingerly on her sleeve and sat at her station and started checking her instruments and said, "No place I'd rather be anyway."

The lieutenant at the sensor station said, "Seven minutes, sir."

Mitch turned to the weapons station officer and said, "Secondaries?"

"Offline." The weapons chief's voice was flat.

"How about mines? Can we drop mines?"

"They won't arm. Too close and inside the minimum safe distance."

With a desperate, sinking feeling in his stomach, Mitch mentally ran through his options, which were getting mighty thin. As if out of thin air, Commander von Kant appeared at his elbow, back from engineering.

After a quick glance at the instruments, she said in a low tone, "The Chief Engineer has teams on it, but he's not going to make it. He says you might want to consider getting the crew off."

Mitch considered this for a moment, then nodded, "Ok, let's do it. If we get them out now, they might clear the minimum...."

"Sir!!" The lieutenant at the weapons station shouted, suddenly, "The lead Elai destroyer just blew up! And another one!" He shouted excitedly, "There goes the third! They're gone!" Mitch looked at Greta, who closed her eyes and blew out a breath, then opened her eyes and smiled slowly. He nodded and turned to the display, which was now showing three slowly expanding balls of plasma, marking the graves of the Elai destroyers and their crews.

"Sir, we have an incoming tightbeam. It's Captain O'Toro and the *Avenger*!" Greta and Mitch traded a relieved look. Mitch moved over to the comm station and tapped the accept button. The screen lit up with a young woman with dark hair and eyes, sitting calmly in her command chair.

She nodded cordially and spoke in a calm voice with a lilting accent, "Mitchell. You looked like you could use a hand."

With a relieved grin, he responded, "Catalina. Excellent timing, as always."

In an arch tone, the other captain replied, "Excellence is all I know how to do, Captain. Do you require assistance with repairs?"

"No, our engineer says we'll be operational in a couple of hours. We would appreciate the overwatch."

The young officer smiled and responded, "Very good. We'll be close, call if you need anything." She paused, then added impishly, "By the way, my Chief of the Boat has informed me that our wardroom prefers imported beer."

With a nod and a grin, Mitch replied, "They'll get it and then some. Give me a few hours to get systems back online and then let's go shark hunting."

With an impish twinkle in her eyes, the young woman nodded, "It is a date, Captain. *Avenger* out."

\*\*\*\*

*Aboard the UEAN* Stalwart, *Task Force 3.2.2 'Escort Force',*
*Draconis 327, Entering high orbit over M3245*

"Admiral, enemy Dreadnought Alpha has been destroyed." The bass rumble of Captain Soklov cut through the silence of the flag bridge. Laura Kensington breathed out a sigh of relief that she didn't know she'd been holding as Soklov continued,

"It looks like the *Infiltrator* hit her with five nuclear penetrators at near point blank range. Less than fifty thousand kilometers."

Laura smiled grimly as Captain Destin muttered, "Jesus. Five penetrators. That'll ruin your day."

"It also appears that the resulting core explosion destroyed several cruisers and multiple light escorts." Soklov added, "Her core explosion was several orders of magnitude larger than anticipated."

Commander de la Cruz stabbed a finger at the display. "How much do you want to bet those big bastards are using an antimatter drive?" She turned to Soklov. "It'd account for how fast those things are, given their mass. It'd also explain why the explosion was so big. They lost antimatter containment when the *Infiltrator* hit them."

"Likely." Soklov grunted, then spoke to the fleet commander again. "Admiral, Dreadnought Bravo and its escorts are moving. Calculating trajectory."

Laura nodded, then turned to the thin, pale officer sitting at another console. "Captain Destin. Status on the drop?"

"Eighty five percent complete, Admiral. The *Phantom Fury* reports that had to take evasive action to avoid debris and that threw her drop timetable off."

"Very good. Notify me the moment that..." Laura began. Captain Soklov broke in.

"Trajectory calculated, Admiral. They're heading for the jump point to 39 Draconis at zero point four." He paused, his face intent on his console. "They have also vectored three surviving cruisers at us here."

"Son of a bitch." Laura muttered, staring at the holotable. "Their fleet commander is trying to cut us off from the jump point and trying to go fast enough that the *Infiltrator* can't get another shot. Those cruisers are to flush us out." She leaned forward, staring at the display. "He's trying to force our hand."

"Extremely likely, Admiral." Soklov tapped his keys for a moment, then spoke. "If we burn hard now, we will beat him to the jump point. If not..." He broke off, looking uncharacteristically worried.

"He beats us and we're stuck until their reinforcements arrive. Clever bastard." Laura finished for him. She paused for a moment, thinking. "It's a good move. We either leave the system or get trapped here. He just retook the initiative." After another few seconds, she made a decision. "Captain Destin, signal the fleet. Proceed at flank speed to the jump point. Tell the *Infiltrator* and *Avenger* that they are to do what they can to buy time for the Marines down there until we get back with reinforcements."

"Aye, ma'am. Signaling the fleet." Laura sat back in her chair, staring at the table and the red symbols of the enemy ships screaming through the vacuum of space at millions of kilometers per minute. After a few moments, she muttered under her breath to the enemy admiral. "Don't get cocky, you clever bastard. You haven't beaten us yet."

# Chapter 11

## "Two Rules of War"

*355th Forward Dropped Resuscitation Team*
*Anvil Station, Inside the Tunnel Complex*

"Thirty six units." Manderson looked up from the datapad. "That's it?"

"Yes, sir." Agawa replied. "A lot of it didn't survive the shuttle crash. Synthblood has a pretty hardy temp range, but hours in subzero temperatures trashed most of it."

"Shit." Manderson tossed the datapad on the tiny table and frowned. "We can't synthesize it?"

"No. It's too complex for the field synthesizers, apparently. The ones on the ship and the ones in the main field hospital element can, but clearly that's not an option now." Running a hand through his hair, Agawa observed, "These surgical teams aren't designed to operate without support from the hospital for this long."

"Shit," Manderson repeated. He was silent for a few moments, then scowled and turned to a footlocker behind him and began rummaging in it.

Agawa watched him dig for a few seconds then said, "There's also the issue of the octo-doc."

Pausing, Manderson looked up. "I saw that. How bad?"

"Bad enough. I guess the specialist with the know-how to fix it went down on the shuttle. Specialist Mathers is working on it now, but he's not optimistic," Agawa shrugged. "Right now, it's a fancy laparoscope. None of the additional arms work."

Shaking his head in disgust, Manderson turned back to the footlocker. After a moment, he pulled out a book. "Here we go."

"Is that a paper book?" Agawa asked, his eyebrows raised. He took the book and looked at the cover. "Emergency War Surgery, Seventeenth Edition...2103." He looked up at Manderson. "United States Army? As in the old United States?" He looked back down at the book. "Wow. This is *old*."

"Right?" The officer turned back to the footlocker, pulled out another book and slid it across the desk.

"Combat Casualty Care: The Evolution of Modern Military Field Medicine." He turned the book to look at the spine. "This one is practically new; published in 2215."

Turning around, Manderson replied with a faint grin. "You're a real comedian, Master Sergeant. You ever consider taking it on the road?" Agawa laughed and opened the book at random. Manderson continued, "Think about it, though. With the octo-doc shot, being out of synthblood and almost being out of stasis pods, we're back to a twenty second century level of medicine."

Sighing, Agawa nodded. "Yeah. I was looking at our quote 'trauma bay' unquote." He grimaced, "It looks like a garage sale for used medical equipment."

"I know." Manderson replied. "We just gotta do what we can with what we have," He rubbed his forehead. "I suspect we're gonna have to make some tough decisions."

"Yeah," Agawa set the book down and sighed. "Yeah. I think so too." He idly flipped the book open at random and read from it, "Triage decisions in craniocerebral trauma should be made on the severity of initial presenting injury. Patients presenting with a Modified Glasgow Coma Score of less than 10 with no signs of neurological protective reflexes should be considered for deprioritization.'" He shut the book and pushed it away from him on the desk. He shook his head. "I get that we're going to have to make some difficult calls here, but this..." He gestured at the book.

"Yeah," Manderson nodded and replied quietly. "Some of these Marines are going to die from stuff that they wouldn't have to if we had the supplies we're supposed to." He tapped the book with his finger. "Some of them in ways people haven't died in a long time." He rubbed his face, then gestured at the book. "There's triage guidelines in there. We can start there."

Agawa shook his head. "I remember on Desolation, we had a heavy lift shuttle go down and had a mass casualty event at our field hospital. It was pretty bad, but even then, we saved a lot of them. We just had to keep them alive to orbit. We had the *Temperance* overhead and she could save anyone. They could even do cerebral resuscitation, if we got people there fast enough." He looked at Manderson and added somberly, "But now…" The stocky medic shrugged. "There's no backup plan."

"Nope. Like I said. Twenty second century." Manderson picked up his datapad. "I'm working out a supply conservation plan. Colonel Douglas and I also put together treatment guidelines. Who gets what and when sort of thing."

Grimly, Agawa nodded silently. After a moment, he spoke. "We don't have much time to train on this. Who do you want doing triage?"

With a grimace, Manderson replied, "Probably you or me. The medical team members will be busy."

"Yeah." Agawa frowned at the book for a moment, then sighed. "Ok. I'll go talk to the troops. Let's get this digitized so we can put it in the helmet display of whoever is outside."

There was the distant tremor of rockets impacting somewhere above them on the surface. A split second later, the comm unit chimed. Agawa picked it up and listened for a moment.

"Got it. We'll be ready."

"Casualties." Manderson's voice made it a statement, not a question. "How many?"

"Ten plus. One of the Marine bunkers took a direct hit." Agawa replied. He stood up. "Looks like it's time to put this old school stuff into practice, sir. You go meet them, I'll get the team ready."

With a grim nod, Manderson picked up his helmet and secured it to his power armor. "Let's go. Keep your ears open for my calls."

The two men stood and moved purposefully towards their tasks.

\*\*\*\*

*Inside the Improvised Aid Station*

"Ok, people. Listen up." Agawa's calm voice cut through the low buzz of conversation. "We have casualties incoming. A Marine bunker took a direct hit from one of those unguided rockets. They are bringing them in now. They're saying ten to fifteen patients, possibly more. ETA is about ten minutes."

There was a moment of silence, then someone muttered, "Shit." Every eye in the room turned towards the six stretchers laid out carefully in the small room.

"Yeah," Agawa replied. "We can't take care of them all. Major Manderson has had to do this before. He will be performing mass casualty triage."

"Like limiting who gets care?" Dahl demanded. "We haven't had to do that for…I don't even know how long." She looked around the small chamber, seeing nods from the other team members.

"That's what triage is for, Captain." Agawa replied, gravely. "And you are correct. We haven't had to do this for a long time, since we usually have a hospital ship in support. We don't now."

"Triage." The blonde nurse pressed her lips together, then spoke slowly and carefully, "I understand."

"We've never done that before," One of the medics protested. "We can't make those decisions without training."

There were murmurs of agreement. "Yeah." "He's right." "I don't think…"

Stepping forward, Manderson spoke. "I get it. We're asking

you to do things that haven't been done outside of emergencies for decades, maybe longer." His voice was somber as he continued, "But if this wasn't an emergency, we wouldn't be talking about this." He looked down at his boots for a moment, then back up at his fellow soldiers. "There's an old saying that my mentor taught me a long time ago." His gaze swept the room. "He taught me that there's only two rules in war. Rule number one is that good men are going to die. Rule number two is that doctors can't change rule number one."

The room was dead silent, broken only by the distant rumbling from the surface as the enemy artillery continued to fall. Manderson's jaw tightened and he pointed up, "Rule three is that no one says we can't try."

The silence continued for a beat longer, then Dahl took a deep breath and looked at the other nurses and medics in the room. "Ok, people. Let's get our equipment checked. We are only going to worry about the ones that show up in here. Trust Major Manderson to do his job and we're going to do ours." She looked around the small room for a moment, then stated firmly. "Like the major says, we might not be able to change rule number one, but we're god damn sure going to try. Let's get to work, people."

Across the room, Colonel Douglas caught Manderson's eye and nodded almost imperceptibly. Manderson nodded back and turned to head out to the hanger, as the staff rapidly checked the trauma bays and prepared for the coming storm.

\*\*\*\*

*Inside the South Hangar, three minutes later.*

"Not my emergency." Manderson muttered under his breath. He took a deep breath and blew it out slowly.

"Sorry, sir?" The Marine corporal next to him asked. "I missed that."

"Nothing." Manderson replied. He looked around at the

large, empty hangar and the massive airlock doors through which the vehicles would cycle with the loads of patients. "It's just how I get myself ready for things."

"What do you mean?" The young man asked curiously.

With the awkward movement that was a shrug in the power armor, Manderson replied. "I take a deep breath and remind myself that it isn't *my* emergency. It's *an* emergency but not my emergency." He gestured at the doors. "I've had to do this before but it doesn't make it any easier."

The young corporal nodded. He looked at the small team of grim faced Marines that were standing nearby, ready to serve as litter bearers. The two grounded pilots stood with them, looking uncharacteristically nervous and out of place in their light flight armor. After a moment the young man spoke. "This quiet...It's unnerving. It's like the lull before a firefight." He looked around the empty hangar. "When you've done everything you can and are just sitting there waiting for the first crack of an energy bolt or explosion to tell you it's go time."

"Yeah." Manderson replied. "It kind of is."

"It sucks," the young man replied. The yellow lights over the airlock door began to flash. The corporal grinned mirthlessly. "And there's the first shot."

Manderson nodded and tabbed his comlink. "War Angel, Triage. Casualties have arrived."

Agawa's calm voice answered promptly, *"Triage, War Angel. Good copy. We'll be ready."*

The massive airlock door slid up and the low slung shape of a Marine ground assault vehicle appeared. It pulled up and came to a stop. The rear doors opened with a hiss and a power armored shape climbed out. It bore red crosses on the shoulder plates. The corpsman slid her faceplate up and called, "I've got eight here, Doc. Where do you want them?"

"Bring them out, I'll see them as you do." Manderson replied, he turned to the corporal. "Litter team, go." The three men sprang into action, moving to the rear of the armored vehicle. A moment later, they reappeared, assisting a Navy corpsman who was rhythmically pumping on the chest of an armored figure on a gurney. The litter moved up next to Manderson and lowered.

"How long without a pulse?" Manderson asked tersely as he shone a light in the man's eyes.

"I don't know. The guys brought him to me without a pulse. I figured I couldn't stop while it was in progress..." The corpsman began.

"He's dead," Manderson stated flatly. "Stop CPR. You're with me." He gestured to the litter bearers. "Deceased. Take him to holding." The litter bearers moved into action, quickly bearing the body of the fallen Marine out of site. Manderson turned to the next patient. The man was grimacing and his face was pale. "Where you hit, trooper?"

"Argh. In the guts. Fuck. Doc, it hurts so much!"

Manderson peered at the Marine's abdomen. The power armor had been opened by the corpsman in the field and a dressing had been placed over the man's stomach. He lifted the dressing and saw a black charred mass and the red-pink shine of abdominal viscera. The officer turned to the corpsman now following him. "Immediate. Armor burn through. Get him inside."

The corpsmen nodded and gestured to the litter teams as Manderson moved on. The next patient was already in front of him. The young woman's face was pale and her arm was missing from the elbow down. Leaning down, Manderson spoke. "Can you hear me, Marine?"

"Yes, sir." The young woman's voice was slow and groggy. Manderson plugged a vitals monitor into her armor, then peered at the damaged limb. After a second, he said, "Delayed. Traumatic amputation with suit aid administered." The litter bearers nodded and moved the wounded young woman away.

The next Marine lay still in his torn and bent armor, eyes blank, his breaths ragged. The side of his face and neck were black with frostbite and the front of his chest was covered with frozen blood. Another corpsman who had her hands pressed firmly on the side of his chest looked up. "He has a burn through. The auto seals in his armor were damaged, so he's got frostbite too."

With a careful look into the young man's pupils and a glance at the vitals monitor, Manderson said, "Expectant."

"Sir!" The corpsman looked up. "We can't just..."

"Keep him comfortable, sailor. That's all we can do." The sailor looked up at him, then back down somberly and nodded. The litter team arrived again to bear the young man away. Manderson moved down the line, performing the cold calculus as old as wartime medicine of those who could be saved and those who could not.

Then as suddenly as it had begun, it was over. The formerly bustling hangar bay was empty of litters and almost deserted. The Marine armored vehicle stood forgotten. The medical officer stood by the rear of the vehicle. Inside was a mess of discarded armor plates, empty IV bags, wrappers from medical supplies and over it all the dark red splatters of blood. The blood was on the floor, the seats and on the handholds. It was tracked around like mud after a rainstorm and a trail of bloody footprints led out of the LAV to where he had performed his somber task. Manderson took a deep shuddering breath and blew it out, closing his eyes to calm his racing heart.

"Where can I help, sir?" A quiet voice broke into his moment of silence. Manderson opened his eyes to see the corpsman that had been with the young man with the chest wound. Her eyes were hollow and her force flat. The power armor she wore was stained with blood up to the elbows and she looked very young and terribly tired.

"Did he..." Manderson started, then stopped when he saw the defeated look in the corpsman's eyes.

"Yes." There was no emotion in her reply. "A few minutes after we went over."

"Did you know him?"

"No." She looked at her bloody gauntlets. "Not really. He

was from Golf Company. I think his name was Anders." She fell silent.

"You did everything you could." Manderson said after a moment. His voice echoed in the still hangar.

"He's still dead," the young woman replied. She took in a deep breath and blew it out. "But what's done is done. Time for that later." She gestured towards the aid station. "I'm going to go see if they need me in there."

"Yeah." The officer turned and silently accompanied the young woman to the busy aid station.

# Chapter 12

## "Derelict"

*Aboard the UEAN* Infiltrator
*Deep Space, Draconis 327*

Ten hours later, Mitch put his hands on his hips and stared at the display over the shoulder of the long range sensor operator. Greta Von Kant, his executive officer, leaned against a nearby bulkhead, quietly.

The young man at the sensor station suddenly pointed and said, "There. Another one, except this one's a lot further insystem. It looks like a mine going off, but it's way bigger." The sailor paused and manipulated the controls and the screen display changed. He said again, "They're getting further away each time and the power of them seems to be variable but whatever they are, they're BIG," He indicated three red dots on the screen, "Those Elai destroyers are out looking for whatever's causing them." Mitch nodded, frowning.

Greta said from behind him, "It has to be Captain O'Toro and the *Avenger*. She's seen what we are after and is luring the destroyers away."

Mitch scratched his head and replied absently, "She's good at the cat and mouse stuff. She was an instructor at the Naval Stealth Warfare School, until the war started." He stared at the screen for a moment and added, "She nailed me more than a few times in training." Glancing at the display he added, "That big bastard is still holding position near the jump point." He straightened up and turned to the sailor at the next console, "Harris, anything from our friend?" He peered at the image of the disabled Elai warship on the screen in front of the sailor.

The young petty officer shook his head, "No, sir. If they're

in there, they're doing a real good impression of being dead."
Tapping a few more keys, he added, "There's a shitload of
radiation from the aft portion, though. It'll probably keep the
back half of her warm, but if these readings are right, their
reactor is either fully melted down or well on the way."

Mitch nodded and asked, "What does the Chief Engineer
think about the possibility of the core going critical?"

Greta, who had moved up and was peering at the sensor
readings over the petty officer's shoulder, answered, "He said
if the core was going to blow, it already would have and that
the auto safety shutdown systems have probably cut in." She
continued after a moment, "He also says 'But then again, these
guys are aliens, so who the shit knows.'" With a faint grin, she
added, "That's a direct quote, by the way."

Mitch chuckled, then frowned and thought for a moment.
He then checked the first console again and said, "Ok. If they
see us, we'll have about forty five minutes to get our team out
of there and vanish. If they don't, we can rummage through
this thing to our hearts content until the fleet gets back in
system." Greta nodded, silently. Mitch started towards the
hatch and said over his shoulder, "Get a boarding party
assembled in the wardroom. I'll brief them personally."

Fifteen minutes later, Mitch entered the wardroom. The
small room was crowded. At the front of the table sat a young
woman with short, wavy hair and the rank of a junior grade
lieutenant. Next to her sat a burly man with his arms folded,
with close cropped red hair shot through with streaks of silver.
On his collar was the insignia of a senior chief petty officer.
The remainder of the table was packed with enlisted sailors
and to the side of the room stood two nervous looking ensigns.
Mitch motioned them to stay seated and stepped in front of the
table and began to speak.

"Ok, sailors. Here's the deal. We have a disabled Elai
cruiser out there that the *Stalwart* zorched a couple days ago
when the fleet was banging heads with the enemy. It's
powered down and adrift, presumably abandoned. We're

gonna get in there and get what we can off of it. Intel, code books, databases, whatever we can get. If we retake the system, we'll take her as a prize. If not, we'll rig her to blow so the sharkies can't salvage her. Captain O'Toro in the *Avenger* has lured the enemy destroyers away, so we have some time, but we cannot assume that will last. Chief Sullivan will fill you in on the details."

He stepped back to let the petty officer up to speak. The massive red headed man said in a loud, clear voice, "Ok, listen up. Here's the plan. We're taking the longboat, since our shuttle went down to the moon and never made it back up. We are going to make entry at what looks like an empty lifeboat port amidships. Once we breach, we will break into three teams. Alpha and Bravo teams will head fore and aft, looking for the bridge and main engineering, to get what data we can. Charlie team will secure the point of entry and maintain comms with the *Infiltrator*." He gestured to the officer seated next to him, "Lieutenant Lopez is going to maintain mission command, with Petty Officer Kim as our corpsman and a security detail at the skiff." He then pointed at the other chief at the table, "Chief Langley, Ensign DeSantis and Bravo Team will take engineering. Me, Ensign Keenan and Alpha will take the bridge. Each team will have two compsystems guys and four sailors on security. We are going to assume that we are going to be in full vacuum so combat armor suits. We also cannot assume that all the sharkies are dead, so we'll also be going in expecting opposition. Assume the worse, be careful and *think*. There is no manual for this. Understood?" His hard gaze swept the small room. The sailors responded with varying versions of assent. Chief Sullivan kept the glare up for a moment longer, then asked, "Do any of you have any questions?"

A sailor said from further down the table in an accented voice, "Chief, how do we know what's valuable?"

Sullivan shrugged and replied, "Use your judgment. If it looks important, grab it. All data pads, grab. All console ports, identify for the system crackers. To my knowledge, no one's ever boarded an intact Elai capital ship before, so we're going to be making it up as we go."

The sailor shrugged and nodded. One of the petty officers asked, "What do we do if we get resistance, Chief?"

With a shrug of his massive shoulders, Sullivan replied, "Shoot 'em. Blow a hole in the hull and space 'em. Bypass 'em. I don't give a shit. Deal with 'em and get to the objective. The nav, engineering and main computer systems are the absolute top priority." The sailor nodded silently, her face grim.

Sullivan gestured to Chief Langley, "Chief, you wanna go over the contingency plans and OPFOR?"

Langley, a stocky man with a shaved head and a sturdy build stood up and said in a calm, confident tone, "We don't know what the crew complement of an Elai cruiser is. Best guess is that it's north of five hundred crew, probably closer to a thousand, based off the wreckage we've scanned before and the Naval intel reports on their consumables use." There was a murmur in the small room as the sailors realized the number of possible enemy aboard the alien vessel. The stocky chief raised his hands, "I realize that seems like a lot, but here's the thing. All the lifeboats are launched and the hull temps are showing that the core of the ship itself is near ambient space temp. This suggests most of the interior is in vacuum. We also disabled her three days ago. Unless the Elai are dramatically different than we are and they aren't, their suits and emergency supplies are likely exhausted by now. Our intel section estimated that there's a seventy-five percent chance of not encountering survivors."

A skinny sailor with a shaved head in the Martian style spoke up, "Chief, twenty-five percent is still pretty goddamn high. Do we expect opposition? What do we do if they do resist?"

Chief Langley looked at Chief Sullivan, who shrugged and said, "If they resist, we shoot them. If they resist too much, we grab what we can and blow that alien piece of shit out of the sky,"

A sailor in the back of the room said in a challenging tone, "How? Their armor is thick as shit. It took a nuclear penetrator to bust the hull on the last one."

With a shrug, Langley answered in a matter of fact tone, "I stripped the core out of an antimatter mine. We'll place it in the hull and pull the pin. Inside the hull, even a reduced explosion without the primary charge will be more than enough to destroy her. The antimatter will see to that."

The room fell silent for a moment, then Sullivan stated, matter of factly, "We're gonna get in. We're gonna take what we can and if we think we can get away with it, take the ship. If not, we're going to blow that fucker to smithereens. Clear?"

There was a murmured mix of 'Aye, Chief' responses from the small group.

The sailor in the back said again, "All right, Chief. We'll loot your sharkie boat for you. But you gotta ask the Captain to let the longboat fly the Jolly Roger. We gonna act like pirates, we wanna LOOK like pirates."

Sullivan gave a crooked smile, "The Jolly Roger, huh? All right. I'll ask. Any other questions?" He stared around the small room, seeing thoughtful, resolute faces, but not hearing any further questions. After a moment, Sullivan said again, "Ok, I'm going to turn you back over to the captain." The big chief paused glaring around the room and added, "Don't fuck this up, or the sharkies are going to be the least of your fucking problems. That clear?" The sailors again murmured agreement. Chief Sullivan turned to Mitch, "Sir."

Mitch stepped forward again and said in a low, serious tone, "I cannot stress enough how important this is. In the old days on Earth, a captured codebook or compsystem could win wars. Be safe, be fast and let's all get home. Understood?"

The sailors responded in unison, "Aye, sir."

Mitch nodded and replied firmly, "Ok. Get to it. Good luck, sailors."

\*\*\*\*

*Aboard Longboat Zero Two Two, six hours later.*
*Approaching derelict Elai cruiser*

The sailor at the controls of the longboat gently tapped the controls. The gentle thrust of the nitrogen jet maneuvering thrusters could be felt through the hull of the small vessel. He looked over at Lieutenant Lopez, sitting in the seat next to him and said, "One hundred meters, ma'am." She nodded silently, her attention focused on the instruments.

Chief Sullivan stood between the two pilots seats, scowling at the thick windscreens in front of him. Suddenly, he pointed and declared, "There. See it? Between that box and that spiky thing. That's the access point."

Lieutenant Lopez looked up and squinted at the area he was pointing, then shook her head, "Gonna be tight."

The sailor at the controls, a stocky young man with red hair and freckles, shook his head and replied, "We can do it. I'll back her in ass first and use the expandable docking collar." He eyes the instruments and then added, "It'll be snug but we can totally do it. Couldn't if we were in the shuttle, so it's actually better that we're in the longboat."

Lopez nodded and said to Chief Sullivan without looking, "Fifty meters. Chief, get your teams ready. I'm cutting the engines." The big man nodded and turned around to face the rear of the craft.

In the rear of the longboat, the sailors forming the teams sat, their backs to the hull. All were clad in combat armored space suits and all carried the collapsing stock UEA M45 carbines. Sullivan regarded them for a moment, then said in a voice that carried through the small craft.

"Ok, this is it. Alpha will be out the hatch first. Sweep and secure the immediate area. Bravo will be right behind. Once the area around the entry is secure, we'll move out and leave security of the area to Charlie team and the command crew." He paused and reached over to the nearest sailor to straighten up a piece of gear on the front of her armor and then said again, "Stay alert in there, people. Starships are dangerous on a good day and that goes double for unfriendly, badly damaged ones. Treat everything like a threat. Don't push any fucking buttons and if you see something strange, speak up. We're going to get in, get what we need and get the fuck out, ALIVE. You all get me?" There was a quiet murmur of assent. His hard gaze swept up and down the rows of seats, meeting each sailor's eyes in turn and then nodded, "Ok. Get set. We're contacting in three minutes. Everyone seal up. From here until we return to the *Infiltrator,* we are on suit air or air piped from the longboat. We can't take chances with contaminants or infectious diseases."

The sailors, previously sitting quietly, suddenly came to life, closing their helmet visors and checking their suit functions. After a few moments, the chief said again, "Alpha, you good?"

Ensign Keenan, a tall, lanky young man shot a thumb in the air, "Alpha is suited up and green across the board, Chief."

Sullivan nodded and looked to Bravo. Chief Langley's calm tone came through the suit radios, "Bravo is green across the board."

Twisting around to the seats in front of him, Sullivan made sure that the two sailors flying the longboat had sealed their visors and, satisfied that the crew was ready, he keyed his radio and said, "Charlie Lead, Alpha and Bravo are green and sealed. Ready to match pressure."

Lopez's clipped tone came across the radio, "Roger, Alpha Lead. Standby for soft dock."

Sullivan crouched and held on tight to the handholds near his shoulders. He could see the sailors linking arms as they prepared for contact with the hull of the disabled warship. They held the brace position for several seconds, then there was a slight bump and an almost imperceptible shift in the internal gravity of the longboat. Sullivan continued to hold on.

Several seconds later he heard the voice of the pilot, "Soft dock achieved. Looks like we have a good seal. Chief, you can get on the door."

Sullivan turned again halfway and gently slapped the sailors helmet. "Nice flying." He looked at Lieutenant Lopez and said, "Any readings from the door?"

Frowning at her instruments, she responded, "Nothing we hadn't seen already. Looks like it's damn cold in there. We probably ought to run thermals on the entry teams. Anything not dead ought to light up like a Christmas tree."

Sullivan nodded and turned to the rear of the boat. Two sailors were already opening the rear hatch. As they did, they exposed a circular hatch, with a very standard looking hatch dog in the middle and no visible electronics. One of the sailors said, "Chief, it looks mechanical. No apparent auto vacuum seals. Looks like when they launch the boats they close the hatch manually, or there's a mechanical system to close it that leaves with the lifeboat."

Sullivan moved about halfway down the longboat, paused and asked, "Can you open it?"

The sailors glanced at each other. One of them muttered, "Well. Here goes nothing." The young woman reached out and placed her gloved hands on the wheel and turned it. To everyone's surprise, it turned easily. After a quarter turn, the hatch started to move towards them. There was a slight gust of wind from behind them as the pressure equalized, then the hatch opened easily. The sailors moved back as the lead sailors from Alpha team moved forward rapidly, carbines at the ready. As they approached the threshold, one of the sailors that had opened the hatch said suddenly, "It's zero g in there. Look."

He indicated a section of wiring suspended in the air right outside of the hatch. Further away, blown clear of the door by the pressure change, were other items. A piece of access panel cover, several bulb shaped items and what looked like a haze of dirt hung in the air. The only light was the circle of light cast from inside the longboat and a dim row of blinking yellow lights along the floor of the corridor. The first two sailors moved out the hatch, nimbly swinging themselves into the zero gravity of the dark corridor. One of them made a sharp noise and then there was the sound of a scrabble in the radio. As this was happening, the second two sailors had swung themselves out into the darkness.

Hearing the noise, Sullivan demanded, "Report, sailor!"

After a second, the sailor responded, "Sorry, Chief. He startled me. I mean it."

The other sailor reported, "There's an Elai out here, Chief. He's dead though."

Sullivan snapped, "Make damn sure!"

With a wry note in her voice, the first sailor replied, "Oh, he's dead. Live ones usually have more limbs." After a pause, she added, "The corridor is still pressurized, but the air sucks. Fifteen percent oxygen, twenty percent carbon dioxide and a whole bunch of other shit. Looks like industrial toxins. Coolant, smoke, burned plastics, that sort of crap. Wouldn't want to breath it." She paused again, then said, "No power we can see aside from those little yellow emergency lights and gravity seems out entirely." They could hear her breathing into her helmet mic for a moment before she said again, "No other Elai except our friend here. I think we're good."

The second sailor said again, "Corridor secure, Chief. We can move out the rest of the teams." Sullivan motioned to Ensign Keenan, who moved smartly towards the hatch and swung himself into the darkness, followed by the remainder of Alpha team. Bravo rapidly followed, led by Ensign DeSantis, with the rear of the small group brought up by Chief Langley. As Langley passed him, Sullivan turned and gave a thumbs up to Lieutenant Lopez and the three remaining sailors, who were setting up small sensor pods and moving them into the hall. She nodded at him and returned the gesture.

Swinging into the passageway, Sullivan immediately saw

the dead alien. It was big for an Elai, dressed in a dark gray jumpsuit and one of its arms had been badly mangled. There was a crude dressing on it and what appeared to be a tourniquet. The terrifying leathery brown face had a grimace on it and the mouth was slightly open, displaying the dozens of terrifying, serrated teeth. The dust floating in a cloud around it was, Sullivan belatedly realized, frozen blood from the injured arm.

Langley, his boots now magnetically attached to the deck, said somberly, "I hope the poor bastard was dead and left here before the boat launched." Sullivan stared at the Elai's body gently floating in the middle of the corridor. Langley added, "Because enemy or not, to be badly wounded, needing help and getting to your boat, only to find it gone with no help coming?" He shook his head, the motion visible through his faceplate, "No sailor deserves that."

Sullivan stared at the body for a moment longer, then responded, "Yeah. Time for that later, Langley. Let's go." Langley nodded and turned and headed down the black corridor, following his team now heading aft.

With a last glance at the dead Elai sailor, Sullivan activated his low light system in his helmet and followed his team, heading forward. They silently moved forward for seemed like an eternity of creeping through the hull of the dead warship, finding nothing but floating bodies and wreckage. Suddenly, the small party came to a stop.

"Hey, Chief. Hatch." Ensign Keenan's voice was low, even though the chance that they could be heard outside of the thick helmets of the combat armored suits was slim.

Sullivan tapped the sailor in front of him and pointed behind them into the dark corridor, then pointing two fingers at his faceplate. The sailor nodded and knelt and brought his carbine up, scanning the darkness behind the small team. Making his way past the nervously alert sailors, Sullivan joined the young officer at the front of the group. He knelt in front of a control panel, which was next to a thick hatch, examining it. Two more sailors were kneeling just past him covering the darkness in front of them.

Sullivan leaned over his shoulder and examined the controls, then asked, "Locked?"

In a distracted tone, the ensign answered, "Yeah. This doesn't look that complicated, though. There's like three buttons and only two big ones."

Sullivan considered this, then grimaced, "Can we go around?"

Keenan shook his head, his face faintly visible in the faceplate in the glow of his instruments, "No. This is the main fore and aft passage. None of those side passages we checked lead anywhere useful. We also haven't found anything resembling data ports. This is the sturdiest hatch we've found so far and well protected usually means important, in a warship." He paused, "Right? Or am I overthinking this?"

Sourly, Sullivan responded, "No. Makes sense." He thought for a moment, then swore, "Goddammit. We shoulda brought a big cutting laser. I really don't like the idea of pushing fucking buttons."

The young officer shrugged and replied, "Well, this is what we're here for. Fortune favors the bold, right?" Before Sullivan could respond, the young man had reached out and pushed one of the large buttons. There was a loud 'click' as the hatch locks disengaged and the massive hatch moved a tiny bit in the frame.

In a mild tone, Keenan said, "Well. Would you look at that."

With a hard glare, Sullivan replied, "Sir...You're fucking killing me. Don't do that again without telling me first."

With a chuckle, the officer replied, "You got it, Chief."

Sullivan motioned to the next two sailors, who nimbly leapt to the wall with the hatch in it and knelt. One of them brought out a box connected to a slender wire and slid it into the tiny crack of the door. After a moment, she said, "Looks like...six or seven of them, maybe more. They look dead. Lots of consoles and shit too. We might have something here, Chief."

Sullivan nodded and toggled his radio, "Charlie, this is Alpha. We have found what appears to be a compartment with system access. Entering now."

The cool tone of Lieutenant Lopez came immediately, *"Understood, Alpha. Keep me posted."*

Sullivan nodded to the two sailors. A third moved up and grasped the massive hatch. The sailors positioned themselves, then at a whispered command the hatch was pulled open. The sailors hurled themselves through, weapons at the ready.

After a moment, the voice of one of them came through. "Clear. Chief, you're gonna want to see this."

Sullivan moved himself to the hatch and swung himself through, followed by Keenan. Pushing their boots onto the deck and engaging their magnetic boots, they looked around. Elai bodies floated in the compartment and several were still buckled into seats at consoles. All of the corpses wore masks, with a tube running to a small pack on their belts.

"This looks like a damage control station or a secondary bridge." Sullivan announced, turning slowly and scrutinizing the compartment. "These guys were probably the crew who stayed to try to stabilize the ship."

Moving into the room, Keenan peered at a console over a dead Elai sailors shoulder and then said, "This'll do for a start. Get Seaman Ross in here." Sullivan nodded and motioned to the hatch where several sailors were watching. Moments later, a sailor flew through the door, nimbly catching himself on the console and clipping his boots down.

He leaned over the ensign's shoulder and peered at the console. After a moment, he said, "Well, it's weird, but not *that* weird. Here, sir." He slipped his pack off and turned it sideways in front of him and opened it up, revealing a modern tablet computer in one half and an old model of computer that had been popular some twenty years before in the other. The older notebook was mounted onto a thick black base. He uncoiled a cable and handed it to Keenan, who reached over the corpse's shoulder, then swore. He handed the cable back and reached down to the side of the body and released the belt. He then gave the body a slight shove, sending it floating to the side of the compartment, where it bumped into several other bodies. Seaman Ross then moved into the seat and buckled himself in and placed his pack on the console and locating a port, pushed the end of the cable in.

The screens lit up and then began to flicker with data.

Keenan slapped the sailor on the shoulder, "Good call, bringing the old Pressbook. Now let's see if that expensive piece of shit they gave us works."

The sailor nodded and replied, "Give me a few minutes to take a look at things before we try to take anything." He paused and tapped a few keys, "It looks like they use a visual operating system, so it's gonna take a few for our system to figure it out for me to get at it."

Sullivan leaned forward, looked at the display and asked, "What are you doing and how long is it going to take?"

Keenen replied, "We're using an older piece of our own equipment to look at their systems. If we figure their state of the art is like thirty years or so behind ours, we need something of comparable tech. That's the old Pressbook." He gestured at the old notebook computer, "When we get that talking with their system, we use that system on the bottom that the Naval Intel guys use. It'll translate as best as we know how and turns the visual data icons they use into something we understand." He pointed at the modern tablet, "That is our system cracker. It's our toolbox to get past their security defenses. It'll probably be…."

Ross muttered, "Adapting biometric access on most of the core systems. Motherfuck." He started tapping at the computer keyboard.

In a grim tone, Keened finished, "Encrypted, just like ours. Shit. This is gonna be tough."

Sullivan nodded, "Can you get in?"

Ross answered, not looking up, "Chief, Me and Ensign

Keenan can get into almost anything if we have the time."

With a growl, Sullivan replied, "Work fast. We might have to unass this place at any second." He moved from the two, leaving them to work on the system and began poking around the compartment. One of the other two sailors suddenly spoke up, "Chief, if this cruiser was abandoned and the crew hit the boats, why are these guys still here? This station looks fully manned. Everyone else is gone, why not them?"

With a frown, Sullivan responded, "Probably the black gang, trying to save the ship." Looking around the compartment, Sullivan counted stations. There were eight stations and eight bodies. He thought about this for a moment, then declared, "Who the hell knows. We wouldn't leave a crew on an abandoned ship, but these guys ain't us. They do things their own way."

Spying a console towards the back of the room, the burly petty officer made his way towards it. There were two Elai still buckled into the seats. He leaned over and noted that the console was different. It was larger with several more screens and with what looked like several data sticks in a slot on the side of the console and several more inserted into the console itself. Leaning past the body, he examined the console. Absently, he put his hand on the shoulder of one of the bodies as he did. Distracted by the data sticks and the console, he was startled to feel it move under his hand. With a sudden feeling of horror rushing through him, Chief Sullivan slowly turned his head to the left, at the Elai who's shoulder he was touching. It stared back at him with its black, pupilless eyes, inches from the faceplate of his helmet.

Sullivan stared at the Elai sailor, who stared back over its bulky respirator mask and didn't move. It slowly closed its eyes again after a moment. Moving as gingerly as he could, he backed away from the Elai, then drew his sidearm and pointed it at the back of the alien's head. The other sailors seeing him looked at him quizzically, then their eyes widened.

Speaking in a low voice, he ordered, "Watkins, Devon.

Cover this fucker. He ain't dead." He gestured at the two sailors near the hatch, "You two, check the others. Make *damn* sure they're dead."

Watkins and Devon moved rapidly, bringing rifles to bear on the still figure still buckled into its seat. Sullivan licked his lips, suddenly acutely aware of how dry his suit air was and said, "Ensign Keenan, call the command cell. Tell them to get the skipper on the horn. Tell him we got a prisoner." With his free hand he pointed at Seaman Ross who was sitting in shock, he snapped, "You keep at cracking that thing. We don't have a lot of time." Eyes wide, Ross nodded and turned his attention back to the tablet screen.

Moving slowly and carefully, Ensign Keenan activated his suit radio and began speaking. No one in the small compartment moved, apart from the two sailors gently prodding the remaining bodies carefully to see if any of them showed signs of life.

After a moment, one of them said, "Chief, this one twitched. What should I do?" The two sailors had backed up and were pointing their weapons at the figure floating motionlessly.

Sullivan gestured to the one still bucked in the station and replied, "Get him over here as gently as you can."

The sailor nodded and, using his rifle barrel, gave the Elai a gentle shove; sending him floating towards Sullivan. Reaching out a hand and stopping the incapacitated enemy sailors' motion, he then backed away, sidearm still trained on them.

Several tense moments passed, then Sullivan said, "I think they're fucked up. The air in here's gotta be bad for them too." He paused for a moment thinking then ordered, "Call Lieutenant Lopez. Have her send the corpsman."

The speakers in his helmet chirped and Lieutenant Lopez's cold voice came through the speakers, *"Alpha team, report."*

"Charlie, Alpha Lead. We got us two Elai survivors in what appears to be an intact and fully manned command and control compartment. The rest are dead and these two appear to be critically ill. Request guidance as to disposition of prisoners and send the corpsman down here to check these sharkies out."

*"Understood, Alpha team. I gotta call the captain and we're sending the corpsman now. Standby."* The lieutenant's voice clicked out. Sullivan regarded the still figures floating in front of him and considered their options.

**\*\*\*\***

*Aboard the UEAN* Infiltrator
*The Bridge*

"Survivors." Mitch Harris set down the handset and looked at his executive officer, "Shit."

Greta Von Kant, the Infiltrator's executive officer, replied with a frown, "Shit is right. What the hell are we supposed to do with them?" She drummed her fingers on the console, then turned to the Chief of the Boat, a tiny woman with close cropped hair and steel gray eyes, "Chief Chara, thoughts?"

The senior noncommissioned officer frowned in thought, her already stern face becoming even harder. After a moment, she said, "We don't have a lot of options, as I see it. We leave them there and they die slow. We bring them here, which is a shit idea for a lot of reasons, or...." She stopped and then shrugged, "We can space 'em. They'd do it to us." Seeing the looks on the two officers faces she added, "Hey, I'm not saying we *should.* Just listing possibilities."

Mitch grimaced, "Let's take spacing them off of the table. Even though they would probably space us, we aren't them." After a pause he continued, "We're gonna need to get creative." He rubbed his nose thoughtfully, then tapped the communicator, "Engineering, Bridge."

After a moment, the speaker came to life. *"Engineering, Ensign Hudgins."*

"Ensign, this is the Captain. Get me the Chief Engineer."

*"Aye, sir. Standby."* The young officer clicked off. As he

waited, Mitch turned to Greta, "If they are in a control compartment, they probably know a lot about the systems. I'd like to take that ship itself but failing that, snatching its databanks and a knowledgeable crewman or two might be the best possible outcome."

Greta traded a glance with Chief Chara and nodded slowly, "Yeah, that would. Better than just raw data anyway. I don't know if we'll be able to use it but someone should be…"

The speaker came to life, "*Engineering.*"

"Commander, this is the Captain. We may need to rig a holding cell for a couple of Elai prisoners. Any thoughts on where we might do this and how fast we can do it?"

There was a pause, then Commander Niece responded, "*With no major bulkhead cuts and not taking working or living space from the crew, I presume?*"

"If possible. Ideas?" Mitch glanced at Greta, who grinned back, knowing the Chief Engineer's love for problem solving.

After a few seconds of silence as the engineer spoke to his team, the speaker again came to life, "*Sir, We have an idea.*"

"Let's hear it."

"*So, you remember how when we were hit by the blast wave, I had to replace a lot of subsystem components; mostly the EMP related protections?*"

"I do." Mitch grimaced thinking of the cannibalized and jury rigged systems all over the ship.

The engineer continued, "*Well, we cannibalized a lot of them from forward missile tube number eight. It had some damage to the launch rails and was going to be a yard job to fix, anyway. We can weld a grate into the tube and stick a door in it. The tube itself is twelve feet across, sixty feet deep and made of reinforced duranium. We can install in a floor so it's flat and place a bunk. I believe that will work as a cell, no?*"

With a grin, Mitch replied, "Works for me, Commander. Get on it. Also, call the surgeon. Ask what he'll need to provide medical care in there."

"*Yes, captain. Give me…..forty five minutes and I'll have*

*your cell ready.*" The engineer disconnected. Mitch turned back to Greta and Chief Chara, "Now. What the hell are we going to keep these guys alive long enough to get useful intel out of them? We'll have to grab it now if we can."

Greta grimaced and asked, "What do they even eat? Suddenly, all those useless pre-patrol briefings seem a lot more relevant."

There was a moment of silence, then Chief Chara said, "Is it worth detouring the boarding party to the sharkie sickbay to grab a buncha shit? Do we even have that much of it mapped yet?"

With a frown, Mitch turned back to the comm console and folded his arms.

"*Conn, Sensors.*" The intercom broke into their conversation.

Commander Von Kant tapped it and answered, "Sensors, Conn."

"*Ma'am, we have some action going on the far side of the system. You should come take a look.*"

Shooting a look at her captain, Greta replied, "On our way." The two officers and the chief made their way forward to the specialized room that contained the *Infiltrator's* long range sensors.

As they entered, a petty officer turned and gestured at a display, "Sir, ma'am. Chief." He sat at the display as Greta, Mitch and Chief Chara looked over his shoulder. He started to speak, "So, I think the Elai are getting wise to us. Look at this." He rewound the display and pointed at a marked target indicating an Elai destroyer, "This here is contact Sierra-2. This little fucker's been all over the place since we got in system. We can tell it's him 'cause his drive is running hot and leaves a distinctive signature." He tapped play on the display and the dots started to move. As the display advanced, he continued to speak, "Now, Mr. Shark here in Sierra-2 is a cool customer. He's moving slowly and cautiously. We think their sensors work better when they move slower. His pal here in

Sierra-6; not so much." He indicated another dot that was moving at a faster pace, "Now, it looks like they're hunting Captain O'Toro in the *Avenger* and that they're using a phased microwave burst emission to get a return signal off of the hull. It'd work too, since our stealth systems aren't really designed to absorb that. Probably takes a ton of power, but those Elai destroyers are overpowered anyway." He pointed at the screen, "Watch here when he pumps out that burst." The spot he indicated showed a brief flicker of something, then was clear again.

Pointing at the spot, the chief declared, "This guy here thinks he's got *Avenger* by the balls and rushes in to try to get her before she can break contact." The Elai warship accelerated and pinged out the microwave pulse again, this time demonstrating a clear return from a ship. The icon for the *Avenger* was very close to the enemy destroyer.

The sensor chief added with a darkly humorous note in his voice, "Too bad for him that Captain O'Toro didn't break away from him like he thought she would and broke *towards* him. He was probably chasing a decoy with that first one. When he pinged her next, she was within two hundred kilometers of him and had her tubes open. Poor bastard probably never even saw it coming."

On the display, the signal for missiles flashed briefly, then the contact icon for Sierra-6 faded. "Two hundred kilometers. Jesus." Greta muttered.

"Right?" The chief tapped the display again. "Now watch this guy." On the screen, the indicator for contact for Sierra-2 had turned around and started to move off, firing the microwave burst at random intervals.

The sensor chief pointed at the screen, "This one here...he's smart. He's starting to figure out that they need to coordinate. They need to go slowly and methodically and work in teams."

The Chief of the Boat declared, "We need to kill that son of a bitch before he gets out of this system and teaches these tricks to the rest of them."

Mitch rubbed his chin and said thoughtfully, "Yeah."

Greta added, "The longer we're in this system without cover, the more dangerous it's gonna get."

The sensor chief blurted out what they were all thinking, "Where the hell is the fleet?"

\*\*\*\*

*Alpha Team, UEAN* Infiltrator *boarding party*
*Aboard the derelict Elai cruiser*

Chief Sullivan cautiously looked at the apparently unconscious Elai sailor in front of him again and then looked at the hatch, just in time to see the corpsman swing in feet first, moving with a catlike grace in the microgravity environment.

The young man moved up next to the chief and nodded through his helmet, "Hey, Chief. Sorry for the delay. I called the surgeon to see if he knew anything about Elai physiology and if he had any advice."

Sullivan nodded back and replied, "Hey, doc. Did he?"

With a broad grin through his helmet visor, the corpsman replied, "Nope. He said and I quote, 'What do I look like, a fucking veterinarian? Just get him over here and I'll see what I can do.'" The corpsman shrugged and added, "So, I brought a couple of rescue bubbles. It'll keep 'em alive and contained until we get back and decontaminated." Not reassuringly, he added, "I think."

Sullivan frowned at this and nodded, "Get 'em opened up. I don't want to stir these guys until it's time to stuff them inside." The corpsman nodded and started removing the inflatable rescue bubbles from the large duffel bags he had in tow and began setting them up.

Hearing muttered curses from behind him, Sullivan turned halfway and looked. Seaman Ross and Ensign Keenan were both staring at the screen of their computer and conversing quietly.

In a firm tone, Sullivan asked, "Problem, gentlemen?"

Keenan looked up and said, "Chief, this is something new. These biometric encryptions... They're incredible. We're using all the tricks we have, but it's like it's rewriting itself, so every time we hit it with the cracker, it has to start all over, since it's basically adapting to our techniques." He paused, "We think there's a dedicated AI driving the security system. It's both awesome and *very* difficult to crack."

Sullivan scowled, "Can you get in?" The young officer looked at Seaman Ross, who just shrugged, his eyes not leaving the screen.

Keenan looked back at the senior enlisted sailor and responded simply, "I don't know. I'm a lot less confident than I was a few minutes ago."

The corpsman finished opening the rescue bubbles and declared, "I'm ready, Chief. We can tag and bag these gomers when you are." Sullivan nodded and the corpsman picked up the bag and gently drifted towards the two motionless Elai.

Suddenly Seaman Ross blurted, "Wait! Stop!" The corpsman caught himself and waited. Sullivan looked at the security specialist.

The young man turned in his seat and said, "Chief, sir. This is sort of a nuts idea, but since this is biometric, why don't we try to use that?"

Sullivan replied, "What do you mean?"

Ross gestured at the unconscious Elai, "I mean, that one there isn't dead. His fingerprints and retina or whatever the shit these guys have will still probably work."

Ensign Keenan tried to rub his chin and startled himself tapping into the faceplate of his helmet. He added, "He's right, even if it requires a passcode after that portion we can probably get through." He paused and added "Hang on a sec." He reached over to the pack containing the computers and picked up a cable. Maneuvering gingerly, he reached over and plugged the cord into the console. Leaning around it, he stared at the instruments and screens then pointed at a section,

"There. See that flat bit with the nub on the top?"

Sullivan nodded, then with a suspicious look at the Elai, reached out and gently grabbed its wrist and pushed the palm of its hand onto the flat area. Nothing happened. After a moment, he adjusted his grip and pushed more firmly. Suddenly a screen illuminated and several symbols flashed on a screen in the middle of the console.

Seaman Ross muttered something, then started typing rapidly. Keenan looked over his shoulder for a moment, then looked back at the chief and said simply, "He's in."

Sullivan released the Elai's hand and motioned to the corpsman, who was standing by with one of the other sailors. They gingerly began the process of placing the Elai in the thick plastic rescue bag and attached a small life support unit. As the two seamen went to their tasks, Sullivan moved over to where Keenan and Ross were staring at the terminal. After a moment, Ross said, "Sir, there's a shitload of data here. We're talking zettabytes. We don't have nearly enough storage space for it all. What should I go for?"

Without hesitation, Keenan replied, "Star charts. Ship technical manuals. Encryption keys. Anything related to ship movements or coordination with other ships. Comm protocols and codes. Tactical doctrine manuals. If it looks remotely valuable, grab it. If you're not sure, grab it. We'll take what we can till we're full." He looked up at Sullivan and said, "Chief, give us fifteen minutes. At the rate we're sucking data up, we'll have filled our portable drives by then. After that, we're ready to get out."

Sullivan nodded and keyed his radio, "Charlie team, this Alpha."

Lieutenant Lopez's voice came back immediately, *"Alpha, Charlie. Go."*

"Charlie, we're in the comp system. Our cracker team says that fifteen minutes and we'll be ready to move."

There was a crackle from the radio, then Lopez responded, *"Understood. Chief Langley is setting his charges in the engine room now. We're gonna blow it so the sharkies don't know we got aboard. He says the superstructure of the ship is so badly damaged that even if we had control of the system, he's not sure she could be towed. The skipper says to scuttle."* There was a pause from the radio, then she continued, *"Get what you can from the systems. As soon as your team is back on the boat, he's starting the timer. Let me know when you head back."*

"Understood, ma'am." Breaking the connection, Sullivan looked around the room. Noticing that the Elai were now sealed into the bags and the thick plastic had inflated, he said to the corpsman, "How are they doing, Doc?"

The young man shrugged, "No idea. This one's not as dark colored as it was a second ago. That's probably a good thing." He regarded the alien for a moment, then added, "I think. Anyway, we need to get them back to the ship. We need to get them treatment. If you're cool with it, I'm going to start moving them to the longboat."

Sullivan nodded and gestured to the two sailors with their rifles, "You two, go with him. Any funny business from them…."

One of the sailors nodded and patted her rifle, "We got it, Chief." Gingerly pulling the unconscious, bagged Elai behind them, the small detail of sailors left the compartment.

\*\*\*\*

*Aboard the UEAN* Infiltrator
*The Bridge*

"Sir. Longboat Zero Two Two has docked and the crew is preparing for decon. The prisoners are on their way to the holding cell now." The young sailor on the communications station paused for a moment, listening to his headset, then reported, "Commander Staley in intel reports the data is being linked and analysis is beginning now."

The captain and his executive officer traded a look, then the exec said, "Helm come to three two two, ahead one third." Underneath their feet, the familiar thrum of the *Infiltrator*'s main engines increasing power could be felt. Turning to Mitch, Greta explained, "I'm keeping the hull of that thing between us and the bulk of their forces. When it blows I don't want even a possibility of being silhouetted."

Nodding, Mitch replied, "Good thinking." He paused and tapped the comm panel, "Sensors, bridge. Any updates on the *Avenger?*"

"*Bridge, sensors. No, sir. After she blasted those two destroyers, she vanished. They're pinging away, but she's gone ghost.*"

"Understood. You hear anything, I need to know about it. Bridge out."

"*Aye, sir. Sensors out.*"

Mitch snapped off the panel and turned to Greta and Chief Chara who had joined them, "Captain O'Toro is doing her 'Harmless hole in space' routine. I don't think the Elai know how many of us are out here." He nodded at the Chief of the Boat, "Chief. How's the cell look?"

The hard faced sailor grinned slightly, "Sturdy. I know the Elai are strong, but the damage control teams welded spare hull rib spars in as bars. The only way out is if we let 'em out." She paused, "If they survive, that is. I checked Sullivans helmet cam footage. They don't look too good."

Greta answered, "No, they don't, but we don't really need them. We got the databases."

Mitch nodded and replied, "Yeah, that reminds me." He tapped the comm panel again, "Intel, bridge."

"Bridge, Intel, Staley here."

"Commander Staley, this is the captain. I wanted to tell you that if you get anything that looks like it might be of use, you need to call me immediately. We may or may not be able to use it for fear of letting them know we've compromised one of their ships, but I still need to know."

"Sir, I was just about to call you. You need to get down here. I think we found something."

The command team traded a look, then Mitch replied, "On our way." He snapped off the comm and swung out of his seat, snapping, "Mr. Horst, you have the conn."

Walking quickly through the tight passageways, the three arrived at the sturdy hatch to the secure intelligence room. Mitch put his hand on the scan plate and said, "Mitch Harris, Captain Zeta Three Six Five Two." The door chimed and the plate displayed the words. 'Assurance Phrase'. This was the software of the hatch ensuring that the person opening it wasn't under duress. Mitch replied, "In west Philadelphia, born and raised, on a playground was where I spent most of my days." Greta rolled her eyes at her commander's choice of code phrase, but said nothing. The door panel chirped and the text displayed. 'Identity, nonduress confirmed. HARRIS, MITCHELL CAPT 3405125'.

The big hatch slid open and the three entered. Lieutenant Commander Staley, a tall, skinny Belter with the traditional shaved head was standing, leaning over the shoulder of an intel tech at a console. He was speaking in a strained voice, "Run the goddamn thing again. Cross reference it with our database."

"Commander." Mitch said.

The skinny man leapt as if he'd been poked and turned. His usually pale complexion was white and his face drawn and tense, "Sir. We have a problem."

With a frown and a glance at Greta, Mitch replied, "Spit it out."

The man swallowed, then said, "It's Earth or ...at least we think it is."

Staring at the man for a second, Mitch tried to decipher what the man meant. "What do you mean?"

The man pressed his lips together and explained, "They use a visual operating system, right? So, we took the easiest things to look for: stellar maps. We were running that as a starting point to scrub for useful data, when Seaman Emory here noticed something." He motioned to the sailor who continued to work while they said. The intelligence specialist continued, "We noticed that there were data packets associated for each star; mostly small files, probably system profiles. We did a side by side comparison of our star charts to theirs to cross reference and see if we could find the Elai worlds and noticed that Sol had a massive data file associated with it."

Mitch and Greta traded a glance. Chief Chara was less patient and snapped, "Well? What's it say?"

The officer shook his head, "We don't know, Chief. It's still encrypted. Seems like there's a secure, compartmented data file there and a big one, to boot."

He swallowed again and said in a clear, high voice, "They know where Earth is and they have what looks like extensive data files on it." He fell silent.

Mitch's stomach sank and he looked at Greta and Chief Chara. The compartment was completely silent except for the sound of the ventilation system.

After what seemed like an eternity, Greta said, "We have to warn them."

# Chapter 13

## "Up Close and Personal"

*349th Special Forces Detachment, 'Thundercats'*
*Fifteen Kilometers north of FOB Anvil*
*Hill 236 'Observation Post Lion'*

Captain Shawn Tulp shifted in his armor, grimaced and adjusted his grip on the bulky shape of the electromagnetic accelerator rifle. He'd had to wear armor for long periods before, but never without even being able to open his helmet. It got damn uncomfortable after a few days. He again swept the scope over the series of ridges and low hills that concealed the three battalions of Elai infantry in front of him.

After a moment, he said, "Charlie."

Sergeant Tran Suk, the unit medic, who went by 'Charlie', answered, "What's up, sir?"

"What are we missing here? What are they waiting for?"

Charlie considered this for a moment, then said, "Well. They own orbit, don't they? So...reinforcements, prob'ly." The slight man said it as a statement, not a question.

"Shit." Tulp slowly moved the scope again and added, "Probably a good bet." After several more moments of silence he asked, "The shelter up and working?"

"Yes, sir. Everyone but you and me is in there and out of their armor. Its tight as hell and smells like ass because none of us have been out of our armor in a week, but it's warm and feels amazing."

Tulp twisted around and looked at the flat area on the rugged hill, just below the crest. The sturdy low slung tent was set up in a waist deep pit and only protruded a few feet above the ground. The nanofiber camouflage tarp over the top of it was held rigid by the nanotubes in the structure of the tarp itself and perfectly matched the dusty gray stone and soil around them. Even from this close distance, it was almost invisible.

"Here they come. Shuttle." Charlie's voice brought his attention back to the ridgeline in front of the well hidden observation post. Slowly panning the view of the rifle scope over the ridgeline, Tulp could see the squat, dark shape of an Elai combat transport moving in low against the horizon then rapidly dropping out of sight. Without raising his eyes from the screen, he ordered, "Get the drones out."

"On it." Charlie was busily tapping keys on the drone control console. As he did, a dozen of the beetle sized recon drones shot skyward. Moments later, several of the larger high altitude drones lifted silently up, their camouflage causing them to blend into the sky and vanish as they rose. Tulp and Charlie lay motionless under their nanofiber mesh and linked their visors to the drones cameras.

Selecting one of the smaller drones, Tulp took it low and fast towards the ridgeline, nearly brushing the freezing rocks. Slowing as he reached the crest of the hill, he ensured that the drone had its camouflage system active and landed it. The tiny drone hit the rock and began to rapidly scurry on its tiny legs. He caught a brief glimpse of what looked like an Elai fighting position and sent the drone wide around it. Several minutes of careful crawling later, he spied a large boulder that overlooked the flat area behind the ridgeline. Sending the drone climbing up the rock, he perched it at the top and panned its tiny cameras around the area.

Hearing a curse from Charlie, he asked without breaking his view, "Problems?"

"Yeah. They greased one of the Ravens. Looks like some sort of laser based anti air system, like our Zeus." There was a pause, then the man added, "We're down to our last two of the bigger drones. I'm keeping them up high as relays. I have a network of the beetles at about a five hundred meters. I don't think they can see them."

Tulp answered distractedly, "Yeah. Link to Three Five, I have one inside on the ground." The small surveillance drone sat motionless as the special forces soldier swung the tiny optical sensors around.

Charlie said, "There. That crevasse." He moved the camera towards a large crack in the rock. From it emerged a double line of Elai infantry, in full combat armor with equipment and weapons in hand.

Tulp squinted at it, for a moment and then asked, "That crack must lead to their LZ." He paused, watching for a moment or two, then asked, "Do these guys look different to you, Charlie?"

Charlie zoomed in on the marching Elai infantry and was silent for a moment. After a few seconds, he answered, "Yeah. Their armor's different. The shoulder piece is a different shape and color and their belts aren't standard. There's more pouches on them." He fell silent for a moment, then added, "They're bigger, too. Look."

The Elai below had fallen out of formation, some sitting, some standing near the enemy soldiers that had been there for hours now, waiting. The Elai that were coming in were noticeably taller by several inches and seemed to be bulkier. The two groups did not seem to intermingle, but watched each other from their respective positions. From the crevasse, a group of four armored Elai made their way. The one in front strode rapidly. His armor was pristine, with a smokey red shoulder plate. The sides of his combat armored suit helmet were also red and he wore a belt with a sword slung on it.

Charlie commented, "Officer for sure. He looks like those other two. Hello. Look here." A similar sized group was approaching the red armored Elai. In the front was an armored figure with a similar sword, who moved with a slight limp. Charlie chuckled, "Hey, look. It's Gimpy. He's still alive."

"Yeah." Tulp answered. He zoomed the camera in to where the two Elai leaders had stopped, several paces apart and were apparently talking, "Too bad we can't hear 'em."

Charlie grimaced and replied, "Yeah. I wish we knew who the fuck these new guys were. They're obviously a different unit."

Below, the Elai in red was gesturing in the direction of the ridgeline. The other figure didn't seem to respond. After another minute or two, the smaller figure in blue turned and limped away, disappearing into a well concealed position in the rocks. The big figure in red turned and motioned to the two big Elai behind him. After a moment, the bulk of the formation stood and shouldered their rifles. Stocky Elai moved up and down the ranks, motioning to various soldiers and adjusting gear. The front of the line began to move, heading for the ridgeline.

"Motherfuck. Here we go." Tulp thought for a moment, then said, "Charlie, get inside. Get out of your armor for a few minutes. We need everyone rested. I think we're about to get busy here. Get Vicky and Top up here with a message drone. We gotta get this out."

"Yes, sir." Charlie started to squirm backwards, then asked, "What about you, sir? You need to get inside too, at least for a few."

"I will. Let me call this in and I'll join you in a few."

Charlie nodded, "You got it, sir."

Tulp turned his attention back to the view of the drone in his helmet and watched the Elai formation. There were now at least a battalion's worth of the new alien soldiers climbing the hill, in three separate groups. He frowned and swung the camera around again. There was no sign of motion from any or the hundreds of soldiers amongst the rocks. Seeing movement, he zoomed the camera in again. There were several blue tinted armor Elai loading a big crate into what looked like a light vehicle. Frowning, Tulp scanned the vehicle carefully. It had no weapons and didn't appear to be armored. The team finished loading and then three of them climbed into the back with the load. Beyond the truck, Tulp could see four other trucks being similarly loaded. After a moment, the trucks started and began to slowly follow the Elai infantry who had now crested the ridge and were picking their way down the far side of the hill, now clearly heading towards the Marine firebase.

Under his breath, Tulp muttered, "What in the hell is going on here?" He keyed his comm system, "Sergeant Tran. You online?"

A moment later, the petite sergeants voice came, "Yes, sir. Sealing my armor now. What's up?"

With a hard look at the trucks as they began to climb the hill, Tulp responded, "As soon as you can get a message drone up, the better. I think our jarhead friends are in for some company."

\*\*\*\*

*Inside the Tactical Operations Center, Forward Operating Base Anvil*

"Observation post Kilo Three reports another wave is heading up. Looks like another push. We'll have an estimate of how many here in a minute or two. The drones keep losing signal from all this goddamn jamming," the Marine on the sensor station reported.

Tony nodded and said to Sergeant Major Jimenez, "Persistent little shits, aren't they?"

The senior noncommissioned officer grunted and pointed at the tactical display and declared, "They're probing. Look. They hit here, here and here." His finger stabbed into the display as he said, "They're testing the defenses and scouting the terrain. Why?"

Tony frowned and replied slowly, "Yeah. Sure looks like it, doesn't it? They're already been over that ground several times. Why do it again?"

The sergeant major scowled and responded, "I don't know,

but I don't fucking like it. Every time these guys mix things up, it ends up with nasty surprises."

"Sir, the drones broke through," the Marine on the sensors called out, "Visual feeds are estimating that we're looking at eight hundred plus foot mobiles and three small vehicles that appear to be cargo trucks."

Jimenez frowned and asked, "Armor?"

The enlisted Marine replied promptly, "Nothing so far, Sergeant Major. Just the trucks." He gestured at the console. "At least, it's all we can see between them blasting our drones and the jamming."

Jimenez turned to Tony and asked, "Worth expending missiles on?"

Leaning on the edge of the display table, Tony thought about this, then asked, "How are we on missiles in the Gorgons?"

With a shrug, Jimenez answered, "Not great. We got a bunch of anti-personnel rounds and a couple good salvos of high explosive. I'd probably save those for armor, sir."

Tony stared at the display and then nodded, "Ok. Unless they look like a threat, save the rounds." He tapped the edge of the display with an armored finger, then said, "Let's get the Gorgons out and in position to dump anti-personnel rounds on this group, though. Those guys up on the line might have a tough time holding them. Who do we have in reserve in case it gets hot up there?"

The short man answered promptly, "Bravo Company from the Second Battalion. They're on a ten minute response. Armor on, helmets and gloves off."

"All right. Keep 'em ready. There's a lot of sharkheads out there." Tony stared at the display for a moment, then said, "It'll be a few before they get up that slope. Let's go check the line."

The sergeant major didn't answer, just picked up his helmet and nodded at a nearby gunnery sergeant, who stepped up and took over the station vacated by the sergeant major. Turning to Tony, he said, simply, "Lets go, sir."

\*\*\*\*

*349th Special Forces Detachment, 'Thundercats'*
*Fifteen Kilometers north of FOB Anvil*
*Hill 236 'Observation Post Lion'*

Sweeping the optics of the tiny drone across the frozen, rocky landscape, Captain Tulp watched the Elai soldiers. Some were in fighting positions. Others were digging shelters, or organizing equipment, or distributing ammunition and air packs. Nothing had changed since the large group of red tinted armor soldiers had left several hours ago. With a frown, he disconnected his helmet feed from the drone and looked at the soldier next to him, Sergeant Vicky Tran.

She looked back through her helmet visor and said, "Something ain't right. These dudes don't look like they're supporting an assault. Where's the reserve? Why aren't they ready to move to exploit a hole in the lines?"

Tulp shook his head and replied, "I don't know, but you're right. Something's off here."

The noncommissioned officer considered this for a moment, then asked, "Wanna risk calling in?"

Shaking his head, Tulp replied, "No. We don't have anything to report. Until we do, I don't want to risk it."

Tran nodded and replied, "Works for me. The less noise we make the better."

Turning back to watch the enemy soldiers below, Tulp replied thoughtfully, "Yeah."

# Chapter 14

## "From the Shadows"

*349th Special Forces Detachment, 'Thundercats'*
*Thirty Kilometers North of Forward Operating Base Anvil,*
*Planet M3245; Draconis 327.*

"There's another one." The young soldier was lying on his stomach on the crest of a ridge, the image enhancer in his rifle scope cranked to maximum. He spoke in a low voice, as if trying to keep from being heard.

Several feet below him, below the crest of the ridge, Captain Shawn Tulp replied in an amused tone, "He can't hear you, Corporal Kim. He's five klicks away and we're sealed in these iron suits."

With a sheepish grin, Kim replied, "Sorry, sir. Habit. I pinged him. Wanna get a drone over there?"

Tulp considered this for a moment, then asked, "How many micro drones do we have left?"

With the awkward motion that was a shrug in the rigid armor suit, the soldier replied, "Seven or eight. Mitch recovered a couple and recharged them. We're good if you want to take a look."

Considering this for a moment, Tulp made a decision. He turned and looked down the hill at the rest of his small special forces team crouched in positions on the downslope of the ridge behind them. Their optical camouflage made them nearly invisible on the shadowy hillside. He keyed his low power radio and said, "Sergeant Chan."

"Sir." A section of nearby rock moved, shimmering and dancing as if being seen through heat waves and moved rapidly closer. As it did, it resolved into a human shaped figure that flopped down next to Tulp. The shimmer faded, revealing the massive dust gray power armored suit of his senior noncommissioned officer, Master Sergeant Sung Chan.

Tulp gestured at the ridge and said, "Kim's got eyes on three Elai about five clicks south. They look like sentries. Let's get a microdrone up and take a look." The big man gave a thumbs up and turned and motioned below. Another section of the rock shimmered as another of the team moved.

There was a brief flicker overhead like a small insect, then Chan said, "Ok it's up. Give it a minute. These things have a lot of cool gadgets in 'em, but they ain't fast."

Tulp slid several feet down the hill and tapped the control in his armor to link his helmet display with Chan's. The view inside of his helmet illuminated to a birds eye view as the drone streamed back information. In the screen, he could see the red arrows pointing out the sentries that his team had identified and that they were on a ridgeline.

Chan grunted and remarked, "Kinda far out, ain't they?" The view changed as the drone banked and slowed and panned back and forth along the ridgeline. Several more red arrows appeared as the software identified additional Elai soldiers. The big sergeant muttered, "What are you little shits up to?"

Tulp said, "It's a sentry line, all right. Think they have good enough sensors to see the microdrones?"

In a distracted tone, Chan responded, "Not sure. They can sure as hell see the standard drones, we know that now. It's even money if the microdrones we lost before were from the Elai greasing them or this shitty ass planet's environment." Finishing the drone sweep, he paused and asked, "Should I push in?"

"Yeah, but slow and make sure you keep the altitude high, so we get a good view before they pop it."

Tulp called up a map overlay and watched the terrain as it populated from the drones mapping software. The big Korean sergeant grunted and eased the drone forward. The beetle sized drone slipped over the ridge and picked up altitude. As it slipped over the ridge, they could see that the rugged terrain sloped down, then flattened out. Several more groups of Elai could be seen in fighting positions in neat lines on the reverse side of the ridges.

With a grim chuckle, Tulp commented, "Reverse slope. Some things transcend species."

"Yeah well, so does fucking artillery, sir." Chan replied sourly. A second later he said, "Oh, hello. What's this?" The noncommissioned officer panned the drone's view and zoomed in on a low slung vehicle, obscured by carefully placed camouflage nets. Behind it was another, then several more, parked in neat rows. Small moving shapes were visible moving all around the area. The software was rapidly tagging them with red arrows in the display. The noncommissioned officer muttered under his breath, "Fuck me. That's a lotta sharkies." After a moment he said, "Captain Tulp, whatta ya think? Battalion sized element? Gotta be the second wave of the assault."

Watching the display, Tulp frowned and replied, "Seems like it. Get more drones up, we need to sweep the whole sector. You know these guys aren't sitting out here in the open by themselves. Start tagging the equipment and see if you can locate any armor or arty."

The big man nodded and turned his attention back to the display. Tulp tabbed his helmet display back to the standard view and reached up and tapped Corporal Kim on the foot. The man looked down at him, "Yes, sir?"

"Keep an eye on those sentries. I'm going to call the boss. If the Gorgons have any ammo left, these fucks are in for one hell of a surprise."

"Yes, sir." The corporal nodded and slid back into his position. Tulp slid down the hill and ended up next to Sergeant Tran, currently manning the burst radio transmitter.

The tiny woman looked up, "Hey, sir. Say the word. I'm ready to record."

Tulp nodded and heard the chirp in his helmet that indicated the comm system was recording. After a moment, he said, "Anvil Station, this is Thundercat Three Five. We have located

172

a battalion sized element of Elai infantry with light tactical vehicles at the pinged coordinates. We assess it likely the second wave. It is highly probable that there are additional forces, so we have a sweep going on now. We'll push up information as we obtain it."

He nodded to Sergeant Tran, who nodded back. After a moment, she said, "Ok. Sent. Now we wait."

\*\*\*\*

"Sir. We have movement on the ridgeline." Several hours later, Corporal Kim's low tone snapped Tulp out of his doze. He rolled over and, after a fast scan of his armor's instruments, crawled up the steep slope to where his seemingly tireless weapons sergeant lay behind his electromagnetic accelerator rifle. As he climbed, he glanced at the time. Two hours had passed since they'd located the mass of Elai troops and called it in and there had been no response, nor any response to their subsequent reports that located three similar sized elements, now bringing the number of enemy troops into the thousands. The comm net seemed to be functional, but what the lack of reply meant, he had no idea. It couldn't be anything good.

Reaching the ridgeline, he slid up next to Corporal Kim and linked his armor display to Kim's rifle scope. In the magnified view, he could see a group of eight Elai, standing on the ridgeline. Two were standing out in front of the group and were facing each other. They stood still, with occasional gestures. Kim cycled the low light imager and the view became clearer. The two were in standard Elai battle armor, but there were flashes of color on the deep black suits. The larger of the two had red stripes on the sides of his helmet and the other had his left shoulder armor painted dark blue. Both wore belts with sheathed swords. The remaining six Elai soldiers, all with the similar blue shoulder markings, stood in a group, alertly watching around them.

Kim observed, "Captain, if those aren't officers, I'll eat my fucking hat. What do you want to do?"

Tulp watched, with a frown and replied, "Nothing. Nothing we really can do." He paused and then added, "Scan right, will you?" Kim obliged, swinging the view of the rifle scope to the right. Coming up the hill from behind the small formation of Elai was a second group. This group was nearly identical to the first, except for a splash of red on their left shoulder. All moved with their rifles at the low ready. They came up and stopped and lined up behind the first group. Kim swung the view back to the two Elai in the different armors, who were standing face to face.

Suddenly, the Elai with the red helmet stepped back and pointed at the group of Elai soldiers. The other didn't seem to respond. After a moment, the group of red marked Elai that had moved behind the first suddenly raised their rifles and fired into the backs of the first. In a matter of seconds, the unaware enemy soldiers were cut down, their bodies landing in a jumble on the frozen soil.

Under his breath, Kim muttered, "Holy shit." Tulp grimaced and didn't reply as the scene continued to unfold.

The smaller of the two figures, the familiar limping Elai officer, in front whirled and looked at the dead and dying soldier. The red helmeted Elai pointed at the dead soldiers as the detachment advanced on the officer of the stricken group with weapons at the ready. The small figure turned to face the one in the red helmet and after a moment, lowered its head and turned its back, in seeming surrender. The turning motion concealed the figure getting a hand on the handle of its short sword and drawing the blade and spinning into a whirl, flashing the blade into the neck of the red helmeted Elai, cleanly separating the head from the body. The headless corpse stood for a moment in the light gravity, then crumpled to the ground. The figure then turned and pointed the sword, the blade now dark with frozen blood, at the group of Elai that had their rifles trained on it. After a moment, they lowered their rifles and turned and walked away. The figure lowered its shorts word, paused and looked at the body of the other figure and sheathed its weapon. It then turned and started down the hill, its gait marked by a limp that became more pronounced as it navigated the rocky hill and moved out of sight.

As the enemy soldiers vanished, Tulp released a breath he wasn't aware he'd been holding and untoggled his view from Kim's rifle. He glanced at the young noncommissioned officer next to him, who looked back.

After a moment, the young man said, "Sir, what the fuck was that?"

Tulp shook his head, "I have no goddamn idea, but Gimpy is one god damn dangerous shark. Did you see how fast he was?" He paused for a moment, then added, "This feels like something command would want to know about." He thought for a moment, then toggled the radio, "Sergeant Tran. We got any messenger drones left?"

The cheerful voice of the communications sergeant came through his helmet speakers, "Yes, sir. One left. I was saving it for something important."

With a wry look at Kim, Tulp responded, "Oh, we have something. I don't know what exactly, but we definitely have something. Get the drone fired up, I'll record a message."

"Sure thing, sir. Give me a minute to get it out of the case, "

Tulp acknowledged absently and rolled over and regarded the direction of the Elai positions. After a moment, he added, "First Sergeant."

The low rumble of his detachment sergeant came through his helmet comm, "Sir."

"Let's get ready to move. I don't know what's going on and we're way too goddamn close to these guys."

"Yes, sir. We'll be ready to move in ten." The noncommissioned officer began to issue orders. Tulp sat for a moment, thinking, then slid down the hill. His small team moved briskly, packing equipment and preparing to move. He stood, thinking, as Sergeant Chan moved next to him. After a moment, he said, "Thoughts, Master Sergeant?"

The big man frowned, thinking for a moment, then replied, slowly, "I think there's a lot we don't know going on here. I think that much is obvious. Internal factions, maybe? I think we always assumed they were one big, happy shark-faced family." He gestured to the ridgeline beside them, indicating the aliens, "We mighta been wrong about that."

Tulp nodded thoughtfully and looked at the ridgeline and replied, "Maybe. That might change things, that's for sure." He fell silent, thinking, then added. "I think Gimpy may be in charge here now."

With a shrug, Chan replied. "He seems to be, doesn't he?"

"Yeah. I don't know..."

Sergeant Tran's voice broke in, "Sir, the message drone is ready. Record when you're ready, then when you're done we can launch it and get the fuck out of here."

Nodding, Tulp turned to his first sergeant, "Find us a place where we can get eyes on all three of these groups. High, but not obviously so."

Chan nodded and replied, "I'll look while you call this in." Tulp nodded and keyed his mic to record his report and hoped his messages were getting through.

After he finished, Kim pointed into the distance. "There, sir. That one." Corporal Kim pointed ahead of them at a hill in the distance.

Tulp squinted at it, then said, "The jagged one that's almost straight up?"

With an unrepentant grin, Kim replied, "Yes, sir. You said defendable, with good sightlines and not likely to be occupied by sharkie patrols. This is the one in the sector that fits the ticket. There's a flat spot on top we can use to launch drones and the Elai can't approach it without us seeing them."

With a frown, Tulp looked around. The hill was one of a series of several jutting up from a ridgeline and about two hundred meters tall. He nodded and replied, "Ok. Take Mitch and sweep it. When it's clear, ping us and we'll move up."

"You got it, sir." The scout stood and motioned to the squad engineer, Sergeant Daniels, who stood with decidedly less enthusiasm and picked up his carbine. There was a brief shimmer as the two activated their active camouflage systems and their outlines faded into the slight distortion that was the only visible sign of their presence. After a moment, the shimmer faded. Tulp turned around and saw that Master Sergeant Chan and the two remaining soldiers were busy engaged in tasks. Sergeant Tran was setting up the burst radio and the unit medic, Sergeant Suk was opening a case with suit consumable packs in it and passing them out.

After a moment, Sergeant Tran said, "Sir, we got a message queued up from FOB Anvil. I'll put it through." She tapped the relevant controls and Tulp's helmet display lit up. The exhausted face of the acting commander of the Marine base, Major Harris, appeared on the small screen.

"*Thundercat Three Six, Anvil Six. We've been receiving your reports. We couldn't reply immediately, as we've been getting hit on the perimeter pretty hard and the damn jamming is constant. It feels like they're trying to tie us up, but we don't know for what. Battalion staff agrees with your assessment that what you're seeing is the reserve force for the current assaults. Keep an eye on them and if they move, we need to hear about it immediately. Update targeting coordinates as you need to. Avoid contact and keep us informed of any more incidents like what you saw.*" Major Harris's image paused and then continued, "*We ran that video of the leadership change through the intel section; and they have no idea. They suspect that it's internal factional power struggles, but don't know how we can use it, if we can at all.*" He paused, then added, "*Avoid contact and keep your eyes open. Our drones aren't worth a shit with the jamming, so you're our only real-time intelligence asset out there, apart from a Raider recon team about twenty clicks west of you. Ironjaw Six is planning something, as soon as his staff get it to us, we'll let you know.*"

*Be safe out there, Thundercats. Anvil Six, out.*" The image disappeared.

Sergeant Chan's deep rumble came immediately, "So, more observe and report. I wonder what they're waiting for?"

Tulp sighed, then replied, "Who the fuck knows. Let's get the troops rested for the move to the hill. You and me on first watch." He moved to the edge of the depression that the team crouched in and sat in the deep shadow of a boulder. He could hear Chan below giving orders to the medic and the communications sergeant and telling them to try to get some sleep. Chan moved up beside him and sat down. After a moment, he sighed.

While scanning the landscape, Tulp asked "Problem, Top?"

"No, not really. It's just these goddamn suits prevent us from doing what I always do in this situation."

"Smoking?"

"No, sir. Brushing my teeth. It's the little things in life." Tulp chuckled at this and shifted, trying to find a position that allowed him to observe the landscape but wasn't uncomfortable. The two sat in silence for a moment.

After a few moments of companionable silence, Chen said, "Sir, can I ask you a question? You don't have to answer it if you don't want to."

Tulp laughed and looked at his detachment sergeant, "Sure, Sung. Not like we have a lot else to do, right?" He gestured at the icy, airless expanse of rocks around them.

The big man paused for a moment, then said, "Listen. I know you haven't been with us too long. What, like six months now?" Tulp nodded, silently. Sung continued, "After the El-Tee bought it, they pulled us in; assigned you to the team, shot us through a round of training and back out into the fray. That's not unexpected, we're too useful to let sit around. Still." Tulp turned to the big Korean sergeant. The man's face was troubled, "Thing is, sir. We heard some rumors about you. They sound like bullshit, but we need to know, you know?"

Tulp nodded and replied, "Ok. Let's hear them."

Sung hesitated, then plowed ahead, "We heard you didn't make major because of bad decisions you made on Paradise that got a lot of your guys killed and that this command is your last chance."

Tulp laughed bitterly, his mind flashing back to those nightmarish months in the jungles of the world known as Paradise.

After a moment, he responded, "All right. You want the story. I guess you deserve that. I have no secrets from you, Top. Not out here." Looking down at the dirt for a moment, he then said. His voice was distant, "I was part of 17th Special Forces Group. I was in command of a technology recovery team. You know- Those ones we used to have before we realized that Elai tech isn't really worth a shit. Anyway, we'd been running around the fucking jungle on Paradise for months. We'd been skirmishing with Elai patrols and hunting down stragglers when they pulled us back to the *Shiva's Wrath*. We rested up and refitted and then we got another tasker. This one was to go down to a secure area, enter a building of some sort and get what tech we could out of it. Simple, right?"

Sung nodded, silently.

Tulp continued, in a slightly distant tone, "There was this major in the 17th Group, acting as battalion executive officer. Major Kenneth." He paused, looked at Sung and added, "A real shitheel of an officer. You know the type." His face tightened at the thought of the man, "He ordered us down on our next drop without our armor, as 'It was a secure area' and we 'needed the austere environment training'. It was to get into an unidentified ruin and search it for technology. I tried to talk him out of it, but he was insistent." He fell silent.

After a moment, Sung prompted, "What then, sir?"

Seemingly startled, Tulp responded, "Oh, we accomplished the mission, despite getting hit by three Elai patrols and losing four soldiers inside of the structure to a goddamn poisonous bug that we probably wouldn't have even noticed if we had

had our armor." His face darkened, "I confronted him about it when we got back up and come to find that the bastard had lied to the battalion commander. He'd said that *I* decided not to take the armor and that he tried to talk me out of it. He called me a liar to my face in front of the battalion commander and threatened me. I guess I was tired, wired and just generally fucked up from the jungle, so I popped him." He paused, reflectively, "I broke his nose on the first shot."

Sung blew out a breath, "Goddamn, sir. Punching a special operations major...wow."

"Fuck that guy. If his dad hadn't been a member of parliament, he'd never have made it to special forces." Shaking his head, Tulp added, "Too bad for him that one of the guys I lost was the nephew of a Fleet Admiral. The UEA Inspector Generals' people were ALL over the place for a few weeks." Tulp shifted on the rock and added, in a reflective tone, "They had to punish me for striking a superior officer, particularly in front of the battalion commander. I got a general officer memorandum of reprimand in my permanent record and 45 days confined to quarters." He made the peculiar movement that was a shrug under the power armor and added, "I was reassigned here afterwards. Probably gonna finish the war as a captain, then be quietly retired. You know the story."

Sung nodded, but said nothing. After a moment, Tulp added, "I coulda saved them if we'd been allowed to bring our armor, Sung." He looked out over the frozen landscape and said distantly, "I think about them almost every day."

Chen nodded, "I understand, sir. I've been there. It hurts. Time will make it better, but it never goes away entirely." Tulp nodded and didn't reply.

After a moment, Chen asked, "What happened to the major you jacked?"

With a grim note of satisfaction in his voice, Tulp responded, "He's back in Sol on Pluto, in charge of a very remote data storage facility. He will never get another assignment as long as a certain Admiral or any of his academy buddies are in the service."

Chen replied quietly, "Not what he deserves, but a form of justice, nonetheless."

"Yeah. I guess." Tulp turned back to watching the rugged, icy landscape and fell silent.

\*\*\*\*

*Inside the Tactical Operations Center, Forward Operating Base Anvil*

"Observation post Kilo Three reports enemy infantry are two kilometers from engagement range. The drones keep losing signal from all this goddamn jamming," the Marine on the sensor station reported.

Tony nodded and said to Sergeant Major Jimenez, "Persistent little shits, aren't they?"

The senior noncommissioned officer grunted, pointed at the tactical display and declared, "Something's bugging me. When they probed the last few times, they hit here, here and here." His finger stabbed into the display as he spoke, "They've already been here and here." He looked up. "Why are they coming into zones they've already probed? If they're looking for weak spots in the line, they have to know that ain't it."

Tony frowned and replied slowly, "Yeah. Sure looks like it, doesn't it? They're already been over that ground several times. Why do it again?"

The sergeant major scowled and responded, "I don't know, but I don't fucking like it. Every time these guys mix things up, it ends up with nasty surprises."

"Sir, the drones broke through," the Marine on the sensors called out, "Visual feeds are estimating that we're looking at eight hundred plus foot mobiles and three small vehicles that appear to be cargo trucks."

Jimenez frowned and asked, "Armor?"

The enlisted Marine replied promptly, "Nothing so far, Sergeant Major. Just the trucks." He gestured at the console, "At least, it's all we can see between them blasting our drones and the jamming."

Jimenez turned to Tony and asked, "Worth expending missiles on?"

Leaning on the edge of the display table, Tony thought about this, then asked, "How are we on missiles in the Gorgons?"

With a shrug, Jimenez answered, "Not great. We got a bunch of anti-personnel rounds and a couple good salvos of high explosive. I'd probably save those for armor, sir."

Tony stared at the display and then nodded, "Ok. Unless they look like a threat, save the rounds." He tapped the edge of the display with an armored finger, then said, "Let's get the Gorgons out and in position to dump anti-personnel rounds on this group, though. Those guys up on the line might have a tough time holding them. Who do we have in reserve, in case it gets hot up there?"

The short man answered promptly, "Bravo Company from the Second Battalion. They're on a ten minute response. Armor on, helmets and gloves off."

"Allright. Keep 'em ready. There's a lot of sharkheads out there." Tony stared at the display for a moment, then said, "It'll be a few before they get up that slope. Let's go check the line."

The sergeant major didn't answer, just picked up his helmet and nodded at a nearby gunnery sergeant, who stepped up and took over the station vacated by the sergeant major. Turning to Tony, he said, simply, "Lets go, sir."

\*\*\*\*

*349th Special Forces Detachment, 'Thundercats'*
*Fifteen Kilometers north of FOB Anvil*
*Hill 236 'Observation Post Lion'*

Sweeping the optics of the tiny drone across the frozen, rocky landscape, Captain Tulp watched the Elai soldiers. Some were in fighting positions. Others were digging shelters, or organizing equipment, or distributing ammunition and air packs. Nothing had changed since the large group of red tinted armor soldiers had left several hours ago. With a frown, he disconnected his helmet feed from the drone and looked at the soldier next to him, Sergeant Vicky Tran. On a boulder several meters above them lay another soldier, holding the drone control panel.

Tran looked back through her helmet visor and said, "Something ain't right. These dudes don't look like they're supporting an assault. Isn't this supposed to be the reserve? Why aren't they ready to move to exploit a hole in the lines?"

Tulp shook his head and replied, "I don't know, but you're right. Something's off here." He pointed at the line of foxholes. "Why are they digging in this far away from our lines?"

The noncommissioned officer considered this for a moment, then asked, "Something's fucky here. Wanna risk calling in?"

Shaking his head, Tulp replied, "No. We don't have anything to report. Until we do, I don't want to risk it. These fuckers are too good at electronic games to take the chance."

With a nod, Tran replied, "Works for me. I guess we standby to standby."

Turning back to watch the enemy soldiers below, Tulp replied thoughtfully, "Yeah."

A split second later, a voice came over the radio. "Captain Tulp, we have something going on up here."

Tulp looked up at the boulder that the sergeant was lying on and asked "What's up, Charlie?"

The medic currently on watch replied, "I don't know. They're all moving with a purpose all of the sudden. Here, let me link you in." He tapped the key that sent his view to Tulp's visor. The image appeared of the Elai encampment. The Elai soldiers were all moving quickly, getting into their fighting positions, or lying prone on the ground.

"Son of a bitch. They're taking cover." Tulp broke the connection and turned to the sergeant crouched next to him, "Get a flash message to Anvil. They're getting ready to..." There was a brilliant flash of light from the south. Several more flashes lit the landscape. In the distance, a ball of brilliant white fire could be seen peeking over the horizon like the rising sun, then fading away, forming the distinct towering clouds of nuclear detonations.

\*\*\*\*

*Forward Operating Base Anvil*
*Primary Defensive Line*

Tony moved in a crouch from the crude improvised staircase built into the side of the crater and entered the trenchline, with the Sergeant Major and a private armed with a rifle right behind him. Moving down the trench, he entered the first bunker. Four Marines were there, preparing the position. Two were manning a mounted Mark Thirty lascannon and the other two were setting cases of grenades near their firing positions.

One of them looked up and nudged the other, "Hey, Corp. It's the Major and the CSM."

The corporal straightened up and said, "Hey, sir. Sergeant Major."

Tony nodded and asked, "How are things going up here?"

With a grimace, the corporal replied, "All right. I wish they'd stop these goddamn probing and get on with it. We know they're out there. We keep getting flickers on the sensors, but between the jamming and the shitty light on this planet, we can't really see them that well until they bum rush us."

The Marine on the Mark Thirty suddenly let off a burst, the green bolts searing into dim light. He paused and then squeezed off another, then said, "Fuckers are moving right below that outcrop of rock. I can't see them except for fast glimpses, but I know they're there."

Tony moved up and took a cautious look out of the slit in the front of the bunker. He saw nothing moving in the dim light. After a moment, he stepped back and said, "Ok. Well, stay sharp. It's going to start any second now."

Sergeant Major Jimenez asked, "You Marines need anything?"

The Marine on the Mark Thirty replied, without taking his eyes off the slope in front of him. "I'd take a hot shower and a beer or five, Sergeant Major."

With a rare grin crossing his weathered face, the senior NCO replied, "You and me both, Marine." He gently slapped the armored shoulder of the corporal and said, "You holler if you need anything, devil."

The woman nodded and turned back to stare down the slope over the shoulder of the Marine on the mounted gun. Tony and Jiminez moved back out into the trenchline. Seeing two Marines carrying a hard sided case, they stepped back as the two set the case down and opened the top. One of the Marines pushed a button. Seconds later, there was a hiss and something shot skyward. A few seconds later, another flew out, then another, until the case was empty. The Marines put the lid back on the case.

Seeing Tony and the Sergeant Major, the private blurted, "Oh! Sorry, sir. Sergeant Major. Didn't see you there. We're just getting more loiter drones up. The last few probes chewed a lot of them up."

The sergeant major nodded and replied in a firm tone, "You carry on, Marines." The Marines nodded and moved off down the dim trenchline with the empty case. Continuing down the trench, they stopped outside the next bunker they came to. A lieutenant and a staff sergeant were standing outside the bunker door talking and paused when Tony and the sergeant major approached. The lieutenant paused respectfully, "Sir."

Tony nodded back, "Lieutenant. You have everything you need?"

The man nodded, "I think so, sir. It's been quiet up here for the last thirty minutes or so since the last probe."

The staff sergeant declared, "And that's what's worrying me. They're up to something, sir."

With a tired grin Tony replied, "Aren't they always? Stay alert." The two nodded and moved into the bunker.

Tony looked at Jiminez, who shrugged and said, "They're tense but ready. We probably ought to get back to the ops center, sir." The two turned to head back towards the stairs.

Tony opened his mouth to reply and felt rather than heard the explosion. He turned and saw a cloud of dust down the trench. As he watched, more explosions hammered around them. Taking two fast steps, they moved into the closest bunker, the first one that'd visited. The Marines inside were sitting on the floor, backs to the bunker walls. Moving into the only space left in the center of the bunker, the two Marines sat down.

Tony activated his comm system, as the roaring of explosions grew in intensity, "Operations, Anvil Six."

The reply came promptly, "*Six, Ops.*"

"Ops, we're pinned down up here on the trenchline under this rocket fire. Captain Saint will be the battle captain until we make it back down there. This is probably the assault we're waiting for. Keep the reserve force ready and get the Gorgons into firing position, with anti-personnel loads, "

The Marine on the radio responded, "*Understood, Six. We'll update as…*"

There was a massive explosion that made the floor shake in the bunker as a rocket hit right outside and then dead silence.

Suddenly, over the local tactical net, Tony could hear someone shout, "Up in your holes! Here they come!"

The Marine corporal snapped, "On your feet!"

The Marines bounced up and took their positions. The gunner picked up the Mark 30 and yelled, "Here we go!"

He began firing, slewing the barrel of the lascannon back and forth. The other Marines were also at the firing slit, adding the blue bolts of their rifles to the green blasts of the Mark 30. Risking a fast look over the shoulder of the corporal, Tony could see the dashing figures rushing up the hill, moving from boulder to boulder, pausing to return fire. The smoky red bolts illuminated the dim slope and gave brief glimpses of the armored figures advancing. There was the bright flash of a rocket motor and then an explosion, tossing the several of the figures into the air. Several more explosions came in short order as the stealthy loiter drones came streaking out of the sky, detonating amongst the onrushing Elai. However, for each flash that illuminated the battlefield, the shapes of dozens more could be seen, relentlessly rushing closer. Over the tactical net, Tony could hear contact reports, then someone shouted into the tactical net, *"Fifteen Meters! We need some help at Three!"* There then came the calm voice of the staff sergeant, ordering a squad to Bunker Three.

Tony looked at the Sergeant Major who said grimly, "Time to call it in, sir."

"Do it." Tony turned back to the firing slit, as Jimenez started speaking into his radio, calling in the missile strike. Watching the slope, Tony could see the figures were very close now. As he watched, he saw one rise up with something in its hand.

The Marine on the Mark Thirty saw the figure and walked a dozen lascannon bolts into the figures chest. It fell backwards and out of sight. Moments later, there was a flash as the grenade went off, throwing several other figures out into the open. The Marines relentlessly poured fire into the figures. Another grenade went off right outside their bunker, kicking up a cloud of dust. A split second later, there was a shadow outside of the slit and then a murderous stream of fire poured into the bunker. Tony threw himself backwards and drew his sidearm. Before he could aim and fire, one of the Marines turned and emptied a magazine at point blank range into the Elai soldier that was firing into the bunker. The shape flopped back into the dust and was still.

Tony rolled over and looked up. The corporal that had been standing next to him was slumped against the wall, with a smoking hole in her chest plate. Her eyes were open and staring. Next to her, another Marine was on the ground, his faceplate cracked and hissing, leaking air. The warm air from inside the man's suit formed a white plume as it froze in the icy atmosphere of the moon. Snatching a can of suit-seal from his belt, Tony leaned over and sprayed the foam onto the man's cracked helmet visor. The sealant sprayed onto the crack and rapidly hardened. As the foam built, the spray of freezing atmosphere escaping slowed, then stopped. Dropping the empty can, Tony reached over the Marines suit and checked his vital signs. Seeing that the man was wounded, but the suit had sealed itself and was providing first aid, Tony looked up just in time to see a muted flash, then hear the rippling cracks of the antipersonnel warheads exploding. The rapid popping went on for about a minute, then ceased.

The Marine on the Mark Thirty said, "Holy SHIT! That was close." He fired a burst into the dust, then stopped firing and said, "All I see out there is bodies, Corporal."

Picking up a rifle, Tony moved up next to the Marine and said, "She's dead." He looked out the firing slit. As the dust cleared, he could see shapes in the distance moving down the hill, clearly retreating. Behind them, they left what looked like dozens of still bodies on the slope. He said grimly, "Looks like we drove them off."

He turned to the sergeant major, who had also picked up a rifle and opened his mouth to speak, when the bunker's firing slit illuminated with a brilliant, chalky white light, which faded, then flashed again, several times in rapid succession. The Marine on the mounted gun screamed and fell back, clutching at his faceplate. Tony blinked, dazzled by the light and fell to his hands and knees as the ground began to buck and roar, tossing the Marines around in the bunker like children's toys.

\*\*\*\*

*349th Special Forces Detachment, 'Thundercats'*
*Fifteen Kilometers north of FOB Anvil*
*Hill 236 'Observation Post Lion'*

The shaking of the ground finally stopped and Tulp climbed to his hands and knees and crawled to the ledge overlooking the Elai encampment. To the south, the direction of the Marine firebase was a towering wall of dust. The blast wave and shaking of the earth had not seemed to affect the prepared enemy troops below. Attempting to activate a drone, Tulp muttered a curse under his breath as the link blinked, 'Signal Lost'.

Next to him, Sergeant Tran said, "Gone, sir. Probably the EMP. Give me a minute. I'll get another couple up." She crawled on her hands and knees to her pack and started setting up to launch another relay drone. Tulp turned back to the ledge and picked up the sniper rifle lying there. He linked his helmet and swept the area below. He could see the Elai moving rapidly, getting up in their positions and readying weapons.

Keying his radio, Tulp said, "First Sergeant. Need you to come take a look at this."

The big Korean moved up next to him and wordlessly linked into the rifle's scope. After a moment, he said thoughtfully, "They're getting ready for an assault. Look. They have crew served weapons set up." He indicated two Elai light weapons that were placed on a small rise, facing the direction of the Marine base.

"Who's attacking them? I don't think the Marines at Anvil have enough people to be out in force and Task Force Hammer is still a long way to the north." Sweeping the scope around, he caught sight of several dozen figures straggling towards the Elai lines and recognized the red armor of the force that had gone out earlier, their armor now battered and scorched. They moved slowly and their previously disciplined lines were gone, replaced by disorganized stragglers.

Shaking his head as he regarded the scene below, Master Sergeant Chan said, "I don't think…" Suddenly from below, there came the red flickering of Elai rifle fire, quickly joined by the two crew served weapons. The red streaks flickered out, catching the staggering figures, cutting them down where they stood. In a matter of seconds, the retreating Elai soldiers had been cut down, crumpling onto the dusty rock of the icy moon.

"Holy shit." Chan murmured, "I think our little Elai internal fight just went hot." Below, the Elai had climbed out of their fighting positions and were advancing past the bodies. Occasionally, one would pause and pump an energy bolt into a survivor as they passed.

Tulp watched the advancing soldiers below and said, "What are we watching here? Why did they send them off and then waste them? None of this makes any fucking sense."

The big sergeant shrugged, "I don't know. Makes sense to me. If you don't mind wasting your assault force, throw them at your opponents to pull them up in their holes, then pop the nukes to make a hole in the defenses. Zorch anyone who runs away. They used to do that sometimes back in the old days in Earth's wars." He watched the Elai soldiers shoot another wounded enemy lying on the ground and shrugged, "Either way, it leaves a lot less of them for us."

Below them, the last of the several hundred Elai troops had moved out of sight into the massive cloud of dust that had followed the blast wave passing over them. The flat area where the Elai had been encamped was empty, now only occupied with abandoned fighting positions, discarded bits of equipment and dozens of bodies.

"Captain, we have the relay drone up. We're trying to establish contact with Task Force Hammer." The petite communications sergeant looked up and declared, "The atmosphere is full of shit. Between the dust and the radiation…" She shook her head and stated, "It might be a while before the electromagnetic interference clears."

"Shit." Tulp thought about this then asked, "Any idea of a timeframe to get ahold of them?"

"None at all, sir. Sorry." She turned back to her portable console.

In the tiny terrain display in his armor's helmet, there was a tiny blinking light, far to the north of them. Puzzled, Tulp expanded his map, examining the display. Advancing from the north were the identification tags for multiple friendly vehicles.

In a darkly cheerful tone, Master Sergeant Chan commented, "Here comes the hammer."

# Chapter 15

## "Breach"

*355th Forward Deployed Resuscitation Team*
*Inside the Tunnel Complex*

The radio chatter was chaotic, but the confusion itself told a clear story. A major assault was under way up above. The tremor of rockets impacting could be felt through the walls. The small medical team clad in their scavenged power armor sat or stood in the aid station listening to the command net. No one spoke, but they all knew what it meant– more wounded were on the way.

After a moment, Dahl stood up and declared, "Major, we're going to be down to field dressings and using medpacks scavenged out of busted suits of armor if this keeps up." She gestured at the surface. "We can't keep those guys alive for much longer if we don't get resupply." She then indicated a Marine in a nearby bed. "Hell. We don't have enough for these guys that we already have!"

"I know." Manderson replied, grimly. "But we don't have a choice. How many are we holding now?"

"We're holding six here that are too unstable for the line medics to manage and another twenty two in the north aid station. There's another fifty or so wounded and out of the fight that we have dispersed to the various company areas under the charge of their aid stations. They're getting the absolute minimum care." The blonde nurse blew out a frustrated breath and ran her hands through her hair. "And the rest...well. Most of them shouldn't even be on duty, but we sent them back to the line."

Manderson nodded wearily and didn't reply. After a moment, he turned to Agawa. "Make sure everyone stays in their armor. Helmets and gauntlets close by."

"Inside, sir?" Agawa asked, raising an eyebrow.

"How comfortable do you feel that we're safe down here?" Manderson replied, somberly. "If things get spicy, I'd like to be able to get out of here in a hurry."

"Fair enough." The stocky medic replied. He pointed at the sailor closest to him. "You come with me. Let's go see if we can scrounge up any more power armor aid packs." The stocky master sergeant and the sailor disappeared out into the tunnel that led to the hangar.

Nearby, the giant medic known as Johansen was standing near a wall with both of his hands on the rock face. He looked up and spoke to Specialist Mather. "There it is again."

The shorter medic frowned and put his hand on the rock and was silent for a moment, then spoke. "I still don't feel anything."

"I'm telling you. I feel it." Johansen insisted, somberly. "It feels like a molecular disruption drill."

"I don't know what that means." The first man replied, acerbically. "I'm from Michigan."

"It's like a crunchy grindy feel." The bigger man replied, moving his hands. "My family have been asteroid miners for two hundred years. If there's one thing I know, it's mining equipment."

"Maybe the Seabees are cutting tunnels?" The younger medic replied.

"In the middle of a major assault?" Johansen shot back, skeptically. "I don't think so."

Watching the two for a moment, Manerson asked, "What are you two talking about?"

"Sven thinks he feels something in the wall." Specialist Mathers replied. "I don't feel it, but he knows about this kind of stuff."

Curious, Manderson took off his armored glove and laid his hand on the cold rock of the tunnel wall. After a moment he spoke slowly, "I do sort of feel something." He looked at

Johansen. "You say it feels like a drill?"

"Yep." The man explained. "An asteroid mining drill. We got used to the feel since it could tell us what the rock density was and if there were any misalignments in the drill beam frequencies." He paused. "It stopped." He looked at Manderson. "Weird. It was just right there."

"Hmm." Manderson thought for a moment, then sighed. "When things slow down, I'll call in to the command post and see if anything is going on, but I suspect that now is probably not a great time for them to investigate this sort of stuff." He gestured at the ceiling as another series of trembling shook the rock above. "It sounds like it's getting busy up there." Looking at Johansen, he ordered, "Keep an eye on it. The last thing we need is a Seabee accidentally driving a boring machine through the middle of the goddamn aid station."

"I will, sir." Johansen replied. He pulled a microphone jack out of his suit and laid it against the wall and listened intently to his suit speakers. After a moment, the big medic muttered, "Gone again." He scowled and said, "I'll try to…"

Suddenly, the floor heaved and bucked under their feet and a deafening roar assaulted their ears. The lights overhead flickered once, twice and then went out entirely and Manderson felt the floor giving away underneath him. He windmilled his arms and fell backwards into the dark, landing roughly on his backside and elbows, striking his head on a nearby folding table holding surgical dressings. There was a moment of noise that sounded like gravel falling onto a metal roof, then a split second of dead silence. A moment later, someone began to scream, in a high pitched, shrill tone, incomprehensible noises of terror. A set of light beams broke the darkness as someone activated their suit lights, then another. The lights danced, sending complex, menacing shadows skittering around the room.

Dazed, Manderson sat up and activated his own suit lights. The floor in front of him that had been the rear half of the aid station was gone, replaced by a pit. Inside the pit, the hulking power armored figure of Johansen was visible. He had an oxygen tank in one hand and was swinging it down at something on the rubble strewn floor. Manderson'e eye was drawn to another flashing set of lights in the pit. The smaller specialist, Mathers, was partially trapped under the body of one of their patients, desperately using an IV pole to strike at a small, black armored figure attempting to rush at him. There was a crash from beside him and one of the wounded Marines that had been lying in the stretchers hit the floor.

"Contact rear! We got sharks in the tunnel!" the Marine shouted hoarsely. Grimacing in pain, he scrambled over Manderson to a still figure lying on the floor behind him and came up with a pistol. Lunging past the stunned officer, the Marine began pouring the bright blue bolts into the smoke and dust filled tunnel entrance that was now visible beyond the pile of rubble. After a few seconds, the smokey red bolts of the Elai battle rifle began to hiss past.

"Get the fuck down, dumbass!" the Marine shouted at Manderson, He turned to yell something else and one of the energy bolts caught him in the side of the head, throwing him to the side. Hurling himself backwards, Manderson fell onto his back, then rolled over and snatched the fallen Marine's pistol. Keying his suit radio, he yelled, "ANVIL OPS, WAR ANGEL CONTACT!! WE GOT SHARKS INSIDE THE AID STATION!" Seeing a shape raise itself over the edge of the tunnel, he raised the pistol. He hesitated, not knowing if it was an enemy or one of the medics down in the pit trying to escape. The wildly flashing white lights from the suits, the red bolts searing out of the darkness flashing like red lightning and the reflections off of the tunnel walls illuminated the dust hanging in the air, lending a surreal, strobe-like effect to the scene. In horror, Manderson realized that the figure climbing up was not human. Its once slick black visor was cracked, revealing a flat black eye and leathery brown skin. It raised a snub-nosed pistol towards him. Manderson raised his pistol reflexively, knowing he wasn't going to make it when the figure lost balance, fell flat on its face, then was jerked backwards into the hole. Where the enemy soldier had been he caught a glimpse of the hulking figure of Johansen again raising the oxygen tank and bringing it down viciously onto the alien with his power augmented strength. There was a strange organic sound, a melodic ringing as the tank hit– like a melon being crushed by a church bell. The giant man roared in a mix of anger and victory, then stiffened as several of the bright red bolts hit him from the rear.

The medic locked eyes with Manderson. His eyes were clear and shot with pain and fear. He spoke one clear word. "Run." He then turned and dove into the dust filled darkness and vanished, leaving only the sounds of rifle bolts hitting armor as he charged. Manderson hesitated for a split second, then rolled over. Grabbing the armored wrists of the fallen nurse behind him, he scrambled for the far door to the aid station, dragging the wounded soldier along with him.

Bursting into the hall, Manderson nearly bowled over Master Sergeant Agawa, who was headed into the aid station at a run. He could see a half dozen of the medical staff in the dim yellow lights in the hallway. Some of them were dragging patients, others pieces of equipment. All were covered in a grim film of dust. Stopping, he gasped, "We got sharks inside the aid station." Gesturing behind him, he added, "They tunneled under the floor. It collapsed after the earthquake and we fell in."

Reacting faster than Manderson could have ever expected, Agawa drew his sidearm and flattened himself against the door to the aid station and peered into the dark room. After a moment, he asked, "Is there anyone else left?"

Handing the still form of the nurse to a sailor nearby, Manderson replied, "Johansen and Mathers went into the hole. So did at least the two patients in the far beds."

"How many sharks?" Agawa demanded.

"At least four or five. Couldn't see very well." Manderson checked the charge on the sidearm in his hand. "Johansen is probably dead. I saw him take a half dozen hits."

"We have to check." Agawa replied. He leaned out into the door peering into the dust-filled room. A split second he ducked back, the red bolts searing past, scorching the opposite wall. "Fuck!" He pushed his pistol around the corner and fired a half dozen blind shots into the darkness. "We have to get the fuck out of here!" He screamed.

"355! GET THE FUCK MOVING! GET TO THE HANGER!" Manderson yelled. He sprinted past the door, putting several blue bolts into the dusty room as he did. He then took cover on the far side of the door, across from Agawa. The dazed medical personnel scrambled for the distant door that led to the hangar, dragging the wounded along with them.

"I can't get the TOC on the line." Agawa called. "The line is dead and the suit radio doesn't have the range."

"I put out a call." Manderson replied, "But we were in contact. I didn't get a reply either." There was a flurry of red bolts and the sound of boots clattering. Agawa again stuck his pistol around the corner and blind fired. Manderson joined him. The red blasts stopped, as did the sounds of movement. A few seconds later, there was a soft click and a disk-shaped object landed in the doorway right in front of Agawa. Again with reflexes that stunned Manderson, Agawa dove forward, swatted the device back into the room and tackled Manderson, bowling them both over. Manderson slammed his power armor helmet closed as the two tumbled– he didn't even remember putting it on. There was a tooth rattling *THUMP* and they could feel chips of stone pinging off of their armor. A moment later, a large cloud of dust washed over them. The yellow emergency lights made the billows of dust look toxic and menacing. A small black figure appeared, staggering through the dust, then collapsed. There were multiple rents in its dusty black armor and a thick stream of dark black liquid poured from the enemy alien's neck. The figure twitched once and was still.

Agawa rolled off of Manderson and yelled, "Let's get the

fuck out of here!" Scrambling to his feet, he hauled Manderson up after him, then gave him a hard push in the direction of the hangar. "Go!" The stocky medic then turned and fired another half dozen bolts into the door, then turned and ran.

A short power enhanced sprint later and Manderson was at the door. Pausing for a moment, he yelled, "Friendlies coming out!!" Then ran through and dove to the side for cover. A moment later, Agawa followed. As the officer rolled over and looked around, he could see the grim determined faces of the remaining members of the medical team, crouching behind crates and pieces of equipment, their weapons pointed at the hatch that they had just exited.

"Is there anyone else left?" A woman's tense voice called. It sounded like Dahl.

"I don't know." Manderson replied, clambering to his feet and moving behind a nearby crate. "I saw Johansen go down and Mathers was tangled up with one of them."

"Get those patients behind the LAV!" Dahl snapped at a nearby corpsman. "Where's the goddamn QRF?" She glanced quickly at Manderson, then back at the door.

"I don't know." Manderson replied and toggled his radio. "Anvil Control, Anvil Control. This is War Angel, priority." He waited a moment, listening to the static and squealing from the radio circuit. "Anvil Control, War Angel. Requesting immediate QRF to the south aid station for enemy in the tunnel, over." He listened again for a moment, then tried again. "Anvil Control, Anvil Control. War Angel. Do you copy?" He looked at Dahl. "I don't think they're hearing us."

"Send a runner." She snapped. "One of the pilots."

"Genova! Moretti!" Manderson called. From the darkness of the hangar, a voice replied promptly.

"Here, Major." A tense voice replied out of the gloom.

"I need you two to haul ass across the crater to the TOC. Tell them we got gomers in the tunnels and need the QRF. Also tell them that the south aid station is out of the fight."

"You got it." Rocco hefted his rifle and looked at Moretti.

"You ready?"

"Fuck no." Moretti replied. "But let's go."

Rocco looked at Manderson. "We'll be back, boss." The two men disappeared at a jog into the darkness, heading for the airlock.

"He's gone." A voice off to the side caught Manderson's attention. He looked over and saw Colonel Douglas, kneeling over a prone armored figure. Manderson pointed at Dahl, "Keep covering that door." The nurse nodded grimly, her eyes not leaving the doorway. Moving quickly, Manderson moved over to the surgeon and looked down. The still figure that he had dragged out of the room was the young flight nurse from the Valkyrie, Captain Matthews. His eyes stared sightlessly at the ceiling and his face was pale. Davoyavich, flight engineer from the grounded rescue ship knelt next to him. Her fine Slavic features were impassive, her face so still it might have been carved from stone. She looked up and Manderson could see the bright sheen of tears in her slate gray eyes.

"He was just a baby." She looked back down at the young man's body. "My son is only a few months older than him." One of her fists balled up. "It's not fair." Her tone changed and hardened. "These fucking monsters. We're going to burn their world for this."

Kneeling, Manderson put his hand on her armored shoulder. "There will be time to mourn later. For now, I need you to pull security." His voice was gentle, but firm.

The woman blinked once, then replied, "Yes, sir." She looked back down at the young man's body, gently laid a hand on the still figure's armored chest and mumbled something in Ukrainian. She then stood and moved to cover the door to the devastated aid station with her snub nosed aircrewman's rifle.

\*\*\*\*

Entering the small personnel airlock that the construction crews had cut, Rocco and Moretti stopped and sealed their flight armor, then checked each other's equipment.

After a few seconds, Rocco asked, "How are you on air and power?"

"78%. Good enough. You?" his co-pilot replied. "You?"

"85%. I'm fine." Rocco replied. He eyed the door and swore under his breath, "Fuck!"

"Yeah," the younger man replied. "I'm sort of regretting talking you into this." His forced grin was clearly visible through his faceplate.

"Wiseass." With a baleful glare at his partner, the pilot hit the switch to depressurize the airlock. There was a blast of air as the pressure changed, then the light over the rough hatch turned green. "Ok," Rocco said. "Let's get to the ops center and get some help, then we can get over to the north aid station and let them know they're on deck." His tone was grim. "Stay low and move fast. I'm gonna be pissed if I have to write a letter to your mother."

"You got it, skipper," Moretti replied, his tone turning serious.

Rocco turned the hatch handle and pushed on the door. Nothing happened. He frowned and then put both hands on the door and leaned his weight into it. "I think it's stuck. That shaking must have jammed it. Help me."

Moving up next to him, Moretti leaned into the door. A few seconds later, he spoke, panting slightly with the effort. "I think it's about there. I felt it move." A few more seconds of pushing, he stood back. "Let's hit it. On three." The two men backed up and counted; and on three, threw their body weight into it. The hatch promptly gave away and sent them both sprawling into the gray-black dust of the surface.

"That was stupid." Rocco growled. "What if we'd torn a suit? These aren't power armor. Fucking hell."

"Well, it worked." Moretti climbed to his feet. "Now we just need to..." His voice trailed off.

"What?" The older pilot rolled over and clambered laboriously to his feet. "Holy shit."

Where the flat floor of the ancient volcano had been clearly visible now stood a towering wall of dust, extending thousands of feet into the air. At the base of the looming cloud, there could be seen the flickering of colors- green, blue and red, occasionally interspersed with sheets of orange that momentarily flashed like lightning. As the two men stood staring in stunned silence, they watched three Marine light armored vehicles tearing across the crater floor enter the dust without even slowing down. A split second after they disappeared, the dust lit up with blue strobe flashing as their mounted lascannons began firing. A moment later, there was a bright orange flash, followed by several dimmer flashes. The distant rumble of the explosions washed over the two men, breaking through the shock. The snapping of UEA rifle fire and the hissing of the Elai weapons was clearly audible between the rolling booms of explosions.

"Holy shit." Moretti started. "Are they...wow."

"It looks like there's a hell of a fight going on over there." Rocco replied, his eyes locked on the scene unfolding across the crater floor. "In fact..."

"We need to hurry." Moretti said abruptly. "If those little bastards come through the tunnels again..."

"Right," Rocco shook his head and checked the compass in his helmet display. "Except there's a problem." He pointed at the right side of the dust cloud, where the Marine armored vehicles had entered. "According to my map, the operations center is under there."

"Shit!" Moretti swore. "How are we going to get to it?" He shook his head. Their command circus is still down, I just checked."

Not answering, Rocco stared at the chaos, then suddenly spoke. "The Valkyrie has a lot stronger radios than these shitty suit comm systems. Maybe we can use those to punch through that crap."

"Worth a try and if it doesn't work...". Moretti paused, then sighed," Well, fuck it. Let's go."

The two men moved off at a jog towards the flat area several hundred yards away where they had set their damaged rescue ship down a week prior. Occasionally they would flinch as a large explosion echoed across the mile wide crater floor.

After a few minutes of running, Moretti panted, "The dust is getting thicker." He gestured at the spacecraft ahead of them. The outlines of the chunky search and rescue vessel were becoming obscured by the billowing dust. Risking a look behind them, he added, "I can barely see the hanger anymore either."

Not replying, Rocco motioned that they hurry and the two men resumed their fast jog. Momentarily, they were alongside the spacecraft and climbing aboard and clambering forward to the cockpit. A moment later, Moretti powered up the life support. As the cabin pressurized, the two men professionally ran the power up checklist, then satisfied that the cabin pressure was holding, removed their helmets.

"Fuck, that sucked." Moretti muttered, still panting. "I need to do more cardio."

"Tell me about it." Rocco replied, trying to catch his breath. He snapped the toggle to the radios and spoke rapidly. "Anvil Station, Valkyrie One." He hesitated a moment, then spoke again. "Anvil Station, Valkyrie One."

"Try the landing and emergency freqs." Moretti suggested, tapping the controls.

The senior pilot grunted and repeated the call several times, then disgustedly replied. "Nothing. It's like they aren't there."

"Well *clearly* someone is alive and kicking out there," Moretti replied. "Look at that shit!" He gestured at the flashes of light from the firefight.

"Doesn't mean their command and control is intact, mister." Rocco replied, acidly. "Visibility is going to shit too. Let me try low light." He reached over and toggled a switch. The screen turned a washed out green and black, with occasional waves of billowing dust. With a growl, he turned it off. "Nope. Too much crap in the air reflecting light."

"Try the landing imaging radar," Moretti replied. Rocco grunted and hit another control. The screen lit up, the billows of gray dust and flashing of the energy weapons overlaid with a computer generated image of the crater. The two men stared in awe at the several hundred meters of collapsed crater wall and the resulting piles of rubble. The landing radar software began tagging identified vehicles as the data came in. A split second later, several large red circle appeared and the onboard threat warning indicator went off.

"We're being targeted! Shut that off!" Moretti yelled. Rocco slammed the switch and the screen went dark. A split second later, the warning indicators shut off.

With a shaky look at Moretti, he muttered, "Little bastards must be targeting active radar."

"Yeah. I don't think we should do that again," Rocco replied, his face white.

"What now?" There was a moment of dead silence in the cockpit.

After a few seconds, Rocco replied. "I don't know." He pointed at the dust cloud. "The Marines are busy. I think we're on our own for the moment."

"And we got compromised tunnels." The younger pilot scowled and ran a hand through his hair. "I guess we go back and tell the major…"

"Tell him what?" Rocco shot back. "That there's no backup plan in case we have to unass the tunnels? Because in case you missed it, the tunnels WERE the backup plan."

"We got all that shit for the field hospitals stuffed into the broken shuttle over on Pad Two. Can we use that?" Moretti persisted. "There's got to be something they can do with it."

Rocco stared at the instrument panel for a moment, then reached up and tapped a switch. A wireframe display of the tunnel as their radar had imaged it appeared. He stared at it for several long moments, then pointed. "Look at that." His finger stabbed at a large protrusion of rock. "See that? Pad Two is behind it and that little ridge there is between the pad and that shit." He gestured at the breach in the crater wall.

"Okay," Moretti replied, studying the image. "What are you proposing?"

"That we use all the hostile environment shelters and the shuttle itself as a fallback aid station." He pointed at the bulk of the shuttle. "It's shot up, but the drives are still ok and it holds pressure. There's our heat and power. We don't even need life support units."

"You mean tents," said Moretti, flatly. "They're reinforced, pressurized tents."

"Well…yeah, unless you got a better idea." Rocco replied.

The two men traded a long look.

After a moment, Moretti muttered, "This idea sucks."

"Yep, but we're about down to that level." Rocco picked up his helmet. "Let's talk to Manderson and see what he thinks." He put on his helmet and sealed it. "You call the Marine HQ and see if you can get them with the main radios. I'll call the Major."

With a last look at the display, Moretto muttered, "Tents. Fuck!" He then put on his helmet and began keying up the radio systems.

# Chapter 16

## "Every Marine a Rifleman"

*Forward Operating Base Anvil*
*Remains of the Primary Defensive Line*

Tony rolled over and sat up. The motion knocked a shower of dust and small chunks of plast-crete from the bunker ceiling off of his armor. Disoriented, he shook his head, trying to clear the wooziness. Reflexively, he checked his armor instruments. Seals intact, servos functional, power within normal levels. Looking around the dusty bunker, he could see the jumbled bodies in power armor starting to stir.

With a burst of profanity, the dust covered armored suit next to him sat up and flipped up its blast visor, revealing the sergeant major. Seeing Tony, the stocky man stopped swearing and asked, "You good, sir?"

Looking around at the groaning and battered Marines and the still body of their fallen corporal, Tony replied, "I'm good. We need to get to the ops center." He stood up and, reaching out, hauled the sergeant major to his feet. Looking Hat the private now tending the Marine who had been blinded on the gun, Tony said, "We'll send a corpsman and reinforcements." Turning to their guard, he ordered, "You stay here, with them. Get this position up."

The Marine looked up and nodded, "Yes, sir. We'll be here." The Marine looked at the bunker's firing slit and declared, "I think the Mark 30 is fucked but we can hold." Pulling the Marine with the burned face up to his feet, he said, "Come on, Martinez. On your feet. You ain't that blind. Link your visor to mine and get on the line, Marine."

With a nod to the three Marines manning the bunker, Tony

and Jiminez exited and entered the trench line. The dust hung heavy in the air, making visibility extremely limited. Tony could see maybe three or four meters, then the swirling gray dust obscured visibility. As they moved, Tony looked down the trench, squinting in the poor light.

Stopping, he said, "Sergeant Major, hold up." He walked a dozen steps down the trench and stopped. He was standing on the edge of a drop off that was where the trench had previously been. The trenchline and the bunkers were gone, replaced by a heap of rubble some twenty meters below them and stretching further into the swirling dust than he could see. Behind him he could hear the sergeant major mutter, "Son of a bitch." Tony pinged his laser rangefinder in his helmet and grimaced as he saw the terrain map update. He stated, "The crater wall has collapsed. We're looking at least a two hundred meter section of rubble- maybe even more."

The sergeant major peered into the dust and announced, "We're wide open, sir. If they hit us, we're fucked." He turned and said in a commanding tone, "Ops center, sir. Now."

The two Marines turned and ran down the trench to the crude staircase and descended into the now dust obscured crater.

\*\*\*\*

Ten minutes later, as they approached the airlock to the tunnel near the operations center, Tony could see shapes in the dust. As they grew closer, he could see Marines and sailors in their combat suits and power armor, moving out of the tunnels. Several of them were setting up portable communications and tactical consoles in a depression in the crater floor, near a large boulder. On the local channel in his helmet, Tony could hear confused chatter.

Moving closer, he saw one of them turn and gesture at him and say "There he is! Major Harris, over here!" The figure beckoned, as the IFF systems in his helmet tagged the man as

Captain Saint, the battalion logistics officer. He declared, "We got problems, sir." The other officer, the personnel officer, Captain Shen, nodded grimly.

Tony looked around at the two staff officers and various enlisted and replied, "No kidding. Where's Major Reyes?"

Shen pointed at the pile of rubble and replied somberly, "We haven't seen anyone from the operations center, sir. We think he didn't make it out."

Stepping up to the display, Tony could see serious faces through the helmet visors. Pointing into the blowing dust, he replied, "Shit. Ok. Well, the crater wall is down on the north face. Not sure how much came down, but we have a big ass hole in our defenses."

Nodding, Captain Saint gestured at the tactical display, "We're getting preliminary laser imaging, sir. Here."

The crater map was glowing on the holo, its usually crisp image distorted and static filled. Tony moved close and peered at it. The blasts had caused a collapse of a three hundred meter section of the north wall of the ancient volcano's rim, leaving a massive pile of rubble.

Tony swore under his breath and asked, "How bad?"

Captain Shen replied, "Not sure. We have at least five hundred meters of tunnel collapsed and the rest of the northeast and northwest sides are unstable as hell. It's why we're out here." He paused, checking to see if the tactical display was set up yet, then continued, "Not sure how many were in that section, but it's a lot. The defenses on top of the collapsed area are gone. We sent out teams to look for survivors, but we aren't finding many." He gestured at the dust, "Between this shit and the EMP, comms are screwed, drones are useless *and* we can't see for shit, so in addition to having our defenses compromised, we're also blind."

A lieutenant in naval construction armor standing nearby spoke up, "Sir, we're stringing cable to the intact defenses, so we'll be able to get comms to what's left of the perimeter, but until we secure that hole..." He stopped and looked at the display before he continued grimly, "You get a defensive line up and we'll get comms to it."

The sergeant major snapped, "Where's the QRF?" He stabbed a finger at the hole and said, "Use them to plug that fucking hole until we get the line reestablished."

Tony nodded and looked at Captain Saint. "Do it. Keep the line intact visually and use runners to communicate back until they get into that rubble pile and dig in." Saint nodded and gestured at a Marine staff sergeant, who sprinted away into the dust.

Leaning over the tactical display, Tony asked, "Who else did we lose in that tunnel, apart from operations?"

With a grim expression, Saint replied, "Supplies, one of the Navy construction crews and their dozer." He shook his head. "We also lost contact with the north aid station."

Tony's head snapped up and his stomach sank, "Entirely?"

Pointing at another part of the map, the junior officer replied, "Yes, sir. All except the Navy surgical team that dropped and the Valkyrie crew. They were posted up over on the far side, in the aid station off of the hangar when the bombs went off." He added, "Major Manderson had his team in their cobbled together power armor, last I saw." The officer motioned towards the collapsed wall. "We got a report of some kind of contact from the south aid station, but nothing since then."

The Sergeant Major snapped at two nearby Marines. "You two. Get your asses over to the south aid station and find out what's going on." They nodded and moved out at a power armor enhanced run.

As the Marines took off, Tony studied the display and muttered, "Shit." Tony shook his head then turned to the Sergeant Major, "What can we do to plug this hole in a hurry?"

Sergeant Major Jimenez put his hands on his hips and stared at the map for a moment, then asked, "Captain Saint, are the Hellhounds still operational?"

The officer tapped the display and three green dots and a

yellow dot shone on the map. He replied, "Yes, Sergeant Major. Looks like Hellhound Four is immobile, but it's at the base of that rubble pile, so it's actually in a pretty good place. The other three are fully functional. Don't know about crew injuries."

The sergeant major nodded and turned to Tony, "Ok, sir. I'd say we get those mechs on the line, one every hundred meters or so with fireteams to support them. Use them as a mobile defensive line until we get trenches dug." He pointed at the map, "That'll help us hold." The stocky man paused and muttered, "I'd kill for some goddamn armor…"

"Sergeant Major?" The engineer officer spoke up, "I don't have armor for you, but I got the next best thing." He gestured to the map, "After we dug the tunnels, the killdozers were parked out in the open, so they're undamaged." He pointed at the map and declared, "They're armored and we have crew served weapons on them. We can cut trenches and defend the line at the same time."

The Sergeant Major raised his eyebrows and looked at Tony, then asked, "How armored?"

The lieutenant shrugged, "Pretty well armored– at least enough to take those Elai shoulder fired rockets without any problems. We can't take on enemy armor but they'll withstand small arms and most infantry portable stuff all right."

Nodding, Tony ordered, "Do it. Get them started cutting trench lines."

The engineer nodded, turned and disappeared into the dust. Jimenez turned to Tony, "It's not perfect, but hopefully it'll get a line reestablished before they hit us."

Tony nodded, "Yeah. Hopefully we get the time to get it established." He looked at Captains Saint and Shen and said, "Get a head count of who we have combat effective and start organizing a second reserve force. That company holding that gap is gonna need help."

Frowning, Jimenez stared at the flickering holodisplay of the crater. After a few seconds, he said, "Major, I recommend we pull a platoon from each company on the crater walls and use them to reinforce the gap. The perimeter is dug in pretty tight, they ought to be ok and if we don't plug this hole fast, we're gonna be in deep shit."

Nodding, Tony ordered, "Get on it." Jimenez turned and started snapping orders to a nearby runner.

There came the crunching of running feet in the dust, causing the men standing at the improvised command post to turn. A private came up, puffing for air. He leaned over and gasped, "Sir, they're here. The patrols are reporting contact in the rubble pile and surrounding tunnels."

Tony looked at the Sergeant Major, who looked back, his face grim, "Well, so much for having time." Tony turned to Captain Saint, "Get moving on that scratch force. We're gonna need 'em." He turned to Captain Shen, "Get comms reestablished. We need reinforcements." The two men nodded grimly and moved to their tasks.

\*\*\*\*

*'Hellhound Lance' Crater Floor*

Captain Chalee nodded at the Marine runner and slid back into the hull of her mech. She keyed the intercom, "Ok, Corporal Yang. Aim for the north wall. Ubuntu, weapons hot." The two crewman acknowledged and as the big walker started lurching towards the ruins of the crater wall, she keyed her radio, hearing the static swelling and surging even over the protected mech's radio system, "Hellhound Lance, Hellhound lead. Advance three five nine, line abreast. Ensure IFF on and go weapons hot." The indicator for her mech's 'identification, friend or foe' system flickered on in her master display.

*"Lead, Two. IFF on, line abreast, copy."* Sergeant Harris's clipped tone replied through the static immediately.

*"Lead, Three. IFF on, line abreast, roger."*

*"Lead, Four. We're deadlined. Our left rear leg is still out; and we're immobile. What do you want us to do? Thad's been*

*out hammering on it, but he says its shot to shit.*"

Tara considered this for a second, then replied, "Deploy the launcher and slave it to me. You guys unass that mech. You're just a target sitting still. Find cover and sit tight."

Sergeant Davis's response came back, "*Ma'am, we're way less use out there than we are in here. We can still use the secondaries and cover the crater floor for stragglers. We'd like to stay with the mech.*"

Tara released the intercom key, pressed her lips together for a moment, then replied, "Four, If you start taking fire, get out. Until then, send a runner to the Marines for a squad for protective detail."

"*Understood, Lead. Four out.*" The connection dropped.

Captain Chalee activated her thermal sights and began to scan the terrain in front of her advancing mechs.

\*\*\*\*

*Forward Operating Base Anvil*
*Improvised Command Post*

"The mechs are moving, sir. Bravo Company is reporting multiple contacts. Their commander says some of them are in those powered suits." The runner coughed and then leaned over, gasping for air.

Tony turned and stared at the holo for a half second, then declared, "We're too far back. With this interference, we're going to lose control of this if we don't get a handle on what's going on."

The sergeant major frowned and then nodded, "I tend to agree, but the closer we get, the higher the risk of having the CP get hit."

Tony nodded and replied, "Well, if we don't, we're gonna get smashed either way. What did that old Marine general say? When in doubt, attack?"

With a grimace, Jiminez replied, "Patton. He was an Army

general, but your point is well taken. Captain Saint's scraped up about a hundred people in his scratch force– mostly support troops. Cooks, mechanics, pretty much anyone he saw. He's going to blow out one of the emergency exits from the intact section of tunnel and hit them in the flank. We just need to hold them until they get into position." He looked at the billowing dust. "Gonna be tight."

Tony reached down and picked up his rifle and smiled grimly, "Alright then, Sergeant Major. You know the deal. Every Marine a rifleman."

Picking up his rifle, the Sergeant Major grinned, "Goddamn right, sir." He turned to the Marines manning the station and ordered. 'Pack it up. We're moving forward."

\*\*\*\*

*349th Special Forces Detachment, 'Thundercats'*
*Fifteen Kilometers north of FOB Anvil*
*Hill 236*

Major Tulp leaned forward and examined the Elai body in front of him. The armor was battered, scorched and had a large hole burned in the chest armor. Spotting something, he reached down to the left shoulder of the body and pulled a soot covered silver disc off of the armor and examined it. It had what looked like a stylized serrated tooth on it, with symbols that he didn't recognize. He turned it over and examined the back, which had only the connecting point and more of the spidery writing.

"Sir, what the fuck happened here?" Master Sergeant Chan was nearby, also looking at the bodies.

Shaking his head, Tulp replied, "No clue, but I've seen this before." He tossed it to the noncommissioned officer, who caught it. As the man looked at it, he added, "I pulled one off of a dead Elai on Paradise. We ambushed them trying to get into this old set of ruins we were trying to exploit, then they brought friends back and tried to overrun us. Damn near succeeded, too."

Chan examined the disk and asked, "Unit patch?"

Tulp shrugged, "Don't know. If it is, why kill them?" He pointed at the direction the Elai main body had gone and added, "They clearly aren't out of the fight yet." Hearing the hissing of hover vehicles in the distance, he turned and raised his rifle over his head and activated his IFF beacon. Approaching in a cloud of dust was a Marine fast attack vehicle, with others behind it. The turret alertly pointed at them, then the barrel raised. The vehicle pulled up and slowed and a power armored head popped out.

A Marine lance corporal popped out, leaned on the edge of the hatch, grinned at Tulp and said, "Need a lift, sir?"

Grinning back, Tulp replied. "As a matter of fact, yes. We'd love one. Need your CO first, though."

The Marine jerked a thumb behind him, "You're in luck, sir. Fifth vehicle back is Ironjaw Six." He looked at the dozens of dead Elai lying around them and said, admiringly, "Goddamn, sir! Did you guys do all this?"

Master Sergeant Chan responded, with a straight face, "That's need to know only, Lance. Call the command vehicle, let Ironjaw Six know that Thundercat Three Two has time sensitive intel for him."

"Roger that, Master Sar'nt." The Marine nodded and disappeared into the hull of his armored vehicle.

\*\*\*\*

Twenty minutes later, Tulp finished giving a brief overview of what he had seen to General Piasecki. He fell silent as the Marine general sat back and frowned, the motion making the metal of the prosthetic in his face glint menacingly.

After a moment, the general stated thoughtfully, "Well, there's clearly internal factions. My divisional intel guys think the same thing. The bigger ones in red are aggressive and well equipped, but don't seem as experienced. The smaller ones in the older uniforms with the blue tints and the other emblem are way more dangerous, due to their tactical flexibility."

Tulp nodded silently in agreement but said nothing.

The general gestured at one of his staff officers sitting at a console in the armored vehicle and continued, "Mitch there thinks that we've got two forces. One comprised of veterans and experienced in dealing with us and the other a new, relatively untested faction." Pointing at the map on the display in between them, he declared, "The area we just smashed through was the blue guys, but we hit three assault shuttles as they tried to lift out a few hours ago that were manned by these red guys. Looks like the troops that came in on them got wiped out by the strike from these guys and the survivors shot."

With an expectant look at the young special forces officer, the general demanded, "Analysis, captain. Don't hold back."

Leaning back, Tulp rubbed his face, then said, "Sir, I think the Elai forces here on this moon are about to fall apart, if they haven't already. What that means for us, I have no idea." He stopped for a moment, then added, "I'd add just this: Keep your eyes peeled. Tell your guys to be alert and report anything weird."

The general folded his arms and regarded the exhausted special forces officer, "Such as?"

Tulp shook his head wearily, "Sir, I'll be damned if I know, but I suspect you'll know it when you see it."

# Chapter 17

## "Under Bright Starlight"

*355th Forward Deployed Resuscitation Team*
*The far side of the Crater Floor*

"The shelters are up, sir and we'll have them linked to the shuttle power supply in the next five minutes. You can start moving the rest of the team in." The voice of one of the Seabees crackled through Manderson's radio. He tapped the acknowledge button, then turned and keyed his suit radio to speak to his team.

"Ok. The hard sides are up and Dahl has surgery and the intensive care beds up and running. It's going to be cold as hell inside, but we'll be able to breathe and they'll keep people alive." He looked at his dwindling team. The weary faces of the remaining medical personnel looked grimly back. "We'll start by moving the remaining wounded we can't push off to the line companies into the shuttles. The rest of the hard sides we'll use for triage and evaluating and treating minor wounds. Everyone got that?"

There was no reply, just tense nods and mutters of assent. Manderson shook his head once, then turned and ordered, "Agawa. Get them moving. I'll bring up the rear."

The NCO motioned to the medical team to follow him. They were lined up behind him, each carrying their weapon and loaded down with as many supplies as they could scavenge. One at a time, they slipped into the emergency airlock and disappeared. Manderson took another look at the hatch that led to the ruins of the aid station. Two Marines were there crouched behind a stack of crates, with a mounted lascannon pointing down the corridor. He shook his head and swore under his breath, then stepped into the airlock.

Stepping out onto the surface for the first time in several days, Manderson was startled at how difficult it was to see with all of the dust in the air. Even with the virtual reality augmentation in his power armor visor, he was almost unable to make out the line of troops several meters ahead of him as they filed towards the improvised aid station. To the north, there was the steady flickering of weapons fire, diffused by the billowing dust. The lack of substantial atmosphere to transmit sound meant that it was a silent light show- a multicolored, flickering display that was almost beautiful, if one didn't think about what the flashing and brief pale orange-red blossoms represented. Manderson gritted his teeth and continued to trudge forward. The gusts of wind buffeted him as he followed the spectral shapes in the dust. Distantly, he wondered what time it was and was shocked when the chronometer in his helmet told him it was near the local noon. The light of Draconis 327 above them wasn't that bright on a clear day, but the dust was so thick as to make it a semi-permanent twilight.

The path twisted and wove around several large rocks. The shape ahead disappeared, leaving Manderson alone, with nothing but the dust and debris left from the constant bombardment half buried on either side of the trail. To the left was the ghostly shape of a stricken Marine assault vehicle. Next to it were several mech legs, their massive bulk twisted and blackened by violence. Smashed open equipment cases, piles of woven duracloth, wire and a thousand other items littered the area– the debris of war. He's seen it before and it was always the same. Shaking his head, Manderson picked up the pace and followed his comrades.

Rounding the corner, he could see bulky shapes of vehicles and buildings ahead through the swirls of dust. The long, flat shape of the damaged assault shuttle was clear; set down on a flat area in a depression in the crater floor. Sprawling out from the large rear doors was a mishmash of portable buildings. A section of duraweave tent serving as a breezeway connecting a battered maintenance shelter caught his eye. Next to it was another Marine LAV with three wheels missing on one side, hurriedly connected with what looked like a section of tunnel liner, sealed with spray foam. As he moved closer, He realized that he could see shapes moving around inside some of the tents, illuminated from behind like some grotesque puppet show. He had a momentary image of himself as a puppet, dancing to the whims of an unseen puppeteer light years away, while around him other puppets in power armor like the one he was wearing danced and jerked mechanically, then collapsed and died as the strings were cut. Manderson shook his head hard, dismissing the vivid image. He was tired, but not that tired. There was still work to do. There was a soft chime from his armor. He glanced at the instruments in the heads-up display and noted that his carbon dioxide scrubber canister only had twelve hours left. He shook his head and silenced the alarm, then picked up the pace and covered the last couple dozen meters quickly.

As he did, he saw two figures in light combat armor raising several flags over the improvised hospital. The first that went up was the ubiquitous white flag with a red cross. Good. Someone inside had realized that the aid stations were no longer marked and decided to mark it themselves. The second was one that he recognized from a distance- off of the tail of the damaged search and rescue craft. It was the figure of a woman with wings, holding a sword and shield, leaping forward as if into battle. A corona of energy blazed off of the shield as she flew forward. The two suited figures ran the flags up the pole, then pushed a button that electrified the nanocarbon tubules, giving them the appearance of fluttering in the wind. They stood motionless for a moment, probably conversing; then a large explosion echoed nearby, causing them to flinch, then run for the improvised airlock nearby. Manderson stood for a second, watching the war angel banner flying over the improvised hospital, then set his jaw grimly and strode forward. There was still a fight going on, he and his battered team still had a job to do.

Two figures in powered armor came around a building. One of them called out, "Major Manderson."

Looking over, Manderson saw that the two were in the armor of the naval construction crews. The two men approached and Manderson could see their tired faces through their faceplates. One of them was an officer with the insignia of a lieutenant, the other a petty officer. The officer spoke. "So, we've got four of the tactical shelters linked with pressure vestibules. Operating rooms and the most critically wounded are in the shuttle. Your power is also coming from the shuttle, so no need for generators." The young man shook his head. "It ain't pretty, but we've got power and heat."

"Almost too much heat." The petty officer added. "We're routing part of the reactor waste heat through the hospital as a heating system and it's almost too hot in a lot of the buildings."

"Yeah and the parts that don't have it are close to freezing." The officer finished. "This job is improvised as hell, but it's the best we can do. Most of my men are cutting defensive lines." He gestured at the petty officer. "I can leave you Micheals. His suit is busted and can't go more than twelve hours without a battery charge, so he needs to stay close to a power source. He can be your onsite support. I have to get back up to the line." The officer turned to Micheals and extended a hand, "Be safe, man."

The petty officer shook the offered hand. "You too, sir. Good luck." He nodded at the hospital. "Try not to come see us, eh?"

"I'll do what I can." The lieutenant nodded at Manderson. "I don't know how much more we can support you, so Chief Micheals is probably it. I'm leaving him with as much equipment as we can spare to patch and repair this place, but we're not at all sure how long it's going to hold up. Keep people in their armor as much as possible and seal all the internal hatches. I don't think you'll have any blowouts but if they hit us with nukes again, all bets are off." He looked to the north, where the flickering colors of the fighting had faded but were still visible and shook his head. "My recommendation is to get back in the tunnels as fast as possible."

"Noted." Manderson replied, "As soon as the Marines say it's safe, we'll move back into the south hangar."

The engineer hesitated for a second, then shook his head again and offered his hand. "Yeah. Good luck, sir."

"You too." Manderson shook the offered hand. The engineer turned to speak to the petty officer again, giving some last minute instructions.

Entering the portable airlock, Manderson felt the buffeting that told him the pressure was equalizing outside of his suit. When the interior door chimed and the light turned green over the top, he stepped forward and opened the hatch. Entering, the first thing he noticed was the slipshod nature of the building. The naval construction engineers had thrown up the pressure tents directly on the ground, then sprayed the ground with plascrete setting agent. The result was a rock hard rough surface, with the footprints and scrape marks of tools in it as the setting agent had hardened the dust as it had lain. Manderson reached up and opened the faceplate of his armor. Immediately, a gust of warm, almost hot air slapped him with a dozen unpleasant scents. The plastic-acetone stink of the flooring, combined with the musty smell of the tent pressure liners were prominent, all mixed with the ages-old smell of healthcare-powerful disinfectant and, underlying it all, the sickly-sweet smell of burning flesh from the operating room.

Inside the entry vestibule, Dahl was waiting. She had her helmet open and Manderson noted a large bruise on her left cheek. "Welcome to Valhalla." The nurse said flatly and gestured for him to follow her.

"What?" Manderson replied. "Valhalla?"

"Yeah. You know. The hall of the dead? Where the warriors go to drink and fight all day, then to be brought back from the dead to do it again for all eternity?" She pointed down a corridor shooting off at a crazy angle and kept walking. "Minimal care ward." Manderson nodded, looking where she pointed.

"How'd it get that name?" Manderson peered down the corridor, noting the ice crystals on the door at the far end of the corridor, then followed as Dahl continued to walk rapidly down the hall.

"One of the Marines has been wounded seriously four or five times now and keeps being brought in, then sneaking back out to get back to his unit. He's convinced he's dead and in Valhalla." She pointed left, then right at a corridor junction and kept moving. "Operating room and sterile processing." She paused, then added, "Plus, I'm one of the Valkyrie crew." She shook her head. "Normally, I'd have him on a psych hold if we had the room, but we don't."

Nodding, Manderson followed, listening as the nurse methodically briefed him. "He's not the only one, either." She gestured at a wall of plassteel that made up one side of the corridor. "Shuttle 215, now known as the hospital powerplant and comm center." She pointed at a vent as they passed by it. "Careful with that. It's a plasma vent turned down as low as the engines will go, but it's still hot enough to burn the shit out of you. We have the other one connected to makeshift ductwork to heat the rest of the place."

"Clever." Manderson observed.

"I guess. It makes some areas hot as hell and in others there's ice forming on the walls. This is critical care." She stopped. "We've got thirty two men and women in there on stretchers. We've got them still in their armor to keep them warm and to monitor their vital signs. Their suits are plugged into a jury rigged charger so they don't run out of power. We're inventorying our medical supplies again, but we don't have a lot left." She paused, then added flatly. "I've got a couple of sailors going through the power armor on the guys in the morgue. They don't need their power packs or aid kits."

Nodding somberly, Manderson replied. "Yeah." He paused a moment, remembering when he'd had to make much the same decision years before, then repeated. "Yeah. It's a hard call, but the right one." He looked Dahl in the eyes. "You're doing a good job." Suddenly, he laughed. "I was going to call you by your first name, but I don't know it."

"It's Susan." Dahl replied, in a low voice.

"Susan, I'm Micheal." He reached out to her and grabbed her armored hand in his and squeezed it. "And we're going to be ok."

A distant explosion echoed off of the walls of the crater and the floor of the improvised hospital trembled.

"Don't make promises you can't keep, Micheal." The nurse replied, with a twist of her lips that was almost a smile. "Follow me. There's a few more things to show you, then we're going to grab Agawa and have a meeting about longer term operations."

"Lead the way." Manderson replied and followed the nurse into the improvised hospital.

\*\*\*\*

Thirty minutes later in the crowded compartment that had been the shuttle's tiny common room, Dahl raised her voice. "Ok. Pipe down, people. Let's get this shit started." She looked at a datapad, then back up. "The reorganized chain of command is Major Manderson, then myself. The senior noncommissioned officer is Master Sergeant Agawa, I'll be acting as the exec." Her piercing glare swept the small compartment as if daring people to challenge the fact. "This is the first staff meeting of the War Angels." She looked down at her datapad. "First, supply." She looked at Agawa. "Master Sergeant?"

"Yeah." Agawa replied. "We did an inventory of all consumable medical supplies and did a pretty thorough scavenging job of the shuttles and damaged vehicles. We've also stripped everything we can from the area support companies without impairing the guys out on the line." He looked apologetic. "Long story short, if we keep on with current consumption of supplies, we've got about twenty four hours remaining at the current operational tempo. We may be able to stretch that to thirty six if we do some improvising, but anything past that?" Agawa shrugged, his normally cheerful demeanor somber. "We're going to be non-mission capable as a surgical element." He looked at a tired looking captain across from him. "Sooner if we run out of anesthetics."

"How much anesthesia do we have left?" Dahl demanded. "I need numbers."

The captain rubbed his shaved head. "Maybe two days? It's calculated in number of major and minor cases and if my math is right, we've got enough for about a dozen major cases and maybe thirty or so minor cases."

"Can we stretch that?" Manderson asked.

The officer hesitated for a moment, then replied, "Not safely."

With a sigh, Dahl replied. "Ok. Call it a dozen major cases left." She made a note on her pad, then looked up. "Thanks, Darryl." Her normally hard expression was compassionate.

The young anesthetist nodded wearily and replied. "I gotta get back to the OR." He worked his way out of the crowded compartment.

"Ok." Dahl replied. "We're ok on food, water, power and air for the moment, so we don't need to worry about that."

"Ammunition." Agawa interjected. "We're low."

"How low?" Manderson asked.

"Low. Two to three magazines apiece." Agawa replied. "Most of us gave what we could spare to the line troops as they went forward to fill the gap."

"Damn. That is low." Manderson frowned, thinking for a moment then shook his head. "Well. I hate to say it, but it doesn't matter that much. If the Elai break through the lines, there's not much we're going to be able to do to stop them." He looked at Dahl. "How much warning will we get if the line breaks?"

"Sir, at this point I suspect the first warning we're going to get is when they show up." Agawa replied, calmly. "I've got some of the less seriously wounded on observation duties in some of the outlying vehicles and buildings, but it's not going to be much time at all. Ten minutes at most? I don't know." She hesitated, then added, "I'm working on a contingency plan, but it's not a good one."

Drumming his fingers on a nearby console, Manderson didn't reply. After a few seconds, he sighed deeply and looked up. "Well. Like I said. It is what it is. Do we have an evac plan for this place yet?"

"Yes, sir. It's not a good plan either." Dahl replied. He lips twisted with the hint of a smile. "It's to go back into the tunnels we just left with as many people and as much stuff as we can carry."

"The tunnels. Jesus." Manderson muttered. "You're right, that's not a good plan either."

"Sorry, boss. Best I could come up with given what we're working with." Dahl apologized.

"No apologies needed." The officer stated clearly. "You're doing a good job in bad circumstances. Keep at it." He looked at the small group of dirty, tired people and added, "You're all doing the best you can. All we gotta do is hang on. The fleet will be back any day now."

"We're hanging, sir." A petty officer in the doorway observed. "But from where I stand it's a long drop from the end of the rope and we're getting damn close."

There were mutters of agreement. A clear voice broke through the murmur. "Where the hell is the god damn fleet?"

"They'll get here when they get here. Until then, we have work to do." Dahl replied coldly. "Now back to work. Report supply issues to Master Sergeant Agawa. Next synch meeting will be at twenty one. Dismissed."

As the group moved towards the door of the compartment, Dahl leaned close to Manderson. "Please tell me the fleet is coming and that wasn't just bullshit for the troops." Her icy blue eyes locked onto his.

Meeting her gaze, Manderson replied. "They're coming." He broke eye contact and involuntarily looked upwards at the ceiling of the small cabin. "They have to."

"Ma'am," the young crewman on the communication console suddenly blurted. "Incoming flash traffic from brigade!"

Dahl gestured at the young man. "Let's hear it."

Nodding, the soldier replied in a numb, emotionless tone, "The operations center is reporting that a company sized element of enemy infantry have broken the lines and are advancing along two three zero." He looked up. "They're ordering us to fall back into the tunnels until the QRF gets here."

Manderson turned to Dahl. "How long do you think it will take to get the most critically wounded out?"

The blonde woman had been leaning over the console, checking the distance of the reported enemy soldiers. "Too long." She pointed at the screen. "That's their last reported position. We're here. If they don't stop, we've got about thirty minutes. It took three hours just to get the patient from the tunnels in here and we've got more wounded now." To the communications tech, she demanded, "What was Rattlesnake's ETA?"

"They didn't give us one, ma'am," The young man replied. "All they said was that 'They were on the way'." Pointing at the screen, he added, "Brigade committed the last of its reserves to the line about an hour ago. I don't know if the QRF was part of it or not. If they were, they're a ways away."

Dahl straightened up and pushed a stray piece of hair out of her face. She pressed her lips together for a moment, then said, "Ok." She clapped the soldier on the shoulder. "Let me know the second you hear from Rattlesnake."

"Yes, ma'am." The man turned back to his console. Dahl looked at Manderson and spoke in a low tone. "The QRF isn't going to get here in time."

"I know."

The woman's eyes bored into him, then she said, "Shall I order the evacuation?"

Manderson took a deep breath and nodded. "Yeah. Sickest first, carried by the walking wounded. Get our surgeons out with them. We can't lose them."

"No. We can't." Dahl hesitated, then shook her head. "Fuck it. I can't stop them, so I might as well tell you. Some of the patients have a plan to defend the hospital in case we have to fall back."

"The patients?" Manderson asked, surprised, "Everyone who can't get back on the line is pretty badly wounded. I don't see how much good they can do."

"Nevertheless, they have a scratch force put together. One of the Gunnery Sergeants has them staged in a tent to the north." She smiled hollowly, "He's an indomitable one, that Marine."

"Let's go see what their plan is."

Dahl nodded and tapped the communications soldier on the shoulder. "Signal Master Sergeant Agawa. Tell him to execute the retrograde plan, immediately."

"Yes, ma'am."

Dahl turned to Manderson. "Follow me. Let's go talk to them and see if we can help them out." She left the compartment and Manderson followed. As she squeezed through the breezeways and tents of the suddenly bustling improvised hospital, she spoke. "Gunny Nichols came in a couple days ago. He's got some pretty bad burns and since we don't have a working dermal regenerator, he's been hanging out here helping us, since he can't get into his armor."

"The pain?" Manderson asked.

"Yeah. It's excruciating for him and he's not exactly the wilting violet type, either. This way." She took a turn and continued speaking. "So the Gunny came to me yesterday and informed me that we're sitting ducks out here and that he and some of the other patients had formed a couple squads to defend the perimeter if necessary."

"He's not wrong." Manderson muttered. "Our ass is flapping in the breeze out here."

"Yep." Dahl stopped at a portable airlock and heaved the door open, then entered. "Close it behind you. This area isn't heated." Manderson nodded and closed the hatch. Even through his thick power armor, he could feel the chill on his face and see his breath puffing in the cold air. Shivering, he turned his suit heater up.

Entering the temporary shelter, Manderson saw about twenty men and women, their armor all displaying battle damage. One man had an arm that was clearly nonfunctional and someone had spot welded the suit arm to his in an improvised sling. He had a large sack at his hip, lashed to his armor. Another woman lay slumped against the wall, her face pale, panting. A man knelt next to her, checking her medical readout. Others sat or stood, checking weapons and stuffing magazines onto their kit.

In the front of the tent was the massive armored bulk of a man; huge even without the bulk of his armor, with dark skin and piercing eyes. The mottled slate gray of his armor suggested that it had been exposed to intense heat, but his face was calm and composed and he moved from person to person in the room, giving instructions and quiet words to each. Seeing Dahl, he crossed the shelter, stepping around the wounded Marines. A limping corporal followed him, her frame seeming like a child next to the massive man.

"Captain Dahl." His voice was a deep baritone, with a flawless English accent. "Good to see you. I've been monitoring the traffic and Corporal Lopez and I have a plan."

"Let's hear it." Dahl replied.

The corporal unrolled a display sheet and tapped the edge. The image turned into a local map. Using his finger as a stylus, Nichols drew as he spoke. "There's a ridge about five hundred meters north of the hospital. We're going to set up a defensive line on the reverse slope and slow them down." He tapped the map. "They'll likely flank here, that's when we're going to fall back and get down to here at these two tractors." He tapped the line. "That's getting close to the hospital, so the security detail can help cover us from their fighting positions as we move."

"What's the plan to coordinate with the QRF?" Manderson asked, staring at the map.

The corporal grunted. "Tell 'em to look for the fireworks. They'll see us."

"Any feedback, sir?" The Gunnery Sergeant asked. "Because if not, we have to get moving. We don't have a lot of time."

With another last, hard look at the map, Manderson shook his head, then looked at the battered Marines in the room and shook his head. "Can they…" He stopped looking for the right words.

Calmly, Nichols replied. "They'll be fine, sir. They're all volunteers." The big man looked at the battered troops with an unreadable emotion in his eyes. "They know what's at stake." He looked back at the officer and gave a half smile. "Besides, I'm not sure you could stop them. Those are their mates back there in hospital."

Manderson shook his head. "I get it, but some of these people should be evacuated." He indicated the Marine nearby with his armor spot welded to his chest. "That guy can't even use both arms."

With a tight smile, the senior noncommissioned officer replied, "No, but what you don't know about that guy is that he's a five time Tau Ceti University zero gravity racquetball champion known for his powerful serve." He indicated the bag at the man's hip. "He can sling those grenades upwards of two kilometers in this gravity and drop them into a space the size of a barrel."

"I guess." Manderson shook his head. "What can we do to help?" He noticed that the gunnery sergeant's armor was emitting a small stream of mist that smoked in the cold from a crack in his chest plate. Pulling a tube of suit putty from his belt, Manderson stepped forward and said, "You got a crack in your suit. Let me." He held up the sealant. Nichols nodded and stooped to allow the officer to apply the patch putty.

As he did, Dahl asked, "How are your burns?"

"They hurt, but I'll be ok." The big man gestured at his neck. "This is the worst of it. The rest I lathered a numbing cream on then about a centimeter thick. It should let me function."

"Gunny, those are second degree burns." Dahl protested. "That numbing cream is going to make them worse. It's not supposed to be used for that." Manderson finished applying the sealing putty and smoothed it down, pressing hard.

The Marine winced as he did, clearly feeling the pressure of his suit pushing on his tortured flesh, then looked at Dahl. "I'll worry about that later." He looked at Manderson. "All set?"

"Yeah." Manderson put the tube away and turned to Dahl. "Everyone who can carry a weapon and isn't actively moving or caring for patients needs to be in the trenches on the hospital perimeter."

"They are." The woman replied. To Nichols she said, "Get moving and be careful. We need you back alive."

With a confident grin, the big man replied, "Oh, I'll be fine. Takes a lot more than a little alien energy weapons fire to kill a Royal Marine." Aside to the hard faced corporal, he ordered, "Form 'em up. Let's get ready to move."

The petite woman nodded once and turned, "Ok, Marines. On your feet. Time to earn that combat pay." The group stood, some of them assisting others, more badly injured and lined up at the exterior airlock. The corporal stood next to the airlock leading to the surface. "Ok. When we drop this, we're gonna haul ass to the main line of resistance at rally point zeta and see if we can get there first. Echelon one, you're with me. Echelon two, you're with the Gunny. If we can, we ambush them and kick their teeth in. If we can't, we'll move to attack and kick their teeth in. Either way, we're kicking their teeth in.

Got it, Marines?"

There was a chorus of affirmative replies, to which the corporal nodded. "Damn right. Seal your armor and keep those weapons on safe. This ain't the god damn army." Catching Gunnery Sergeant Nichols eye, she gave a thumbs up, then sealed her armor. The massive NCO nodded and looked at Dahl. "Is it too late to ask you on a date?" His eyes twinkled and he put on his helmet.

"You gotta live for that." Dahl shot back, her voice breaking. "Go kick some ass, Gunny."

"Kicking ass is all I do, Captain." He closed the visor or his helmet and turned to face the troops. On the outside of the visor was a holographic imprint of a laughing skull smoking a cigar. His augmented voice boomed from the speakers. "Ok, Marines. Time to go kick a little shark ass. Who's with me?"

The Marines responded with the ancient, guttural cry of their corps. "Uh-rah!"

Manderson and Dahl watched for a second, then turned and stepped back through the airlock and hurried towards the communications center in the wreck of the shuttle. As they did, Manderson's radio came to life.

*"War Angel Six Actual, this is War Angel Ops."*

Keying his radio, Manderson replied. "Go for Six."

*"War Angel Seven Says the first group of patients is staged and ready for evac."*

Overhearing the conversation, Dahl replied, "Those gomers are ten minutes out. If they get past Gunny's troops, they're going to be caught in the open."

"Right." Manderson replied and keyed his radio. "Ops, Six. Tell them to stand by. We'll move them when it's clear." He hesitated a second, then added, "Advise brigade that we're holding the first wave of evacuation until the enemy infantry is neutralized." The soldier acknowledged and signed off just as the two officers entered the operations center.

"Pull up our personnel tracker on the screen." Dahl snapped. The soldier at the operations station tapped several keys and a three dimensional map of the improvised hospital and the surrounding terrain appeared. Two lines of blue dots were moving rapidly out from the hospital. "Open their comms channel, now."

The soldier nodded and tapped more controls. Immediately, they could hear Nichol's voice, his breathing heavy from the exertion of running in power armor. *"Echelon One, get to the ridge and dig in. Get their attention. Echelon Two, come to two three five and hustle. We'll get behind those boulders and hit them from the side once Echelon One engages. Go, go, go!"*

On the screen, the two lines started to diverge, with one peeling off to the side and speeding up and the other spreading out, line abreast.

There were several seconds of silence from the communications panel as the blue dots representing soldiers moved into place.

Suddenly, over the circuit, someone shouted. *"Contact left!"* A blue dot flashed, indicating the soldier had opened fire. Suddenly a dozen or more red dots appeared on the screen as the Marines' power armor targeting sensors detected contacts. Another voice reported, *"We got six of them in the open by that flat rock."* The channel was suddenly flooded with contact reports.

Corporal Lopez's icy voice broke through the chaos. *"Squad One, get the Mark 30 up. Two, cover them!"*

One of the red dots blinked, followed by another, replaced by a tiny red 'x', followed by one of the Marine's changing to the 'KIA' symbol. A voice yelled, *"Emmanual is down! I think he's dead!"*

*"Stay on the fucking line!"* Lopez shouted. *"Keep fire on those fuckers. Check left. LEFT!"*

The red dots indicating the enemy grew more numerous and closer. Marines and enemies fell, their lives ending coldly being displayed as their status changed on the display.

*"Gunny, we could use some help here."* Lopez called, her breathing ragged. *"They're trying to flank us."*

"*On it.*" Nichols replied. "*Echelon Two, hit em!*" The second line of Marines that had been moving into position opened fire, their position markers flickering as they did. The enemy soldiers, instead of facing the new threat, accelerated their attack, rushing towards Lopez's beleaguered force.

"*Lopez, they're trying to get in close with you so we can't fire.*"

"*I see it.*" Lopez snapped. "*Squad Two, fall back to that wrecked LAV. Squad One, stay on that gun!*"

The five remaining Marines from the second squad leapt up and rushed rearward to the cover of a wrecked vehicle. As they did, another symbol changed- another Marine fallen. The four soldiers from first squad remained at the Mark 30, pouring lascannon fire into the oncoming enemies. Suddenly, three of the symbols at the lascannon position winked and changed to red. The fourth was yellow. Manderson and Dahl watched silently.

Several seconds later, Lopez yelled, "*Antigua! Report!*"

There was a pause, then a voice thick with pain replied. "*Antigua's dead. I think they got a grenade in on us.*" There was a pause and then the voice added, "*I think I'm fucked, Corp. My suit is leaking bad and I think I'm hurt again.*"

"*You hang in there Marine!*" Lopez ordered. "*Gunny, do you have eyes on him?*"

"*They're around me now. One of them just looked at me and kept moving. I think they think I'm dead,*" the Marine replied. "*I think...*" He hesitated, then his voice came back stronger. "*Is there anyone left around me?*"

"*I see his position.*" Nichols replied, flatly. "*But he's got a dozen of them around him.*"

"*Corporal Lopez,*" the Marine called again, the pain still clear but his tone firm.

"*You hang in there, Maarten! We're coming for you!*" Lopez yelled. "*Gunny!*"

"*No time, Corporal.*" Maarten replied, numbly. "*I'm disengaging my suit core safeties. Get everyone clear.*"

"*Suppressing fire on the left!*" Lopez shouted. "*Pin them down!*" She drew a deep ragged breath, then replied to Maarten. "*I understand. We're clear. Do what you have to, Ben.*"

Maarten's breathing could be heard in his helmet. "*Ok, they're off. It'll take a few…*"

There was a blink on the monitor and a slight rumble could be felt through the floor of the operations center as the Marine's armor power core detonated. Five of the enemy indicators winked out on the display.

"*Echelon Two, hit em!*" Gunnery Sergeant Nichols powerful voice ordered. The remaining dots from Nichols element surged into action, rapidly closing the gap between the remaining Elai infantry and their position. The two forces collided, with red and blue dots mixing, flashing and winking out.

"What is happening?" The soldier at the operations station whispered, his face pale.

"They're fighting hand to hand." Manderson replied flatly. "Notify Rattlesnake that we have Marine elements in close quarters combat and that extreme caution is advised when engaging enemy hostiles."

"Yes, sir." The soldier bent over his comms station and spoke into his mic. A few seconds later, he looked up, "Rattlesnake is ninety seconds out, sir."

"Alert the trauma bay." Dahl ordered, flatly. "I want litter teams moved to the north side exits. The second our perimeter sees them, I want those litter teams out there. Do it now."

"Yes, ma'am." The soldier acknowledged. The chaotic mix of red and blue flashed and moved on the screen, but the radio was quiet. For what seemed like an eternity, the two officers watched in silence. Suddenly, Lopez's voice broke the silence. "*Rattlesnake, this is War Angel QRF. We have you in sight bearing two two six, six hundred meters. Advise we have troops in close contact with the enemy.*"

On the screen, the boxes indicating the vehicles of the

installation quick reaction force appeared, rushing rapidly towards battle. The red dots began to drop rapidly, then suddenly, there were no remaining.

A few seconds later, Lopez called, *"Echelon One, clear. No remaining hostiles in sight."* Another unfamiliar voice replied a few seconds later, his ident tag flashing as Private First Class Edsel. *"Echelon Two, all clear."*

*"Where's Gunny Nichols?"* Lopez demanded.

*"Gone."* Edsel replied flatly. *"We have three effectives remaining."*

Coldly, Lopez replied. *"Understood. Hold your position for now."*

*"War Angel, Rattlesnake Seven."* The communications panel suddenly spoke.

Manderson keyed his radio. "Go for War Angel."

*"Brigade has reestablished the line and no more should be getting through. They also say you can hold off the evacuation of your position for now. Advise you withdraw your QRF back inside of your perimeter. We will hold a blocking position here for the time being."*

"Understood." Manderson replied, wearily. "Thanks for the help, Rattlesnake."

*"Happy to. Those gomers got damn close. We didn't realize you had a QRF force ready to go."*

"We didn't." The officer replied, grimly. "Those were patients defending the hospital."

The line was silent for several seconds, then the Marine NCO replied somberly. *"I understand. Can't say I wouldn't have done the same, if it were me."* He paused again for a few seconds, then added, *"I've got some of my guys helping bring them back to you."* He hesitated and added, *"All of them."*

"We appreciate it, Rattlesnake. War Angel Six out." Manderson sat the handset down and stared at the display. Lopez's four remaining Marines and the three left from Echelon Two had joined up and were slowly moving back towards the hospital.

Dahl was leaning heavily on the table with both hands, staring at the display. After a few moments, she spoke in a hollow voice. "Is it always like this?"

"No," Manderson replied. "Sometimes it's worse."

"How much worse can it get?" She gestured at the display. "We just watched those people die to save us and we don't even know if we can give them medical care by the end of the day."

"It can always get worse." Manderson looked down, then back up. "But regardless, we still have a job to do."

"God, you suck at being comforting." The woman replied, shaking her head. "I know you mean well but Jesus, Mike."

"Thanks," Manderson replied. "I think." His communicator unit chirped and he looked down at it. "Master Sergeant Agawa just pinged me. He says that there's more patients on the way from the line."

"Back to work," Dahl replied. She pushed her blonde hair out of her face and picked up her helmet. "I'll be in the trauma bay. Let brigade know how short on supplies we are." She shook her head, suddenly looking very tired and very young. "Not that they have any to give us."

"Right." Manderson replied. For a moment, his eyes strayed to one of the cameras showing an exterior view. There were Marines carrying litters with shrouded shapes on them. He watched for a moment, then swallowed hard and turned to his communications panel to once again try to scrape up supplies that would keep them in the fight. Picking up the handset, he saw his hand was trembling. Summoning every scrap of willpower he had, he stared at it, commanding it to stop.

After a few seconds of concentrating, the shaking stopped and Manderson keyed the handset. "Anvil Station, War Angle Six Actual, priority."

The handset hissed and spluttered. "Anvil, War Angel, come in." There was no reply. With a frown, he looked at the comms operator.

"Sorry, sir." The soldier replied, apologetically. "It's all this shit in the air. Sometimes we get them, sometimes we don't. I'll keep trying and call you when I get through."

Manderson nodded, set the handset down and rubbed his face. He could feel the tic in his cheek starting again. The exhaustion threatened to wash over him like a tidal wave. Blowing out a hard breath, he forced himself to focus and headed off in search of Captain Dahl. Striding down an improvised hallway, he suddenly stopped. His head was spinning and his heart was pounding in his ears.

He paused and leaned against the durasteel of the wrecked shuttle hull to steady his balance. He took a few deep breaths and muttered to himself. "Shit." He was tired, but so was everyone. "Keep it together, Mikey." He straightened up and said to himself in a forced confident voice. "Just a few more days. You got this." He hesitated, then nodded firmly and strode off into the maze of improvised tents in search of the captain.

# Chapter 18

## "Damn the Torpedoes"

*Task Force 3.2*
*Interplanetary Space*
*Aboard the UEAN* Stalwart

"Admiral, all ships signal condition Zebra and report ready for jump." The communications officer spoke in a calm, clear tone, breaking the silence on the flag bridge.

"Two minutes to jump," Commander Destin reported from his console.

"Very good, Commander." Admiral Laura Kensington watched as the holographic display updated in the center of the room. The imposing bulk of the two fleet carriers, the *Shiva's Wrath* and the *Athena's Bow* dwarfed the smaller but still deadly cruisers formed around them. The carriers had brought four more cruisers with them, bringing Kensington's battered force up to a total of nine heavy cruisers, two light cruisers and the four carriers.

"We're getting a signal from the *Shiva*. Standby." The communications officer frowned at the screen for a moment, then added. "It's in plaintext, open frequencies."

"Show us." Kensington ordered, leaning forward slightly. At the front of the dimly lit compartment, the holoscreen lit up. The words hung in the air for all to see.

*'THE ALLIANCE EXPECTS EVERY SAILOR SHALL DO THEIR DUTY'*

The commander at the communications station turned to look at Laura. "That's all. I don't know what it means."

With a quiet laugh, the admiral replied, "I do. It means

Admiral Phillips is British and is expecting a fight." Laura frowned for a moment, then smiled tightly and ordered, "Signal the following: 'Close with the Enemy'. Send it in plaintext. He'll know what it means." The watch stander nodded and turned to his console.

"Thirty seconds to jump." The calm voice of Commander Destin reported. The words displayed on the screen in the front of the compartment captured her attention. 'DO THEIR DUTY' burned itself into her mind.

A few seconds later, Laura felt the puzzling sense of disorientation that was always associated with a faster than light jump. The holotank in the middle of the room flickered rapidly, updating. Shaking her head to clear the disorientation, the admiral carefully counted to thirty, then backwards down to zero to clear her mind, then spoke. "Commander de la Cruz, report."

"Yes, Ma'am. Dreadnought Bravo appears to be holding position approximately halfway between the jump point and Objective Onyx. There are ten heavy cruisers in the primary group, with the dreadnought centered in their formation. There are also several destroyers, which appear to be performing anti stealth screens."

The holo tank displayed the formation of the enemy fleet. It appeared to be hanging still in space, despite screaming through the void at thousands of kilometers per second. The imposing bulk of the massive alien warship dominated the center of the holotank. Commander Destin continued, "Intercept in three hours, forty two minutes at current course and speed."

"Very good. Signal the fleet to maintain the current course. Notify me of any changes in enemy formation or course immediately." Laura replied.

"Admiral, preliminary analysis from the intelligence cell suggests that the Elai commander strategy is planning on protecting his dreadnought from missiles with the cruisers' main weapons and protecting the cruisers with the dreadnought's main particle cannons." A transparent red sphere popped onto the screen, encompassing the enemy fleet. "This is the maximum effective range of the particle cannons, as projected from our last encounter." He looked at the Admiral. "It is a formidable and effective defensive strategy. Since we don't use cannons as primary weapons systems, there is little in current naval doctrine that is of assistance."

Leaning forward and staring at the screen, Laura chewed her lower lip, thinking. After a few seconds, she spoke without taking her eyes off the screen. "Captain Soklov. I need options. Get the intel and ops cells on the carriers together and get me courses of action. You have one hour."

"Aye, Admiral." The stoic Russian officer rumbled and turned to his console, slipping on a headset.

"Commander Destin, Commander de le Cruz, start running back all fleet engagements in this system from the initial actions and forward your observations to Captain Soklov's working group. Let's see if they have any patterns we can exploit." She pointed at the holodisplay. "This bastard's smart and we've already underestimated him once. He's not going to do that again."

"Aye, Ma'am." The two officers turned to their tasks.

Sitting back in her chair, Laura frowned at the holoscreen and muttered, "You're a tough bastard, you scaly little shit. But we'll crack you yet."

\*\*\*\*

"Admiral." Captain Sokolov's rumble interrupted Laura's concentration. "We have worked up several options for your consideration."

Setting aside her datapad, Laura replied, "Let's hear them."

The officer tapped his console and the main display blinked. "Based off of the first encounter with the dreadnought, we believe the most likely course of action for the enemy fleet will be to maintain his cruisers inside the range of his primary weapons systems." The display blinked, showing the range of the primary cannons encompassing the supporting cruisers. "This way the cruisers provide anti-missile support to the dreadnought and the dreadnought keeps the cruisers covered." The Russian paused, then added, "The enemy's primary strategic objective will be to prevent us from reinforcing the Marines on the ground. It is also highly probable that he will endeavor to utilize his superior armor and close range firepower to cut us off from our jump point, should we not engage him upon system entry. Failing that, the most likely course of action will be to fall back to the jump point to their home system and engage us should we attempt to enter their home system."

"No surprises so far," Laura grumbled. "Solutions?"

"We have two primary courses of action and a contingency developed." The display changed. "Option one. We will assume a modified Delta-Two formation centered around the carriers. In this variant of Delta-Two, we will use the fighter wings as a first line anti-missile screen, to allow the cruisers to buy time to engage the dreadnoughts escorts. The recommended course of action for this is to conduct several passes, eliminating several cruisers per pass. Once the screen is reduced, the dreadnought can be engaged with long range missiles."

Frowning, Laura thought about this. Delta-Two was a flat formation, shaped like a disc. The proposal was to hurl the disc at the edges of the enemy formation and whittle them down while not giving a concentrated target for the enemy to focus on.

Captain Soklov continued, "It risks our cruisers coming into particle beam range, but if the maneuvers are timed right, the time in effective range will be minimal."

"Numbers?" Laura demanded.

"The operations cell has determined that if the maneuver is timed properly, there is a seventy percent chance of reducing the enemy escorts to fifty percent within three passes." He looked at his console. "They estimate losses will be moderate, with the leading cruisers taking the bulk of the enemy fire."

Nodding, the admiral replied, "Very good. Option two?"

"Yes." The display blinked and reset. "This option is less subtle. It is a derivative of the Angston Maneuver, intended to break through minefields. We will use this formation to break through the enemy screen and attempt to inflict fatal damage to the dreadnought in one pass." On the screen, the fleet formed into a long, thin shape, with the heavy cruisers and fighter escorts in the front of the formation, followed by the lighter cruisers and the carriers. The thin formation on the screen stabbed directly into the enemy cluster, taking fire from all sides. It dove deep into the enemy fleet, racing past the massive dreadnought, pouring fire into it as it passed.

In a dispassionate tone, the Russian officer continued, "This is a much riskier option. The damage to the lead elements will be severe and there is no guarantee that we will fatally damage the dreadnought on the first pass. It is unlikely we will be able to attempt this maneuver a second time."

The admiral stared at the display, slowing it down as she thought it through. After a few seconds, she asked, "What are the dissenting options?"

"There are three, all of which involve bypassing this force to directly reinforce the Marines on the surface. In all of the simulations, the Elai naval forces cut us off from the jump point and inflict critical damage to the fleet, be it attritional, or when the bulk of their home defense fleet arrives. They are not viable, but should you wish to view them, we have run the simulations."

"And your recommendation?"

"Ma'am, we recommend option one. It presents the lowest cost to risk ratio, with the added benefit of not engaging the dreadnought directly until the escorts have been reduced."

Resetting the display and rerunning the first maneuver option again, thinking. After a few moments, she nodded. "Option one it is." She looked at Captain Sokolov and

Commander Destin. "Work up the maneuvering package and push it to the fleet."

"Yes, ma'am."

"And get me Admiral Philips on tightbeam."

"Aye, Admiral." Laura sat back and stared at the screen, her mind troubled.

\*\*\*\*

*Aboard the UEAN* Infiltrator
*Deep Space, Draconis 327*

"Captain Harris?"

The communications watchstander's voice broke into Mitch's light doze. He sat up in his command chair. "Yeah?"

"We're getting encrypted signals from the fleet. It's being broadcast widebeam."

"I'll be in comms." Mitch stood up and stretched. His back ached from the long hours on the bridge, staring at the enemy formation they'd been shadowing for days now. Every approach they'd made, they'd been driven off by the destroyers.

Making his way forward to the communications room, he encountered Commander Von Kant. "Morning, sir."

"Good morning." Mitch opened the hatch and gestured his executive officer through, then followed her. "Let's see what Laura has cooked up for us today, shall we?"

"Can't wait," The other officer replied sourly. "Let's hope she's got a good plan. That big fucker is making us work for it."

"Morning sir, ma'am." The communications tech greeted them. "I've got your message decrypted and on display here." The sailor gestured at the wall screen. The details and orders of the maneuvering package took a few moments to scan, then Mitch pointed at the bottom of the message. "Stealth warships will maintain close distance and engage targets of opportunity as the tactical situation permits."

The two officers exchanged a look, then Von Kant observed, "Well, at least she's not going to bog us down with details."

"No kidding." Mitch considered the message for a moment longer, then cleared it and pulled up a system map. "Ok. Let's do some math and get the intercepts worked up. Once we get a plan in place, let's drop onto a message buoy and let the *Avenger* know."

"Gonna be a bar fight, sir." The exec observed.

"Yeah." Mitch grinned, "But you know the thing about bar fights?"

"What?"

"It's the guy coming out of the dark with a chair that you gotta worry about."

"Are we the guy with the chair?" The woman asked sardonically.

"If our plan works and if we can get a clear shot and if those escorts are distracted."

"That's a lot of 'if's'." Von Kant observed.

"Yeah," Mitch frowned at the display. "It sure is. Let's get to work on reducing some of them."

\*\*\*\*

*Aboard the UEAN* Stalwart

"Ten minutes to contact." Soklov's baritone rumble broke the silence in the compartment.

"Very good." Kensington glanced at her personal display, then ordered, "Assume combat formation."

"Aye, ma'am." Soklov replied and turned to his console.

"Admiral, I'm getting an urgent message from the long range sensor data analytics cell." Commander Destin reported, frowning at his console. "They're reporting multiple nuclear detonations on the planet's surface." He paused reading the message, then continued. "They are small, fifteen to twenty kilotons and have all been detonated on or in the primary Marine Firebase." His tone took on a sardonic note. "Intel assesses it as unlikely that these are defensive in nature due to the proximity to allied positions."

"Trust intelligence to tell us the obvious," Kensington quipped. "Thank you, Commander. Not much we can do about it now except to win this fight and get there to assist them."

"Yes, ma'am." Destin replied.

The silence held in the compartment, becoming almost unbearable. Kensington had had enough. "Did I ever tell you guys about the time Admiral Ozawa got drunk and tried to ride a mechanical bull?" She asked, mischievously.

There was a burst of nervous laughter and Commander de la Cruz asked, "Not the perfect image of an officer, Fleet Admiral Ozawa, surely?"

"Oh yes. The very same." Kensington checked her timer, watching it count down. "We were junior officers. I was a junior lieutenant and he was a lieutenant commander on the old *Kaga*." Kensington laughed remembering. "We had just made port at Theta Indi A and the Japanese crew were going to take us Yanks out and show us 'How real Japanese sailors party'."

"And how do they party, Admiral?" Soklov asked, suppressing a smile.

"With lots of exuberant toasts and lots of sake." The admiral shook her head. "So much sake." She laughed at the memory, "Anyway, one thing led to another and the night kind of got out of control. It ended with about most of the air wing officers and a half dozen line officers at a western themed bar on the seedy side of the port."

"What is a western themed bar?" Asked Commander Destin, curiously. "We don't have them in the Belt."

"It's a bar themed like the American old west. Cowboys and Indians and loud rock music. Stuff like that." Kensington paused, trying to think of how to describe it. "Except, it was a

Japanese bar, so more like the American bars than actual American bars. Like…"

"I have been to them." Soklov rumbled, "Exaggerated Americanness."

"I see." Destin replied politely. He clearly didn't.

"Anyway, we got to this bar and we were already drunk when we got there and Commander Ishimura challenged then-Commander Ozawa that whoever fell off the mechanical bull first would buy the drinks for the night." She looked at her staff, seeing them more relaxed now. "Well, Ozawa's honor wouldn't stand for that, so he stepped right up, climbed onto that bull and fell right off, he was so drunk."

"Takes a real sailor to get that blasted." de la Cruz observed.

"It does indeed," The admiral agreed. "So we helped him back on, he grabs with one hand like the bull riders did, shouts this traditional Japanese battle cry and the guy starts the machine." Placing her hand over her heart, Kensington declared, "As god is my witness, I have never seen a naval officer fly that far in a gravity field."

The staff burst out laughing, the tension broken. Soklov asked, "Did he buy drinks?"

"He sure did!" Kensington laughed, shaking her head at the memory. "Years later, when he was captain of the *Junryo*, I was assigned as the new commander of the air wing. I was sure he'd forgotten, but when he welcomed us aboard, he shook my hand, looked me directly in the eye and asked me with a dead straight face if I'd been quote 'to any good American places lately' end quote. I almost died trying to keep a straight face." The console chirped and the admiral looked down. "Two minutes. Run your survival checklists."

The crew immediately went into the familiar motions of the pre-combat checklist. Tugging her uniform collar up around her neck and sealing it, Kensington then reached to the side of her command chair, feeling the survival helmet in its clips. She then checked her gloves and fist sized liquid oxygen tank on her belt. Satisfied, her emergency equipment was here it should be, she rolled her shoulders, took a deep breath and locked her eyes on the display.

"Sixty seconds." Sokolov reported impassively.

There was a chime from a console, then a split second later, Commander Destin shouted, "They're changing formation and heading! Up six, port three seven!" He hesitated, then added in a quieter controlled voice. "They're forming behind the dreadnought."

"Thirty seconds." Sokolov reported flatly. "They are using the Angston Maneuver against us, relying on the dreadnoughts armor to blow a hole in our formation."

"No time to change formation now." Kensington cinched her command chair seat belt tighter. "We'll adjust after this pass." She took a deep breath and blew it out slowly as the timer approached zero. There was a half second of silence, then an ear splitting noise, then blackness and the smell of burning plastic.

\*\*\*\*

*Aboard the UEAN* Bravado

The deck stopped trembling and Captain Ripley Piaseki snapped, "Damage control, report."

"Damage to the port side, frames thirty two, thirty three and thirty six. Scattered pressure and power losses. Personnel accountability underway," the damage control officer reported, her eyes locked on her console.

"Captain, the *Stalwart* is falling out of formation." The sensor watchstander reported. "She's got heavy damage to the port side and her engine core power is fluctuating." He hesitated, then added, "The enemy have vectored two destroyers and a heavy cruiser at her. Thirty minutes to engagement range."

"The *Shiva* is signaling that Admiral Phillips has assumed command of the fleet. He is ordering all formations and functional ships to come around for another pass. The maneuvering package is being transmitted next." The officer on the communications station called. Ripley noted with pride that the bridge crew was terse, but kept their voices under control.

"Captain! We're getting a signal from the *Stalwart*! She's sending a shuttle with high priority cargo. Captain Kayser is sending rendezvous coordinates now."

Ripley and her executive officer traded a look, then the big Swede blinked in realization. "The Admiral," He stated flatly.

Looking back at the display, Ripley frowned, running the intercept numbers in her head, then ordered, "Helm, slow to zero point three. Comms, signal the *Shiva* that we are slowing to pick up a high value shuttle from the *Stalwart* and will rejoin the fleet on the third pass."

"We're going to be alone out here." Commander Knutson observed.

"We'll be long gone before they can get to us." Ripley replied. She stared at the display, then muttered under her breath, "I think."

\*\*\*


*Aboard the UEAN* Stalwart

The dim red emergency lights popped on, sending pools of murky red light through the smoke filled compartment.

Coughing, Laura Kensington croaked, "Report."

"My console is dead, Admiral," Captain Soklov reported. "I have nothing."

"Mine too." Destin replied from his position. "That means primary and auxiliary power is out in this section."

Commander de la Cruz had a handset in her hand, the earpiece pressed to her ear. "Understood. We'll be ready." She hung up the handset. "The bridge says they're sending someone down to help us."

Kensington shook her head angrily. "We can't wait. We

need to get comms reestablished."

Suddenly the thick hatch to the flag bridge popped open. The passageway beyond was filled with the dancing beams of lights from helmets and battle armor.

The large figure of a power armored Marine clambered through the hatch. "Admiral. Captain Kayser has instructed us to get you to a shuttle."

"Are we abandoning the *Steadfast*?" She asked, startled.

"No, ma'am. You're transferring your flag."

"That's my call, not his." Kensington replied angrily as the Marine moved into the compartment to assist her.

"Not this time. The captain needs you off the ship right now," the Marine replied, handing her survival helmet. "Time to go, ma'am. Helmet on."

Unsnapping her seatbelt, Laura slid her gloves and survival helmet on and sealed them as her staff did the same. She clambered through the small hatch and into the passageway, seeing that the emergency lights were on here as well and that the smoke was accumulating in the air. Two Marines in hulking power armor each took an arm and started hustling down the passageway, her feet barely touching the floor. She could hear the commotion of her officers being similarly hustled along behind her. There were alarms hooting and she could hear a muffled voice booming from the ship's public address system.

"NOW HEAR THIS. HAZMAT BLACK DECK EIGHTEEN AND NINETEEN, SECTION FOUR THROUGH EIGHT. REPEAT, HAZMAT BLACK. RADCON TEAMS TO DECK EIGHTEEN IMMEDIATELY. REPORT ANY AMBIENT RADIATION RISES TO YOUR LOCAL DAMAGE CONTROL TEAM LEADER."

Flashes of once pristine corridors twisted and torn by the immense forces of the enemy weapons could be seen as she was hurried along through the ship. Here and there, helmeted and suited sailors could be seen moving rapidly, their faces grim and focused. There was a sudden shaking, a moment of queasiness as the artificial gravity fluctuated, then returned.

"DAMAGE CONTROL VAC TEAM THREE TO THE FORWARD DCON LOCKER SIX IMMEDIATELY. FIRE SUPPRESSION TEAMS TO DECK EIGHTEEN IMMEDIATELY."

The small group rounded a corner and Laura could see the round door of an emergency escape shuttle standing open. Two enlisted crewmen stood outside the hatch, shouting for them to hurry.

One of them, a senior chief, cupped his hands and yelled, "SIXTY SECONDS! MOVE IT, MARINES!" The other was pointing towards a second hatch. "Half here, half there! Move!"

Reaching the hatch, the admiral was propelled unceremoniously into the shuttle and found herself shoved all the way forward, ending up in the empty co-pilot's seat, as her staff piled in behind her. The pilot, an ensign who looked all of twenty three years old, turned and shouted at the enlisted man at the hatch. "Get your ass in, Chief! We gotta go!"

The man yelled back, "Wait! The captain says he's got more coming."

"We're at capacity! We can't wait if we want to make the rendezvous!"

In the passageway, three more sailors appeared. Two were young; junior enlisted sailors shepherded by a stocky petty officer. Each of the junior sailors was carrying a briefcase sized object. One of them, a wide eyed blonde woman, barely out of her teens, clambered in and sat in the last seat, clinging tightly to the object in her hands. Her face was white. The other two figures flashed past the hatch, clearly heading for the other escape shuttle.

The ensign yelled, "That's the chief's seat! She can't stay!"

Leaning in the hatch, the chief made a fast count of the passengers, then called to the pilot. "This is directly from the captain." The young woman looked at the senior enlisted sailor for a moment, her eyes wide.

"You'll be fine, ma'am." He jerked his head at Kensington. "Get the admiral off." He stepped back and slapped the hatch seal controls and the rear doors snapped shut. Only his face was visible through the tiny porthole, then that too vanished.

The pilot's eyes narrowed and her lips tightened. She nodded once and flipped her VR visor down. "Strap in people. We're going for minimum safe distance." She reached for the console, snapped two switches, then slammed her hand on a large red button on the console. There was a sudden push against Kensington's back as the ejection rockets fired, making it hard to breathe with the force of acceleration. After a few seconds, there was a loud crash from outside of the hull and the shuttle began to tumble wildly. Through the front windows, Laura could see the blackness of space, then a snapshot of the *Stalwart*, ugly black scars on the once pristine sides of her hull and plumes of white fog spewing out as atmosphere vented into space. The stabilizer rockets fired, jerking the shuttle into another tumble, this time slower. The wounded starship was again visible, but this time there was something else behind it- a bulky, sharklike shape with red sparkles on its nose and bright pinpoints of light growing rapidly larger. The anti missile laser turrets on the *Stalwart* began to sparkle defiantly with a ruby light as the lasers engaged the incoming warheads. The shuttle rolled and jerked as it tumbled through space, jerking Laura's eyes from the dying warship.

Unconsciously, Laura reached for the controls, decades of experience as a space fighter pilot kicking in, then stopped herself. She toggled her intercom, "Pilot, do you need assistance?"

Panting, the young officer replied, "I think…" The rockets fired again and the tumbling slowed again. "I think…yes." She blew out a shaky breath. "Yes. We're ok." She rapidly tapped the controls, then put her hands back on the stick. "I think there's a propellant leak on the port side. It destabilizes when

we accelerate, so I have to manually correct as we speed up."
She had her eyes locked on the instruments. "Can you run
comms?" The shuttle shook and wobbled as the pilot
corrected.

"You bet your ass I can." Kensington replied and reached
for the radio. "Who are we being picked up by?"

"*Bravado*, I think." The ensign replied, her voice now
steadier.

The admiral keyed the microphone and seeing the shuttle's
call sign on the console in front of her, spoke calmly.
"*Fortuna*, this is *Stalwart* escape shuttle two seven, requesting
immediate pickup on the pinged bearing."

The response from the Bravado's communications
watchstander came immediately, "*Stalwart* Two Seven,
*Fortuna*. Maintain course and accelerate to point three five if
possible. You are pre-cleared for emergency docking in bay
four."

"Understood, *Fortuna*. Be advised that there is a second
shuttle behind us that will also need priority clearance." Laura
reached out to activate the short range sensors and scowled
when the display flickered and died.

"We've got them as well, Two Seven. Seven minutes to
dock."

Kensington acknowledged and looked at the pilot. "What's
your name?"

"Ma," the woman replied, her voice still slightly shaky.
"I'm May Waters."

"That's a lovely name. I'm Laura." The admiral reached
over and patted the woman's arm through the thick survival
suit she wore. "You're doing a great job, May."

"Thank you, ma'am." The woman risked a glance at the
Admiral. "I can't believe I've got an admiral as a co-pilot."
She laughed, the tension in her voice clear.

"This might come as a surprise to you, May, but I was once
a young ensign assigned as a shuttle pilot." Kensington
laughed, also feeling the tension. "But I never had to evacuate

a ship like that." She looked at the young woman. "That was some damn fine flying."

The pilot was silent for a moment, then asked, "Is the *Stalwart*..."

"I don't know." The admiral looked at her console. "My console is dead."

"Well." The woman's jaw set determinedly. "Captain Kayser is a hard man to kill. They're going to be fine. They have to be." The pilot's console chirped. "Ok. We're on approach."

The next few minutes were silent as the young pilot accelerated as hard as the damaged shuttle would allow and slowly matched speeds with the massive warship, slowing as quickly as it could. The massive bulk of the warship appeared in the blackness of space ahead of them, rapidly turning into what looked like a vast, metal wall. Ahead was an open shuttle bay, the yellow docking lights flashing. The ensign deftly approached the bay and tapped the controls, matching speeds with the warship, then deftly rolled the battered shuttle into the bay. It gently touched down with a slight bump. There was a tremble and a banging transmitted through the hull as the massive bay doors flew closed, a moment of queasiness as the Bravado's gravity field took hold, then the shuttle was silent.

Ensign Waters ran through the shutdown sequence, then slumped in the pilot's seat, shuddering, making a noise that was half laughing, half sobbing.

Unstrapping herself, Laura patted her on the shoulder. "You did great, May. You go sit down and come find me when this is all over." The ensign nodded wordlessly.

The rear doors of the shuttle popped open and several suited sailors with visors open stood there. "Admiral Kensington?" One of them called.

"Here!" Kensington clambered out of her seat and headed towards the hatch.

The sailor saw her, nodded and toggled his comm unit. "Inform the captain that Backblast is aboard." Laura looked up at the use of her old callsign, surprised that people remembered it. She worked her way to the rear hatch.

Pausing at the exit, Kensington spoke to the young sailor who had been pushed onto the shuttle at the last moment. "What did Captain Kayser want on board so badly?"

The young woman uncovered the box in her lap and Laura could see it was a reinforced carrying case, made of hard material, with a bright silver plate with writing on the outside. "It's the ship's logs, ma'am."

"What does that say?" The admiral pointed at the plate.

"It's the *Stalwart's* motto. '*Hold Fast*'," the young woman replied, looking at the officer with wide eyes. "The captain has it everywhere. He says it's important."

With a half smile, the admiral nodded. "That it is, sailor." She patted the young woman on the shoulder. "Get those logs to the Bravado's crew."

"I will, ma'am."

Climbing out of the shuttle, Kensington motioned to the sailors, "Bridge." She ordered and followed the sailors at a fast walk into the depths of the warship.

## Chapter 19

### "Close With the Enemy"

*Interplanetary Space*
*Aboard the UEAN* Bravado

"Captain, we've reestablished comms with Forward Battery Three Alpha." The damage control officer reported.

Commander Ripley Piaseki leaned over the damage control officers shoulder and spoke to the helmeted and suited figure on the screen. "What's your status, chief?"

The petty officer replied, his voice with the muffled sound that helmet survival microphones always had. "We're back online, ma'am. It won't pass an inspection, but she'll fire."

"Our sensors are reading you're still in vacuum. How are you on restoring pressure?" The young officer demanded.

"The hull is holed somewhere under the body of the cannon." The older sailor replied with a grimace. "I could patch it in a few minutes if I could get outside but from here, I'd have to take the battery back offline to get to it."

"How are you on survival bottles?"

"We have plenty," the sailor replied. "We're good for probably six plus hours."

"Good." Ripley replied. "We have a team cutting through the hull from frame fourteen now. Damage control says an hour tops, but it might be longer if we have to maneuver."

"We ain't going nowhere, skipper." The chief gestured at the bulk of the laser battery. "And we can fight if you need us to."

"I know you can." Ripley replied. "Hang in there, sailor. We're going to get you out of there." She broke the connection and turned to her sensor officer. "Status of the *Stalwart?*"

"She's going at it with those destroyers now. She seems to

be holding her own." The watchstander gestured at his display. On it, the green emblem representing the heavy cruiser was volleying missiles at one of the Elai destroyers while dodging incoming missiles with an agility that belied the damage to her systems. The sensor officer added, "She can probably handle them, but that cruiser is another story." He pointed at the enemy cruiser screaming towards the wounded warship.

"Anything we can do from this range?" Ripley's executive officer asked, somberly.

"No. We have the admiral aboard now. We can't chance it." The young officer stared at the display, her lips pressed tight as she watched a volley of missiles from the Steadfast overwhelm one of the destroyer's defenses, detonating the enemy ship in a ball of white light.

"Admiral on the bridge!" A nearby sailor called.

"As you were." The admiral ordered as she entered.

As Admiral Kensington worked her way through the compartment packed with people and duty stations, Ripley ordered, "Comms, signal the fleet in the open. *Bravado* has assumed flag duties. Helm, make your course two three six, mark seven, speed zero point six and prepare to rejoin the fleet after this pass."

Pointing at the comms watchstander, Admiral Kensington ordered firmly, "Belay that. Captain Piaseki, what is the status of the *Steadfast*?"

"She's beat up but holding her own against the destroyers. She won't last long against that cruiser though." Ripley replied.

"Very good." Kensington replied, calmly. "Captain, have your watchstander signal Admiral Phillips on the *Shiva* that he is to press the attack on the enemy and that he retains command of the fleet for the time being." She smiled humorlessly, "We wouldn't make it into formation in time anyway." She pointed at the display. "Captain, engage and destroy that enemy cruiser if you please." The older woman moved to the observer seat on the bridge and regally sat down, like a queen assuming her throne.

Ripley hesitated half a heartbeat, then replied. "Yes, ma'am!" She whirled and began to snap orders. "You heard the Admiral, Mr. Stone. Mr. Casey, make your course one eight zero, mark two, ahead flank." She reached down to the arm of her chair and snapped a switch, activating the shipwide intercom. "Attention. This is the Captain. We will be engaging the enemy in approximately ten minutes. All hands make ready for emergency thrust." She closed the circuit and stared hard at the display, thinking fast. After a few seconds, she spoke, "XO, set all warheads in forward tubes for maximum yield. Alert all batteries we will be engaging in close quarters combat." The giant man nodded once, acknowledging the order.

On the display in the front of the compartment, the *Stalwart* accelerated, heading towards the nimble enemy destroyer as if to ram. The tiny ship slipped aside, volleying salvos of small missiles into the hull of the *Stalwart* that exploded on contact, leaving a rippling series of flashes against the hull. The cruiser suddenly spun around on its axis and fired the main drive. The massive plume of actinic white fire from the fusion drive exhaust caught the smaller warship, stripping away hull plating and tearing deep into the superstructure. The drive flame ceased and the larger ship pivoted again and accelerated past the now drifting partially melted wreck of the destroyer, which was being rocked by a series of smaller secondary explosions as her systems failed.

"God damn can that man drive a ship." Ripley's executive officer muttered under his breath.

"Yeah, but that cost him a lot of time. Look." Ripley pointed at the intercept numbers on the display. "They're going to beat us to him by a couple minutes."

"Captain, the fleet is preparing to make a second pass at the enemy main bod," the sensor watchstander called. "Thirty seconds."

"Route those reports directly to the admiral," The captain

ordered. "Weapons, time until intercept?"

"Seven minutes, forty seven seconds at present speed." The weapons officer responded promptly.

In the bridge observer's chair, Admiral Kensington stared at her display, with Captain Soklov looking over her shoulder. The fleet was once again rushing towards the enemy, still in the flat, disc shaped formation, with the enemy still in the densely packed column, led by the dreadnought. "What is he doing?" she muttered. "They hit us hard the last time…"

On the screen the human ship's formation was shifting at the last possible second. It rotated from a flat disc to an open circle, with the enemy passing right through the middle. The human ships poured fire into the alien warships from all sides. The flashing of explosions in the enemy formation marked the deaths of several of the cruisers as the two formations once again raced away from each other.

The screen blinked and the damage numbers updated. Another Alliance cruiser, the *Unyielding,* was drifting, with extensive damage to her hull and systems. Most of the rest of the ships were reporting damage of various levels. On the display, the enemy formation once again curved around for another pass, once again diminished but still deadly.

"That isn't going to work again." Soklov observed. "I hope Admiral Phillips has another trick up his sleeve."

"Me too." Laura replied. Under her breath, she muttered, "Godspeed, Tom Phillips."

\*\*\*\*

*Aboard the UEAN* Infiltrator
*Alongside the Enemy Fleet*

"There it is." Commander Von Kant declared. "They just gave us our opening."

"They sure as hell did." Captain Harris replied. "Helm, come starboard to zero three five, down mark two. Weapons, prepare a targeting solution on that big bastard. Set the starboard tubes with multi warhead splitters and the port with penetrators."

"Aye, sir. On it." The crew acknowledged efficiently.

"Blind 'em with the first wave, knock them out with the second." Von Kant murmured. "I like it."

"Yeah, well. You can congratulate me if it works," Mitch muttered. He raised his voice, "Time to intercept?"

"Two minutes, seventeen seconds." The Chief of the Boat replied from where she stood by the weapons officer. "Skipper, they're gonna be right pissed when these go off. What's your plan to get out of their formation?"

Harris smiled humorlessly. "We're gonna give them the old switcheroo. Kappa-Two."

The Chief nodded thoughtfully. "Well. That's interesting." She shrugged. "It's as good an idea as any." She turned to the defensive weapons officer. "Load Kappa-Two into the decoy drones and stand by to launch them the moment we fire the main tubes."

"You got it, Chief." The lieutenant tapped at her console, then nodded in confirmation. "Done." She looked at the senior enlisted and lowered her voice. "Does this work?"

"In theory." With a smile that only showed in the wrinkles in the corners of her eyes, the sailor added, "I don't think anyone has ever used it in combat."

"Shit." The defensive weapons officer muttered. "Well, here's one for the textbooks." She tightened her seatbelt.

"Thirty seconds to the engagement window." The weapons officer reported flatly.

The captain nodded acknowledging the report. The bridge was silent as the stealthy warship maneuvered. Moments later, a console pulsed.

"In range, weapons hot." The weapons officer reported.

"Match bearings, open all tubes." Commander von Kant ordered.

"Tubes open, weapons targeted." The commander on the

weapons station reported. "On your mark, captain."

"Fire tubes one through ten." Captain Harris ordered. The familiar hum and thump of the electromagnetic accelerators hurling the two ton missiles into space shook the ship.

"Tubes one through ten fired, missiles away. Commencing roll and firing tubes eleven through nineteen." The nitrogen jets puffed, rotating the warship on its narrow axis, exposing the second set of tubes. "Tubes eleven through nineteen fired, missiles away. All missiles running hot and true."

"Defensive weapons, execute Kappa-Two." The captain ordered. "Engineering, shut down the main reactor, emergency power only." The two thumps as the decoy drones left the ship could be felt. Seconds later, the lights dimmed and the ventilation fans slowed, leaving the bridge in a deep, quiet murk, illuminated by only instruments and the red emergency lights. The captain turned to Von Kant. "XO, spread the word throughout the boat. Shut it down. No electronics more powerful than a flashlight. I want this boat dark and quiet."

"You got it, skipper." The slender woman hurried aft, her orders clearly audible in the quiet compartments as she moved through the ship.

On the main display, the two drones were steadily moving away from the now shut down and drifting warship. One was running hot, blazing with light and putting out a large fusion drive trail. The other was ghosting along on an entirely different vector, giving off as little energy as possible, nearly invisible.

The defensive weapons officer suddenly muttered, "I get it." She pointed at the screen. "That's the drone and the enemy is supposed to think that's the drone." "She pointed at the other decoy. "But that one looks like a stealth ship coasting under full EMCON, but we're here exactly where we fired these things from, because that's the last place anyone sane would stay." She stared at the screen. "Just floating along in space like a lump of garbage."

"A very expensive, well trained lump of garbage, but yes."

The chief clapped the ensign on the shoulder. "Nice work." The senior enlisted sailor turned to the captain. "What now, sir?"

"Now?" Captain Harris sat back in his command chair calmly, "Now we watch the fireworks."

\*\*\*\*

*Aboard the UEAN* Bravado

"Two minutes to contact," The sensor officer reported. "The *Stalwart* has engaged the enemy cruiser." In the screen, the battered Alliance cruiser had attempted to accelerate away from the closing enemy warship, but was unable to maintain a lead due to the damage. As the crew of the *Bravado* watched, the *Stalwart* suddenly flipped again and fired her main drives, slowing dramatically. The Elai cruiser in close pursuit didn't change speed, resulting in the *Stalwart* coming alongside the enemy warship, her anti missile laser batteries blazing, leaving glowing trails of molten metal in the enemy ship's hull. A split second later, dozens of short range missiles intended for anti fighter defense were ripping across the void between the two ships.

Almost belatedly, the enemy warship's own anti missile defenses went into action, striking down many of the missiles, but leaving them unable to concentrate on the Stalwarts own laser batteries, which systematically began to focus fire on the enemy ships turrets.

"Captain, the *Stalwart* is inside the minimum safe distance for ASM's. She'll be caught in the blast." The weapons officer reported breathlessly. "The combat systems are warning against it."

Staring at the display, Ripley focused for a moment, then snapped, "Mr. Stone, signal the *Stalwart*. Tell them ahead flank when we pass on their port. Mr. Casey, I want a close pass to the son of a bitch. Weapons, prepare to fire everything you have except for the Mark 19 ASM's."

"How close, captain?" Lieutenant Casey was rapidly tapping his instrument panel.

"As close as you can get without hitting her," Ripley replied, her eyes locked on the display. "We need to hit her hard."

"Message sent, Captain," Ensign Stone reported. "*Stalwart* acknowledges flank speed upon passing."

"The enemy is slowing, ma'am," The sensor officer reported. "They see us."

"It's going to prolong our time in their engagement envelope." The weapons officer reported. "We will be exposed for one minute, thirty seconds."

"Understood," the young captain spoke without turning, "Weapons, you get one shot at this. Hit them hard. Melt the batteries if you have to."

"Understood, ma'am." The weapons officer tapped furiously on his console.

"Sixty seconds to contact."

Commander Piaseki tapped her intercom, activating the ship-wide circuit again, "This is the captain. Sixty seconds to contact. Fortune favors the bold!" She shaped the switch off and tightened her seatbelt. She took a deep breath and watched the timer roll backwards to zero.

"Contact!" The sensor officer shouted. The deck began to tremble and the ship rang and shook as if a giant was striking it with a giant hammer.

Clenching the arms of her command chair, she focused on the display in front of her. The weapons officer was reporting in a calm voice. "All port anti missile batteries firing. All mark five and nine short range launchers firing." He tapped his controls. "All batteries, Weapons. Conduct emergency coolant dumps as needed. Keep those guns firing." On the display, the symbol for the *Bravado* pulled alongside the enemy warship, her laser batteries blazing, volleying the tiny anti missile rockets as she did. The distance continued to close and the ship trembled and shook as the enemy returned fire.

From what sounded like a hundred yards away, Ripley could hear the damage control officer reporting in a droning, mechanical voice, "Hull breaches on decks seven, eight and nine, frames ten through fifteen. Scattered power losses on the port side. Forward Battery Three Alpha is not responding. Forward Battery Four, Five and Seven are reporting emergency coolant dumps, but remain online. Pressure loss, left number seventeen passageway…"

"We're clear!" The sensor officer shouted.

"Status on the *Stalwart*?" Ripley demanded.

"One second…She's just now clearing the minimum safe distance. We're good!"

"Helm, flip one eight zero, cut engines. Weapons, fire everything!"

The *Bravado* again flipped in space, pointing her nose at the now receding enemy warship and began volleying the large anti ship missiles at her opponent.

"Weapons away!" The weapons officer shouted.

"Mr. Casey, flip one eight zero, ahead flank!" The ship again flipped and fired its powerful main drives, accelerating away from the enemy cruiser.

"Damage control, report."

"We've got vac teams headed to seal the breaches on the midship decks. The power failures appear contained. No damage to engines, or primary life support. No radiation leaks reported. Personnel accountability is under way now."

"Very good." Ripley took a deep breath and was startled to find she was drenched in sweat. She wiped her forehead. "Mr. Casey."

"Yes, captain," the young officer replied, in a calm voice.

"How close exactly did we fly to that cruiser?"

"Six point two three kilometers, ma'am." Mr. Casey turned from the helm for a moment. "I could have gotten a little closer, but decided to play it safe." He grinned, unrepentantly.

"You're a maniac," Ripley replied, with a shaky laugh.

"But nice flying." She raised her voice. "Nice work everyone." She looked at the weapons officer. "Status on the ASM's?"

"Nope." The weapons officer shook his head angrily. "She fired off three drone decoys that got three of them and smoked the rest with her anti missile lasers."

"Damn." Ripley swore. "I thought we had her." She turned to the sensor station. "Where's the *Stalwart*?"

"Two three seven, mark four, moving at zero point five. They can't get her now; not before Captain Kayser links back up with us."

"Can they catch him?"

The sensor officer stared at his display, then replied, "Not unless they want to be caught or he's a lot more badly damaged than we think."

"Ok." The captain turned to her executive officer. "Lars, get below and check on the damage control efforts. I want accountability and casualty numbers, yesterday."

"Aye, aye, Captain." The giant Swede unstrapped and left the bridge.

\*\*\*\*

As the buzz of the warship's operations continued around her, Admiral Kensington focused on her display. The massive Elai dreadnought was curving around for another pass on the main human fleet, which had turned and was accelerating towards the enemy. The display chimed, indicating updates, then flashed. The indicators for a half dozen impacts appeared on the enemy dreadnoughts hull and red damage indicators popped up, as did another ship with an Alliance style drive signature that the combat systems hadn't been tracking. Two of the enemy cruisers started to change positions to engage the newly appeared stealth warship, but before they could, the two formations crossed each other again. Caught out of position and away from the dreadnought's protective fire, the two cruisers crumbled quickly under the combined fire of the

Alliance fleet and vanished into bright balls of light as their drive cores overloaded.

As the two fleets drew apart again, Kensington took a deep breath and stared at her display. The Elai dreadnought was damaged and of the original ten cruisers that had escorted it, only four remained. As she watched, the enemy fleet adjusted course and engaged their main drives. Hoping against hope, she checked their course and confirmed what she suspected-the enemy fleet was heading for the jump point towards their home system.

Standing behind her chair, Captain Soklov muttered something in Russian, then said, "Well done, Admiral."

"We're not done yet." Kensington tapped her control to record a message. "Task Force 3.2, well done. Maintain pressure on the enemy fleet, but do not pursue them closer than two light minutes from their jump point. Stay between them and the planet." She hesitated, then added with a weary smile. "Fine work, Tom. We're almost done here." She closed the message and ordered, "Send that to Admiral Phillips."

The communications officer replied, "Yes, admiral." He paused, then added, "Ma'am, we're actually getting a signal from Captain Beck on the *Shiva* now. I'll route it to you."

The display activated on Laura's command chair. Captain Beck's image appeared. The stocky, middle aged woman sat in her command chair, her face composed, her voice controlled and formal. "Admiral Kensington, the enemy fleet is breaking off. I have ordered the stealth ships to keep pressure on the enemy fleet, while the main body maintains a screen between the enemy and the planet. We will await further orders." The woman paused then added in a somber tone. "I also regret to inform you that Admiral Philips and his staff are dead. During the last engagement, the flag bridge sustained a direct hit from the enemy particle beam cannon. There are no survivors." The woman sat up straighter. "I will retain tactical command of the fleet for the time being and am awaiting further orders. Task Force 3.2 out."

Laura closed her eyes for a moment, took a deep breath in then blew it out slowly. She tapped her communications control. "Captain Beck. Acknowledge last. Detach the Assault Carriers to my formation and continue current operations. Admiral Kensington out."

The admiral closed her eyes again and rubbed her face with both hands, then sighed. She opened her eyes and saw that Commander Ripley was looking at her. The Bravado's captain looked very young and very tired. The two women exchanged a long look before Laura nodded once. Ripley returned the nod and smiled sadly before returning her focus to her ship.

## Chapter 20

### "Dust and Shadows"

*Inside the defensive perimeter, Firebase Anvil*

Tony moved rapidly in a crouch through the blowing dust. Seeing a large boulder, he moved behind it and knelt. He was immediately joined by the sergeant major, the engineer lieutenant and two Marine NCO's. They moved into the small depression behind the rock and opened their tactical display. Tony leaned around the boulder and peered into the dust. Seeing a runner coming, he waved at the Marine, who sprinted to them and dove behind the rock into cover.

Hauling the woman to her feet, Tony ordered, "Report, Marine."

The private shook her head, dazed and replied. The nameplate on her armor read 'Euwing'. "Sir. They're all over the place, popping in and out of the dust and in our positions before we can react." She looked down at her armor and rifle which was splattered with a dark coating and said, "Lieutenant Rodriguez is dead. Gunny Okono is running Bravo company. Not sure about the others." Looking past Tony, her eyes widened. The private snapped up her rifle and yelled, "Down!" and began to squeeze the trigger, firing sharp blue blasts into the dust. Tony flopped to the ground, dragging Jimenez down with him. After a moment, the Marine said in a shaking voice, "Clear!" She kept her rifle trained on the swirling dust.

Rolling over, Tony looked in the direction she had fired. Barely visible in the dust about fifteen feet away was a crumpled figure, lying face down. Euwing said again, "This is what it's like all over the line, sir. They pop up outta nowhere and it gets up close and personal." She continued to scan the dust for a moment, then added bitterly, "I killed the one that got the L-T with my knife."

Sergeant Major Jimenez patted the Marine on her power armored shoulder and replied, "You did your job, Marine. So did Lieutenant Rodriguez. We just gotta hang on until help gets here."

The woman turned and looked into his eyes through his visor and replied, "They'd better make it fast, Sergeant Major. I don't know how long we can hold out in this shit."

Leaning around the boulder again, Tony peered through the dust. He swore under his breath. He turned to the staff sergeant crouched by the portable tactical display and asked, "Where are the goddamn Gorgons? They're supposed to be supporting the line!"

The staff sergeant opened his mouth to reply, but before he could, the dust cloud to the right of them illuminated a brilliant green. A muted roar could be heard. The light disappeared, then again, the brilliant flashes of green, this time interspersed with explosions. The green flashing from the powerful lascannons grew in intensity, illuminating the entire area in an eerie flashing green light. The staff sergeant grinned and pointed into the dust, "There's one, sir." There was a ripple of light, then a series of cracks as antipersonnel rockets exploded a split second later, seemingly right in front of the armored vehicles position.

Tony shook his head and muttered, "Damn. Whatever they're shooting at, it's close." He shook his head and turned to the engineer lieutenant, "Anything from the killdozers?"

The young man shook his head, "My last runner said they had started cutting trenches, but I haven't heard from them in a while. They're out there somewhere."

To the front of the small group, the dust started flashing red and Elai energy bolts started searing past. Tony pulled his head back and turned to the right, watching the mech crew, obviously seeing whomever was shooting, start walking streams of green fire through the dust.

One of the staff sergeants looked up and shouted, "We

got...." His helmet faceplate was suddenly a smoking hole. Inside, where his face was a second before, only a shapeless red and black mess remained. His body knelt where it was for a moment as the power armor servos tried to keep it upright, then fell slowly forward. In one motion, the remaining Marines dove prone. As one, they brought their rifles up, aiming into the blowing dust. Tony scanned the dust and activated his low light system in his helmet. The image immediately washed out with the reflected light and he shut it off and strained his eyes.

Suddenly, Euwing shouted, "Contact left!" She popped up on one knee and opened fire. Tracing her shots, Tony could see shadowy figures running and diving behind rocks, appearing and then vanishing in the dust. Two barely visible shapes opened fire from behind a rock, pouring a stream of red bolts at the Marines. Tony laid as flat as he could, hearing the bolts searing overhead.

After several seconds, the fire ceased and there was a startling silence. From behind him, Tony heard a surprised grunt and rolled over. There was a dark armored figure in the depression with them, kneeling on Euwing's back. The young woman was screaming incomprehensibly. Shocked, Tony raised his rifle. Before he could fire, Sergeant Major Jimenez popped up onto his knees and swung a fist at the figure's faceplate, hitting it with the augmented strength of his power armor. The figure fell backwards and the NCO fell over with it, tumbling out of the depression and out of sight. Another two shapes were rolling on the ground. Tony reached over and grabbed the first thing he could find, a dark armored boot. Bracing his feet, he yanked as hard as possible. There was a terrible screech and he could feel a sickening crunch from the extremity. The Elai kicked at Tony with its other leg. He leaned back, trying to keep the boot away from his faceplate. Suddenly, the Elai stiffened and then went limp. Tony looked down at the Elai's body and saw the engineer lieutenant, his face pale through his helmet visor, holding the handle of an entrenching tool that was embedded deeply into the alien's helmet. Tony nodded at the man and released the leg. He rolled over, just in time to see the Private Euwing clamber back to her knees and hurl a grenade into the dust, then drop face down and cover her helmet with her hands. Tony snatched his rifle and, hearing the explosion, popped up with his rifle at the ready, followed by Euwing. Seeing two Elai writhing on the ground a dozen feet in front of their position, Tony joined the Marine in pumping several bolts from his rifle into the bodies.

The aliens' bodies jerked as the bolts hit, then went still. Tony stopped firing and watched the dust intently. Hearing another motion behind him, he whirled and pointed his rifle. Upon seeing the sergeant major climbing back into the depression, he lowered his rifle. The man was covered in dust, sticking to the blood freezing on his armor.

Sitting down hard, he looked at Tony and in a strained voice, said, "Shit."

"Yeah." Tony looked at the man and asked, "You ok?"

Jimenez nodded and looked down, "Yeah. Not mine, sir." He rolled over the body of the staff sergeant and seeing the hole in his faceplate, shook his head and said again, "Shit." His voice was tense. From the left and the right of them, the brilliant green flashes illuminating sheets of blowing dust told them that the Gorgons were once again firing.

Tony cautiously looked out and then said, "Sergeant Major. Take a look. You see anything?"

The older man crawled in next to Tony and stared into the dust. Suddenly there came a blue flash, flying over their heads, then another. In front of them, the dust lit up with a sudden fury of blue and red flashing, mixed with occasional stray bolts flying over their heads. After several seconds, the firing died down and there was nothing visible in front of them but the blowing dust. Private Euwing popped her rifle up again, her sharp eyes picking up something in the dust. The small group all trained their rifles on the dust as a figure raced at them. Tony breathed a sigh of relief as the figure resolved into the armored shape of a Marine. He skidded to a stop, flopping down next to the prone Marines.

Jimenez growled at the young man, "Report, Marine."

Panting, the man replied, "Sergeant Major. The flanking force has linked up with the line. We're pushing them back."

Tony demanded, "How many Marines are left in the flanking force?"

The Marine shook his head, "Don't know, sir. They took a lot of casualties. Captain Saint is dead, so is Sergeant Kimbro. The remaining troops are in the trench line with Bravo company. The bad guys are falling back."

Tony turned to Jiminez and said, "Well, it looks like we held 'em."

"For now." The noncommissioned officer looked into the dust and muttered, "That trick won't work twice though."

Tony nodded wearily. "Yeah. Suggestions?"

With a hard expression on his face, Jimenez looked at the blowing dust, then replied, "Not much choice. We sit here, we get wiped out." He looked back at Tony, "Let's go get 'em."

Tony smiled humorlessly, "When in doubt, huh?" He picked up his rifle and checked the charge on the ammunition pack.

"Attack." Jimenez nodded, "You got it, sir." He turned to the Marine runners and said, "Marine, Get the message to the line companies and the mechs. Advance to contact."

\*\*\*\*

*Task Force Hammer,*
*Command Vehicle*

"General. Hammer One-Six and One-Two are reporting contact with multiple enemy foot mobiles." The shaven head, hard faced lieutenant colonel paused, then added, "They are deploying infantry for an attack."

General Piasecki nodded absently as he stared at the screen.

A staff sergeant reported, "Sir, we're getting incoming signals from the fleet." He stopped and then grinned and said triumphantly, "It's Admiral Kensington! The message reads, '*A- Reinforcements inbound. Hold the line, Marine. -L'*.'" He added, "It looks like the entire Fifth Fleet is here!"

Piasecki sat quietly for a moment, then asked, "Is the *Bravado* with them?"

The Marine stared at the console and then replied, "Yes, sir. She's with the fleet. She's reporting minimal damage." He frowned and added, "It looks like the *Bravado* is now the flagship, even though the *Stalwart* is still with the fleet. Don't know what that's about." He looked up, "Why do you ask, sir?"

The Marine officer shook his head silently, blew out a breath and his usually rigid posture sagged a tiny bit. "No reason." The old Marine replied. He then turned to the colonel sitting at the console, "John, tell your boys help is on the way. Get them deployed in a line abreast sweep. We need to push them back, nice and methodical." The officer nodded silently.

The staff sergeant spoke again, "Sir, we still don't have comms with Firebase Anvil, but we did get a drone up over the dust cloud." He tapped a key, pulling up the static filled drone feed. The dust cloud obscured much of the screen, but there was the distinct flickering of red and blue tinting the dust clouds. The sergeant commented, "There's a hell of a firefight going on down there."

Piasecki glowered at the screen then turned and said to the task force commander, "Colonel Mecham, get in there and relieve those Marines!" The hard faced colonel nodded silently, keyed his mic and began to give orders to the task force.

\*\*\*\*

*Forward Operating Base Anvil*
*Outside the Perimeter*

Tony stepped over a still Elai body and carefully scanned the area in front of him. The dust had started to lessen somewhat, allowing him to see twenty meters or so, further at times when the dust plumes allowed. The line of advancing Marines in front of him was just barely visible in the dust and occasional red and blue flickers lit the billowing dust clouds. To the right, the brilliant green flashing of the Gorgon's secondaries firing lit the cloud again. There came one last long burst of red bolts streaking over them, then nothing.

Over the tactical net, Tony could hear the harsh whispers of the noncom's ordering the Marines to hold. Taking a knee, Tony stared into the rolling dust. Hearing someone come up next to him, he glanced over and saw the sergeant major, who was also staring intently into the dust.

After a moment, he said, "Why did they stop shooting? They gotta still be out there."

Tony shook his head, "No idea. Think it's a trap?"

The sergeant major was quiet for a moment, then responded, "I don't know. The Elai are a lot of things but this isn't like them. They usually lay a counter ambush if they know we're following." He glanced at Tony and then added, "We gotta keep the pressure on though, sir, or they'll reorganize, come back and kick our teeth in."

"Sir." A runner came up to them in a crouch with his rifle in one hand, "Something weird's going on up here."

Tony glanced at the sergeant major, "Weird how?"

The Marine runner replied. 'I don't know. There's like these little red flags up everywhere and they aren't shooting anymore." He added, "We know the little fuckers are still there. We can see them moving every now and again under cover."

Tony considered this, then said, "Sergeant Major?"

Slowly, the senior enlisted man replied, "Flags don't sound like an ambush to me, sir." After a moment, he added, "If anything, it sounds like a surrender." He looked at Tony and shrugged, "If they aren't shooting, lets see what happens next."

Turning back to the runner, Tony ordered, "Ok. Tell the line companies to hold here. If you're shot at, shoot back, but if they aren't firing, don't shoot." The man nodded and ran off into the dust. Tony took a knee and blew out a breath and muttered under his breath, "And now, we wait."

# Chapter 21

## "War Angels"

*355th Forward Resuscitation Team*
*Improvised Aid Station, The Crater Floor*

"The Marines are attacking," the young sailor on the communications station of the shuttle reported. He paused, listening to one of his headphones. "The battalion commander had ordered a general counterattack across the lines." He twisted to look at Manderson. "Apparently the Elai are falling back and Major Harris is trying to keep them running."

Shaking his head, Manderson muttered, "I guess. Feels like a Hail Mary." He turned to Dahl, who stood beside him. She was still in her full armor, but her helmet was off. Her normally stylish hair was damp with sweat, there was a large dark smudge on one of her cheeks and there were dark circles under her eyes. "How are we on supplies?" When they had inventoried them about twelve hours prior, they had been critically low and the consumption rate was far higher than their supplies would withstand.

"We're out." The exhausted woman replied, simply. "We have no remaining synthblood and all of the donors on site can't give any more or they won't be able to work. We're out of medpacks for the suits, we have no more ventmasks remaining. We're out of all fluids and pain medications except for what's in our suit medkits and I'm like ninety percent sure most of us have been using those for the patients."

"Damn." Manderson replied. He looked at the communications panel for a moment, watching it lighting up with dozens of different frequencies and signals. After a moment, he shook his head and declared, "We can't stop."

"Clearly." Dahl replied, flatly. "But we can only do so

much with improvised dressings and no supplies for resuscitation."

"We're going to have to tighten our triage standards again."

"I don't know how much more." Dahl's voice had a strained note in it. "I've got a three section tent of dying men and women without enough pain medication as it is." She looked down at her armored gloves, still stained with blood and grime. "None of the nurses have any narcotics left in our suit kits. We've used them all. Same with the medics." She looked up and smiled tightly. "We're of the opinion that if we get hit badly, the best thing to do is to just open our suits and go to sleep."

"Stop." Manderson ordered, firmly. "That doesn't help."

With a shaky sigh, Dahl nodded. "I know. But…"

"No buts, Susan." The officer replied. "When I was on Desolation and we were cut off and about to be overrun, I told myself 'When the worst is happening, it can only get better." He gestured around them. "This is about the worst it can get." He paused, then added, reflectively. "Until it does get worse, I guess."

"Yeah?" The nurse replied, "Well, we have a saying in air med, too. 'It gets worse before it gets worse'." Her eyes flashed defiantly. "Fortunately for you, I thrive on misery. Unfortunately for you, it's usually other people's."

Despite himself, Manderson laughed, "You are a fighter, aren't you?"

"The jarheads got their fight and I got mine." She grinned, tiredly. Her comm unit chirped and she looked down at it. "I gotta go." Dahl turned to leave the shuttle cockpit that had turned into the command post for the improvised hospital. She got to the hatch and hesitated. "For what it's worth, sir; you're doing a great job too- but you really do suck at inspiring people."

"You've mentioned that before." Manderson replied with an exhausted laugh. "Call me if you need me."

"We've got more casualties coming in, sir," The sailor on

the comm panel reported. "Fifteen or so. The Marines are just piling them into an armored vehicle and bringing them here."

Still in the hatch, Dahl replied, "How many critical?"

"I don't know," The sailor replied. "They're not even sending proper casualty reports anymore. I don't think they have a battalion aid station anymore. I haven't heard from them for quite a while."

"We can't sustain that. They need to be triaging them before they transport."

"Yes, ma'am, but I'm not even sure they have many line medics left."

"Find out." Dahl ordered. "Sir, we need to get an evac system back in place."

"Yeah, we do." Manderson considered this for a few seconds, then spoke. "I can go up closer to the line and get an aid station re-established. That'll help ease the load on us." He looked at Dahl. "Who can we spare?"

With a short sharp laugh, the nurse replied, "In reality? No one. For this? I'll find a couple of medics." She jerked her head. "Let's go." She turned and headed out of the hatch. Manderson picked up his helmet and followed closely behind.

Fifteen minutes later, Manderson clambered into the back of a battered Marine light armored vehicle and sealed the hatch. As the engine started and the vehicle started to lurch across the rocky ground of the crater, he looked across from him at the three suited figures sitting there. In the middle, he recognized Master Sergeant Agawa. The implacable man nodded and gestured at the suited figure next to him.

"Sir, this is Seaman Hess," the young sailor nodded wearily. Agawa gestured to his right. "This is Kante M'Binga. He's a shuttle systems contractor who was an emergency medical technician at the Tau Ceti Fleet Yards in college." The massive man nodded and grinned cheerfully, his teeth shining white in the dim light.

"Major. It is a privilege."

Opening his helmet and raising his voice over the noise of

the engine, Manderson called, "You're a long way from Tau Ceti, sir."

M'Binga shrugged and replied, "As are you from Earth, Major."

Looking back at the two, Manderson shook his head and spoke, "I want to thank you both. We're damn short of medics and for you two to volunteer to come up here is incredibly helpful."

The sailor laughed and shrugged. "It's fine, sir. I'm not much use at the hospital anyway. My equipment was lost in the shuttle crash and it's not like people are getting dental exams right now anyway."

Tilting his head and scrutinizing the young man, Manderson asked, "You're a dentist?"

"Dentist's Mate," the young man laughed tiredly. "I was up for Petty Officer next round of boards. Guess it'll have to wait."

Despite himself, Manderson laughed. "Ok, Seaman Hess-promotable." He grew serious. "You gentlemen are going to be running the aid station up there. We're going to help you get it up and going, but then you two are going to be it." Looking intently at the two men, Manderson added in a serious, hard tone. "I don't know when we're going to relieve you. I don't know if you're going to get any more supplies than we're leaving with you." He gestured at the three large rucksacks of medical supplies that Dahl had managed to put together before they'd left and shook his head. "Hell. I don't know much of anything, except this. You two have got to triage the wounded coming through. Send us the most critical only- the ones we can save. Treat the lightly wounded as best as you can and keep the ones we can't save comfortable." His eyes searched their faces intently. "That's your job up here. Is that clear?"

"Yes, sir."

"I understand."

"Good. Agawa gave you the new triage guidelines, right?"

The two men nodded again, silently. "Good." He looked down at the floor of the LAV. It was covered in crushed energy drink cans, wrappers from medical equipment, dirt, large stains of dried blood and crunchy chunks of pink suit sealant foam. Shaking his head hard, the officer looked back up. "Listen, fellas. I've been here before. No supplies, no reinforcements, no options." Looking past them for a moment, he remembered suddenly the fighting on Desolation and how very desperate he had felt as he realized that security had broken down and that he and his team were cut off. He shook his head, refocusing. "At least here, you aren't alone. There's thousands of Marines out there and we're about a klick behind you." Leaning forward, he stated flatly. "Your main job is triage. It's a cold job. It helps to think of them as machines and go down your checklist. Don't think too much about them as a person." Seeing the worried expression on both of the men's faces, he added, "Trust me on this one. There will be time to process all of this later. For now, we need to sort out who can be saved with the resources we have and that's going to take sticking to the script." Looking from face to face, he asked, "You stick to the script. You two got that?"

"Yes, sir." Seaman Hess replied. M'Binga nodded silently.

The intercom crackled to life with the voice of the young Marine driving the LAV. "Sir, we're at the rendezvous point. First Battalion is sending a runner to escort you in."

"Got it." Agawa replied. "Seal up." The four men closed their suits and exited the LAV. Moving away from the rear of the vehicle, they crouched near a large boulder and waited silently. About fifteen yards away were the remnants of a Marine fighting position. Two power armored bodies could be seen lying silently in the dust, one of them slumped over the twisted remnants of a Mark 30 lascannon. In front of the position contorted in the dust lay a half dozen of the black armored Elai infantry.

Seeing the young sailor looking in horror at the scene, his white face visible through his helmet visor, Manderson prodded him and said, "Take a deep breath." The man did as he was told, then nodded, his face still pale.

"You ok?" Agawa asked, watching the interchange.

"No, but what choice do I have?" The man replied, tightly.

"Fair enough." Above and around them, the dust still billowed and blew. The reflections from the energy weapons still flickered, but seemed less intense than previously. Occasionally a sheet of yellow-white light would flash through the darkness, rapidly shooting away into the gloom. It was quickly followed by several more flashes of light.

"What is that?" M'Binga asked, pointing at the lights.

"Probably the Gorgons." Agawa replied. "That's an anti personnel rocket being fired." He leaned around the rock and peered in the direction of the fighting and added, "That's good. That means the bad guys are at least a kilometer away. They can't fire any closer than that."

"Oh." M'Binga replied. His eyes were wide as he took in the surreal scenes.

"*War Angel?*" A low voice came over the suit radios. "*You there?*"

"We're here." Agawa replied on the local frequency. "By the boulder to the left of the LAV." Two hulking figures emerged from the murk- Marines in their armor.

"We're from First Battalion. We're here to escort you to the aid station. Follow us. We have a new site picked for you, but it's a ways away," the Marine gestured, then turned and slipped into the dust. The second Marine, a somber faced young woman with heavily scarred and pitted armor paused and said, "Eyes open. This area ain't as secure as we'd like. They keep slipping through the goddamn lines."

As they moved through the dust, Manderson noted that he could definitely see further. The dust was clearing up. The six men trudged through the dust and jagged chunks of rock, with the only words occasional muttered curses as one of them stumbled.

About two hundred meters further, the Marine in front

stopped. "There. To the right of that big rock, there's a tarp. See it? It's about fifty meters up that rockslide. That's it." He pointed into the distance. He turned to Manderson. "We gotta get back up to the line. Good luck, sir. Hope I don't see you again."

"Same here," Manderson replied. "Thanks, Marine." The two Marines moved off into the distance, heading towards the sounds of fighting. Suddenly, the noise died down, with the flashing fading out until it consisted of only a few flashes here and there. A single series of bright green flashes came from over the ridge, then the whole area fell silent. Manderson looked in the direction of the fighting and listened intently.

"What does that mean?" M'Binga asked in a low tone. "Is the fighting done?"

"Probably doesn't mean anything good." Agawa replied. "Keep going."

The men made their way to the overhang. Underneath it was a field tent, with a single airlock. The men crowded their way into the tiny lock and stood silently as the pressure rose, buffeting them with gusts of wind. Stepping out of the lock, they could see that the Marines had used a combination of plast-crete sealer and tents to make a small pressurized aid station, similar to the improvised hospital. There were a dozen or so Marines lying wounded– some of the more critically injured being tended by the less injured. A few armored figures could be seen rushing from patient to patient. No one spoke to them until a Marine sitting on the floor next to the airlock slowly looked up. His eyes were glassy with pain and his right arm was crushed and scorched. His helmet was off and sitting in his lap. "Are you from the fleet?" His voice was dazed.

"No. We're from the hospital." Hess replied, kneeling to check on the man.

"Oh," the Marine replied and fell silent.

Stepping forward, Manderson stated loudly. "Who's the senior medic here?"

"There's no medics left, sir," The wounded Marine replied. "It's just Charlie now."

"Who's Charlie?" Hess asked the Marine, opening the panel on his armor and checking his vital signs.

"He's the cook from Golf Company." The Marine grimaced as Hess opened his armor and changed the medpack. "It was him and Adams, but Adams went out to get supplies and never came back."

"Where is Charlie?" Manderson asked.

"Here." From the next tent, a youthful voice replied. In the tent vestibule, a man stepped into view. He was in a light combat suit, not power armor; and his suit gauntlets and the front of his suit were stained dark with blood. "Are you a medic?"

"Yes." Agawa replied. He set the rucksack of supplies down and ordered Hess and M'Binga, "You two. Start treating these men. Identify the most wounded for immediate transport. The Major and I will take them back."

"Yes, Sergeant." Hess replied and set down his own aid bag and set to work. Manderson stepped closer to Charlie.

"How long have you been without a medic?"

"Uh." Charlie looked down at his wrists, then shrugged. "I don't know. We had one, then he went out to support the counterattack and didn't come back. When I realized it was just me, I grabbed my buddy Adams and now he's gone too." He shrugged, helplessly. "A couple of hours maybe? A day? I don't know." He looked around, looking helpless. "I've been doing my best, sir."

"You're doing fine." Manderson reassured him. "I've got two medics I'm going to leave here with you." Regarding the man, for a second, Manderson asked, "The Marine said you were a cook. You have been managing this aid station all by yourself?"

"Yes," Charlie replied. "After the medic left, there was no one else so I just did what I could." His voice quavered. "I did my best, but so many of them I couldn't do nothing for except bandages and painkillers." He looked around. "I sent the most badly wounded back to the rear. I heard the hospital had set up someplace on the surface and that they had plenty of supplies and stuff."

Reaching out, Manderson gently squeezed the cook's shoulder. "You did well, Marine. Listen to Seaman Hess and Mr. M'Binga. They're going to help you get organized and we've left you all the supplies we could spare."

"Yes, sir." The young man took a deep breath and looked at Manderson. "It can't go on much longer. One of us is going to have to give in."

"Yep. But it ain't gonna be us, is it?"

The young man wiped his nose on his suit sleeve and replied simply, "Nope. Not us."

"That's right." Manderson gave the man a final pat on the shoulder. "Not us." He turned. "Agawa."

"Sir." The stocky senior medic turned from where he had been leaning over a patient.

"You have patients identified for evac?"

"Yes, sir." Agawa replied calmly. "Those two over there and this guy." He gestured at the Marine on the floor. "He's technically walking wounded but his suit's damaged. His heater's busted and if they lose pressure in these tents, he's in trouble. He can sit in front with the driver."

"Ok." Manderson replied and turned to Charlie. "Litter bearers?"

"I've had those dudes moving people for me." He gestured at a pair of burly Marines in the next tent in badly damaged armor, hastily repaired with armor fabric and sealant foam. "Their armor is beat up, but they can hold pressure and move stuff. They're waiting on an armorer to bring replacement parts to get back into the fight."

"That'll work." Manderson gestured at the Marines. "You two. Take this guy." He pointed at one of the patients that Agawa had identified. "Me and the Master Sergeant will take this guy." Moving to the end of a stretcher, he stooped to pick his end up and waited for Agawa to grab the other end. The implacable medic picked up his end and the two litter teams and the dazed Marine headed for the airlock. As the first litter carried by the two Marines cycled through, Manderson turned and called to the young cook. "Charlie."

"Yeah?" The man replied, not turning around.

"You're doing a hell of a job. Just hold on a little longer. I'm going to see if I can get some more people up here to help."

"I'll be here." Charlie hesitated, his back still turned as if he was going to say something more, then he merely raised a hand in acknowledgement. He then vanished without a further word into the next tent as Manderson and Agawa carried their precious cargo into the airlock.

The walk down to the flat area was silent, the only sounds the puffing of breathing inside the men's helmets. When they got to the bottom of the hill that used to be the crater wall, the armored vehicle was gone.

"Where the fuck did it go?" Manderson demanded, as they set the stretcher down. He motioned to the two Marines that they could leave and the two men clambered carefully back up the rock pile towards the aid station.

"To get fuel. Sorry. They messaged me while we were up there and I forgot to tell you." Agawa replied. "They'll be back. They said ten minutes, but who knows." He checked the vitals on the injured Marine next to him, then glanced up. "Oh. Look. It's cleared up."

Manderson looked skyward and saw the hard points of stars above them. As he watched, he could see the hard sparks of blue white moving steadily among the fixed points of the stars, clustered in groups. His armor carbon dioxide canister alarm chimed again, demanding a change, but he was out. He'd given his last fresh scrubber away. He couldn't remember when, but it was a while ago. Absently, he silenced the alarm again and turned his eyes back up to the silent drama overhead. There was another burst of flashes and the points of light flared and moved in their silence dance.

"Looks like someone's still got ships up there." Agawa observed.

"Yeah. Let's hope they're ours." Manderson muttered. He shook his head and looked back down, letting his eyes sweep across the crater, finally able to see more than immediately around him. It was a wasteland of craters, wrecked equipment and piles of rubble.

"Wow." Agawa said quietly.

"Yeah. They really did a number on this place." The officer fell silent for a few seconds, then Manderson shook his head bitterly. "We don't even know why the god damn war started. You know that?"

"I don't know about that." Agawa replied. "I saw what they did to the colonists out in the Frontier. It was pretty ugly."

"I guess," Manderson replied. Seeing the makeshift ambulance approaching, he was silent for a minute, then added, "It's going to be hard to get the people past this." His eyes moved to the fighting position. While they were in the aid station, someone came and removed the bodies of the Marines. The Elai soldiers remained where they'd fallen. The dust had coated their armor, leaving the still figures the same color as the surface of the moon, like life sized realistic sand sculptures of fallen soldiers. "I wonder what they do with their dead." Manderson said absently, staring at the remains. "All the time I've spent around them and it never occurred to me to find out."

The Marine with the mangled arm that had been quietly sitting in the ground suddenly spoke. "I seen it." He looked up. "I saw it on Solace and again on Paradise." He struggled to get to his feet and failed. Agawa reached out and silently pulled the man up.

"Thanks," the Marine said. "They take the bodies and lay them flat and cover them with a blanket. They put their weapons and things that were valuable with them and put a knife in their hand, then they cover their eyes with a cloth." He looked at the dead Elai dispassionately. "We don't know why they do that, but they did it for fallen humans too so maybe it's a religious thing."

"Maybe." Agawa replied. "Humans have a million religions and death rituals, it stands to reason that so do they." Grabbing the handles of the first stretcher, he waited for Manderson to grab his end and said, "On three. One, two…three." The men lifted and moved towards the LAV. The rear door opened and two soldiers in light combat suits jumped out and moved for the other casualty. The injured Marine moved forward and awkwardly climbed into the front of the LAV.

After securing the patient, Manderson climbed into the LAV. As his armor connected to the LAV comm system, his messages lit up. Rapidly scanning them, he swore under his breath, then called to Agawa. "There's more wounded in route to the hospital. A bunker took a direct hit from a rocket. They're going to beat us there."

"Damn." Agawa's face was grim. "We can't catch a break, can we?"

"Doesn't seem like it."

"Sir?" The driver spoke over the intercom. "I've got an all forces broadcast coming in over the general freq's."

"Let's hear it." Manderson traded a glance with Agawa, who just shrugged.

"It's text, sir. I'll push it."

*FROM: COMGENFIRSTMARDIV*
*TO: ALL UEA GROUND FORCES*
*SUBJ: TEMPORARY CEASE FIRE*
*BODY: ALL FORCES WILL CEASE OFFENSIVE OPERATIONS AT 1345ZULU 15NOV2246////DEFENSIVE FIRE TO PROTECT POSITIONS AND PERSONNEL AUTHORIZED////HOLD CURRENT POSITIONS AND AWAIT FURTHER ORDERS////*
*SIGNED: BG PAISEKI COMGENFIRSTMARDIV*

"A cease fire, huh?" Agawa muttered, after they read it. "I

wonder who won?"

"So it seems." Manderson replied. "And it's damn hard to tell. If we did, it sure doesn't feel like it was us. Anyway, it doesn't change our job much."

"That's true," Agawa replied. The LAV lurched to a stop and the two men sealed their helmets and prepared to re-enter the chaos of the overwhelmed hospital.

## Chapter 22

### "Under a Scarlet Banner"

*Temporary Marine Command Post*
*Outside of the Perimeter of Anvil Station*

Forty five minutes later, Tony turned to the sergeant major and said, "Ok. Not a peep from them. It feels like a cease fire, but man. It's hard to tell. I think we gotta take a look."

In a sour tone, Jimenez replied, "I don't like it, but I agree." He nodded at a runner, "Tell Sergeant Knut to take a patrol out and find out what the fuck's going on. Tell him to be *extremely* careful and if anything looks off at all, to get the fuck out."

The runner nodded and ran off towards the line of Marines, who had now dug a line of shallow fighting positions. Ten minutes later, the Marine came sprinting back and skidded to a stop. Panting, he said, "Sir. They're just sitting there."

The sergeant major replied, "What the fuck do you mean 'sitting there'?"

The young Marine replied, "Sergeant Major, exactly that. They're just kneeling. They look like they're waiting for something."

Another Marine ran up in a crouch and reported, "Sir. There's a couple of them that walked out and are standing in front of our lines!"

Tony and Jimenez traded a look. Tony said, "Surrender? This isn't how the ones on Paradise surrendered. Those guys just sort of wandered out of the jungle and handed over their weapons." He looked in the direction of the Elai lines and frowned.

The sergeant major shrugged, "No idea, sir." He stared thoughtfully across the lines at the Elai positions.

Suddenly, Tony's helmet speakers crackled to life, spitting

static filled but understandable words, "*Anvil Six, This is Hammer Six Romeo.*"

"Ha! Hot damn, we got comms again!" Tony exclaimed, then keyed his radio, "Hammer Six Romeo, Anvil Six actual."

The radio operator replied, "*Anvil Six actual, Hammer Six Romeo. Standby for Ironjaw Actual.*" There was a pause, then General Piasecki's gravelly voice replied, "*Tony. Glad to hear you're ok. What's your situation?*"

Tony looked towards the enemy lines, now able to see the thin banners the Marine had reported earlier and replied, "Beat up but operational, sir. They're stopped shooting and appear to be waiting."

"*Same here. The Navy just blasted 'em outta orbit and my intel boys think they might be offering surrender terms. You see anything that looks like officers or leadership?*"

Peering towards the enemy lines, Tony replied, "Apparently two of them just walked out and are standing in front of the lines." He paused for a moment, then asked, "Since the cease fire seems to be holding, what should we do, sir?"

Immediately, the general replied, "*Go talk to them. See what they want.*" The older Marine paused, then added, "*The Navy is on the way and their fleet has bugged out. These guys are alone out here, caught between us. They have to know their situation is untenable.*" There was another moment of silence, then he added, "*The Elai are a lot of things, but stupid ain't one.*" There was a surge of static, then the general's voice continued, "*They give you any shit, pull back and the Navy's gonna fry their ass from orbit. Use your judgment and be careful, Tony.*"

"Yes, sir. I'll call you in a few. Anvil Six actual, out." Tony disconnected and then turned to the sergeant major, who regarded him impassively.

"So. We're gonna go talk to the sharkheads." Jiminez stated flatly.

Tony sighed, "Yeah. Division intel thinks this is a surrender."

"Shit." The sergeant major looked towards the Elai lines, then said thoughtfully, "Think we ought to send a junior officer?" He paused, then added, "You are the acting battalion commander, sir. What if they have some weird shit thing that kills you?"

Tony considered this, then countered, "What if sending a junior officer is seen as offensive and they attack?"

Jimenez shrugged and replied, "Dunno. That's the problem with aliens, sir. They do alien shit." He motioned to a Marine nearby and ordered, "Marine. Get something to put a white flag up on and hustle." He pointed at another Marine and ordered, "Private, go find Captain Shen and bring him here." The Marines nodded and hurried off. The noncommissioned officer regarded Tony, then said, sounding amused, "Well, sir. You're about to make Marine Corps history. First Marine to try to make peace with aliens."

With a grimace, Tony replied, "I guess. I'd rather kill them but I'd prefer not to lose any more Marines doing it."

The Marine came running back with a long, slender antenna and a white square of cloth on the end. He gestured at it and stated with a grin, "Whip antenna from a busted comm relay and a piece of armor sealant cloth."

Impressed, Tony replied, "That was fast!"

The sergeant major grinned and replied, "The ingenuity of the enlisted can be a powerful force for good, when they want it to."

The brief moment of levity faded, as Tony stood and looked towards the enemy lines. He stared for a moment, then said, "Ready to do this?"

In a sour tone, the noncommissioned officer replied, "No. But we got no fucking choice, now do we?" He motioned to Captain Shen, who had moved up to their position and was crouched behind the boulder at the tactical console, "Captain Shen. The major wants to talk to you."

The young man looked around, then moved over in a crouch, "Sir. What's up?"

Looking at the young officer for a moment, Tony said gently, "We need you to go out and make contact with the Elai and offer them surrender terms."

The younger man considered this for a moment, then sighed and replied, "I'm the last officer available that doesn't have a direct command, aren't I?"

Tony smiled wryly and replied, "Well, yes– but you're also one of the only guys we have that's taken the Elai language course."

"Shit." Shen observed, then hastily added, "I mean- shit, sir. It wasn't a very good class. I seem to remember mostly it was a bunch of whistling and chirping and stuff. It was an easy grade, since even the instructors can't speak it."

With a dry chuckle, Tony replied, "I made the same mistake once. I let my commander know that I had taken an Elai psych class and ended up interrogating a prisoner on Paradise." He gestured at the Elai lines and added, "In any case, you're the best and currently the only option." He paused, then asked, "You ready?

With a grimace, the young captain replied, "No. Not really." He sighed and motioned at the enlisted Marine standing next to them with a small box, "Hook me up."

The Marine stepped up and attached the box to Shen's belt, then plugged the device into his armor. On the display inside Shen's helmet, a string of text displayed, then showed the message. *'System Ready- Receptive: Auditory input, visual display. Transmit: Auditory input, auditory transmit.'*

With a frown, Shen tapped the switch, then said, "Test, test, test." The box on his waist whistled and clicked, translating the words as proficiently as the software could manage into the Elai language. He clicked it off, glanced at Sergeant Major Jimenez and said, "Ok. I'm ready."

The sergeant major gestured at a nearby stone faced staff sergeant. The man held a rifle, half a dozen energy grenades on his belt, a regulation pistol and an enormous vibroblade machete on his hip. He nodded somberly and said, "Sir, I'm

Sergeant Morris. I'm your escort." Shen nodded and handed his rifle to a nearby Marine, leaving him with only his sidearm and his traditional Marine combat knife in its sheath on his belt.

The Sergeant Major leaned in close to Shen and Morris and said, "No fucking around. Get in, deliver the message and get out. These guys give us any bullshit, we pull back and the Navy fries them from orbit. Got it?"

Shen replied, "Yes, Sergeant Major." Morris just nodded silently.

With a hard expression. Jiminez regarded them for a moment then jerked his head at the enemy lines and said, "The Major and I will be here waiting. Go."

The two Marines turned and started towards the line of hasty fighting positions about a hundred yards in front of them. The dust was settling, with only occasional eddies and billows now whispering around. Their boots puffed up dust with each step.

As they walked away, Tony looked up at the sky. The stars and the looming mass of the gas giant were once again visible. As he watched, there came a single flash above them as something exploded in the dark of the sky, then faded away.

Looking back down, he could now see the two alien figures, patiently waiting for the two advancing soldiers. Without taking his eyes off of the two men advancing towards the enemy, Tony said, quietly, "Stay alert, but nothing provocative. Rifles at the enemy lines, not at the enemy leaders." Jiminez nodded and quietly whispered orders into his radio.

The Marines on the line acknowledged silently with acknowledgement pings from their armor and lowered their rifles slightly. Passing them, Shen stepped out into the space between the two forces, with Morris to his left and the Marine with the white flag right behind. Covering the dozen meters between them in a few moments, he came to a position about ten paces from the two still Elai and stopped.

The Elai in front of the enemy defensive line were both wearing the characteristic slick black combat armor, with a deep blue stripe down the side of the helmet. One of them, instead of the standard issue utility belt, wore a belt with an ornamented buckle and a short, sheathed sword on it. The one with the sword confidently walked forward alone, halfway to where Captain Shen and Sergeant Morris stood and stopped expectantly. Shen noted that the Elai limped slightly as he approached, but that it did nothing to alter the impression that this Elai was very much in charge.

Motioning to Sergeant Morris to stay put, Shen stepped out and walked up to the enemy leader. He stopped two paces in front of the Elai. Standing still for a moment, the two regarded each other, then the Elai began to speak, its whistles and chirps forming a fluid, melodic speech. After a moment, the translation appeared in Shen's helmet visor.

*"Name Broken/shattered/destroyed claw <Untranslatable 1> belong <Untranslatable 2> Three group Seven subgroup. Request war master/leader/director. Discuss/negotiate/agreement for acquisition integration/mix/absorb <Untranslatable 2>. <Likely interrogative> ((Untranslatable 1- Likely group/political affiliation proper name; require more data. Untranslatable 2- Likely unit name/designation; require more data.))*

Shen considered this for a moment, then activated the translator and said slowly, "I am Captain Andrew Shen. I speak for the commander of the First Marine Division. I can negotiate on his behalf." He paused for a moment, considering his words carefully and then said carefully, "Your fleet has been defeated. You are surrounded and outnumbered. If you cease fighting, you and your men will not be harmed." The translator on his belt whistled and chirped. The Elai's shiny black visor revealed nothing, but it's alert posture told him that the enemy soldier was listening intently Shen added, "You have fought with honor and skill."

After a moment, the Elai replied in its language and the translation appeared a moment later.

*"Agreement. Conflict cease. Preserve life. <Untranslatable 2> Three group Seven subgroup enter sea soldier clan. Honor in victory. Grace in defeat. Strength in unity."*

There was a roar overhead as a flight of Apparition space/ground fighters made a low pass over the battlefield, as the fighters from the carriers arrived. The Elai looked up at them impassively, then reached up to its left shoulder and removed a palm sized silver disc that showed three curved lines with a slash across them. The enemy officer looked at it for a moment, then carelessly tossed it aside. The alien then reached for its right hip and removed a small knife and presented it hilt first to Shen. Unsure of what to do, Shen reached out and accepted it and looked at it carefully. It was about five inches long and the blade was a deep shimmering black metal. The hilt was oddly curved and the handle was formed to fit the Elai hand perfectly. Shen looked back up at the Elai, who was standing expectantly. The alien stood for a moment, then pointed at Shen's combat knife on his belt. Shen considered this for a moment, then reached down, unsheathed his knife and presented it to the Elai hilt first. The Elai gravely accepted the weapon and inspected it, testing the weight and balance, then placed it carefully into his belt. He then stood quietly, waiting.

Shen frowned, thinking, then said, "I accept your surrender. Your men will be well treated." Cocking its head, the Elai listened to the translation, then replied.

*"Sea soldier clan ferocious <Untranslatable 3> Glad/happy/joy conflict/flight/struggle end between clans. United clans now battle/destroy <Untranslatable 4> Jagged/Uneven teeth clan. Clan sea soldier provide/give*

*air/water/aid to sea soldier clan three group seven subgroup. Low/out/short critical. ((Untranslatable 3: Likely slang; require more data. Untranslatable 4: Proper Name, possibly military unit. Cross reference with 'Jagged Fang' from datafiles.))*

Shen nodded and replied, "We will provide supplies." The translator whistled and chirped and the Elai stood impassively. Shen said again, "You fought valiantly. The attack into the crater was very clever." He paused, then asked, "Why did you kill the soldiers in the red armor?" After the translation software said, the Elai shook its head violently.

*"Three group Seven subgroup not <Untranslatable 4>. Jagged/Uneven teeth clan improper war conduct. Improper actions. Refuse/avoid/deny clan entry. Punished/treated as per code/law/protocol. ((Untranslatable 4: Proper Name, possibly military unit. Cross reference with 'Jagged Fang' from datafile))*

The alien officer paused, regarding the hulking shape of the Marine in his powered armor, then continued.

*"<Untranslatable 4> <Untranslatable 5, 6> Consumers of excrement/waste. Impolite/rude/unruly followers of ancient/old/outdated traditions. Irrelevant/useless/improper for Broken/shattered/destroyed Claw. No longer bound by clan law. No respect, no surrender/quarter/capture possible/allowed/desired. <Untranslatable 7, 8>*
*((Untranslatable 4: Proper Name, possibly military unit. Cross reference with 'Jagged Fang' from datafiles. Untranslatable 5, 6: Likely regional dialect, likely profanity/slang. <Untranslatable 7,8: Likely regional dialect, likely colloquial phrase, possible religious reference, require more data))*

The Elai officer paused, then took a step closer to Shen. He reached out and tapped the eagle, globe and anchor on Shen's armor that the UEA Marines had adopted from their predecessor services from the wet navy days on Earth. He then tapped the spot on his left shoulder where he had removed the silver disc and chittered.

*"Require clan sea soldier sigil/emblem/insignia. Much valor/bravery/fortitude sea soldier conflict with broken/shattered/destroyed claw. Clanbond forged on forsaken/forgotten/abandoned ice/frozen/cold world. Brotherhood/kinship/family formed forever. Much sorrow. Sing/perform death/loss song, enter clanbond. Sing victory song. <Untranslatable 9> ((Untranslatable 9: Stylistically related to Untranslatable 7,8. Possible colloquial phrase, Possible religious reference; require more data.))*

Shen nodded and replied, "Have your men stack their weapons and we will provide air and water." The translator chirped and tweeted as it relayed the message. The Elai tilted its head slightly but didn't reply. He paused, unsure what to do next, then came to attention and saluted. The Elai regarded him curiously, then laid its suited hand on its chest armor and inclined its head slightly. Shen released the salute. The Elai looked him up and down once more, then turned and strode back to the other Elai, who waited patiently. There was a brief exchange of gestures, then the second Elai turned and gestured at the kneeling enemy a dozen yards away.

Shen watched the two aliens walk back to their lines, then turned and trudged back to Major Harris and Sergeant Major Jiminez, who were crouched behind a boulder, about twenty yards behind the Marines lines. The four Marines started making their way back to the improvised command post.

"Well, sir?" Jiminez asked. He looked slightly amused.

Shen replied in a thoughtful tone, "I don't know." Seeing the amused look, he asked, "What's so funny, Sergeant

Major?"

The shorter man shook his head and replied, "Nothing at all, sir. You did a great job in a shit circumstance. Had it been up to me, we'd have wiped these fuckers out."

With a tired laugh, Tony replied, "You might get your chance. I'm not entirely sure of what the fuck we agreed to."

With a grimace, Jiminez replied, "I say that, but I prefer not to lose any more Marines. I say if they still wanna fight, we just fall back and let the Navy drop rocks on 'em." They fell silent momentarily as they walked.

As they approached the depression behind the rock where the temporary command post was set up, a staff sergeant popped out and waved at them. "Sir! Sergeant Major! We got something going on!

Picking up the pace, they moved back behind the rock. Tony peered at the tactical display. The sergeant, a man named Thornton, shook his head. "No, sir. Here." He flipped a switch on the console and suddenly, through their helmet speakers came a low, haunting humming, with a sub melody woven through it. It was both mournful and triumphant, alien but somehow familiar.

Tony listened transfixed for a few moments, then asked, "Where's this coming from?"

Sergeant Thornton replied, "It started from the Elai lines as soon as you left, sir. They're broadcasting it on all local channels."

Thoughtfully, Shen commented, "I feel like I heard this in that class. It sounds kind of like a mourning song. They sing it when they lose something or someone." He paused, then added, "It's different than that, though. It's mourning mixed with something else." He fell silent again, listening, entranced, then added absently, "It sounds…triumphant."

A runner came sprinting up and gasped, "Sir! We got Elai all over the place! They're standing up!" Tony whirled around and hit the magnifying feature in his helmet. As he zoomed in on the enemy lines, he could see the Elai were standing up, shouldering their rifles and helping their comrades out of their fighting positions. Short, burly Elai were moving around pointing at things and directing the now standing enemy into orderly lines.

As Tony watched, the number of enemy seemed to keep growing, as far more than they had suspected, climbed out of their hidden positions and fell into formation. After a few moments, one particularly stocky Elai moved to the front and motioned to the Elai with the sword, who stepped forward. As he did, the mournful song over the local channels ceased. There was a moment of silence and then the Elai began to fall into marching columns and began moving briskly towards the Marine's lines. As they passed the halfway point, each of them removed their knife and badge and dropped them into a rapidly growing pile.

The sergeant major muttered, "Lot goddamn more of 'em left than we thought. Glad we decided not to push on them." He turned to Thornton and snapped, "Tell the line companies to make a hole to let 'em through and not to fucking shoot!" Thornton nodded and turned to his radio.

As Tony watched, a Marine private climbed out of his fighting position at the front of the line. He held up a hand and pointed at the lead Elai's rifle. The Elai soldier looked at his rifle and then pointed at the Marine's rifle. The Marine pointed at the rifle again and then pointed at a nearby rock. The Elai seemed puzzled but set his rifle on the rock. The Marine gestured that the alien continue past him. The next alien followed suit and neatly set his rifle on the rock. Soon, the entire column was quickly and compliantly stacking their rifles as they marched through.

Sergeant Major Jiminez shook his head and said sourly, "I think these guys were planning on keeping their rifles."

With a slow nod, Tony replied, "I think so. I don't think they think they're captured. I think they think they're joining us." They continued to watch the column of alien soldiers passing by in silence. Suddenly Tony added, "There's a lot here we're still not seeing."

Jiminez only grunted in reply as the two watched the deferred enemy marching past.

Three assault shuttles flew low overhead and settled down about a hundred yards behind them, promptly disembarking dozens of additional Marines, their power armor clean and uniform and moving energetically. Three armored figures made directly for Tony's improvised command post. The armor IFF markers identified them as they drew close.

The tall one, with a tag that read 'Colonel Makenzie', said in a calm, commanding voice, "Major Harris, Colonel Makenzie, from 2/1. We're your relief. Where's your commander?"

Tony shook his head and replied, "Colonel Nelson was hit in the drop, sir. I've been acting CO for Fifth Battalion since we hit the surface." He gestured around them, "This is FOB Anvil." He paused, then added, "Or what's left of it."

The tall colonel looked around at the devastated ruins of the crater fortifications, the burned out hulks of crashed fighters, the battle scarred and smoking missile mechs, all surrounded by exhausted Marines in scorched, filthy power armor. Taking in the sight of the Elai marching quietly into the rear with a wary line of guards, the man shook his head.

After a moment, the tall marine officer commented, "Looks like a hard fight, Major." He looked at Tony and added, "You guys did a hell of a job. Sorry it took us so long to get here to help out. The Navy took a beating getting us here."

Tony just shook his head silently, watching the fresh troops fanning out to the Marines positions, bringing power packs, water and ammunition. Behind them, he could see the plastic bubbles of the temporary shelters going up in the crater floor, the bright lights visible through the dim light.

Colonel Makenzie said firmly, "Why don't you get me up to speed here, Major. We have shuttles inbound to get your guys up to the *Phantom Fury* and get checked out." He looked at Tony closely, then added, "Hold on a bit longer, major.

Another week and we'll have every last one of your guys out of here." He gestured to the column of docile aliens, "Since these guys don't seem like they want to fight anymore."

Sergeant Major Jiminez muttered, "Shoulda been here an hour ago, sir. These little fuckers are something else when they want to be."

Colonel Makenzie motioned to Tony, "Let's get you into a shuttle, get a drink of non-recycled suit piss water and you can brief me on the tactical situation. Sergeant Major, I'll let you work with Sergeant Major Covington and my staff to get the men organized and a relief plan in place. My staff will get you what you need."

The two NCO's nodded and replied, "Yes, sir." As they started towards the defensive positions, Tony wearily followed Colonel Makenzie to the assault shuttle.

\*\*\*\*

An hour later, Tony finished briefing Colonel Makenzie. As he did, a Marine stuck his head up from a communications console and said, "Major Harris. General Piasecki would like to be debriefed. He's got a CP set up with the bulk of his forces about twenty clicks north, on the far side of the radiation zone." The Marine paused and added "He wants to see you in person, sir. We have a shuttle on the way for you."

Tony tiredly nodded his thanks to the Marine and walked to the shuttle's airlock. His armor had been cleaned and recharged while he was inside and the feeling of climbing into clean armor was a relief. Cycling the lock, he stepped outside and moved away from the assault shuttle that was serving as the relieving force's command post. Seeing that the landing area nearby was empty, he sat down on a rock and keyed his mail service. Now that the data links to the fleet were reestablished, he could see several pieces of mail waiting for him. One was from his mother in Philadelphia, another from his uncle Bo in Tau Ceti and then the one he was looking for.

Seeing Elizabeth's name, he smiled and decided to wait to open it.

Leaning back and looking at the gas giant hanging in the star studded sky, he keyed the record feature in his armor and said, "Hey Liz. I know I haven't written in a while, but we've been busy out here. I don't know what they're telling people, but it's been tough. These Elai... man. These guys can fight. I guess I don't need to tell you that."

Pausing for a moment, watching a group of ten of the aliens quickly and methodically digging through the rubble with a vigilant Marine standing guard, he continued, "They fought like hell, then just surrendered out of the blue. It was weird. One minute they were shooting and fighting like demons and the next, they weren't and are acting like they're part of us. It's the strangest thing. I think there's so much more to them than we know. All we know of them is war, but there are complexities here we aren't seeing."

He paused again and looked back up at the sky, "Onyx is something else. It's really spectacular. It's beautiful, in its own way. There's this orange and red gas giant over this moon. It flickers with deep lightening and has these swirls of reds and oranges. It's incredible. It looks like a Chinese lantern." He sighed, watching a small dark spot against the gas giant grow rapidly and turn into a transport shuttle. He said into the letter again, "I have to go, my ride is here. Before I do, I want you to know that there's not a day that goes by that I haven't thought about you. It sucks out here, but the thought of seeing you when I get home has made the long, crappy days bearable."

The shuttle landed and the doors popped open. A ground crew hustled up and connected a fuel line and the crew chief leaned out and gestured at Tony.

Tony stood up and continued, "I love you, Elizabeth Suarez. Save me a spot on the beach, you and I have some catching up to do. In fact, I believe I owe you dinner. I'll see you soon." Tony stood and boarded the small transport shuttle.

Buckling in, he leaned back in his seat and watched the view as the shuttle lifted. The wreckage of the crater was astonishing from above and he shook his head at the devastation. He checked his chronometer and seeing that there was about thirty minutes until he landed, decided to close his eyes.

He had just closed his eyes when there was a tremendous *BANG* from underneath the shuttle and the engine took on a sickly whine. Popping his eyes open, he could see the horizon through the open shuttle doors swaying back and forth as the pilots tried to control the shuttle. He grabbed the handles next to his seat and hung on as the shuttle started to spin. Tony took several rapid breaths and then suddenly thought about his mother's lasagna and how it was a shame that Elizabeth wouldn't ever get to… There was a sickening drop, the sensation of tumbling and then everything went black.

\*\*\*\*

*Aboard the UEAN* Shiva's Wrath
*Combat Information Center*
*Low Orbit over M3245.*

A console chimed and a watchstander called out, "Captain Beck, Marine TACAIR is reporting that a heavy transport shuttle callsign 'Daredevil Five-Two' has crashed on the surface of the planet." He paused and added, "No enemy fire in the area, probable mechanical failure."

Captain Beck nodded calmly and ordered, "Helm, slow to one third. Prepare the flight deck for rescue operations and alert the CAG. Dispatch search and rescue."

The watchstander nodded, then paused listening to his headset. He said again, "Marine TACAIR reports that combat search and rescue have been dispatched. They are requesting additional space based assets."

Nodding to the Air/Space Operations watchstander, the

captain ordered, "Get them what they need. All search and rescue flights are to get priority launch status."

"Yes, ma'am." The watchstander returned to his tasks as the massive warship continued on its path over the shattered world.

# Chapter 23

## "Evacuation"

*The Improvised Field Hospital*
*Crater Floor*

"Ok, sir. The Seabee CO just called. His engineers just certified the tunnels. They say we're good to start moving patients back in," the radio in Manderson's helmet crackled.

"Good copy. I just finished inspecting them with the engineering team," Manderson replied. He took a deep breath. His head was pounding and his suit air felt stuffy and thick. "Let Master Sergeant Agawa and Captain Dahl know we can start the move."

"*Understood, sir.*" The radio fell silent and Manderson started trudging the several hundred meters back to the improvised field hospital.

Suddenly his radio blared to life, "*Sir, we just got an air raid warning from battalion! We got fast movers inbound!*"

He could hear sirens starting in the background as he broke into a run. "Get people on the floor!"

The communications tech yelled, "Sixty seconds out!" The line went dead.

Looking at the hospital and realizing it wouldn't be much cover anyway, Micheal looked around and, seeing two boulders forming an overhang about a dozen yards away, raced towards them, seeking what minimal cover he could find. A split second after he reached the rocks, there was a flash of movement overhead. Three sleek, streamlined shapes could be seen outlined for a split second against the gas giant. Gasping, Manderson sagged down against the rock in relief. The fighters were friendly- United Earth Alliance Navy Apparition fighters. The three fighters flew low over the crater and vanished over the ruins of the far wall. The officer stood woozily and keyed his radio. "Ops, this is Six. Those are friendlies...Repeat, those are friendly fighters." He stared for a moment in the direction the naval fighters had vanished, then continued plodding towards the hospital.

"*Six, ops.*" The radio came to life again. "*Yes, sir. I think we just reestablished comms with the fleet. All sorts of things are going off in here and updating. Captain Dahl wants to know if we're still moving to the tunnels.*"

"Tell her I'll be right there." Forcing one foot in front of the other, Manderson made his way down the rocky trail. As he approached the flat area in front of the hospital, he could see several power armored figures outside. The armor ident tags popped up showing Master Sergeant Agawa, Captain Dahl and one of the Valkyrie pilots. There was a low rumble from behind him. He paused and turned in time to see a massive fleet assault shuttle clear the top of the south crater wall, its bulk belied by its grace in flight. The shuttle moved quickly and surely towards the landing pads near the hospital. Forcing himself to move more quickly, he joined the small group waiting at the hospital entrance just as the shuttle landed in a cloud of dust.

After a few seconds, the exterior landing lights went on, lighting the area up brighter than Manderson had seen in days. The massive rear equipment ramp started to drop, as did the side ramps and people began to exit as Manderson watched numbly, his head swimming.

Three people approached at a fast pace. His armor pinged, identifying Colonel Assad, the field hospital commander. He was flanked by Colonel Loyo, his operations officer and the hospital sergeant major.

Assad stopped in front of Manderson and surveyed the hospital for a few seconds, then looked at him closely. "Looks like a hell of a fight, Mike." He held out his hand to shake Mike's.

"Been a long couple weeks, sir." Manderson replied,

reaching out for the man's hand. The colonel's voice sounded like he was speaking from the bottom of a deep well. "We've got a lot of people that need evac." He wobbled, his head spinning. "We need to start with…" Blackness rushed up at him and he had the sensation of falling.

Distantly, he heard voices from the darkness.

"Mike? MIKE!"

"Catch him! Catch him!"

"Ok. Lower him down. Good. Corpsman! CORPSMAN!"

There was the sensation of activity, then hands started pulling at his armor and distantly he wondered what was happening, then decided he didn't care and let the darkness wash over him as the voices continued.

"Ok, he's got suit pressure."

"Mick, readouts?"

"Vitals ok, oxygen ok. Jesus. Look at his CO2. His scrubber canister is toast."

There was the sensation of movement, then tugging. "Ok. Swapped it out."

"Yeah. Let's get him on an aux scrubber and get him loaded. Hyperoxygenate. Hit him with twelve point five grams of oxypentate."

"Ok." Clicking, then a hiss. "Got it."

"Dee, this dude's armor aid kit is empty. No fluids, no pain medications, no anti-shock, no spare scrubbers, nothing."

"The fuck is he doing walking around with nothing in his aid kit?"

"Whatever, we'll figure it out later." A pause. "Colonel, he's gonna be ok, but we need to get him out of here."

There was a murmuring, then the voice responded. "Yes, sir." There was a motion of rolling back and forth, then a tightening on his chest and knees, then the first voice again. "One, two, three." The sensation of being lifted came and then gentle swaying.

Micheal opened his eyes and saw a helmeted, power armored figure looming over him, outlined against the stars.

The corpsman glanced down and seeing his open eyes, spoke soothingly, "We got you, sir. We're getting you out of here." Manderson closed his eyes and let himself fall into the darkness.

\*\*\*\*

*Aboard the UEAN* Bravado
*Low Orbit, Draconis 327*

"Admiral Kensington, the enemy fleet is approaching their jump point. Looks like they're leaving the system."

From the observer's chair, Laura nodded. "Thank you. Keep me…"

"Ma'am! We've got multiple Elai warships at the jump point! They've got reinforcements!"

"Main display," The admiral ordered. "Forward this feed to my staff."

On the screen, the massive bulk of the Elai dreadnought and its surviving escorts faced the newly arrived flotilla of Elai warships of a half dozen cruisers and numerous destroyers. For several long moments, there was no motion from either of the enemy flotillas. Suddenly, the combat systems display pulsed and showed the markers for dozens of anti-ship missiles leaping from the newly arrived ships towards the battered dreadnought. The dreadnought immediately returned fire with its massive particle cannons, immediately crippling several destroyers and a cruiser. The two formations dissolved into a chaotic mess of ships firing missiles at close range and maneuvering wildly. Kensington watched the melee with her head tilted to one side, thinking.

"What the hell are we watching?" Commander Piaseki demanded. "Admiral?"

Slowly, Laura answered, "Captain, if I knew I'd tell you." She watched the scene unfollow in awe and horror.

On the screen, the newly arrived ships had concentrated fire on the dreadnoughts' escorts, picking them off one by one. In return, the massive warship methodically used its superior firepower to systematically tear the opposing warships to scrap. In moments, it was over. The dreadnought, with several new scars on her armored hull, was alone, her escorts destroyed, along with all of her attackers. A moment later, the cannons flashed again, targeting something in a debris field, then again. Small shuttles could be seen slipping out of the warship and racing towards other wrecks.

"They're shooting up lifepods, Admiral." The sensor officer reported. "Those shuttles are recovering others, though."

"I will never understand these monsters." Ripley muttered. She raised her voice. "Orders, Admiral?"

Still staring at the display, Kensington replied slowly, "No changes for now. Whatever they're doing, it means less of them for us to deal with." Looking up from the display, she ordered, "As soon as you can raise General Piaseki, please patch him through. I'll be in my stateroom."

"Yes, ma'am."

**\*\*\*\***

"Laura." General Piaseki's image showed up on the screen. He was still in his power armor and had the helmet off. The confines of an armored vehicle could be seen behind him.

"Alex," The admiral replied. "How was it?"

"Rough." The old Marine replied, flatly. "We lost a lot of good Marines down here."

"Yeah." The admiral sighed. "We didn't do so great either."

"But we're here." Piaseki replied. "And you made it back. That's a win in my book." He regarded his old friend for a moment. "How bad?"

"Bad." Laura rubbed her face, feeling the soul crushing weariness threatening to overwhelm her. "We lost seven cruisers and a dozen destroyers. Another half dozen so badly damaged they'll need major fleet yards to even see if they can fight again." She paused, then added with a sigh. "Probably about seven thousand sailors. We're still figuring out how many." She fell silent again for a moment and added, "Tom Phillips and Anders Halleck didn't make it."

"Damn." The Marine fell silent for a second then spoke, "They were good men." He bowed his head for a moment, "And those ships. Good sailors."

"Yeah." Laura fell silent for several seconds, then spoke. "Alex, something happened right as the Elai fleet left the system. They started shooting at each other. They destroyed as many of their own ships as we did."

"We saw something similar down here," the Marine replied. "My intel people are saying it was very focused and seemed almost ritual in nature. They think it might be a defeat thing." He shrugged. "Then, again they admit they're only guessing. We don't know anything for certain except that we have about three thousand alien prisoners."

Laura's head popped up, "Prisoners?"

"Yep." Piaseki replied, "They fought like demons, with us and each other and then just stopped. My battalion commanders are saying they seem like they want to join our side." He paused, then added, "Well, one faction of them does at least."

"Could they be breaking up internally?"

"Seems like a possibility." Piaseki admitted. He frowned, his prosthetic making his face look terrifying as he considered this. After a moment, he sighed. "I don't know. Hell, I'm just a beat up old Marine. They told me to take this rock and we did. Where we go from here ain't up to me. I got my hands full trying to find all my Marines."

"I hear that." Laura replied, simply. She regarded the man for a few seconds, then sighed. "I'll get my staff to start working on what to do with thousands of alien prisoners."

"Yeah," the Marine grimaced. "Nothing is easy out here, but they're compliant and helpful enough fellows, now that they aren't shooting at us. They'll mind their manners."

The console in front of Laura chimed and she frowned at it. "Hang on. Priority message."

Pulling up the message, she read through it, then her eyebrows shot up. "Alex. You need to see this." Tapping her controls, she forwarded the message.

The old Marine scowled at the message for a few seconds, then looked up in shock. "They attack Mars and kill millions then…surrender?"

"Apparently so. This came in just now with the courier ship." The two officers stared at the message in silence. After a moment, Laura said, "I've heard about Operation Avalon. It's a civil relief task force with teeth." Her console chimed again and she looked at it. "And there's an order package." She looked up at the Marine General. "I think it might be over."

"Seems like it." General Piaseki rubbed his chin thoughtfully, then added slowly, "Now comes the complicated part." He made eye contact with Laura. "What happens next?"

She gazed back, her worried expression telling. "Alex, I'll be damned if I know." The two officers fell silent.

\*\*\*\*

*Aboard the UEAN* Phantom Fury

Micheal Manderson opened his eyes. The ceiling was clean, with a frosted light. There was the murmur of voices nearby. He turned his head, his neck screaming in protest. He blinked hazily and tried to remember where he was.

"It's about god damn time you woke up." A woman's voice broke into his examination of the room. He turned his head and saw a trim young woman in a khaki uniform with blonde hair sitting next to his bed. She set down a datapad. "I told them that the brain damage wasn't going to affect you that much since you're clearly an idiot."

"Hey, Susan." Michal replied with a wan smile.

"Six times." Dahl pointed at him. "You silenced your god damn $CO_2$ alarm SIX times." She glared angrily at him, "You know you could have died, right?"

"There was a lot going on," Manderson replied. "I meant to get to it."

"Meant to get to it." She glared at him for a few seconds, then shook her head. "Anyway." She set the datapad down. "You're lucky, Mike. An idiot, but lucky."

"Where are we?" Manderson asked, peering around. Curtains hung on either side of the bed, restricting his view.

"You're in the sickbay on the *Phantom Fury*. You've been here for about three days."

Suddenly, the memories began flooding back and he tried to sit up, "Did the hospital get evacuated?"

With an amused half-smile, Susan replied. "Yes. After you went down, Colonel Assad got things moving. The evacuation actually went pretty fast." She regarded him for a moment, then added, "We saved a lot of Marines down there" She paused, then added pointedly, "You saved a lot of people down there."

"I just did my job," Manderson muttered. "Nothing special."

"Yeah?" Dahl countered, "Well, Colonel Assad disagrees and told me to give you this to prove it."

She produced a slim, flat box and handed it to Manderson. Taking the box and opening it up, he stared at the gold, emblazoned shape of an Earth Alliance Cross. She smiled as he stared at it, then said, "You did good work, Mike." She leaned over the bed and gave him a kiss on the cheek. "I'll see you around, big guy. She stood up, the scent of her perfume in Manderson's nostrils.

"Where are you going?" He asked.

"I'm not going anywhere." The nurse replied with a smile, "I'm going back to my Valkyrie squadron. You, on the other hand, are heading home."

"We're not all going home?" Manderson asked, confused.

"No. Scuttlebut around the fleet is that something big is happening. Surrender, maybe. Maybe the scaly little bastards have had enough and are crying uncle." She looked down at him and added, "The *Phantom* is headed back to Sol." She gestured vaguely, "The rest of the fleet that's not beat to hell is being reorganized and sent to the Elai home system."

"I don't understand." Manderson protested. "I can still do my job. I have to come."

"The fleet doctors disagree." Dahl regarded him, tilting her head. "So do I." She smiled suddenly. "Get some rest, Mike. I'll come see you before you head home." She turned and took a couple of steps, then turned around. "And thank you." She hesitated. "For everything." She opened her mouth as if to say something else, then turned and hurried out of sight.

Manderson watched her vanish in the distance, then looked back down at the Alliance Cross in his hand, sighed and collapsed back into his pillow. After a moment he muttered, "Going home, huh? We'll see about that."

\*\*\*\*

*Aboard the UEAN* Bravado
*The Captain's Stateroom*

The communicator chimed and Commander Piaseki looked up from her terminal. Glad for a relief from the seemingly endless paperwork required of a ship's captain, she tapped the communicator. "Piaseki."

"Captain, we have Major General Piaseki on the line for you."

"Put him through." Ripley closed the paperwork, it could wait. General Piaseki's scarred and frightening image appeared on the screen. Ripley rested her hand on her fist. "Hi, Daddy."

"Hi, pumpkin." The old Marine smiled at his daughter. "How are you?"

Pressing her lips together, Ripley blinked quickly, trying to keep the tears away. "It's been a long couple of weeks."

"Same here. It's been something else. How's the *Bravado?*"

She took a deep, shaky breath. "I lost sailors, dad." The tears began to flow down her cheeks. "I've never lost someone before."

The Marine nodded, quietly. After a second, Ripley wiped her eyes. "How can you do this, dad? It hurts so much. I would give anything to have them back. Anything."

"It never gets any easier, Pumpkin." Her father answered gently. "You do the best you can and follow all the rules and still sometimes good Sailors and Marines die because that's how war works." He paused and looked down for a moment, then back up at his daughter. "All you can do is make their sacrifice worth it."

"Maybe if I'd just..." Ripley began

"Stop." The general said gently. "You can 'maybe' and 'what if' and 'should have' yourself into eternity. It doesn't help," he paused, then continued. "Your duty now is to your crew. Honor their sacrifice and remember that you got far more home than you lost."

"I know, but..."

"No." The man replied firmly. "No buts. You're the captain of a starship. Those crew are your family. They need you to be strong; and not have you second guessing yourself. Believe in yourself. If not for you, then do it for them."

Ripley wiped her eyes and sniffed. "But where do I turn?"

"To me." He regarded her for a long moment, then added gently, "I would give anything to give you a hug right now, but the best I can do is some fatherly advice. Wash your face, straighten up your uniform and know that I and your mother and your crew are proud of you."

"You used to say that to me as a kid," Ripley laughed through her tears.

"I'm nothing if not consistent," the Marine agreed with a

smile.

The two fell silent for a long time. Eventually, Ripley spoke, "Mom will never understand, will she?"

"No. Neither will your brothers." He smiled. "But you always have your old man."

"I do." An alert chimed at her desk. "I gotta go, dad."

"My too." He regarded her closely for a moment, then added, "I love you, Ripley. I'm very proud of the woman and officer you've become."

"I love you too, Dad." She touched the screen. "You be careful down there."

"I will. Take care, pumpkin."

"Bye, Dad." The call ended. Ripley sat still for a moment, staring at the gently rotating UEA Navy symbol on the monitor, then took a deep breath, wiped her face and went back to work.

# Chapter 24

## "Full of Grace"

*Draconis 327, M3245 'Onyx'*
*Crash site of Daredevil Five-Two*

Tony awoke with a start, disoriented. He was lying on his back and it was dark outside of his suit helmet. His ears were ringing, his vision was a blurry mass of colors and he could hear a low, insistent hiss. Blinking his eyes, he realized that the colors he could see was his helmet display flashing with alarms. In block letters in the lower half of his visor blinked the word 'EMERGENCY' alternating with 'SUIT COMPROMISE'. With a shock, he realized that the hissing was his armor leaking. He tried to reach for his suit sealant cans on his belt and found that he couldn't move his right arm; it seemed to be blocked by something. As he reached for it with his left hand, he opened his mouth and croaked, "Activate Trauma System."

The suit's onboard computer responded in its dry, calm voice, "*Trauma System autoactivated at 1832. Medical Emergency. Treatment initiated for multiple traumatic injuries. Right arm- vascular compromise, Auto-tourniqueted. Right leg- Major fracture detected, Immobilized. Blunt abdominal injury suspected. Multiple broken ribs suspected. Internal bleeding suspected. Fluid, analgesics and anti-shock administered. Emergency. Vital signs critical. Seek medical attention.*"

Tony got his left hand on the can of sealant and pulled it out, nearly dropping it. He blinked hard to clear his eyes and spoke, in a louder voice, "Activate suit diagnostics."

The suit promptly replied, "*Suit Status: Power: 15%. Armor integrity 45%. Breach detected to right arm, auto sealed. Left helmet seal damaged-continuing pressure loss. Breach overpressure system active. Trauma system: Active. Camouflage system: Offline. Damage to right arm medial and lateral servos, inoperable. Damage to right leg servos, operating at 50% capacity. Communications network link: Unavailable. Impact protection system: Expended. Oxygen generator: Damaged, reduced output. CO2 scrubbers, online. Water reclamation system: Offline. Primary heating systems: Offline. External lighting system: Online. Emergency beacon activated at 1832. Suit incapable of extra atmospheric operations. Seal breaches immediately. Seek shelter immediately. Emergency."*

Tony pulled the can to his left arm, feeling his body screaming in agony at the motion. He pointed the can of sealant at the left side of his helmet and pulled the trigger. The pink spray flew out of the can and stuck to the armor and immediately began to harden. Hearing the hissing continue, he held down the can's nozzle. The can spluttered, empty but the hissing in his helmet continued. Tony caught his breath and dropped the can and reached for his belt to feel for another can of the foam. As he did, the hissing stopped as the sealant expanded and hardened. He closed his eyes for a moment and breathed a sigh of relief.

The onboard computer said in its impersonal voice, *"Pressure integrity restored. Overpressure system to standby."* The blinking words in front of his helmet now only flashed 'Emergency'.

Coughing and feeling a stabbing pain in his ribs, Tony looked through his helmet visor and realized all he could see was a sheet of metal, about fifteen inches in front of his face. He reached up with his left and pushed on it. The piece of metal didn't budge. Gathering all of his strength, he pushed again as hard as he could, feeling pain searing through his ribs and chest. He fell back, coughing, feeling the sharp stabbing pain in his back and chest, like a knife being driven into him.

After the coughing and pain receded somewhat, he

whispered, "Emergency override- Left arm servo power output."

The suit chirped, then replied, *"Unable to comply. Suit power critical. Recommend power cell replacement. Power conservation measures will commence at 10%."*

Tony gritted his teeth and squinted his eyes shut and tried to think. When the suit hit 10%, it began to shunt power to essential systems. Life support, heat and the trauma system. Everything else either shut down or was reduced to bare essential functions. When it hit 3%, emergency stasis was initiated. He had to get out of here and fast. He reached down to his belt again, to where the spare battery packs were located behind his waist but couldn't get his arm behind himself and was unable to shift the broken chunk of the fuselage enough to reach it. After a moment of struggle, he stopped and swore, realizing how very winded he was. He was panting and light headed from just moving his left arm around. He let his head fall back in his helmet, exhausted. He could feel his head spinning and was seeing spots flashing in his eyes. Vaguely, he realized that he was trapped and dying but the thought didn't seem to bother him as much as he thought it should have.

He let his body relax and his mind began to wander, with random memories drifting into his mind. The flickering neon sign over the stand on Tenth and South streets where he got water ice in his boyhood home in South Philadelphia. The snow crunching under his skis in the Pocono Mountains from his post college ski trip before he left for the Marines. Elizabeth lying her head on his shoulder in a dark compartment on Paradise. Mass at midnight on Christmas with his family at the church their family had attended for over a century in South Philly and the comforting bass voice of Father Okonu, the parish priest. The familiar words he'd known since a child came to his lips.

"Hail Mary, full of grace…"

His suit chirped and the display flashed and read: 'Power

Critical: Power conservation mode initiated.' The lights outside his helmet went dark, as did most of his display. The constant chiming in his helmet went silent and all he could hear was his breathing.

"The Lord is with thee, Blessed art thou amongst women and blessed is the fruit of thy womb, Jesus." Tony took a deep breath. The pain in his chest seemed further away now. He blew out the breath and noted distractedly that there were ice crystals forming inside the edges of his helmet visor.

"Hail Mary, mother of God. Pray for us sinners, now and at the hour of our deaths…."

There was a strange feeling in his legs and abdomen, as if someone was shaking him. He blinked and blew out another lungful of air, seeing the white cloud as his warm breath hit the cooling air in his helmet.

He squinted his eyes tightly shut and felt the hot tears in the edges of his eyes squeezing out onto his cheeks and running down his face.

"Hail Mary, full of grace…" he whispered. The only response was the silence of his armor and the icy atmosphere outside. He opened his eyes and saw a timer clicking in his vision. The display now read: 'Emergency Stasis initiation in 8:55, 8: 53, 8:52…'

Tony whispered, "Pray for us sinners, now and at the hour of our deaths…" He took another breath, now feeling the sharp bite of the rapidly cooling air.

Suddenly, there was an explosion of pain from his right side, flashing into his vision, blinding him with a brilliant white light in his eyes. He squinted his eyes shut and began to scream, but all that came out was a tortured moan. After a moment, the pain eased but the light remained. Forcing his eyes open, he squinted against the light. The piece of metal that had pinned him down was gone, replaced by a bobbing and moving brilliant white light. It moved closer and Tony could begin to make out a shape behind it. Turning his head against the glare, he squinted his eyes shut. The brilliant light flicked out. After a few seconds he turned his head back and looked again and then started in shock. Looming over his faceplate was the slick black visor of an Elai combat helmet.

Tony stared up at the slick black visor for a moment, then let his eyes move down the alien's body. The left shoulder had a disc with three curved lines with a slash through them. On the Elai's left arm was a band of what looked like cloth. On the cloth was a symbol in bright red that Tony couldn't make out. He looked back up at the alien who stood motionless, staring down at him.

After a moment, the Elai tilted its head then reached for Tony's chest and opened his suit control panel. Surprising himself with his strength, Tony reached up to push the alien warrior away, but was startled when the alien casually pushed his power armored arm aside and peered at the instrument panel. The alien studied it for a moment, then turned its head and motioned. A second slick armored head appeared and also looked at the panel, whistled at his comrade then looked up at Tony's faceplate. The Elai with the armband looked down and reached out of his view for a moment. Suddenly, to Tony's horror, it brought what looked like a snubby black pistol up to his faceplate. The alien soldier pushed the barrel against his helmet and Tony instinctively turned his head away and squinted his eyes shut. After a moment, he heard a strange noise. It sounded like whirring and was coming from inside his helmet. He turned his head back and opened his eyes and saw that the 'barrel' of the device pushed against his helmet was drilling through his faceplate, down by his chin.

Tony again tried to reach up to push the alien away, but again the black armored figure easily pushed his arm down, seemingly effortlessly. A second later, the drill bit broke through, letting tiny bits of plastic fall into his helmet. His suit computer chirped and the words displayed in large block letters: *'EMERGENCY. BREACH DETECTED- VISOR. SEAL IMMEDIATELY. EMERGENCY'*

The drill bit withdrew leaving a dark circle made of metal

in its place. The Elai pulled the device away from his faceplate, then reached out of sight again. After a moment, the alien reached up again and connected something. A split second later, he felt a rush of warm air against his chin. The Elai soldier then reached over to his hand, picked his wrist up and moved it into his line of sight and placed a brick sized box with a tube attached to it in his armored glove. The Elai then firmly pushed his hand with the box onto his chest and did something that Tony couldn't see. He could feel the box in his hand, but it was now stuck to his armor. He clung to the box like a drowning man to a lifeline and kept his eyes locked on the Elai. The Elai straightened up and turned. Another black suited arm appeared over his helmet, handing the Elai a package. The second alien took it, then leaned over Tony's helmet visor and chirped and whistled in its birdsong language. It motioned to his right arm, then leaned back. There was suddenly an explosion of pain from his right arm. Tony screamed and blacked out.

\*\*\*\*

Sometime later, Tony woke, disoriented. He was gently rocking back and forth, in a gentle, rhythmic manner. Confused, he blinked a few times and tried to remember what was going on. His eyes wandered to his helmet display. There were a dozen damage indicators gently blinking, but he appeared to have pressure. He grimaced and tried to reach to his faceplate but realized that he couldn't move his right arm. Suddenly, memory started to flood back. The shuttle crash, being trapped in the wreckage and the Elai soldiers pulling him out. He strained his eyes, trying to see something out of his helmet, but all he could see was the black of the sky and the hard points of stars far above. Dark shapes in front and above him occasionally blocked out the starlight. After a long moment, Tony realized he was being carried and breathed a sigh of relief. Suddenly he remembered that his suit was almost out of power and let his eyes move to the power indicator. It read forty five percent. Groggy and confused, he tabbed open the log and noted that a battery change had been performed about an hour ago. Not remembering doing it, he racked his brain, then it hit him: The Elai. They must have swapped out the suit battery for the spare on his belt.

Thinking about this for another moment, he decided that while it was weird that they knew how to change the batteries on a suit of Marine infantry power armor, it was also comforting that they hadn't just let him freeze to death. He'd always been afraid of freezing. There was a red flash over his head, but it didn't matter too much to Tony. He idly wondered what they planned to do with... There were several more red flashes above him. Suddenly Tony fell, landing with a hard crash and knocking his head against the inside of his helmet, landing in a slight sitting position, his back against a rock. Confused, he looked up and saw one of the black shapes raising something to his shoulder. Tony wondered what it was then the Elai began to fire. The smokey red of the bolts backlit the Elai's armor each time as he squeezed off shots as fast as he could and he could see the rocky terrain reflected in the alien soldiers visor with each shot it fired. Seeing the Elai's armband, Tony realized it was the one who'd given him aid earlier. The Elai crouched and started to reload, as another burst of the red flashes came from somewhere out of Tony's view. The other Elai was firing, the pulses snapping through his field of vision.

It occurred to Tony that the Elai were usually pretty deliberate marksmen and for them to be firing this fast, there must be a lot of targets or...whoever that was out there was really, really close. There was a flash from behind him and he felt something thump against his helmet, then the other Elai fell forward next to him. He could see a large hole in the alien's armored pressure suit. A trail of smoke rose from the wound. The Elai in front of Tony looked over at its fallen comrade and hesitated a moment. It then popped back up and opened up again, squeezing off rounds as fast as the rifle could fire.

After a few seconds, it crouched back down and dropped the rifle and pulled its sidearm, looked at it, then holstered it. It popped up to look over the rock, then ducked when a particularly close burst of fire came at it. The return fire didn't seem as ferocious but was still steadily flickering over the depression they occupied. The Elai looked at Tony, then reached down to his right leg and manipulated something, then came up with Tony's pistol. Tony watched idly as the Elai racked the slide on his sidearm, then popped up and sent a half dozen bright blue bolts into the air randomly. The Elai repeated this several times, then stopped and looked at the pistol.

Tony shook his head, distractedly. He and a lot of the other Marines had complained for years about the energy cell size on the M5 Personal Defense Weapon. It just didn't last long enough. He'd have to write a letter about this...

The Elai dropped onto its hands and knees and crawled over him and placed the empty pistol in his left hand. Tony was surprised at this and watched fascinated as the Elai then drew a wicked knife from its belt, held it flat against its forearm, then suddenly collapsed bonelessly across Tony's lap and lay completely still.

Perplexed, Tony joggled his knee to startle the alien. It didn't move. He joggled harder, but still nothing. With a frown, Tony tried to figure out what was going on, when he saw a figure appear over the edge of the depression with its stubby rifle at the ready. A split second later, another appeared, a few steps past the first. Their rifles alertly tracked both Tony and the Elai lying motionless across him.

As it stepped closer, Tony could see that these Elai were different. These were bigger and carried different equipment. One of them stepped right next to Tony and leaned forward to prod the Elai lying across Tony with its rifle barrel.

As it leaned over him, Tony made an impulsive decision

and spoke in a hoarse whisper to the computer in his suit, "Activate riot control systems-stun."

The suit chirped and activated the integrated stun system built into the gauntlets of his armor. Tony opened his hand and grabbed the Elai's ankle. The contact points built into the fingertips and palm activated, sending a surge of electricity through the alien's suit. It stiffened then crumpled slowly. The second Elai turned in confusion and then the alien lying motionless across Tony's legs leapt. In a single motion, it went from lying face down onto its feet, driving the long knife into the other Elai's neck, thrusting up into its helmet. It then jerked the knife out; leaving a spray of flash freezing blood and a plume of white atmosphere venting from the suit. The Elai then whirled and leapt on the other, who was on its hands and knees, recovering from the shock Tony had delivered from the riot control system in his gauntlet. There was the flash of a blade against the stars, then the knife was driven hard into the back of the Elai's helmet, where it met the neck of the suit. Another spray of white atmosphere and dark blood and the alien collapsed, twitched once then was still.

The Elai with the armband stood still for a moment, pulled the knife out and cautiously peered over the edge of the depression. Apparently satisfied that there were no more of them, it sat down heavily. With a swift move, it stuck the knife into the frozen ground tip first and then sat still for a moment. Feeling lightheaded and detached, Tony noticed bemusedly that the Elai was trembling. He thought about this for a moment, decided he could empathize and passed out.

# Chapter 25

## "Never Leave a Fallen Comrade"

*Secondary Tactical Operations Center*
*Forward Operating Base Anvil*
*September 15, 2246*

The dim light of the operations center glinted off of the metal and plastic half of General Piasecki's face as he leaned towards the sweating officer standing nervously in front of him. His voice was calm, but radiated menace, "I don't give a good goddamn, Major. You get those teams back out there and you keep looking. You keep looking until you find that shuttle."

The man replied with a stutter, "Sir, we're trying but..."

Pointing a finger at the man, the General declared, "No buts. Find them. It's been twelve hours. They don't have much longer."

"Sir, there's a lot of resistance out there. The second faction of Elai are still active and organized and are shooting at the Valkyries." The man swallowed hard, then added, "We can't set them down. It's not safe."

Piasecki held the glare for a moment longer, then growled. "Oh, they're shooting at my medevac birds, are they? I can fix that." He then turned and snapped at a nearby Marine, "Marine, get me Task Force Hammer's CO on the horn." Turning back to the officer in front of him, he said firmly, "I'm going to reroute Task Force Hammer. You and your search and rescue assets now fall under him. Report to him immediately."

"Yes, sir!" The Marine replied in a relieved tone. He snapped to attention, then rushed out of the room.

Across from him, coms spoke up, "General, Colonel

Mecham is on the line."

With a grunt, Piaseki moved over to the station and snapped the control. The image of Colonel Mecham lit up. Calmly, he replied, "General."

"Jonathan. I have a job for you and it's not going to be easy." Piasecki sat down and regarded the shaven headed officer for a moment with a frown, then said, "I'm gonna need you to take first and second battalions east, into the mountains. We have a bird down and those red suited bastards are running around shooting at the Valks."

The other officer considered this for a moment, then replied calmly, "Ok. Need twenty minutes to get a plan together. Can probably roll in an hour or so." He paused, then asked, "Just personnel recovery?"

With a nod, Piasecki replied, "Yes. Get in, secure the crash site, recover our people and get out. Smash any Elai that try to stop you, but don't go chasing them. Any that resist we're gonna leave out there. Nothing they can do then but slowly run out of air and power." He added, "You'll have full air and naval fire support, as well as all of the armor you need."

The taciturn officer replied, "No problem. I'll get back to you with a plan, sir." Piasecki nodded and broke the connection.

He turned to the map table, the holo the terrain to the east of Firebase Anvil. He leaned on the edge of the table and stared at the display. After a moment, he muttered, "Hang in there, Tony. Help's coming."

\*\*\*\*

*Aboard the UEAN* Infiltrator
*Interplanetary Space, M3245*

"Conn, Sensors." The intercom on the arm of the command chair came to life.

Greta Van Kant looked up from the duty roster she was

reviewing and tapped the control, "Sensors, Conn. This is the XO."

"Ma'am, we have new sensor contacts, but they're different than anything we've seen. When you have time, we'd like to run it by you."

"I'll be right there." Greta stood up and set the clipboard down. She motioned to a nearby ensign, "Keenan, you have the conn. I'll be in sensors." The ensign nodded and slipped into the command chair. Greta turned and moved forward. A few moments later, she entered the dim sensor compartment.

One of the officers turned and nodded, "Commander."

Nodding in return, she replied, "Lieutenant O'Hara. What do you have?"

Gesturing at a nearby station, the man responded, "Well, ma'am. We're not really sure. Have a seat; I'll run some data with you." Greta sat down at the display and the man tapped a control.

As the display came to life, the lieutenant described what they were seeing, "So, this is a replay of the engagement of the cruisers from the screening force for Task Force 3.2 smashing the Elai in the last engagement." The screen showed the short, sharp clash between the opposing fleets and the rapid destruction of the Elai cruisers. Pausing the display, the sensor officer said, "Now watch. Keep your eye on these two Elai cruisers right here right after the *Venganza* trashes them." He pressed play and the symbol for the *Venganza* led two other UEA cruisers on a firing run. The three cruisers flashed by a damaged Elai vessel, which exploded and broke apart under the fusillade. The Alliance ships curved nimbly around and repeated the tactic against the sole remaining Elai cruiser which futilely spit a swarm of missiles, then detonated in a massive explosion. The trio of warships then accelerated off and the lieutenant froze the display.

Greta looked at him and shrugged, "Ok. Whatever you're seeing, I missed it. I watched it in real time when it happened yesterday and I don't see anything different."

"So did we, until we ran it through standard post processing. Here. Check this out." He tapped a few controls and the image rewound and zoomed in on the second Elai cruiser. The officer said, "Keep your eyes on the Elai ship and the missile exhaust in particular." He then hit play again and adjusted the action to half speed. Greta squinted at the ship and watched the hard specks of light streaking in from off the screen. The sparks of the missile exhaust vanished for a split second, then reappeared and impacted on the hull. The Elai vessel shuddered under the impacts, then a split second later, detonated. As the brilliant white fireball of the core detonating grew, there was a dark shape against one side of it that was briefly visible, then vanished in a split second. The replay ended and the lieutenant reset the display.

Cocking an eyebrow at the screen, Greta commented, "Was that…"

Pushing a control that brought up a freeze frame of the fireball, O'Hara replied, "Yep. It's a ship. One we weren't tracking before. Look." The screen showed a dark mass silhouetted against the explosion.

Greta leaned forward and examined the image closely and commented, "Well. I guess that answers the question as to whether they have stealth ships." She glanced at the sensor officer and asked, "Can we track it?"

With a cocky grin, the officer replied, "Ah. I thought you'd never ask." He tapped the display and said, "See, now that we know it's there and because it was exposed to an antimatter core detonation at relatively short range it was saturated with medium energy gamma radiation, we can track it. It leaves a trace signature that we can look for."

He tapped a control and a plotted course appeared, running from the engagement site back towards the gas giant. Greta nodded and then leaned back for a moment, drumming her fingers on the console. Abruptly she stood up and clapped the sensor officer on the shoulder, "Good work, O'Hara. Keep on it. I'll let the Captain know." She glanced at the display, "In the meantime, find out a way to detect and track these things. This changes things."

O'Hara nodded, "We're already on it, ma'am." Greta nodded and left the compartment in search of the captain.

\*\*\*\*

*Crash site of Daredevil Five-Two*
*Twenty kilometers east of FOB Anvil*

"Colonel Mecham, Blackjack Three-Six has located the crash site."

The hard faced colonel looked up and nodded. The armored vehicle hit a particularly large bump and everyone inside the tight command compartment lurched.

The enlisted man listened to his radio again for a moment, then reported, "Blackjack Three-Six reports that they engaged an Elai patrol at the crash site. They report that it looks like Elai faction two. They were apparently attempting to secure the scene." He listened again and added, "They are pursuing the remaining Elai from the patrol. Bravo Company is securing the crash site and beginning the search for survivors."

Mecham nodded and replied, "Tell them to keep pushing on that Elai patrol. These Elai have a nasty habit of turning around and counterattacking, particularly when we think they're whipped. Tell them to locate their main element, then call for air support."

"Yes, sir." The Marine started whispering into his headset.

Colonel Mecham leaned around and spoke to the vehicle commander, "Sergeant Norris, ETA?"

The vehicle commander replied immediately, "About a minute, sir."

With a nod Mecham replied, "Got it." He turned to the grim faced Marines in the back of the assault vehicle, "Ok, Marines. Hats closed." He picked up his helmet, attached it to his power armor and sealed it. Several seconds later, the sergeant at the rear door gave a thumbs up. A moment later, the light over the rear door changed, indicating that the cabin was depressurizing. The rear ramp swung open and the four Marines climbed out. Colonel Mecham looked around, getting his bearings. Seeing the dancing lights of power armor in the distance, he set out at a fast walk over the broken terrain. The two Marines on his security detail fanned out to either side of him and his executive officer next to him. His exec was a slightly pudgy and usually cheerful major named Zabramski. Today, however, he walked in silence next to Colonel Mecham. A few moments of hard walking later and they reached the crash site. Colonel Mecham stopped and put his hands on his hips and surveyed the wreckage of the shuttle. It had impacted on its belly and then rolled several times, before hitting a large boulder and coming to rest. There were pieces scattered for a hundred yards in a trail.

Seeing him, a nearby officer came over. His armor IFF tag identified him as 'Captain Hill'. He said grimly, "Sir. We have located five of the crew; all KIA."

Mecham nodded silently, his eyes roaming the debris field. After a moment, he said, "Manifest had seven. Three crew and four passengers. Who have we found?"

Captain Hill replied, "Both the pilots and the flight engineer were still in the fuselage, sir." He indicated the mass of the shuttle next to them. Mecham turned slightly. The nose art was battered and scraped but visible, showing a grinning cartoon devil on a flying trapeze. The captain paused, listening to radio traffic in his helmet, then continued, "We just located two ... correction ... three more, all KIA." He listened for another moment, then added, "There's another chunk of the fuselage over that rise. That's where they are." He indicated a terrain feature about thirty yards away.

Wordlessly, the colonel started walking over to the other piece of the ruined shuttle. Coming to the top of the small rise, he could see Marines climbing in and around the wreckage, attempting to remove the bodies of their fallen comrades.

Major Zabramski turned aside, poking at a large chunk of wreckage leaning up against a rock a few feet away.

Suddenly, Mecham heard the man exclaim, "What the hell...." Mecham turned to see the man leaning over and turning his armor lights up. Curious, the colonel moved up next to his exec and stared at what the man was looking at.

In the brilliant light of their suits, there were several items lying in the dust. One was a standard UEA power armor suit battery, lying half buried. Next to it were several pieces of plastic wrap, an empty suit sealant can and a hard sided case, sitting open on the ground. In the dust was a confused mash of bootprints and a large dark stain on the cold earth of the moon. Zabramski swung the light and centered them on a piece of equipment– an unfamiliar shaped backpack, in a pattern that was clearly not of UEA origin. A set of deep footprints disappeared into the dark, the size and shape too small to be Marines. The tread pattern was unfamiliar, but the marks of a set of power armored legs being drug was clearly visible.

"Oh, brother," Mecham muttered.

Zabramski replied, "You can say that again, Colonel."

Tabbing his radio, the colonel said, "Hooligan Two-Two, this is Hammer Six actual."

The crew in his command vehicle answered, "*Hammer Six actual, Hooligan Two-Two. Go ahead, colonel.*"

"Hooligan, I'm gonna need you to get me an uplink to FOB Anvil. I need to talk to Ironjaw Six actual. We have probable captured personnel." He paused a moment, then added, "Also: relay to Blackjack Three Six that we may have friendlies under the control of Elai faction two. Use extreme caution when engaging."

"*Roger, Hammer Six. We'll patch you through when the uplink is established. Standby.*" Mecham could hear Zabramzski ordering a Marine detachment to follow the tracks and starting to organize a pursuit.

His radio crackled again, "*Hammer Six Actual, Standby for Ironjaw Six Actual.*"

After a few seconds, Mecham's radio spoke with the familiar gravelly voice of General Piasecki, "*Jonathan. What do you have for me?*"

With a grimace, Mecham replied, "Nothing good, General. Let me bring you up to speed..." He quickly started bringing the general up to speed on the situation.

\*\*\*\*

*Unknown coordinates, Onyx*

Tony opened his eyes and realized that he was moving again. He was slumped back in a reclined position and moving slowly but he was moving. Confused, he raised his head and saw that he was strapped onto a litter. The end of the litter he was facing was being drug on the ground. The stretcher was shorter than he was, so his armored boots were dragging on the ground. He looked further down and saw his right arm for the first time. The plaststeel of his armor was torn and mangled and he could see the dark, frozen mass of flesh through the rents in the armor. After a moment, he laid his head back and blew out a breath and thought about this. His right arm was gone, that much was certain. There was a flicker of motion out of the corner of his eye and he turned his head. As he did, he caught sight of something moving extremely fast. A moment later, he felt a series of tremors through his feet as the ground shook.

Suddenly his head lowered and he was lying flat on the ground. The Elai soldier appeared over him and checked his suit control panel then looked into his helmet. Seeing him awake, it tapped his helmet then reached behind him with one hand, while pulling his body forward. After a second, it let him go and Tony slumped back against something, now in a reclining position.

The alien soldier crouched, watching him intently then chirped at him. After a moment, Tony nodded and said in a cracking voice, "I'm good." The Elai watched a moment longer, then pulled a device from its belt and started manipulating its controls.

As the alien worked the instrument, Tony looked around. He realized that they were near the crest of a decent sized hill, overlooking a large valley. There was another flicker of motion and Tony caught sight of a pair of UEA Banshees flying in close formation past the hill. There was a flicker underneath them, then they pulled up simultaneously and disappeared into the distance. As they did, there was a series of hard flashes of light in the valley below and several seconds later the trembling of the ground as the ordinance exploded and transmitted their energy into the rock.

Tony checked his instrument status in his helmet, but his communications were still out. It made sense– the transmitter was on his right shoulder and he'd been hit pretty hard there. Idly, he checked his rescue beacon to make sure it was still transmitting and then turned his eyes back to the scene below.

In the valley, he could make out fires burning from whatever the Banshees had bombed and as he watched there were several flashes of light as damaged pieces of equipment exploded. In the distance, he could see the Banshees curving back around for a third pass. The Elai soldier had stopped trying to use the piece of equipment and was watching the Banshees. The two squat aircraft had lined up further down the valley again and slowed down. As they approached, their noses lowered and began to spit a stream of green fire towards the ground. Tony watched, fascinated as the lascannon bolts hit the ground and remaining pieces of Elai equipment and spit sparks. Again the squat ground attack craft swept past, then curved around. The Banshees made one last pass, this time low and slow, then accelerated abruptly and vanished over the horizon.

There was a whistling noise from the Elai, who was staring at the devastation. After a moment, it shook its head and turned back to the piece of equipment in its hand. A few button presses later and a green light shone from it. The Elai then set the box carefully on a rock and turned back to Tony and chittered again.

Tony muttered to himself, "I'd kill for that translator right now." He shifted slightly and checked his suit power level. It seemed to have stabilized, now that the breaches were sealed. He wondered how long he had before his arm, or what was left of it, would start to be a problem. The Elai had sat down and was hanging its arms over its knees in an oddly human manner. It sat motionless, staring up at the stars.

After a moment, Tony could hear the Elai begin an idle hum, which rapidly grew more complex as he listened. The hum undulated up and down, interspersed with a whistling that climbed and dropped with the humming. Tony let his body relax and listened to the melodic singsong. It reminded him of the monks back on Earth, if they had a whistling section in their choir. He let his eyes wander up to the hard points of the stars above. The moon was facing away from the gas giant and the hard speck white that was Draconis 327 shone like a beacon in the starfield. Tony took a breath and ordered his armor to play his last letter from Elizabeth.

The screen lit up and showed her in a duty uniform, sitting by a window overlooking the barren but beautiful Martian landscape. She looked tired, but Tony was struck as always, by the deep brown of her eyes. He listened to her voice and let himself get lost in the words.

*"They put me up in the Huxley Hotel, which is super fancy but it just feels way too nice. The Navy guys are telling me that this is pretty standard for them. Again; typical, but I don't need to tell you. I'm sure they make the Marines sleep outside in space suits while the Navy has luxury hotels!"* Tony grinned slightly to himself about this, thinking about his current situation.

The image looked down at her hands for a minute, then back up at the camera and said, *"I don't know where you are, but you be careful. We have a lot of things to do and I need you in one piece to do them."* Elizabeth smiled, then continued, *"In case you are unclear on that last bit, you may consider that an order. I do outrank you for the time being."* She made a mock serious face for a moment, then stuck her tongue out at the camera and laughed, *"Ok. I gotta jet. I need to go get breakfast, then I'm going to go fly in a small shuttle through the Martian winter winds…. Actually, on second thought, maybe just coffee."* She smiled at the camera again and spoke, *"Don't forget what I told you before. You owe me dinner and interest is accruing rapidly, my friend. I'll see you soon."* She kissed her fingertip and gently touched the screen, *"Be safe, big guy.".* The recording ended.

Rapidly blinking to clear tears from his eyes, Tony closed the player and looked back up at the night sky. He blinked again and then frowned. There was a shimmering distortion in the stars above him, that grew rapidly to block out the stars, looming over them. Rocks and dirt began to blow around, as the craft got closer. Tony could hear the clicking as the debris hit his armor. The Elai next to him stood up, moved beside him and crouched protectively, trying to shield him from the flying dirt.

A moment later there was a slit of faint green light in the dark wall that now loomed next to them. The slit rapidly grew into a door and revealed the green lit interior of the craft. Several dark figures leapt nimbly out, rifles at the ready and took up positions several yards away, alertly staring into the darkness.

As they swept past Tony, he could see that these Elai were different. Over the slick black face armor were compact goggles, with multiple ports pointing out in different directions. They all wore dark armored suits, with a different type of armor that Tony had never seen before. Two of the Elai moved right up to Tony. One of them peered into his helmet briefly, the goggles giving it a spectral, haunting appearance. It then chittered to Tony's companion, who responded in the same fluid, melodic tones. Another Elai was doing something to the external air supply on Tony's chest. After a moment, they abruptly laid him flat, then before he could figure out what was happening, rolled him left and right. A moment later, he was wrapped securely in a dark colored blanket and being strapped to a stretcher. A few seconds of work later and he was hoisted into the air and maneuvered towards the waiting aircraft.

Tony knew he should be scared and that every moment he was getting further from rescue but couldn't help being faintly impressed at the casual way that these new soldiers hoisted him and his two hundred kilogram suit of power armor into the air like a sack of potatoes.

He was passed into the aircraft and felt straps going across his chest and legs. All he could see was the dim green overhead lights and various pieces of equipment.

Several seconds later, he could feel the aircraft shudder slightly and saw several shadowy helmets around him as the Elai soldiers piled back in. There was a whine as the engines increased in power and Tony could feel the floor drop out from under him as they lifted into the sky.

Idly, he wondered how long they'd taken to get him and realized that it couldn't be more than ninety seconds. Whoever this new unit of Elai were, they were good. Very, very good.

Suddenly, he had a vision of one of the Valkyrie pilots that he'd worked with back on Paradise. That little Puerto Rican colonel...what was her name...Elise. That's right. He grinned at the thought of being in the hands of the Elai equivalent of Elise and her med evac crew. This suddenly struck him as terribly funny and he began to laugh in hysterical exhaustion.

One of the Elai leaned over him and chittered. He recognized the armband and stopped laughing long enough to say, "You're going to need a name if we keep meeting like this."

The Elai responded in a singsong warble, then turned away. Tony laughed, deliriously, "All right. You patched me up? I'm gonna call you Doc." Doc didn't respond and Tony laughed again. "Ok, Doc. You're the boss."

The aircraft dropped suddenly, then banked hard and tilted back. There was a sudden surge of pressure on him as the boosters fired and he felt the ship tremble as it launched out of the icy atmosphere. Tony stopped laughing and made sure that his emergency beacon was still active. His situation wasn't good, but he was still alive and he had a promise to keep.

\*\*\*\*

*Aboard the UEAN* Infiltrator
*High Orbit, M3254*

"See, sir? Right there. It just changed course again. They can *totally* see the mines." The sailor flipped up his VR goggles and tapped the screen for emphasis.

Lieutenant O'Hara frowned and said, "We can't even find the goddamn things without the beacons and our sensors are orders of magnitude better. How the hell do they see them?"

The sailor shrugged, "Dunno, sir, but it allowed it to get into a damn low orbit. Ten to one it's doing personnel recovery."

With a sigh, O'Hara replied, "Yeah. Probably." He picked up the communications handset and hit the number for the bridge. As he did, he complained, "You know, every time we think we have these little bastards figured out..." He tabbed the handset. "Conn, Sensors."

"*Sensors, Bridge.*" Captain Harris's unmistakable tone came from the handset.

"Sir, contact Charlie-Two is actively avoiding the stealth mines the fleet left in orbit. We're not sure how yet."

There was a pause, then the captain replied, "*I'll be right down. Bridge out.*"

O'Hara set the handset down and frowned at the display. The sailor had his VR goggles back down and was manipulating the controls. Several moments later, Captain Harris entered the compact compartment, followed by

Commander Von Kant.

O'Hara gestured to a nearby screen, "Sir, ma'am. Check this out. Charlie Two can see the mines." He rewound and replayed the several deliberate course corrections the Elai stealth ship had performed to avoid the stealthed mines in orbit over the planet.

Harris watched silently with his arms folded. After a moment he asked, "How is he doing that?"

O'Hara shook his head and replied, "No idea, sir. Whatever he's using, we don't have it. *We* can't even see the damn things unless we program 'em to be seen."

Commander Von Kant spoke thoughtfully, "Well, we know their other ships don't have it. They lost two destroyers to mines during the first evacuation attempt."

With a frown, Captain Harris stared at the screen for a moment longer, then said, "Ok. Thanks, Lieutenant. Let us know if we see anything…"

The sailor on the console suddenly started and spoke up, "Lieutenant O'Hara! I have something here!"

Leaning over the sailor's shoulder, O'Hara stared at the screen, then muttered, "What in the hell…" He sat down and typed for a moment, then leaned back and said in a shocked voice, "Captain…You aren't going to believe this, but we have a distress beacon out there."

Harris, who had been watching quietly, traded a look with his Exec. The slim woman asked, "What ship is it off of? I thought the fleet got all the lifepods picked up."

The enlisted sailor replied, "It's not a ship beacon, sir." He reached up and flipped an overhead toggle and continued, "It looks like a combat suit."

Frowning, O'Hara replied to the man, "Run it again. We shouldn't get them this high up."

The sailor responded, "I did, sir. It's a combat suit emergency beacon. Looks like it's from the First Marine Division." He tapped for a moment, then said, "Sir, can you confirm this? It looks like it's close to Charlie-Two."

---

O'Hara nodded and went to work on his station. A few seconds later, he said, "Yep. The signal is definitely moving towards Charlie-Two."

Greta turned to Mitch and said quietly, "Sir. Those beacons don't go off unless someone sets them off."

Grimly, Mitch replied, "I know." He paused. "O'Hara, do we still have a hard fix on Charlie-Two?"

"Yes, sir. He's not getting away from us again. We have his drive signature now."

The enlisted man reported, "The signal is gone, sir." He paused and then said, "Charlie-Two is breaking orbit. I'll have a course calculated for you in a moment."

Mitch said abruptly, "We'll be on the bridge. Let us know if anything changes. Do NOT lose that contact." He turned and left the compartment at a fast walk, Greta right behind him. He spoke quickly, "Greta, I think those bastards are taking prisoners off of that rock. We have to follow them. Are the Thundercats aboard yet?"

Greta replied, "Yes, sir. They got on board about an hour ago. They're refitting to go back down to help finish off some of the holdouts in the tunnels."

"Tell them to hold on that." The two officers entered the bridge and Captain Harris started snapping orders, "Helm, set up a pursuit course for contact Charlie-Two. Communications, get me a tight beam to Task Force 3.2's commander. Flash traffic." He turned to the chief of watch, standing nearby. "Bosun Higgens, call Captain Tulp from the Thundercats and have him come speak with me at his earliest possible convenience." He frowned and turned to the weapons station, "Ensign, get a team to start breaking out and warming up the secondary torpedo stores and get me an inventory on consumables for a long range patrol."

There was a chorus of 'Aye, aye, sir' as he snapped orders. He turned and spoke quietly to his executive officer, who was standing quietly with her arms folded, "What else do we need, Greta?"

She looked him calmly in the eyes and said, "If you're thinking what I *think* you're thinking: A full battle fleet. But since we can't do that...I think we'll be ok, as long as we stay quiet."

"We can be quiet." He met her gaze and then said in a low tone, "We can't let them just slip away with our people."

The woman returned his gaze steadily, then replied, "No, sir. We can't."

The helmsman called out, "Sir, course plotted and laid in. Looks like it's heading for the jump point towards Elai space."

Mitch looked Greta in the eyes for another moment, then turned and said firmly, "Helm, ahead two thirds. Follow that contact."

The deck began to thrum as the stealth ship picked up speed and turned to follow the enemy ship as it slipped into the darkness.

## Epilogue

*Operation Cold Forge was deemed a resounding success by the leadership of the United Earth Alliance. While both the First Marine Division and the Third Fleet sustained heavy casualties, the overall objective of seizing and securing the moons and interdicting all fuel refining operations in Draconis 327 was achieved. The Elai were trapped, low on fuel and surrounded; with their final defensive line around their home system broken and apparent civil conflicts starting to break out. But, as the ancient axiom went: "A trapped enemy is often the most dangerous."*

Preview
Valkyrie Book IV: Armistice

## "Insolent Dragon"

*January 4th, 2249*
*Alpha Draconis III*
*Unnamed island off the coast of Landmass Two*
*Objective Dragon*

Captain Shawn Tulp laid on his stomach and stared through his armor visor down the hill at the complex in the valley in front of him, noting again the sturdy towers and thick walls surrounding it. Outside the walls, there were clear fields of close cut grass and beyond that, low shrubs. On each of the towers hung a red banner, with an unknown symbol on it. As he examined the scene, he scowled. In his helmet speakers, he heard the low, calm voice of his detachment sergeant, Master Sergeant Chan.

"Sir, Team Three reports launchers set and sighted and is moving into assault position. Teams One and Two are in breach position and awaiting the signal."

"Roger." Tulp tabbed frequencies, switching to the laser comm system that was set up behind him and his NCO's position. "Raider Five-Six Actual, this Dragon Six Alpha. All Dragon Teams in position. Awaiting your signal."

There was a momentary burst of static as the signal bounced up to the incoming destroyers, then the cheerful voice of the Marine Raider commander came back. *"Copy that, Dragon Six. We're three minutes out. Enjoy the light show."*

"Copy that. Dragon Six out." Tulp tapped back to his local net. "All Dragon teams– Blast shields down. Ten seconds." The round lights in his helmet display blinked as the team leaders acknowledged the warning. He reached up and slid the thick durasteel blast shield closed on his helmet, the shimmering of the optical camouflage on his arm distorting his view momentarily. His display dimmed, then brightened as it switched to the augmented view from his suit cameras. He turned his attention back to the complex below.

Suddenly, the entire valley lit up with a chalky white flash of a small tactical nuclear weapon detonating several thousand feet overhead. As the flash faded, he could hear Master Sergeant Chan snapping, "All teams: Execute! Go, go, go!"

Blinking rapidly to clear his eyes, Tulp watched as the presighted rocket launchers carefully positioned around the prison began to fire their payloads of surface to surface missiles into the bases of the towers. Several seconds later, the tower closest to him collapsed. Almost simultaneously, another tower collapsed. In his helmet display, the computer outlined shapes of the assault teams leapt from the low shrubs and sprinted across the low ground, towards the breaches. Their active camouflage made them look like apparitions as their augmented speed allowed them to cover the hundred meters or so of open ground in a matter of seconds. The shapes vanished into the clouds of dust as they breached the compound.

Tulp listened intently as the radio erupted into the chaos of combat. *"Two, there's one! Door, left side!"*

*"Got him. Another behind that crate!"* In the background, the bark of the M45 assault rifle's energy blasts could be heard. The terse words continued as the special forces team swept through the compound.

Several seconds later, the cold voice of Sergeant Kim crackled through the radio. *"Dragon Six, Dragon Three Lead. Primary objective secure. Moving to secondary."*

"Understood, Three. Six out." Tulp tabbed the radio. "Raider Five-Six Actual, Primary Objective Secure. Stick One is clear to drop in the main courtyard."

The Marine commander's reply came immediately, her voice sounding as if she was being shaken. There was a loud roar in the background of the radio. *"Understood, Dragon Six.*

*One minute. Kinetic strikes on the air defense should be hitting any second."*

There was a series of brilliant streaks from the sky, striking several nearby hilltops, leaving towering clouds of dust. The ground bucked underneath him as the shock of the orbital kinetic rounds transmitted through the earth.

"God damn. So much for those missile sites." Chan muttered. "Those gotta be fifteen ton rounds, at least."

With a humorless chuckle, Tulp responded, "Well, Master Sarn't. You know the Marines. Never use a scalpel when a sledgehammer will work." The burly Korean sergeant just grunted. Tulp's radio crackled again.

*"Six, this is Two. We got a strong point here. Mounted weapon, cutting off our extraction route. He's got us pinned."* The tense report was punctuated by the familiar hissing of a heavy lascannon bolts streaking by the pinned down special forces team.

"Two, Six. Raiders are hot dropping in the courtyard in thirty seconds. Keep your heads down and paint it for them."

As he spoke, there was a low hissing, which rapidly grew to a deafening roar. Raising his gaze, Tulp watched the fireballs screaming in from overhead. As they grew closer, the flame tails reversed as the retrorockets fired, slowing them down. As they got to within ten meters of the ground, the drop pods burst open, the remnants of the pods falling in all directions. Out of them fell the bulky armored shapes of the Marine Raiders. Their shoulder mounted lascannon were already firing and the high powered gauss rifles that they carried were spitting hyper velocity tungsten rounds even before they hit the ground. Tulp watched as dozens of the Marines vanished into the central courtyard of the compound. Almost immediately, he could hear the cracking of the gauss rifles and see bright flashes of explosions as the Marine infantry and the grenadiers began to go to work on the surviving Elai inside the compound. Snapping his eyes back to the walls, he saw the remaining raiders rapidly forming a perimeter around the complex.

The radio crackled again, awash with static from the electromagnetic interference from the nuclear weapon overhead. *"Dragon Six, Dragon One. Main gate secured. Two's moved past the strong point and is clearing what looks like a barracks. We're moving up to support."* Sergeant Sung sounded out of breath and the crashing of his footsteps could be heard in the background as he reported.

"Two, Six. Understood." Further down the wall, the main gates slid open and half a dozen of the massive raider suits poured out and fanned out on either side of the gate and took cover, weapons trained on the road leading to the now open gate.

*"Dragon Six, Raider Five-Six Actual."* The Marine commander's voice was much clearer now that she was on the ground.

"Actual, Six. Go."

*"The courtyard is secure, as is the command center. The central computer banks are a flaming wreck and so is their armory. The barracks are on fire, but there's still some resistance inside. It's being neutralized now. Your team Three is making contact with the prisoners. Let the swabbies know they can send our ride."*

"Understood, Actual. Any word from the blocking force on the road?"

*"We have our 1st Platoon with a heavy weapons squad about three clicks down the road waiting for them. It's our recon platoon, so they know a thing or two about ambushes. If these sharkies send a QRF, they are in for a double dose of hurt."*

With a dark grin, Tulp replied, "Acknowledge, Raider Actual. Start getting our people organized. Extraction will be here in two-zero minutes. We'll be down there momentarily. Dragon Six out."

Standing up from their hide site, he and the stocky NCO moved towards the prison complex. Reaching the wall, they scrambled over the rubble and entered the courtyard. Rifles at the ready, they cautiously looked around, then relaxed. Several of the buildings around them showed blast damage and all had dozens of holes from both the special forces energy weapons and the Marine gauss rifles. The Raider teams were positioned around the courtyard and atop buildings and walls; clearly in control of the area. No living Elai could be seen. Several dead alien bodies were scattered around the courtyard and more were visible in a street leading away. One of the massive armored figures turned and gestured at him. Deactivating his camouflage system, Tulp and Chan walked over to the Marine Commander. The Raider's power armor was massive, festooned with weapons and spare ammunition. A skull imprinted into the dura-plast visor gave the armored figure a terrifying visage.

Tulp opened his helmet visor and offered a hand. "Captain Tulp, 348th Special Forces, OPDET Alpha. We're off of the *Infiltrator.*"

The Marine popped her helmet, revealing a diminutive woman with dark, curly hair. She grinned widely. "Captain Lieberman, Second Raiders." She cheerfully gestured around them. "Nice place you got here. Sorry we fucked it up."

With a return grin, Tulp replied, "It's ok. The neighbors suck anyway."

"Ha! 'Bout to get a whole lot worse!" The woman retorted. She paused, listening to her radio, then said, "Ok, sir. Your Team One just finished clearing the northwest sector. Dunno why they're reporting through my guys. Maybe a fried radio." She listened again. "And we just made contact with the ranking officer here. My guys are bringing her over to assist in the evac."

Tulp nodded, as his own radio cracked, *"Dragon Six, Dragon Three Lead."*

"Three, Six. Go."

*"We got an entire cell block here fulla sharkie prisoners; maybe thirty-five or forty of them. They aren't doing anything,*

*just watching us from inside the cells. What should we do with 'em?"*

"Standby, Three." Tulp turned to Master Sergeant Chan. "We got a cell block full of Elai prisoners."

The burly Korean sergeant frowned, then shrugged. "Well, we ain't here to take prisoners. I say we leave 'em." He paused, listening to his radio, then said, "Three is still taking fire from the barracks. I'm going to go take a look." He sealed his helmet and strode off into the compound.

Captain Lieberman, who'd been listening in added, "I agree. We don't have the room for prisoners on the evac shuttles."

Shaking his head, Tulp responded, "No. We can't leave them. We're gonna zorch the whole site from orbit as we leave. I understand the sentiment but we can't just leave them locked up and bomb them out of existence. Let's wait till the last shuttle is boarding, then as we withdraw, we'll unlock and tell them to run like hell. That way they get at least a chance and we aren't greasing prisoners."

"Belay that, Captain." A firm, clear voice broke into their conversation. A short, blonde woman in a worn navy uniform with the rank insignia of a rear admiral was striding up, escorted by two of the Raiders. She stopped in front of Tulp and Liberman and asked in a crisp, professional tone, "Who's in operational command of this force?"

"I am, admiral." Tulp replied. "Captain Tulp, 348th Special Forces."

"Good. Admiral Svetlana Kvint, formerly commodore of the Third Fleet's Cruiser Division Six." She waved an arm at the wrecked prison around them. "I am the ranking officer here at the Waldorf. I need to speak to you about the Elai prisoners here."

"We were just discussing that, Admiral." Lieberman replied.

With a firm look, Admiral Kvint pointed at Tulp. "Captain, those Elai are critical to the war effort. Among them there are the equivalent of seventeen general and flag officers, several prominent scientists, a dozen mid-level nobility and most importantly, five matriarchal females. They MUST be extracted." She looked from face to face, her eyes piercing. "They are of extreme value to the war effort."

Tulp looked at Lieberman, who shrugged, "We can probably stuff a hundred and fifty or so more on board, but it's gonna be a problem getting all of your SF guys out too."

Turning back to the admiral, Tulp asked, "Admiral, it's going to be tight. Why are they so important?"

Kvint frowned and replied, "Because those five females *alone* represent their entire clans, which means tens of millions of Elai and their assets *each*. The others are extremely influential, either politically, religiously or civilly. You rescue them and those clans are ones that will willingly assist us in the ending of this war."

With a sidelong glance at the Marine captain, Tulp replied carefully, "The war is over, Admiral. We're here with a relief force. The Elai fleet is hulled and adrift and there's no organized planetary defense."

With a cold smile, the woman replied, "Not OUR war, Captain. The Elai *civil* war; which I assure you is *far* from over."


Valkyrie: Armistice
Summer of 2024

*Thanks*

*My deepest thanks go out to my wife, for supporting my crazy idea to write books and supporting me as I did. You're the best, honey; I love you to the moon and back. Thanks also to John, my editor and friend and Shawn; my hypercaffinated, profanity spewing muse. Last, but definitely not least, I'd like to thank you- my readers. You have stood by (mostly) patiently waiting for me to write more of this series, providing feedback, encouragement and criticism and you're awesome for it. Thank you all. Book IV is well under way and pandemics, wars and life notwithstanding, this time there won't be such a long delay between books.*

*Valkyries never die!*

Humanity engages in a desperate struggle with an alien species for this side of the Orion Arm. Spaceships die in instantaneous bursts of light and turn into vapor, but on the ground, Marines scream and lie wounded in the mud and blood, praying for the Valkyries to come save them. They aren't wishing for death and a Nordic goddess to take them to Valhalla, the wounded are calling for the pilots of the 348th Field Hospital MEDEVAC to dive through fire and hell to come save them. Because they know that ... Valkyries never die!

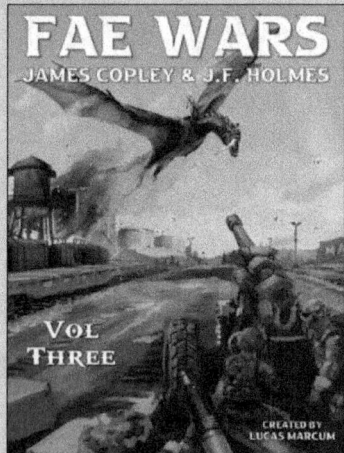

# FAE WARS

# Check out all of Cannon's books!